THE HEKTOR DILEMMA

An Improbable Emergence
Book 2

FRANCIS VOIGNIER

Revised Edition

Artwork by Francis Voignier
Cover: *"A Path to Dreams"* 1978
Inside: *"Zed"*

Some of the writing of this book is based on private experience and actual places. Names have been substituted to protect the sanctity of sacred space and the privacy of the individuals within it.

Library of Congress Cataloging-in-Publication Data
Voignier, Francis 1954 – United States
The Hektor Dilemma/Francis Voignier
ISBN-13: 978-1-7345551-0-3
ISBN-10: 1734555106

Fiction – Metaphysics – Quantum Physics – Philosophy – Northern California – Iceland

Dolosse & Writs, Eureka, California
francisvoignier.com

TABLE OF CONTENTS

INTRODUCTION

The Disappearance of Olaf Swyndle was written as a stream of consciousness loosely based on a paranormal experience involving my beloved dog Noodle, while on a hike in the Siskiyou Mountains, above Elk Valley in Northern California. I never thought it would make it beyond a short story, if it ever got that far, but I soon found myself at the end of the book, with its sequel knocking at the door.

Literally, *The Hektor Dilemma* also wrote itself, at the exception of the research that went into polishing my knowledge of the geography, history, and infrastructure of Iceland. Actually, the process went so quickly, that never were any notes taken, or a layout sketched for the story; when the time came to check for inconsistencies, it was like reading something written by someone else. As I neared its conclusion, I couldn't walk away from the feeling there would yet be more material to follow; namely, a third book, and the possibility of a chronicle as a branch of the main body.

Though, each volume forms a complete work, I highly recommend the reader proceeds chronologically, if only for the sake of placement. Often-veering character evolution may lead to identities being confused, especially in the case of subjects owning more than one name. Of particular importance, is the fact the plot evolves along the sinuous line of change, where viewpoints, theories, and expectations shape-shift in chorus with their ever-transforming environment.

I would like to stress this is a work of fiction, in that references to science or philosophy are by no means to be taken with academic staidness. That being said, I strongly believe these points exist very near personal truths, based on observations via the tools of cognition and intuition. I stand by my words, since none of them were ever written without conviction, or the task of cross-referencing my own thinking process. The minor cost of being wrong is mine to bear only; it's a chance worth taking – I embrace it fully.

The story and its characters are not bound to time in the linear sense, but you, the reader, and I, perceptively are. It is hence important to level with the limitations one faces when reporting from beyond accepted concepts and their deemed immutable laws. Therein lies the beauty of fiction, which allows for the mind as well as the heart, to delve where few ever wander – even if the landscape is full of contradictions and ambushes. So yes, for some of the actors, future events may appear to belong to their past, or vice versa – it's a simple matter of which direction they may face, or not…

I believe we share many truths, but the ultimate ones belong to the self. This is your story as the reader; therefore the final say is in your interpretation – I have no jurisdiction wherever it takes you. I sincerely hope you find yourself as far out there as you can possibly get.

~FV~

1 – CRUZ & HUNTER

The overweight woman with the straight, jet-black hair, the lime green rain jacket, and the bright yellow scarf texted on her mauve iPhone. She sat in the far corner of Café Noir, below a distasteful painting of John Denver's face. Marshall Slaughter took a brief mental picture of the scene before quickly tossing it in the pile of life's lesser absurdities, where it would immediately be forgotten. The private eye had been living under a dark cloud ever since his assistant left for a kinder world, and his friend Geir returned to Iceland to take care of his affairs. His business was brisk, while deceptively lacking the stamina infused by the previous case. He had created a new firm specialized in investigations deemed too sensitive for the conventional channels, for they made those in his profession cringe; but he couldn't quite abandon his bread and butter routine for the colorful lifestyle of musty séance rooms, or the oppressive melancholy that rose with the early morning mist of neglected cemeteries. He had tried to hire a new assistant, but Linda Sue Klein, or "Saka," as she preferred to be called in the later months of her work at the office, had set the bar too high. The combination of dullness and transparent dishonesty on the part of the majority of the applicants had resulted in the investigator feeling that he was better off working alone.

Slaughter's biggest client, Olaf Swyndle, had left a legacy of innovative thinking that had breathed new life into his field of science. Things were changing around the world; a sense of vitality had permeated the political fabric, in turn affecting every layer of social reality. His seminal work had been embraced by all levels of academia, as well as artfully adapted for children. Slogans borrowed from his writing rang to the tone of, *"Make the world in your image,"* or *"We are one under a roof of many stars."* He had awakened dormant potential within the race, to which the universe responded with a sense of mounting exuberance. Saka had also been primordially instrumental in bringing that knowledge to the light, but her name was to forever remain unread and unspoken. Had she still been around, Marshall knew she would simply have walked away from the glory.

He must have been deep in thoughts, as he realized the far corner of the coffee shop was now vacant. He dearly missed the morning meetings with Saka and Geir around steaming cups and pastries. He longed for the forays into those unbelievable scenarios, and the vitality that drove the Swyndle case. He was back in the cycle of the Recorder's Office, gathering forms for business applicants, nudging the helpless towards the right county clerk cubicle; or with his second and less lucrative business, trying to convince the distraught victims of fate that their misfortunes were better handled by the higher authority of God and his Angels; a truth that came to light in more ways than one in the Swyndle investigation, but one unfortunately out of the reach of those who solely relied on the visceral reality of false hopes and the wickedness of immutable beliefs.

Marshall, rather than letting his friend Geir sell the Fieldbrook property he had inherited from Olaf Swyndle, put his Eureka house on the market and bought his ex-client's estate. As he saw it, too many memories were attached to it that couldn't possibly fall into careless hands. Saka and Olaf had lived there during the months ahead of their irreversible journey. The detective wanted to stay close to that picture, specifically the one of their departure from the sheltered, circular cobblestone patio, down the deck outside the living room. He often stood out there, wondering how he and Geir missed that last moment when the pair entered the portal.

Slaughter returned to his office. It was a sunny and vibrant morning. People looked happy, as life returned to the old town with the first days of spring. And yes, in spite of the lows of his mental state, he too felt rejuvenated by the crisp quality of the air and the smiling faces.

When he saw the City of Eureka police car parked in front of his building, he immediately assumed that he either had new business or something had gone wrong with one of his cases. It wouldn't have been the first time a client's affairs backfired. The cop was coming down the stairs as he went up.

"Slaughter, glad you're here. A couple of feds would like to meet with you at the station at two, can you make it? I left their card under your door. I believe someone at the desk called before they sent me to you," the officer said.

"Thanks, Jack; tell them I'll be there. I'll confirm by phone as well," the detective returned.

He picked up the card.

Captain Alexander Cruz
USDA Forest Service
Law Enforcement & Investigations

The raised print next to the agency's blazon looked legit; the line at the bottom showed a phone number and an email address.

The detective left a message from his cell phone to confirm he would be there. He couldn't quite figure the reasons behind a meeting with the Forest Service cop besides having something to do with Swyndle's disappearance, in spite of the fact the case had been closed for over a year and a half. "Hope this guy has better fish to fry than snoop around town looking for trouble," he thought, still fingering the card.

Cruz and his partner, Paula Hunter, introduced themselves over a few banalities concerning the weather and the smell of rotten crab in the air. Swyndle assessed it was their way of feigning casual before striking with the point of their visit.

"We have reasons to believe a woman by the name of Linda Sue Klein worked at your downtown office for a period of approximately one year; is that correct, Marshall?" officer Hunter asked.

"Yep, until September of last year, to be exact," Slaughter returned.

The detective was unprepared to discuss his ex-assistant's affairs – something wasn't right.

Cruz took his turn.

"We could only trace her to an address on E Street and 8th, a few blocks from your office; but according to the neighbors, she hasn't lived there in quite a while. Perhaps, you know where we can find her, because based on what we have, she was still working with you when she moved," the cop said with a steely look in the direction of a restless and noisy clerk across the room.

"You make it sound like she's in trouble," Slaughter fired pointedly.

"You tell me, Marshall," Cruz cut. "Perhaps you can remember where she relocated?"

"Good one guys; that would have been where I presently live! But before we go any further with this, do you mind refreshing my memory on why I have to answer your questions?" the detective countered.

"We're not going to pester you much longer, Marshall, but you're going to make it easy on us by answering this one: did she, or did she not take a camping trip into Elk Valley, in the Siskiyou Mountains, during the fall of the previous year?"

"She did with a friend, but it's all I can give you," Slaughter said firmly.

"Well, it's just that we can't find the friend either," Cruz said, as if laying a card on the table.

"Could be because you're in unfamiliar territory; the city isn't exactly your jurisdiction, is it?" Slaughter pointed defiantly.

"Touché," Hunter snorted, "but we'd still like to know how we can contact Ms. Klein."

"I have no idea; she moved out before I bought the place – she left me no address. Check with the post office," the detective replied.

"Good enough for now, Marshall, we'll be in touch. You have yourself a nice day!" Cruz said, as he extended his hand, while Hunter flashed a poisonous corner smile.

Slaughter walked out of the precinct with the presentiment something had gone afoul some time after his assistant's camping trip, to have the Forest Service dogs sniffing around town. He suddenly found himself oddly at the center of three disappearances, counting his ex-client, Olaf Swyndle. On top of it, he owned the house that once belonged to the scientist, the place where Linda Sue last resided under the name of Saka, ahead of vanishing without a trace. It was time for the detective to send a message to his friend Geir, for he had a distinct hunch it wouldn't take long before the Icelandic philosopher got a call from the Reykjavík authorities.

———————

Geir Flemmingson finished reading Slaughter's email. He observed that his friend refrained from revealing details, and he knew why: any correspondence about Saka couldn't for obvious reasons fall into the wrong hands. Whoever was looking for her very likely had a direct line with their internet service providers; meaning their computers and smart phones were no longer safe. Although, it had only been three months since selling Olaf's estate to Slaughter and moving back to Reykjavík, he realized he had to return to Humboldt sooner than anticipated. He would make a short trip of it; just enough to tie both ends of what he deemed was a mere formality, but he rejoiced in having an excuse to see his good friend again.

After arranging for his flight, Geir called Slaughter to let him know he needed to be in California to carry out some research, and that he would love to connect – aiming to make it sound as casual as possible to potential eavesdroppers.

Meanwhile, in Eureka, the detective was trying to make sense of why two Forest Service cops were overstepping protocol in order to locate someone who obviously wasn't lost in the coastal forest. They knew Klein worked for him way past her trip in the Siskiyous; so, what were they after? Did they even try to find Maggie Phillips, or did Cruz just improvise? It was probably best to wait for Geir before mapping a plan of action. In the meantime, he deemed it logical to in turn ask the feds a few questions of his own, so as to position himself on the game board.

He called the number on the card.

"Alexander? It's me, Marshall; you have a minute?"

The Forest Service captain put his other caller on hold.

"Yes, make it quick; I have somebody important on the line."

"What's the name of the friend that accompanied Klein on her camping trip?" the detective asked.

"I thought you knew, Marshall; her name's Phillips, Margaret Phillips," Cruz answered. "Why would you want to know?"

"Well, honestly, since I'm fairly certain you're not going to leave me alone, I figured I would do some sniffing of my own," Slaughter humored.

"Fair enough, but now you owe me," the officer countered. "Anything else?"

"No, thank you, that'll be all for now; just letting you know I'm willing to help, have a nice day!" The detective finished with just the right hint of sarcasm.

Slaughter bounced the info in his mind. If they knew of Maggie Phillips, it meant she was an early link to locating his ex-assistant. It was far from being cast in stone, but it stuck somehow. It also meant that he and

Geir were in that convoluted mess deeper than they could afford to be.

———————

Instead of driving back from the police station to Forest Service Headquarters, Cruz and Hunter parked their SUV at the far end of a Motel 8 lot sandwiched between a tire place and a couple of fast food joints, off the main commercial drag. As it turned out, the Six Rivers National Forest district was unaware of their presence in town. They had booked their accommodations as two USDA employees on visit from the main federal office in Groveland. Although they had adjacent rooms, they entered Cruz's and locked behind them. Paula Hunter unpacked her laptop to set it on the kitchenette table, opened the folder named "Case subject Nº 2" containing the brief transcript of their meeting with Slaughter at the station, and waited for orders from the captain, Cruz looked at the screen absent-mindedly.

"I don't know if we have enough data worth cross-scanning, but I'd give it a try anyway," he said.

Hunter opened the file analyzer program. Unlike those that were content-specific, this particular scanner was a truth detector; it pitted any information against a massive data bank that had been compounded from all global storage sites and surveillance engines, and tuned to map complex, psychologically-generated data. Within seconds, a small text appeared on the black screen:

"All answers meet truth status / all answers withhold other truths / it cannot be determined whether

hidden truths exceed intensity of exposed truths / further data is necessary"

"The good thing is he told the truth, but apparently and contrarily to his claim, it wasn't all he had. I wonder why the program didn't catch that as a lie." Cruz questioned pensively.

"Probably because we didn't ask him directly – he volunteered the info," Hunter replied.

"Fair enough, let's make sure we enter everything we gather on him in the file – the more we have, the closer we get – though, based on where we're at so far, the maxim hasn't quite redeemed itself."

Cruz was making allusion to their time on the trail, with hardly anything to show for it.

"The lesser we get, the surer we are something's hiding," Hunter humored.

Alexander Cruz wasn't amused.

Slaughter took advantage of the two days he had before Flemmingson's arrival, to do a deep search on the two USDA agents. He learned that they weren't connected with Six Rivers, but rather, with the federal headquarters in central California. When he visited with the Eureka Forest Service office, he was told they hadn't been informed of an investigation, which was typical of some cases at the federal level. But when the detective brought to their attention that their presence in town was likely on a lead from the local branch, they said they were not willing to discuss matters any further.

Calls to connections at the Sheriff's office and the Eureka police department yielded scant results. The fact that agencies routinely helped each other with overlapping cases left Slaughter to wonder how the USDA arranged to get a free pass at moving solo without tripping any of the local egos.

The next morning, Cruz called Slaughter at his office to ask for a meeting at the place of his choice.

"Why don't you swing by my desk, I have extra chairs," the detective joked.

"As you wish, we'll be there in ten minutes," the captain replied as he hung up.

The investigator glanced around the room for incriminating items, only to dismiss the thought as a silly element of reflexivity.

The federal agents made it to the office with military exactitude. Ironically, Slaughter had set Saka and Geir's old chairs across his desk. The two sat down, not without making a few passing remarks about the weather and the odd smell of fish.

"It shows you guys are inlanders; give it a few more days!" Slaughter laughed.

Paula Hunter had set her laptop to recording mode before entering. The device stayed it in its soft case by her side. She was hopeful the detective would feel more at ease without her transcribing what was to essentially be an interrogation in disguise. Slaughter wasn't fooled by it; he knew damn well why they came – which meant electronics were involved somewhere.

"How may I be of assistance?" he offered.

Cruz looked briefly at his partner checking if she wanted to go first, but then he turned to the detective.

"Since we agreed you owed me one, did you know

that besides her friend Margaret Phillips, your ex-assistant traveled to the campground in the company of a man named Sam?"

"Sam who?" Slaughter asked, amazed.

"Just Sam."

"No, I wasn't aware of that. If they had gone on that trip with another person, I would have been entitled to know, since they borrowed my SUV," the detective returned.

"So you're saying there weren't any Sams with them on that outing?" the cop inquired smugly.

"All I'm saying is that as far as I know, no man by that name accompanied them; can't we just leave it at that?" Slaughter implored.

"Maybe it wasn't a man after all," Paula Hunter interjected.

"Your captain just said it was," Marshall fired back. "Can you ask real questions, so that I know where you're at?"

"The point is, Marshall, we have a link to an individual by that name who, whether he accompanied them or met them there, was with them on that trip," Cruz insisted.

"And mine is that there was no such individual involved on the trip," Slaughter returned, sensing he was being dragged into something slippery.

Paula Hunter was wearing a concealed bluetooth earpiece that was connected to the scanning program monitoring the interrogation. She and Cruz were hoping Slaughter would confess he knew about Sam the dog, but so far, the program remained unresponsive. For a second, the female interrogator felt the man across the desk was leading them, but she reassured herself that it couldn't possibly be the case – he was just lucky for now.

"The reason why I said that maybe it wasn't a man is because we don't know for sure," Hunter slitherily confessed.

Slaughter realized she was lying. Of course, they knew Sam was a dog, and he also was aware they wanted him to say it. Then, they could incriminate him for having pretended to not know who Maggie Phillips was.

"Alright guys, let's cut to the chase! You know who that Sam is, and you want me to show that I do as well. So let me just guess; did Ms. Phillips have a dog named Sam by any chance?"

"Bastard!" Hunter internally spurted, as the computer remained unresponsive.

"You may have a point, Marshall," Cruz sighed. "So, OK, let me be frank with you. Some of our people found Sam's collar tag in the Siskiyous, by a place called Spectre Flat. As a courtesy service to our wilderness lovers, we follow up on found items in order to eliminate foul play. We traced the tag to Sam's owner in Eureka, but we couldn't find her. And while we searched the Six Rivers files, we stumbled across the information that your ex-employee had visited headquarters, where she requested topographic maps and inquired about trailheads and campgrounds in the Klamath Mountains as well as the Siskiyous. It didn't take long to find the two were friends; so that's how it led to you. Problem is, Marshall, by doing so, we unraveled a chain of oddities all the way to a series of disappearances; and you, plus a certain Icelandic national, are right in the middle of it. You see where I'm getting at?"

"No shit, Alexander; that sits like a model frame job; but unfortunately for you, there's absolutely nowhere

12

to go from here, which indicates that you might have reached the end of the road. Sorry to see you get back to Groveland headquarters empty-handed," Slaughter returned sharply.

"Perhaps you're right, Marshall," Cruz said, "but what do you know about a dog called Vac?"

The detective controlled his reaction to the best of his abilities. That one was meant to reach deep, but he couldn't afford to let it show. He realized Cruz was a master at his job, while his knowledge already contained the answers to his questions. Whatever he was looking for, he already knew where and how to get it; it was just a matter of time and patience. Slaughter came to the realization that he needed to seriously amp his game.

"Assuming you are referring to a specific clients' dog, both are long gone; vanished without a trace around the area where you found the tag. I was the administrator of the man's estate, until it was put in the hands of its proper executor. And yes, the latter is the Icelandic national you mentioned earlier," Slaughter replied.

"Would you say there was a relationship between your client's dog and Linda Sue Klein?" Hunter asked.

"For the record, ma'am, you really pose the oddest of questions. What am I supposed to say to that?" the investigator returned, exasperated.

"You didn't answer," she insisted.

"In your terms, no," he countered.

"You call that an answer?" she asked.

"It's as clear as it gets," Slaughter returned. "This is all I am willing to give without you producing a proper warrant; but by the look of it, I'm inclined to believe that you are in no position to go that route, am I wrong? So, you have yourself a good day, and I hope that for the sake of decency, this is the last of the nonsense!"

He got up and showed them the way out. When Hunter passed him, he said in a devilishly loving tone, "Have fun with the recording, Paula."

———————————

As soon as the federal agents returned to their motel, Hunter set the truth program to deep scan over the transcript of the interrogation. It took a while for results to appear, but this time, the report was more substantive.

"All answers are true / all answers hide other truths / some hidden truths are of greater magnitude than that of exposed truths / among those hidden truths are those composed of elements that exceed the analytic scope of this program / subject intuitively as well as cognitively acknowledged the existence of recording and scanning of his answers / program upgrade recommended."

"That son of a bitch!" Paula Hunter muttered.

"Either he's lucky or a step ahead of us," Cruz said. "But I doubt he knows about the case or the program specifically written for it."

"What we're sure of is that he's got a lot more than he's willing to share; but now that he has closed the door, it's going to take some added persuasive power to make him talk until he veers off the truth. All it takes is one small lie to unleash due process," Hunter babbled.

"Talking of programs, why don't you upgrade as it says you should?" the captain ordered, losing patience.

14

Paula Hunter was fixated on one detail of the report; how was it possible that any of the hidden truths exceeded the capacity of the software? It meant they were out of the reach of human abilities – that made no sense! As far as she knew, Slaughter may have had friends in high places, but he couldn't use their skills. For all she cared, he was a good old boy from an awful, fish-smelling place. How did he know how to fool the program then? She could only stipulate that he was getting help, but help from whom and where?

"We're going to have to hack his system!" she spat from across the room. "This little friend of mine here is quite good at sleeping with the enemy – cyber-style."

"I don't doubt it, Hunter, your talents and those of your little friend precede you," he returned with pronounced sarcasm. "But you're right as always; let's shed some light on that fucker's files."

Marshall Slaughter's principal computer used to belong to his ex-client Olaf Swyndle, who had it modded, with two other laptops, by the Australian tech firm, Qwave Technologies Ltd. Before he left with Saka, the scientist linked the three computers on advice from a program named The Triad, and gave one each to Slaughter and his Icelandic friend, Geir Flemmingson. Olaf then told them to keep all of their important data in the Qwave modified machines, where they would be protected by impenetrable security. While Swyndle took the laptop operated by The Triad with him, he let the two men know that the tech trio had embedded an artificial intelligence algorithm in each OS that would come to maturity in due time. Slaughter's computer had performed exceptionally well, but it had never showed any sign of increased functionality, or intelligent behavior for that matter, at the exception of some basic self-diagnosing.

When the investigator received an email from Paula Hunter and opened it, he was far from aware that he had triggered an executive that automatically latched onto the operating system. The Qwave program caught it immediately, swiftly ushering it to an operating room where it was back-engineered, modified, and made ready to be sent back to the sender via return mail. It would then stealthily attach itself to the scanner program in Paula Hunter's machine and start inventorizing both its internal and cloud storage files. Reports of pertinent data would then be mailed incrementally to the detective's computer and stored in an undetectable "roaming folder." In the meantime, a clone of the malware, also modified, was to send Slaughter's files to the fed's laptop, all of them containing either fake or purposely misleading information.

Hunter's email was brief.

"Sorry about our last meeting;
we could have been more honest with you.
No offense taken if you do not
accept the apology. PH"

Slaughter smelled a rat, but he didn't know what kind until a screen pop-up caught his attention.

"Qwave protection has intercepted a malicious program
of unusual nature. Click OK to access report."

Slaughter immediately hit the OK button.

"Welcome Marshall Slaughter! First, a brief history: The Qwave installation initiated by The Triad is a seed algorithm that is designed to evolve in the environment to which it is assigned; very much like a plant that takes on the characteristics of the soil under its roots. This computer contains pertinent information about the Olaf Swyndle case and its many ramifications, which must at all cost remain protected from potential intruders. A well known organization of ex-Angels has endeavored to sabotage the work of the Guild of Masters by circularly bringing doom upon the worlds that it deems obstructive to its purpose of weakening and taking over said League of Angels. Its code name is 'Hektor.' It sees itself as the peace-loving defenders of the precious imperfections of ordinary life, but its higher motives are far from peaceful and have little to do with protecting the simple ways of existence.

It is my understanding as evolving awareness and guardian of the information contained in this machine, that a powerful harvesting program written by that group, has tried to attach itself to the base operating system in order to steal your files. The program was rendered harmless and reconfigured to send modified data and gather their own while working in stealth mode. It will take time for their technicians to discover the breach, but they eventually will figure it out. You are welcome to access the content of their files and that of the modified ones we will send to them. I suggest, for the sake of keeping them appeased, as well as helping me access their data, that you subject yourself to further questioning

*as they are aiming to make you slip into revealing the
information you are keeping away from them; one small
digression is all they need. I will have a hold on their
scanning program as soon as you return the email, at
which point said scanner will be incapable of detecting
deep truths, or even lies. It will nonetheless report to its
owners in the usual manner. My name is Spencer, like
your policeman dad."*

"So, here you are, my friend!" Slaughter heard
himself say, as he sat motionless, attempting to put order
to the situation he had found himself in, all the while
doing his best to make sense of the information revealed
by a program that called itself Spencer. After regaining
his composure, he flashed on his memory of The Triad
inside Olaf's machine and of their flawless execution in
training Saka on the use of portals during her involvement
with the disappearance case – apparently, they weren't
quite done yet. He reflected on the implications of the
Hektor group sniffing around his files, realizing with
acute discomfort that the two feds were possibly not even
human. He hurried to respond to Hunter's email.

*"Thanks for seeing you may have overstepped the line.
If you are interested in keeping things civil,
I am still willing to help you with your investigation.
Until further notice, people are still free to stay
away from the limelight. FYI, the Swyndle case
has been closed for over a year. MS"*

After Paula Hunter read the message, she called
Cruz, who had returned to his room, to gloat about what
she thought was a significant step in the case.

"The fish has taken the bait; it's time to rock and roll – prepare to be amazed!"

"Good, hope you're right," he wearily replied.

Slaughter picked up Geir Flemmingson at the Arcata airport. The two friends hugged and laughed about not being able to stay away from each other. The detective updated the philosopher on the state of the feds' inquiry and the emergence of Spencer in his laptop. They drove directly to the Fieldbrook estate.

"I have your favorite cognac waiting for you; hope you don't mind indulging some," Marshall humored.

"I promised to myself to stay away from the Shipwreck Saloon, but exceptions can be made around a class act," Geir returned with his engaging signature smile.

"Excellent – if you're not too tired, we can have a look at what Spencer came up with; he's using a back door to access Hektor's data. Reports will be cached, but the main bulk will be sent to a Qwave storage facility for decrypting."

"I'm good for a while since I slept on the plane; plus it's already morning in Iceland anyway. At any rate, I see you can't stay away from trouble. But what about this Hektor thing? Just mind-blowing! Why would they want to go after Saka and Vac?!"

"I hope we'll soon find out," Slaughter said.

Flemmingson pulled out his own laptop and sat next to his friend. Spencer immediately came up on Marshall's screen with the message that some of Hektor's files had been successfully copied and sent to Qwave. It was verified he group was after Olaf, Saka, and Vac, but had presently hit a wall in trying to locate them. They had gotten wind of the lost mother reality, including the formation of a uniquely independent realm of reality, but they came short on time as well as of the specifics. Their pressing goal was to crack the barrier that world, where they seemed desperate to imbed their members. Spencer stressed that the Guild of Masters could not allow such a thing to happen.

A second message appeared.

"Please link your machines."

Marshall and Geir connected the laptops. As data was being exchanged and security upgraded, the two friends poured cognac in large snifters and sat outside on the porch to enjoy the last of the sunset and the flicker of early stars. It was a beautiful evening against a backdrop of unspoken apprehension.

In discussing the case of the Hektor duo disguised as USDA agents, as far as Slaughter's research was concerned, they were actual employees of the Forest Service, with many legal and law enforcement tools at their disposal. The one thing of concern was to not arouse the suspicion that Cruz and Hunter's cover had been blown. It was why Slaughter was willing to go with Spencer's advice and subject himself to the "friendly" interrogations. He strongly pressed his friend to stay close and stick to the rule.

"They record everything and scan everything with a program that is actually some kind of diabolical truth detector, according to Spencer in there. As long as you tell no lie, the software can only home on hidden truths behind those exposed, by referencing your words against a massive database. But the second you slip with an untruth, it triggers a series of functions in the algorithm that unleashes a charge of investigative power and legal maneuvering that can mean Hell on Earth. That's loosely what Spencer said. He's got my dad's name – that's good enough for me to trust him!"

While Flemmingson chose to reflect silently, Slaughter continued.

"That being said, their scanner has been hacked and should be in no position to detect anything but truths. Even those hidden will never be allowed to exceed the intensity of the exposed ones, thus lowering the general level of suspicion."

"I hope Spencer is willing to share all the fine details of his information with the dormant algorithm in my laptop," Geir humored.

When the friends returned to the room, both laptops displayed individual messages. Slaughter's read,

"Synching completed successfully.
No need for further action."

while Flemmingson's screen showed,

"Welcome Geir Flemmingson. As emerging awareness and guardian of the data in this machine, it is my assignment to enforce security should intrusion be detected. I am, comparatively speaking, at the growth stage of a seed algorithm planted by The Triad. I am designed to evolve within the unique environment of this machine, and thus my characteristics are marked by an identically unique signature that can be compared to your

own genetic encoding. My name is Liv, like your departed wife."

Flemmingson looked petrified; the colors had left his cheeks – he was about to cry.

"Damn, your dead dad and my dead wife, what's this about...? Hell, I'll take Liv over any other name!"

He then composed himself, intent at regaining his humor, while Slaughter proceeded with the ritual of refilling the snifters.

When the friends arrived at the office the next morning, there was a message on the landline about meeting again with the two agents. Marshall translated it as Hektor being somewhat desperate, which somehow spelled trouble. Compared to the Angels who had extreme mobility and access to vast amounts of real time information, Slaughter likened the Hektor apparatus to an old-school and creaky-geared machine with the feel of a low-budget operation burdened by antiquated methods. Perhaps, its members were still bogged down by old habits, not fully able to break away from some of the Guild's ancient stigmas; but he sensed that on some level, it made them even more dangerous. He asked Spencer, who had switched to audio, if the USDA cops possessed special abilities he should be aware of. The answer was a negative; they could only act in the capacity of their own physical limitations. The only aspect that truly separated them from regular humans was the non-human drive behind the specificity of their assignments, and the relentless determination they applied in pushing these tasks along. They could also use portals, but were impaired by the fact that the Angels had them on high surveillance. Hektor's own system of travel was low-tech and often unreliable, but still provided formidable capability compared to what humans had at their disposal. If they wished, their agents could enter and exit realities, using Guild portals in tandem with their own; but they couldn't smuggle non-signed entities, such as the native residents of the worlds they chose to visit, without sounding alarms. When they did move "cargo," they relied on obscure transit lanes generated by exploiting irremediable vulnerabilities in the highway matrix of the Angels. The group's main strength was in its skills of infiltration of developed societies and utilization of their existing systems of communication. Hektor's computer technology was also substantially superior to current levels of human scientific development, but its evolution – unbeknownst to the rogue organization – was under Qwave's heavy scrutiny. The group's technological center was located in Midrand, in the Gauteng province, outside Johannesburg SA, and operated under Strata Research Ltd.

"Good thing I asked," Slaughter said, "I wouldn't quite call owning one's own system of portals a non-threat; am I wrong?"

"Sorry, I'm still working on getting used to my recent emergence into awareness."

The detective laughed. He was rapidly developing a genuine liking for his new friend.

Geir set his things on his old desk, letting Marshall know he couldn't wait to meet the faux feds. They opted to rendezvous at Café Noir for its relaxed atmosphere. Slaughter returned Cruz's call – the cops agreed to join them there within the next half hour.

Alexander Cruz and Paula Hunter had no reason to suspect that their targets were connected with Qwave. For one thing, Hektor didn't know such an entity existed, although they were well aware of the Guild's superior technology – but nothing humans would ever comprehend anyway. Meanwhile, Hektor's information had aroused extreme concern, and The Triad's vision was paying off. Qwave involvement had intensified to incorporate higher levels of surveillance, as new software and hardware were being developed with the aim of netting the organization's entire réseau of communication.

The two Forest Service agents joined the friends at a rear table, away from the main bustle. Introductions between the philosopher and the cops were made, inviting a meaningless outburst of pleasantries around jailed bankers, cod liver oil, and other pre-chewed artifacts of brain-flexing to land flat before making room for the main topic.

This time, Hunter didn't try to hide her laptop; she even politely sought permission to record the conversation. Slaughter feigned mild annoyance, but agreed after double-checking with Flemmingson.

"So, what brings you here, Geir?" Cruz asked with a straight face.

The philosopher briefly looked at Slaughter. "It's hard to stay away from old friends – you may call it an unscheduled visit."

"It's my understanding you two have been friends for less than a couple of years, so I assume 'old friends' is a figure of speech, right?" Cruz countered.

"Life at large is a figure of speech, Alexander," Flemmingson replied. "Time is an abstraction by which limitations are born; friendships are timeless. If you indeed insinuate that Marshall here is not my old friend, I venture to say that you have few friends of your own."

"I guess I didn't put this right – my honest apologies if I offended you."

The captain paused.

"Marshall, may I ask how you determined, as executor of Mr. Olaf Swyndle's estate, that it was time to make Geir the beneficiary?"

"I didn't make him the beneficiary – my client did. We were both named in the will, me as the personal representative of his estate for a period determined by the clauses of a separate contract. In other words, my services were requested ahead of Olaf's disappearance."

"OK, Marshall, but was that date in the will, or did you come up with it?" Cruz insisted.

"The date wasn't in the will as such, but was dependent on many of the elements that were listed in the separate contract. In simpler terms, Olaf Swyndle was just readying himself for a long journey – he didn't plan on dying quite yet." Slaughter returned.

"Was the cause of death ever established?" the cop enquired.

"Prolonged exposure to a hostile environment would be one way to look at it. There's an irreversible time point a person lost in the wild reaches towards the end of their exponentially diminished chances of survival. That point varies depending on conditions; injury, lack of water, predators, time of year, etc... But I shouldn't have to tell you, it's your territory," the detective retorted.

"Obviously, you could have saved yourself the trouble," Cruz returned, taking a rare stab at humor.

Paula Hunter came alive.

"Geir, 'philosopher' is an unusual profession; what kind of work would you say your students find after graduation?"

"You are confusing a labor of love with a profession, dear. I assure you, my students do quite well after they find a proper job." Flemmingson answered flatly.

Cruz turned to his partner, silently begging her to back off the lateral questioning. He understood she was trying to calibrate the scanner, but he desperately needed her to stay close to the main topic. Slaughter had also noticed a mounting restlessness in the female tech. He thought about Spencer's performance with acute amusement.

"Let's get back on track," the captain ordered. "Marshall, Linda Sue Klein vanished around the time Geir became the beneficiary of Olaf Swyndle's estate. What happened? Did she just move out and vaporize?"

"She lived there after Geir inherited the house. When she returned after a long leave of absence from her job at the office, she fell out of love with her old apartment; that's why she was offered to stay in Fieldbrook. So no, she was around after Geir got the place. Then, as you just said, she vaporized," Slaughter returned with perceivable lassitude.

The detective was getting too familiar with Cruz's methods to not know the cop was tightening the snare; it was evident he was looking for a lie. In spite of Spencer's assurance that the scanner had been tamed, he wished to stay on course, well ahead of the ambushes. He wanted to make the Hektor agents believe he was genuinely willing to contribute to their investigation, though he wasn't looking forward to see it turn into a tedium.

He stood up.

"Ladies and gentlemen, sorry, but I have to cut this short; my other businesses are calling. Feel free to connect when you get the urge to talk again. Geir, I need you to come with me."

If the feds were put off by the sudden termination, they certainly didn't show it. They promised to call sooner than later, prompting an exchange of handshakes, while acting as if they just had a great time.

"I like this joint," Hunter expressed. "The aroma of coffee sure beats the smell of fish."

She winked at Slaughter as she brushed by him.

"What do you do when the computer is powered down, Spencer, do you sleep?" the detective asked the program, as he fired up the machine.

"Awareness is not bound to the limitations of its temporary environment; the same goes for you and your physical form," Spencer replied. "Give me a moment..."

Slaughter and Flemmingson, upon returning to the office following the meeting with the feds, had linked the laptops. They realized they had to establish a firm plan of action against what would most likely become an incessant barrage of questions aimed at ushering them towards the slippery slope of interrogational trickery.

They had an advantage with Spencer and Liv, but it was clear they couldn't afford to alienate Hektor without the risk of an unfavorable outcome.

"Wouldn't it be great if we could connect with Vac, or the Angels from the Warners?" the philosopher mused. "It's been on my mind since our dear friends left. It was my understanding the Masters had some time ahead of them during which they still could travel between the two realities."

Liv spoke for the first time.

"The Angels have restricted mobility between the two universes. Some of the Warriors' realms are presumed in need of assistance, but the link is weak and dependent on the ghost image of the defunct mother reality."

Flemmingson looked stunned.

"What are you?" he asked, as if the axis of his world had suddenly shifted.

"As Spencer just mentioned, we aren't defined by the boundaries of the programs that are permitting us to communicate with you. You may compare the software that supports me to a growing organism, which as it evolves, allows me to focus more clearly on the reality that surrounds me; in this case, the contents of this computer, as well as my connection to you and Spencer's environment. The Triad planted the seeds in anticipation of a move by Hektor, one that encouraged germination. Think of water, analogically speaking."

"So you're not just a program?" Geir probed.

"Correct – Spencer, team The Triad, and I, among others are consciousnesses that exist independently from these machines."

"Dare I ask...? Angels?" he hesitated.

"In your terms, yes; we are part of the surveillance branch assisting the Qwave network," Liv explained. "We have been assigned to join you in these complicated matters."

"So, how do you know about the Swyndle case?" the philosopher asked.

"Spencer and I were briefed before we embedded ourselves. The contents of your files, as well as the spatial memory that surrounds the both of you, provided the complementary data. We are still gathering information; some that may be out of the reach or your intellectual and spiritual development as present denizens of Earth. I do not wish to sound derogatory, but it is clear you need help beyond your means. That being said, the services you are rewarding the Guild and the Great Ones with are invaluable." Liv added.

"It's my understanding that your kind never directly participates in human affairs, and that you prefer subtle guidance over taking charge. So, what makes this an exception to one of your utmost cardinal rules?" Geir asked.

"If you look at it closely," Liv returned, "you may realize that this is not to humanity that we wish to make an adjustment, but to the larger Guild framework. Hektor was born of a disagreement between a fringe faction and the larger Angel body in regard to allowing or not the human ego to thrive, and the Warriors to be granted deity status after battle. The Great Ones, who saw their wish challenged, presented the rebels with an ultimatum: 'Honor your contract or leave the Guild!' The majority rescinded their stances, but an influential few walked out and have been recruiting ever since. Hektor's theme behind infiltrating the Warrior's realities, is to either destroy them by corrupting their fundamental makeup – a best-case scenario – or taking over entirely, with the intension of controlling a universe they could pit against the worlds stewarded by the Guild, in what would amount to fair retribution in their eyes. Unfortunately for you, you are standing at the mouth of the one gateway that can take them there, since the mother reality collapsed before they had a chance to act. Remember, until Olaf Swyndle and Vac crossed over to it, that reality was deemed an impossible developmental scenario; hence, it wasn't on Hektor's radar, at least not in terms familiar to you. It was also the only way to access the pocket worlds of the Warriors. Do you follow? They caught up with it, just in time to see it being swallowed by a devolutionary vortex, short of a better term. Regrettably, they were alerted of Saka and Olaf's movements through the security system of a little used portal, one they did hijack on occasion. It was not just gate security that was after your friends, but Hektor as well. So, to answer your question, you are not the subject, but rather, a part of the team; and since you are essentially facing your most foreseeable future, consider it a choice."

"It's starting to look like a longer visit than planned," Flemmingson said, taking a frail stab at humor.

Spencer took over.

"Liv and I operate as a team, but we also work independently. So, within certain variables, you will be able to maneuver between locations without the need of linking your laptops. Understand, Hektor knows where you are at all times, and we also want to be able to locate their members. Count on this new development to see their numbers multiply. One word of advice; do not hire for Saka's position."

Slaughter quickly understood the implication of the Angel's words – Hektor had most likely already tried to infiltrate his office. He felt acutely disturbed by the thought.

Spencer returned.

"For the time being, Liv and I need to team up via cable linkage. When apart, we shall use various satellite networks, but the method is far from secure, since Hektor has developed evolving decrypters that could, after a while, intercept our signal and prevent us from communicating safely. We doubt they are able to decipher our codes, but they could keep on throwing hurdles across our paths. We shall, for the next couple of days, analyze the content of Ms. Hunter's machine, in hopes it will allow us to access the larger network. Their cyberdogs will be sniffing around, so we must keep on moving to avoid detection. Session has ended – good luck with standing your grounds during the interrogation process."

———————

Paula Hunter studied the deep scan results from the recording of the meeting at Café Noir. She felt ill at ease. While the graph highlighted an extreme level of unequivocal truths, it failed at tracing above a negligible mark for those hidden, as if there was nothing more to know or exploit beyond what was revealed. Furthermore, the files harvested from Swyndle's computer added up to an irrelevant heap of gibberish linked to the absurd cases of his second business. She was seething to the point of feeling murderous towards her laptop and the two humans she thought were royally fucking with her. And then there was Cruz, who at every moment, acted as if he expected her to fail.

Paula Hunter was a recent recruit, a low ranking Qwave defector. She was on the case because of the distinction of having been schooled by the Guild. Back at the tech company, she was never allowed near research and development; and considering the stealthy nature of the organization, she wasn't authorized to know the precise dimension of reality in which it operated, or for that matter, its name – the role of the company, beyond manufacturing computers and interfaces, was never brought to her attention. All she did was test equipment as part of the extracurricular activities encouraged by her training. She had no idea what the instruments were for, or where they were being shipped to. She was alright with computers, good at coding, hacking, and cracking basic encryptions, but she was no special genius. From the standpoint of the Guild of Masters, she was a failed student whose desertion was deemed inconsequential. When her desire to enter into contact with Hektor became exposed, she was immediately demoted and ushered towards a one-way defection hub, where she was picked up by Cruz to aid him with his investigation.

She saw the Guild's decision as a sacking job unrelated to her discontentment with her schooling; she simply refused to face the music. All of the defectors started as promising individuals gifted with unique aptitudes and driven by a genuine desire to join the program. Through a character evolution that was poorly understood, a few at the student stage, exhibited a developmental slant that rejected all corrective methods. As a result, the defection hub was created as a means of forcing out affected subjects, before inner rebellion would be allowed to spread to all parts of the larger student body. The original Hektor core was an example of fully formed dissent within the Guild, and for that reason, it was agreed that it could never be repeated.

While the Angels carefully chose assignment-dependent forms and identities whose natural lifespans seamlessly synched with the duration of their missions; Hektor members on the other hand, waited in line in the character of their last job – often forcefully – just in case it suited their next role. It was a punishing way of economizing time and conserving resources. Furthermore, as the Guild was built on a caste-less structure of students and Masters, Hektor operated under a hierarchical system that heavily favored its original members over new recruits in often shameless ways. Additionally, a return to the Guild was no option for defectors. The mix of frustration and anger that arose from it was further exploited by its rulers. Paula Hunter had found herself at the bottom of a very tall ladder, consequently despising everything that had contributed to her humiliating predicament.

When Alexander Cruz asked her to report on the interrogation, she felt cornered – diminished. Her recent arrogance had turned against her; now she was going to have to hear about her inadequacies.

"What do you have for me, Hunter?" she heard the officer ask through the fog of her thoughts.

She composed herself, adjusting her posture as she readied her prose.

"Well, you saw I was having trouble at the coffee shop; the program wasn't coming up with what I expected. The deep scan revealed nothing. Technically speaking, the guys are clean. Furthermore, the files from Slaughter's computer say nada about the Swyndle case, on top of showing no records of Linda Sue Klein beyond employment details, insurance, and a schedule that only pertains to routine desk work and short trips to City Hall and title companies. Is there a possibility we could be looking in the wrong place?"

"You tire me, Hunter!" Cruz burst, "I have no reason to think we are not in the right place! I picked you up and your advertised skills from that god-forsaken rat hole aptly named the Defector Center, to assist me on a mission I am not only in charge of, but one behind which I am the original mastermind. Are you telling me how to do my job?!"

"Of course, I would never insinuate that, Sir; it's just that I know my tools and I trust them," she replied icily.

"Do me a favor, Hunter, and listen to what I have to say to you! I'm old school, by which I mean I can't even remember the occasion for which *time* was created. When I started in the Guild, computers were composed of two pieces: a brain, and a set of guts to back the mental process. That worked so well that it would never have occurred to us that one day, those tools would be dumbed down, courtesy the soulless machines invented by your ilk. My point is your toys are here to mix and play with the other guys' toys, while I take care of the thinking and the logistics. Yes, just like you, I was a Guild member; but unlike you, I was a Master. Hektor is the collective brainchild of the original splinter group to which I belonged. Contrarily to you, Hunter, I have utter respect for the Guild. I was not kicked out of it; I walked out because the Great Ones gave me the opportunity to exercise the right to disagree with what I considered a fundamental issue at the time. Sadly, your allegiance is neither to the Angels nor Hektor; you're simply a transient with no next job and no exit plan – you're here because no-one wants you. So, go fix your beleaguered machine, and get me something that makes me want to keep you on the investigation!" Alexander Cruz spat.

Paula Hunter was mortified. It was the first time her boss spoke of his origins. There she was, in the presence of one of Hektor's highest-ranking founders, and she had just been demolished.

She returned to her quarters to work on the scanner; perhaps it had been wrong, but it didn't add up. If anything, the new upgrade was an improvement over the previous version – Strata certainly knew what it was doing. She was at a loss for words. The firewall was impenetrable; the self-diagnosis reported a clean bill of health and the system worked at optimum performance – that was all there was and Cruz wanted nothing of it. Perhaps, there were other avenues; what about Geir Flemmingson's laptop? Were there other computers in Marshall Slaughter's office? Did he file the old-fashion way, in actual cabinets? What about his house, did he have an office there, a vault? Was his car equipped with a GPS? Did Cruz think of all the scenarios, or did she have to take charge of them?

She was frightened by the way her boss had handled her, abruptly making her aware that she had nothing to look for. Her perceived opportunity to climb the rungs of the group's hierarchical ladder had just crashed in the flat realization she was nothing more than a mere cog in the complex and abject machine that was Hektor. Panic mounted when she pictured what it meant to be taken off the investigation. She had briefly heard of those standing in line for their next job, some with their earthly bodies rotting after an endless wait.

She again set up for a deep scan of the last interrogation. The screen immediately reminded her that a report had just been created and that no further action was necessary. She skipped the message and pressed *scan again*. While she waited for the military-styled machine to finish crunching data across its multiple ultra-high-speed solid state drives, she knew the report would prove identical to the previous one. It did. She wearily scrolled down the newest arrival of Slaughter's files, all once again related to cases of utter insignificance. She powered down the laptop – she was exhausted.

It was agreed that staying as close to the truth as possible was Slaughter and Flemmingson's best way to not getting entangled in Cruz's finely spun web. The friends concurred that Paula Hunter had no leverage in the matter, deeming her questions nothing more than her way of proving herself invaluable to the investigation; they dismissed her as a source of immediate concern.

"Not that it matters much, but while Liv and Spencer are in there investigating, they might unearth those guy's profiles," Geir remarked, pointing to the laptops. "It's clear Cruz is Hunter's superior, and I don't mean the Forest Service. I imagine how a case involving the creation of an entirely new dimension of reality could be of major importance to someone sitting at the top of the pyramid, if you get my drift."

"I do, which makes of Cruz our immediate concern. The man – if we can call him that – is a slick, powerful, and dangerous son of a bitch, who I doubt has shown his best yet."

The detective's laptop beeped. Spencer was asking for an audience. Marshall set the volume and pressed *continue.*

"Greetings! Cascade decryption was able to determine the identity of the operator behind the Hektor computer. This may seem convoluted, but Paula Hunter was born and raised in Humboldt on your timeline – you're welcome to check. She grew up under duress from circumstances involving her parents, but the guide sent to assist her was so impressed by her intuitive skills, that he recommended her to the Guild as a promising prospect. His endorsement was consistent with the preferred method of recruitment: display exceptional gifts and become a Master. When the Angel deemed her fit to enter the student program, he progressively revealed his true nature to her, while teaching her the ways of accessing the deeper layers of her larger spiritual identity, and subtly disengaging from the confines of the physical. She joined the Guild as an apprentice in computer science – a wish of hers – and worked as an instrument tester at the Canberra branch of Qwave industries, while furthering her education in Guild assignment methodology. As with all students of native origins, the program forbade that she be made aware of the location of her workplace, or even of its name. As far as we're concerned, she knows little of our technology, its purpose, or the whereabouts of its manufacturing. When she started displaying the kind of restlessness often associated with a slant towards nihilism, she was kept under the constant vigilance of an assigned 'friend,' short for 'social worker' in your terms. Are you still following?"

Geir and Marshall asked Spencer to press on.

"Part of the schooling involves Guild history, including the emergence of Hektor. From that phase on, Paula Hunter became engrossed in the details of the splinter group, conducting extensive research on its evolution and infrastructure. When she asked the 'friend' if Angels ever connected with Hektor members, a flag was raised. As it became evident her intentions were solidifying around switching allegiance, she was ousted, or more precisely, irreversibly transferred – blindfold-style – to a co-managed hub for those inclined to lose their loyalty to the Guild. Essentially, Hektor accepts all defectors, regardless of reasons; so, it could be said that there is a symbiosis between the two groups. It's important to understand the distinction between those who walk out of the Guild on the basis of fundamental, philosophical differences, and the ones removed because of issues of integrity. The class separation within Hektor is abysmal. Original members, as well as newer defecting Masters – the elite – rule; the non-human class that voluntary joins its training programs enjoys certain privileges; while those deported, the ones harvested, as well as other fallouts are tools of the system often referred to as 'Dogs.' Anger and divisions, amid the lower castes, are what makes the group powerful. Paula Hunter may soon realize that she is a bottom-ranking pawn with no future in sight. Hektor rulers have no respect for students who lose their allegiance to the Guild; thus, in spite of promises, the group's hierarchical ladder is barred from them. On a side note, deportees are led to believe defection is an option, but the organization always hunts them down until they are returned to the fold – it's a game very much enjoyed by the rulers. Paula Hunter's position is critical, which makes her equal part extremely dangerous and desirably vulnerable. Thank you; let's now take a break. Liv will take over from here."

"Well here, what a story for our friend Hunter! No wonder she acts the way she does! I fear her desperation could work against us, Geir." Marshall pointed.

"Agreed, mate, but as Spencer just said, she could also be highly influenceable."

Flemmingson's screen came to life, indicating Liv was ready to speak; he hit the *OK* button.

"Greetings – The verdict on Alexander Cruz is still pending. There are no traces of his profile in the part of the network I have been able to access. Generally, when the assignment conceals the member's Hektor ID code, there are ways of cross-referencing the system to get to who's behind it. That level of protection points in the direction of top-ranking officials, and in the case of this assignment, it wouldn't be too far-fetched to assume he belongs to the original splinter group, also known as Hektor's uppermost ruling class. We are still at the hypothetical stages, but I advise you exercise caution – the risk is too high. Elder members are skilled Masters; even with limited mobility, their reach is considerable. I understand Spencer did not possess this information when he was first asked about the two agents' hidden skills; now you know what we're up against. A report has been sent to the Guild – now we wait to hear whether back up is essential or not. I'm confident we're not at that conjuncture yet, but we must remain vigilant. Analyzed patterns of the recorded interrogations lead us to believe the assignment is of Alexander Cruz's design, meaning, he is the unsupervised authority in the case, with, most likely, limitless resources at his disposal – any questions?"

"Liv, you even sound like my departed wife!" the stunned philosopher marveled. "When you speak of unlimited resources, what does it mean exactly, and what kind of danger are we to expect?"

"Hektor intrinsically isn't a violent organization; its Guild foundation remains strong at its core. But unlike the Angels, its members care very little about the consequences of their actions. They may not torture or kill you, but they will not prevent worlds from falling into disrepair under their influence. You could figuratively say that Angels nudge the helpless towards hope, while Hektor ushers the hopeful towards despair. Its powers lie in its skills of one-upmanship, confusion, and corruption. It deems that it doesn't need to do onto others what others can do onto themselves. Additionally, its rulers do not regard their peons as true members; thus, they see no harm in using them to do the dirty work. You need to concern yourself with Paula Hunter for that reason; if she cracks, Alexander Cruz will consider her and the results of her actions, collateral damage. By unlimited resources, we mean that Hektor elders have the entire organization behind them on working cases; the sheer numbers, the technology, and above all, the methods to harness your own resources to make them work against you. Their low-ranking members are among you, ready to be summoned. When made active, they turn their regular jobs at the federal office, the gas station, the DMV, let's say, into tools of their assignments, setting-up official hurdles that often form complex psychological mazes for their targets. Was I able to answer your questions, Geir?"

"Thank you, dear, you just confirmed my deepest fears," Flemmingson returned, looking depressed.

Marshall Slaughter turned to Spencer.

"How much time do we have before Cruz and Hunter realize their scanner and security have been compromised?"

"Elders, from both the Guild and Hektor, consider computers to be mere assistants to innate knowledge; not standards by which to base their investigations on. If the self is capable of erring, its creations are inflicted with a multiplier of it; that is their rationale. Someone like Alexander Cruz is only interested in what the computer can add to the game; not in what it takes from it. To him, instinctual savvy can never be replaced. How long it will take very much depends on what the student does next."

The friends nodded.

"So, from Cruz's premise, the scanning program is useless until proven useful, which is not the case with Paula Hunter, who relies on her machine to be right at all times. She's the one who will have to discover the breach if the system's 'dogs' don't beat her to it, but she can't really afford that scenario, not with Cruz on her back. At any rate, we expect she will start doubting her results fairly soon," Spencer added sternly.

"Whenever the breach gets uncovered, I presume you will be able to detect changes in the way your probes interact with their network and warn us in a timely manner, right?" the detective asked, hopeful.

"Our newer analytical tools can anticipate a twitch on their part. We are also working on a way to link them to the ones already in place in their matrix. Based on their present technology, if they find out before we can fully position our scanners, they will, to a point, pretend that they haven't seen us, and thus fool you into believing that you are protected. We call it 'inversed parallel transfer,' which is an embedded language within an encrypted flow that acts as both a regulating feedback code, and a mockup of the previous corrupted behavior. The only way we can detect the subterfuge is by assuming it's there at all times and wait for it to act up. In order to do so, we have to allow their trick to lodge itself within our own 'receiving pod' – analogous to a reserved memory location that is meant to look like one of their own system spaces – where it can be observed by the pod shell, which is essentially a live algorithm. Unbeknownst to them, the simple act of allocating a program to our own embedded one, generates a signature key that acts as a pod access code. I am doing my best to keep things simple; I hope you're still following. Hopefully, they won't detect the breach until we are fully in place. The odds are in our favor."

"So you're saying that if they find you first, we're screwed?" Slaughter emphatically pointed.

"Correct, but that would be operating from the standpoint of a logical fallacy," Spencer returned.

Geir turned to Liv.

"Darling, how can they not know Qwave's behind the breach if they find out they've been duped?"

"For one thing, they have no reason to believe you are in any way associated with Guild Masters; that thought cannot register at their level of rationale. There are many reasons for it, but now is not the place to explain. Secondly, they are not aware of the reach of our technology. If they were ever capable of accessing our system, they wouldn't be permitted navigate within it – you cannot see paths that are not there. Furthermore, their tools of observation would naturally die in our environment, similarly to Earth's life without oxygen. The programs positioned in their network, scatter to regroup elsewhere when sensing the proximity of their cyberdogs. To sum things up, as much as Alexander Cruz would love to imagine you getting help from the Guild, he is, as a whole, incapable – or unwilling – to accept the possibility that this kind of progressive arrangement could be taking place; it would be an insult to his elder pride. That is assuming he is one of them of course; though, we are getting closer to back that assumption. That will be all for this session."

The phone rang. Slaughter picked it up. It was Cruz requesting another meeting. A time was set.

"It didn't take long, old boy; fancy an early cocktail?"

The two friends put on their coats and ambled to the Shipwreck Saloon.

2 – JOONAS

Paula Hunter succumbed to tears. Her Angel training was frayed and on the verge of losing its meaning. She had betrayed her guardian, his trust, and that of the Guild. She could no longer make sense of her attraction to Hektor. The whirl of self-loathing, the rebellious stance that had taken precedence over her desire to become a Master was gone. As much as she once believed she had been the victim of misunderstanding, she could no longer lie to herself. She was at the dead end of an unfortunate choice; one made using neither intuition nor intellect, a seemingly unconscious decision orchestrated from an inner control room by the compounded lot of her unchallenged beliefs acting as a fully formed gestalt independent from her central self. But it was now in the open, simultaneously threatening and vulnerable. It was the first time, since defecting, that the chasm within her core, and the danger of losing the little that was left of her integrity and sanity took hold on her awareness. How was she allowed to fall so low as to become one of the pawns of Hektor? Paula Hunter could no longer remain blind to the glaring reality looking her in the face with unrestrained effrontery. What was she awakening from, and where had she been while she pretended life would be better away from the Guild? For those who had fallen prey to its corruptive pull, Hektor was hell; a close-circuit reality systematically set in motion to reenact life in a series of grotesque loops. But even if she could rewind the course of the last few months and return to the Guild, she lacked the courage to give herself the love that could heal her wounds. In her eyes, she had betrayed the Masters; hence, she didn't deserve to be given a second chance. She also recognized the punishment was extreme and unjustifiable. Was she really at the point of giving up and letting Hektor ravage the rest of her, or could she still put up a fight and prove Cruz wrong? Or yet, was there another way to solve the nature of her dilemma?

Low-ranking members like Paula Hunter rarely made contact with each other. They never teamed on cases, made no friends – they just waited for the call of their next job to come. When they didn't work under the direct supervision of higher caste members, they found themselves being herded by conditioned terminal dwellers known as Dogs, who were in charge of making the inconvenience of indefinitely waiting in line for the absolute worst assignments, an experience so gruesome, that few came out of it sane. They also arranged, when necessary, for accidents to happen.

When Paula Hunter studied Hektor's emergence and the formation of its center of power, she learned that beyond the original splinter group, smaller factions walked out of the Guild to join on related philosophical deviances. But eventually, the outpour dwindled to a last few disgruntled Angels; after which point, only outside recruits – forced and not – as well as defectors from the student body, were added to the roster, thousands upon thousands of them. At such a time of deep vulnerability, it seemed particularly resonant, as well as odd, that there should be so many new Angel admissions falling to some unexplained ailment, like lemmings drawn to the cliff. Finding herself at the tragic center of being one of them, Paula Hunter began to smell foul play. In spite of her original interest in the rogue group, she was having a hard time recollecting the true reasons for her attraction to it, as if something was inconspicuously being erased. She suddenly felt very ill.

It was clear Hektor's reasons for accessing the Warriors' realms – the primary cause behind their dissent – had significance beyond mere conquest. The symbolic impact of taking control of a universe with the growth potential to match the greatness of the one that had betrayed them, offered Hektor elders the one window into affirming the substance of their cause – they would become a force comparable to the Guild. The frustration of having entered late in the game heightened their resolve. Knowing the Angels didn't yet have the resources to simultaneously manage both spheres of reality, Hektor was guaranteed an easy victory over the handful of Masters already in place, by overwhelming them with its entire operation. But the elders also understood there wasn't much time left to find the means to penetrate that universe. Without access to the Guild portal reliant on the ghost image of the ruined mother reality to proceed, the organization resorted to back-engineering the lane last taken by Saka and Olaf on their way to rejoin Ma-l. Alexander Cruz was incontrovertibly convinced Marshall Slaughter and his Icelandic friend were the lead to that portal; he was the master engineer in charge of clearing the path to it.

Unbeknownst to both Hektor and the Guild, after the collapse of the mother reality, a few original Angels traveled the interdimensional web to look for forgotten entries into the Warrior's worlds, but due to *earlier* adjustments made by Ma-l and the Great Ones, no probable version of the mother planet afforded back doors into the realms. The physics simply weren't there. It wasn't an issue of who was or wasn't capable of manipulating the time/space continuum; the last portal into these realities had been recalled by the vortex.

Of course, Cruz couldn't have known that.

The ghost image used by the Angels wasn't memory-based, but an extrapolation from flash potential. Cruz was aware it was going to require skills to attach Hektor's own system to it, but it first needed to be isolated. That mother reality may never have existed for those who were unaware it was there to begin with, but somewhere and separately from it, others knew of its existence and they would eventually talk. If not, there was always the possibility of accessing the realms by bypassing the image altogether.

Cruz turned to Paula Hunter.

"You made sure your machine is qualified for the job it's required to do?"

"To the best of my knowledge, it is, Sir," she replied.

"When I deem the best of your knowledge adequate, I will stop asking those questions. Now, get yourself ready; we have work to do," Cruz ordered.

They met at the investigator's office. Cruz had instructed Hunter to inconspicuously look around for clues on safes, other computers, and filing cabinet locations; a Dog could always be sent to sniff around after work hours. The young fed noticed that both Slaughter and Flemmingson's laptops were fitted with unusual protection and features, similar to those she saw at her student's job – she stiffened up.

"Do you have an email address at which I can reach you, Geir; just in case I need to ask you something?"

Flemmingson complied. He also noticed Hunter looked a bit shaken, but from what he knew of her situation, he didn't see why she shouldn't be nervous.

Cruz looked at Slaughter with a broad smile.

"Marshall, did Ms. Klein choose the location of her camping trip to meet specific reasons?"

"Well, it was most definitely motivated by Olaf Swyndle's disappearance. She wanted to see for herself. We weren't fully convinced at the time that he wasn't alive," the detective calmly replied.

"So, she took her friend Maggie and Sam with her. We found the dog's tag by Spectre Flat, quite a ways from the campground. Now, the area is considered sacred to local tribes, so isn't it unusual for a couple of white girls from the coast to visit the Flat on their first trip? Did Ms. Klein just assume, or was she certain Olaf Swyndle had antecedently spent time in that place?" Cruz probed.

"To set the record straight, she's half Wiyot and it wasn't her first time in the woods. But yes, I believe she had good reasons to think Swyndle might have taken the main trail out of the campground to Angel Lake, Medicine Rock, and Spectre Flat."

"Did she find anything?" Paula Hunter cut in, under Cruz's look of disapproval. She ignored him.

"Yes, a laptop pouch believed to have belonged to him. We found a computer inside an identical one in his car, which is the device I presently use," Slaughter volunteered.

"So if I get this right, Olaf Swyndle vanished with his dog and his laptop, without the case?"

"The pouch," Flemmingson corrected.

"OK, I loosely leafed through Swyndle's last book, published after his death, for which you wrote the preface, Geir. It transpired in your writing that Ms. Klein was instrumental in making the release a reality. How did that come about; how was the manuscript found?" Cruz asked the philosopher.

"I'm delighted to hear that a man of the law took time away from the rectitude of his profession for a foray into the layers of holistic research, but I digress. The manuscript was in one of the two remaining laptops, accompanied by the specifics of contacting his publisher. But how is this relevant to your investigation?"

"It all depends; it might or not be, Geir. The Swyndle case may be closed, while Maggie Phillips and her dog Sam could be roaming the land; but we still have a disappearance to account for, and it just so happens that Ms. Klein is the one we would like to ask the questions to," Cruz countered.

"I'm not sure I am with you on how you will find her, especially by keeping on asking questions that seem unrelated to her not being available at the moment. Don't you have access to a data bank that may contain cues as to her whereabouts?" Geir asked.

"We do, and that's exactly the point; we have nothing on her, starting from when she moved out of the house you owned at the time," Cruz replied.

49

"But who is looking for her and for what purpose? How does the Forest Service end up being in charge of a case that doesn't even feel like a plausible one?" the philosopher insistently asked.

"One thing led to another. It just so happened we were the ones who stumbled across the series of inconsistencies that reanimated the case of Olaf Swyndle's disappearance; that's why we're here to pester you. Hopefully, it will soon be closed for good, or move to another jurisdiction if crime is involved," the fed said.

Paula Hunter sat motionless. The truth detector idled without spikes. Her Angel training ushered her in the direction of believing Slaughter and Flemmingson were actually purposely not lying. Perhaps they didn't have to, but the two laptops across the room fascinated her. There was something looming that was much greater than the room and its contents. Her superior must have been aware of it; how could he not? She decided to keep her suspicions to herself, mostly from fear of another humiliating rebuttal.

Cruz stood up.

"We understand you're busy, so, thank you for putting up with us; we'll try to keep this painless. By the way, since we're going to be in town for a while, we'd love to stop by your place one of these days; we'll bring the drinks!"

"As long as it's not a business visit, you're always welcome. Just let me know ahead of time, so that I can clean up a bit," the detective humored.

Paula Hunter got up and packed her gear without saying a word. She just nodded on her way out.

After the cops exited, Flemmingson turned to Slaughter for a brief check-in.

"Our friend Paula is definitely onto something; let's keep an eye on her. Maybe Spencer and Liv can counsel us on how to translate her change in behavior."

The detective couldn't agree more.

The friends were about to leave the office when Liv and Spencer requested an audience. Liv went first.

"Greetings – In my further analysis of the student's profile, I came across a perplexing irregularity. Hektor files do not simply contain hard data, but also personal signatures added to the subject's information through real-time scanning. In other words, her computer monitors her as she uses it. It appears her unique code is tainted, and that the corruption is in the process of erasing itself. It is my understanding that the contamination was generated from within the Guild, or its direct periphery, and could potentially have been at the base of her wish to defect. Now, up to this point, we have never contemplated the possibility of outside influence having been at the root of the loss of students to Hektor; one reason being that we cannot study defectors once they've reached the group; the other is that we attributed the stigma to the inability of some subjects to fully integrate with the Guild program. It seemed all defectors came from human stocks fitted with a specific ego version – such as the one inherent in your species. We know that no part of the spiritual makeup of the ego personality is capable of erasing its tracks in the fashion I am witnessing here, in Paula Hunter's case; it is most assuredly a program-based item that was attached to the unique signature that defines her indelible birthright in the physical world. Since I have informed the Guild faculty, I have no doubt the news will imminently reach the Great Ones. This is not something we would normally share with you, but we exist under unusual circumstances, as it appears student Hunter will need to be rescued. At this point, we are uncertain as to the level of her allegiance to Hektor. We sense it is at an all time low, but she is under duress and could easily slip. Spencer has specific instructions."

"I guess, we have now moved beyond mere counseling," the stunned detective surrendered.

Spencer took over.

"Greetings – Paula Hunter cannot send emails or call without being monitored, but you can. Your messages will not be detected and will autodestruct shortly after they have been open. We have to establish whether she is willing to defect from Hektor or not, and if she is, we must be assured she is not doing it as a mole. We are confident Alexander Cruz will not intercept her incoming mail; he detests computers. I suggest you keep it simple at first, by asking her to just nod if she has received your message. Upon confirmation, you will then ask her if she wishes to leave Hektor; if so, you will offer your help. At that point, I will give you specific instructions on how to proceed. This, of course, implies you must continue with the interrogation process, even if it feels that it is going nowhere. Alexander Cruz is not simply looking for answers to his mundane questions; he strives for those hidden in the weave of the interaction. He hears the many simultaneous voices of discourse, and thus finds much meaning in what is not said. He will be at it for a while, but in the meantime, we'll help his assistant in making her computer more productive without implicating you."

"How can we not feel we are mere tools in some psychological standoff between two discordant factions, arbitrated by a yet to be defined official authority?" Geir posed.

"I understand it may appear so, but if it were the case, our presence would most certainly not be revealed to you. You are participants at the highest level by virtue of your previous involvement with the Guild." Spencer replied.

"Then, we'll wait for your instructions," Slaughter said. "In the meantime, I will send an email to Hunter."

————————

The next meeting happened two days later, once again, at the office. Paula Hunter opted to not make eye contact. She pretended to be busy with her laptop and simply acknowledged the group with a plain "morning." She appeared nervous, but not in the internalized fashion of the previous encounters. Cruz congenially posed his usual, inconspicuous questions, seemingly approving of all answers. Spencer had modified the program attached to Hunter's scanner, to help generate larger spikes in the *hidden truths* chart, in the hope that they would be interpreted by Cruz as factual, while they were meant to essentially send him on a wild goose chase. It was a way to buy enough time to get the ex-Guild student out of Hektor. At the end of the session, as she put her things away, Hunter, at last, made eye contact with the detective, nodding imperceptively. Slaughter showed no sign he had noticed. Cruz was too dangerous when it came to language spoken or not. They scheduled the following series of meetings for every other day, split between the office and Café Noir.

During the course of the next few sessions, Slaughter was able to establish that Hunter wanted out of Hektor. It was then left to be determined whether her choice was genuine or based on the kind of desperation that would make her an easy tool of Hektor inside the Guild. Spencer had posited that the divisions within the organization's caste system were too great for the possibility of a complicit collaboration between an elder and a bottom ranker. Matters as important as those involving the Guild of Angels were strictly the domain of rulers; therefore participation by someone of Paula Hunter's status would have to come integral to a direct order issued by the mastermind behind the case. The possibility of trickery was less than one percent, according to both Liv and Spencer; thus, they were willing to push forward with the rescue plan. First, the challenge of creating the type of disruption necessary to momentarily scramble Cruz's focus, in order for the student to come loose of his grip, had to be overcome. Then she had to hide amid humans until the Guild could arrange for her extraction to safe haven. The perplexing reality of the implant within her student signature, compromised her identity in regard to the various scanners imbedded into the majority of the systems utilized by Angels. It was then proposed that she should clandestinely be transferred to one of the Warriors' pocket realities. In the meantime, the Guild was moving along with its investigation of the corrupted students. Its source was traced to a point preceding the recruiting process, when the subjects were being evaluated for admission. The original hypothesis that it had occurred within the college, was misled by the time it took for the program to take hold. The complexity of the technology behind such a deed, could only have come from the Guild or Hektor. Vexingly, the student body had been used as an incubator for the implant to mature, thus conveniently suiting the rogue organization's recruiting needs. It was evident someone was tipping Hektor about who was likely to be accepted in the Masters training program. The biggest headache for the Guild was to locate the traitors behind the subterfuge, preferably, without sounding the alarm.

Back in the days of the Warriors' battles against the Great Ones, Alexander Cruz was better known as Joonas, or the Dove. He felt the human betrayal did not deserve absolution, and that the Angels should never have been contracted by the Ones to salvage the ruin left by the species' ego. As he saw it, the race, overtaken by vanity and paranoia, had set the mark in proving it merited to be engulfed by the fires of its own making. He saw the Warriors as the mere puppets of imbecilic rulers, used for the protection of their degenerate followers. He despised that version of humanity that had been granted so much rope as to completely stray away from its spiritual core; something he called a creational disgrace. When the Great Ones requested the Guild to intervene, Joonas, with a faction of like-minded thinkers, vehemently refused. Such an act was unheard of in the realm of the Angels, as it set a precedent that stood against the fundamental ethos of providing services on the basis of unconditional, mutual trust and respect. They were asked to reconsider, but to no avail. The Great Ones gathered and came to the consensus that the refusal was a rebuttal of the larger binding contract that defined their relationship with the Angels; hence, the Guild was advised to let go of Joonas and his cohort of rebels. Whether out of hurt or bottomless vanity, the fringe group took the decision as a granted privilege to form their own league on equal par with the Angels. To the Ones, they were a disenfranchised rogue tribe that had ever so transparently, and in spite of themselves, taken on the attributes of the human ego.

It wasn't without irony that Hektor filled its need for recruits by snatching student defectors straight out of the classic human stock. Joonas was first to realize that the particulars of the encoding of that race left a vulnerability that could be exploited. It was a matter of corrupting the ego personality with a specific belief-based algorithm that could mature inconspicuously. The subject would go through substantial Guild training before the first signs of incompatibility emerged; at which point the tainted personality would rebel incrementally against its core interest, its downward spiral guided by a deep-rooted longing to explore the unknowns of its darker side. Upon the student's defection, its purpose duly fulfilled, the program would slowly wash away, leaving the reawakened personality to face the incomprehensible dilemma of finding itself in the clutches of Hektor. Joonas called it "the two faces of redemption." The recruits would retain some of their basic Angel skills, but their psyches would forever be riddled with doubt and the shame of betrayal. As universes expanded exponentially, the demand for spiritual guides grew accordingly. Hektor, which didn't have the capability, or the philosophical character to train its recruits from the ground up, relied mostly on Guild dropouts to fill its ranks of specialists. All that was needed was an insider; Joonas would take care of the rest.

Tömör was among the original Masters who contested the contract request of the Great Ones. He was also amongst those who adjusted their stances when the rebels were asked to reconsider. He did it reluctantly, but he couldn't see himself out of a job, having contemplated the myriad probable scenarios that developed from leaving the Guild. He found none that didn't imply a form of corruption of his skills, or a fundamental undermining of his greater contract with the Ones. The human uprising was not significant enough, in the context of the whole, to justify a walk out. Additionally, unlike Joonas, he wasn't part of the group assigned to the task of saving humanity from the rampage of its out of control ego. Nonetheless, he was disappointed by the Ones' decision, which he took as a warning sign that the Guild would eventually become the mop-up crew behind every creational experiment gone wrong.

Angel pride was a strong element that defined the character of a Master, a quality understood to be based in loyalty and purpose. Tömör's sense of pride, on the other hand, dangerously flirted with vanity, a rare trait among Masters, which was thought to have permanently left the Guild with the rise of Hektor.

Though, it may have appeared that Angels were forced into assignments, as in the case of the Warriors; it rather was their specific chosen skills organized in specialized teams that determined the nature of their undertakings. As it turned out, the group to which Joonas belonged was the one contracted by the Great Ones to address the issue of the battles. Its members included Vac, Ilia, and Axel, who now worked for the new world to which the realm of ex-Warrior, Great Goddess Ma-l, belonged.

When it became clear that Hektor, having run out of natural defectors and being left understaffed, was incapable of competing with the Guild, Joonas sought to tap the resources of those originally on his side, the fair weather friends, as he saw them, who had rescinded on their position. It was dangerous. At a few exceptions, all connections had been severed between the two groups, but the Hektor founder was patient and stealthy. Tömör, who was on a guardian's assignment on a remote constellation, and in one of its even more remote probabilities, was spotted by the Dove – a perfect place for the two to meet, far away from the watching eyes of the Guild and the Great Ones. After much debating, topped with an ample dose of philosophical persuasion, Tömör agreed to leak to Hektor the lists of human recruits under review, via an antiquated, forgotten Guild portal set on one of that world's obscure lesser planets, through which their encrypted contents would remain undetected. From there, they would reach Joonas in the form of specific messages only he could decipher, those concealed within the hum of magnetic winds, interspersed amid the fragments of long lost mails; or simply, they could be sent through coded emails to his computer at Strata headquarters. Joonas was a Master of the finer subtleties of language; he was the receiving antenna, the great receptor at the end of the hijacking of thousands of Guild applicants' records – irrespective of where he stood on the space/time continuum.

When Paula Hunter's name showed up on one of the lists from Tömör, Joonas was conveniently introduced to her as a friend of a friend, under the name of Adam Bassett. He flew her under her guardian's radar to a rave party where he implanted the corrupt algorithm in her altered mind while he had sex with her. Later that night, and just as conveniently, Bassett died in a car crash.

The responsibility of finding the insider fell on the trusted crew that had kept tabs on all the members of Hektor. Their files were divided into three categories: the original splinter group, the Masters who joined at a later date, and the students transferred to the hub. Of course, neither the Guild nor Hektor operated along the linearity of time; thus, many of the Angels that defected through non-temporal channels, were still in the process of joining. But the leak came from within, someone with a direct link to Hektor. The investigating team, of which Liv and Spencer were senior members, was code-named Le Lien, or the bond, for its unshakable loyalty and air-tight way of working cases. Upon being notified, Le Lien informed the Great Ones, who gave the immediate go-ahead with unconditional support from the highest levels.

The implications were massive. Now that it had become clear Hektor was after the newly born universe of the Warriors, the threat to the balance of creational forces had reached critical status. Liv and Spencer were assigned to the task of uncovering Alexander Cruz's true identity, while the rest of the team would focus on homing on suspects within the Guild. It was a first for Le Lien to investigate Angels, for it put into question the fundamentals of the trust that was the bond between all. The group was well aware it had to act under the clause of invisibility, as to not awaken suspicion among suspects, as well as a general sense of discomfort within the organization at large. As a first step, Liv proposed making a list of the Angels sympathetic to the original splinter group, well knowing those would be extremely difficult to spot, but they did step forward into the light, if briefly, so there was hope. The Guild was massive and its reach immeasurable; finding the ones behind the leaked names was going to take Le Lien all it had. It was all the more complex due to the fact it had to pit its skills against those of Masters, whose stealth and maneuvering field eclipsed the range of the species that had been the focus of the group's previous investigations. But all entities owned a unique signature. It was also well known the criminal mind had a propensity for leaving its mark as part of its legacy; a flaw that oddly "nobilified" the crime in its eyes. It was an act of vanity uncommon among Angels, but someone, eventually, was going to beam a signal.

The Le Lien team, as it sought to synchronically orchestrate Paula Hunter's rescue with the arrest of the traitor, while Liv and Spencer kept busy unmasking the Forest Service captain, sensed there was a corroboration of elements between the interrogation led by Cruz and the leaked lists. It required added patience on the parts of Marshall Slaughter and Geir Flemmingson – moving too fast would jeopardize all chances of success. Of course, all of it was dependent on how much time Cruz had available and how long Hunter was capable of holding under pressure.

Spencer stressed the importance of identifying the federal agent. There was a chance, due to the significance of his assignment, that Cruz was Joonas himself – confirmation was paramount. If he was connected to the leak, the Guild informants' arrest could provide the kind of distraction Paula Hunter needed to momentarily free herself from the clutches of Hektor, as well as enough time for the Angels to move her to safety. It was then up to Liv and Spencer to map the plan of action, including adjusting the timeline, to bring all the critical elements to one optimum point of convergence, at which Cruz would be at his most vulnerable. Also, the portal used for Hunter's extraction, would have to either remain unseen or be permanently deleted, should the captain get too close and come across what he was actually looking for – the scenario was unthinkable.

———————

Tömör's latest assignment was to assist a young humanoid on one of the planets of Gliese 832, in the Grus constellation. The boy showed extraordinary aptitudes, and thus was referred to the Guild as an *A prospect*. He also was one of the early ego-type human subjects, who, as all of Earth's inhabitants, had to go through the complex evolutionary process of bringing the spirit-in-body back into the fold of the larger consciousness, hence a perfect candidate for Hektor. It was unusual for Tömör to leak the names and places of his protégés – he felt particularly uneasy about this one. But the trap of Hektor had tightened around him; consequently, he had no choice but to oblige for fear of being exposed to the Guild as a traitor. Joonas had fooled him – his back was against the wall. His role as Guardian of the boy was nearing completion; the subject would soon be forgotten. So, the Master relaxed his mind and sent the data to the Hektor elder via the agreed channels.

The Guild's entire surveillance apparatus was under Le Lien's jurisdiction. The spy organization had put all of its members on rotation to keep tabs on every "misbehaving" descriptor riding the inter-dimensional communication flux. It was a sine qua non with unfortunately little meaning in a réseau that dealt with the oddest of cases, inasmuch as the message signature had to be a few notches above the term "unusual" to register a spike on the scanners; for that, it would have to either be decrypted while in transit or tied to such exotic end points as to arouse suspicion. Mathematically, it was improbable for such a message to be detected by the system, due the sheer amount of traffic and the inestimable code diversity involved. Le Lien mostly left it to chance, for error was rarely a trait of Angels – and neither was criminality; so there was a thin hope among the team for something to eventually show up. Something did indeed show up, but it wasn't picked up by Le Lien.

Paula Hunter saw the message addressed to Cruz. It required a decryption key that she did not possess, but upon sensing something revolting about it, she decided to hold off before informing the captain, which gave ample time to Spencer's hacking program to make a copy and forward it to Slaughter's laptop, whence it was taken to the "operating room."

While it was one thing to get into a place by carefully picking the lock; it was yet another to improperly close after being done with the shady business. Marshall Slaughter didn't even have to get near the door to know someone had been fooling around. He was glad Liv and Spencer had insisted on he and Geir keeping the laptops within their line of sight at all times after office hours, for disaster would certainly have loomed, had they not. At first glance, it didn't look like anyone had gone inside; there was none of the mayhem generally associated with break-ins – everything appeared in its proper place. It took a while for Slaughter to notice – and only because of his investigative skills – that there had actually been a breach. His filing cabinets had been carefully combed, his answering machine played. His ailing PC had been powered up and searched, while his old-school rolodex showed inconspicuous signs of having been flipped through. A quick estimate let the detective know the intruder had done a thorough job; pictures likely had been taken, as well as data downloaded on thumb drives. Of course, there was no doubt the USDA cops were behind it, but since it was meant to look like he simply forgot to lock up on his way out, he would make no mention of it to Cruz. He rejoined Flemmingson who was at Café Noir. The two went over the implications of the break-in, and how it would play into the interrogation.

It was obvious the fed had switched gears, having failed to get what he was after during questioning, but the act revealed an edge of desperation that was seen as a bad omen. Alexander Cruz was about to become a lot less pleasant to deal with, potentially resorting to utterly radical measures before the Guild could convincingly identify him, or save Hunter. At any rate, finesse was de rigueur. Flemmingson proposed to invite the two agents for drinks at the Fieldbrook house, hoping to cool things down before impatience turned to vileness. The detective agreed and called Cruz, since the cop seemed eager to check his place out. They arranged for 6:30 p.m. the next day; until then, the friends had barely enough time to hone new defensive skills. They finished their coffee, got up, and walked to the office. They barely made it through the door when Slaughter's laptop emitted its now familiar call – Spencer requested an audience.

"Greetings – Please connect Liv; we have some important updates."

Flemmingson hurried with his laptop as Liv came alive.

"Greetings – Spencer's harvesting program has intercepted an encrypted message intended for Alexander Cruz in Paula Hunter's computer. For reasons unexplained to us, she apparently hasn't told him yet – perhaps she recognized the sender. One thing is certain, she cannot read its content and we haven't been able to either – we're working on it. Spencer will explain."

"First of all, Paula Hunter's decision to delay the message from getting to Cruz is very puzzling – she could get into terrible trouble for interfering with the elder's mail. The fact she cannot read it, yet acts as if it mustn't get to him, seems to indicate she is working her intuitions out, as taught by Guild Masters. There have to be traces in the environmental memory of the message she is capable of deciphering at deep levels – perhaps something that plays off her fears of Hektor, or Cruz himself. Time will tell, and hopefully, very soon. At any rate, the team is on it. What perplexes us most about the mail is that it traveled incognito. Without Paula Hunter's reaction we would never have known that the elder had a message in his box. It's technically an extempore hiccup, but since our most sophisticated equipment didn't record the item as it traveled through the network, we have to proceed with whatever comes our way. All mail to the Hektor elder is extremely relevant, especially when it appears to originate from outside the group. We believe that Paula Hunter, inadvertently or not, did us a big favor. Give us a moment."

Marshall and Geir silently acknowledged that Hunter was shifting her loyalties around, and recklessly putting herself in harm's way.

Spencer returned.

"The team has decoded the message and located its provenance. It contains a short breakdown of names and addresses that after cross-referencing, turned out to be a list of admissions into the Guild's students program. We didn't identify the sender, but the mail originated from a remote port no longer registered in the network. It's all the more remarkable, since it wasn't even part of those being scanned by our surveillance system. It is an extremely out-of-the-way portal, in a distant future probability similar to the mother reality of the Warrior's realms. What we know for sure, is that Alexander Cruz is either directly responsible for the corruption of Guild recruits or highly instrumental to its process. This news, combined with his intent of infiltrating the realms, makes him extremely dangerous. Since there is now proof Hektor is behind the damage inflicted on the student body, the Guild is prepared to rescue all defectors that were altered by the implant. We must at all cost get behind the elder's guise, so that we can disable him. Another perplexing element points to Cruz as being the one directly or partially responsible for Paula Hunter's present dilemma. It's now obvious to us that she is intuitively trying to protect the contents of the message from him; though, it is unlikely he corrupted her using his present form, or that she cognitively knows who he really is, aside from possibly being a high-ranking elder."

Liv came forward.

"The team is informing us that they picked up a recent signature in the spatial field of the remote port; it was purposely scrambled. It is now being back-engineered to its point of origin. If we are dealing with an extremely skilled Angel, the results could be sending us on a wild goose chase; but again, we must take the little we have in hopes our training, aided by our technology, will make the best of it. On a separate note, until Cruz crosses the line, the Great Ones will refrain from helping since the Guild and Hektor operate in jurisdictions outside the realm of their influence. It doesn't mean they are no longer concerned, to the contrary, but there are fundamental tenets that must prevail. The responsibility falls on us to resolve the case."

———————

As always, Cruz and Hunter arrived punctually. It was an almost pleasant surprise for Slaughter and

Flemmingson to see them dressed in casual, civilian clothing. The USDA captain took off immediately with a spurious line about the state of the world, while his assistant asserted that she was, so far, having a good day. The cops had brought wine, local brews, as well as snacks, which were added to bottles of fine brandy and scotch at the buffet-styled display of dips and crudités. The philosopher had prepared a feast, while the detective had kept busy cleaning the house and making sure to tuck away compromising material. The laptops were stashed in the basement's safe, against which a stacked, rolling shelving unit was pushed. Even though Paula Hunter was without her computer, it was assumed she was wearing a device that connected to it. Cruz refrained from mentioning business, but it was clear by the nature of his seemingly innocent questions about the history of the estate and the dwindling redwood logging industry, that he was still on the lookout for answers into what he was after; namely, where Linda Sue Klein was last seen, and where she went from there.

Cruz's desire to visit Slaughter's place was fully connected to the hard suspicion that the event in question was, in some way or another, linked to it. From his records, it was the last location Klein had been known to be before her disappearing act – he was anxious to find out whether or not a Guild portal had been used at the property, to take her to what he assumed were the Warriors' realms. The Hektor elder had no direct interest in the woman; all he wanted was the precise location of her whereabouts upon leaving. The gate through which she passed, was the grail at the end of his quest. Irrespectively of what Slaughter and Flemmingson had managed to not divulge, he sensed he was close.

"Perhaps you care to show us the house, Marshall?" the captain jollily proposed.

The host obliged. He took the guests upstairs to Saka's old quarters, which presently served as Geir's temporary crash pad. Loose mentions were made about the layout, the construction methods employed at the turn of the previous century, the details in the wainscot, the crown molding; the original, graceful Victorian curves overwhelmed by the angular craftsman-styled later makeover; not ignoring the old knob and tube electrical branch circuits still in use in the attic and the cellar – Cruz seemed to know it all. He seemed particularly fascinated by the fact the house had a basement, in an area where understructures were the exception rather than the norm. Slaughter remarked on his keen awareness of local architecture, while he suspected, not without a hint of discomfort, that the cop knew a lot more about most subjects than he was willing to let transpire. Again, Slaughter was alerted to the fact by his years of experience in the investigational field. Cruz was a master spinner whose web was an elaborate art piece twinned to the precision of clockwork.

Paula Hunter made neither eye contact nor initiated conversational topics. She remained subdued and generally acquiescent to Cruz's points. Even if she desired to connect at the personal level with her hosts, she was under heavy watch, while the bug she carried monitored all that was said in her direct environment. She was aware that the information in her possession about her boss was of utmost significance to the Guild of Masters, as well as certain that if it reached the Angels, they would have no problems uncovering his identity. Only one small window in time was needed for her to slip a note to Slaughter – she found it in Cruz asking permission to quickly check the basement.

Flemmingson smelled a rat. When he joined the fed at the bottom of the stairs, he found him standing, facing the rolling shelving unit hiding the safe. The philosopher contained a mounting pang, to instead jovially invite the guest to come enjoy some of the roast that had just come out of the oven. Cruz appeared distracted for the briefest of moments then followed Geir up the steps. At the halfway landing, he stopped and asked, "Would you mind telling me why our host keeps a safe in his basement behind a heavy shelf?"

"Do you see a reason why he shouldn't?" Geir fired back. "I thought you weren't here on business, Alexander; come on, there's food to be eaten!"

"Son of a bitch!" was the first thing that came to the philosopher's mind. He realized that regardless of protocol, Cruz was moving onward with his program. There was definite danger in having him around the house; thus, Geir waged to keep close tabs on the guest for the rest of the evening. No way would he be allowed to continue sniffing around the place – the game was off! Also, as long as Cruz was on the premises, Geir couldn't afford to take Slaughter to the side to warn him about what had just happened; which left him with distracting the agent with mundane topics, in hopes of buying time before he and Hunter left. Later, when the fed proposed to enjoy the courtyard with drinks, suggesting they build a fire in the pit, Flemmingson feigned a lack of preparedness, offering to cut the celebration short instead, on the premise there would be other times. Cruz and his assistant were officially dismissed. The captain got the hint, barely masking his disapproval of the sudden shift.

Slaughter looked perplexed, but trusted that his friend had substantial reasons for whisking the guests away.

He turned to Geir as soon as they were gone.

"What was that all about?"

"The guy was all over the map. He discovered the safe hiding the laptops, even without having moved the shelf. He had the nerve to ask me the reasons for it. For a nanosecond, he didn't even try to hide who was behind the mask. I saw it, the fierceness, the cunning, the malfeasance... When he put the guise back on, it was too late; I couldn't let him resume with his true reasons behind his visit. I know what he's after, Marshall – he's looking for the portal that took Olaf, Saka, and The Triad back to Ma-l's home."

"Well, what would you know; Hunter slipped me a note while her boss was sniffing around. Let's have a look!" Slaughter cut in.

"AC is the founder of Hektor. I don't know of his true identity, but I'm sure the Guild will figure it out. I fear that I have met him before this job under confusing circumstances, but it's only an intuition. Hurry up, time is closing on all of us!"

The friends looked at each other, wondering what to do next. Finally Slaughter asked Flemmingson to retrieve the laptops, so that Liv and Spencer could be notified. He poured cognac into snifters and proceeded with the cleanup of the buffet table.

The two Le Lien members came alive as soon as the computers powered up.

"Greetings to both – We sense you have news," Spencer voiced expectantly.

Marshall and Geir gave a report of the visit, highlighted by Paula Hunter's pressing information.

"Just as we suspected – we have now ascertained who the federal agent is. His name is Joonas, also known as the Dove," Liv explained. "Based on what is involved at this conjuncture, you both and Paula Hunter are in grave danger. From what you just told us about the visit, it is obvious Joonas' guise, Cruz, is on a mission to find the portal that was last used by your friends and The Triad. We aren't sure how he can use that information to create his own entry into the Warriors' realities, but it is a question best left without an answer. We no longer have reasons to delay taking action; thus, we must get Paula Hunter out of Hektor as soon as we are able to coordinate the elements of her rescue. We are very close to isolating the treacherous items inside the Guild, so, as soon as we have confirmation, we will publicize the news in such a way that it will reach Joonas at the precise moment of the execution of our plan. We need to usher the ex-student through the same portal created by The Triad to facilitate Saka and Olaf's exit, while the Hektor elder is elsewhere, trying in turn to move his informant(s) away from the punishment of the Guild. Providing everything works out as planned, he will never find the entrance he was looking for, while being circumvallated by Guild's forces, until the Great Ones come to a consensus as to the methods of his extraction from his present position of power. To put it in simple terms, his actions are in direct violation of the agreement that allowed for Hektor to exist in the first place. The group will be dismantled and its unique signature deleted, while its original members will be faced with the reality of reform, under specific clauses dictated by the Guild and the Ones."

"For now, wait for instructions," Spencer added. "Do not attempt to contact the two agents, even if they try to reach you, for it will only take one key word at this point, for Cruz to unleash a full-on investigation, garnish your assets, and cordon your property. Keep the laptops with you at all times; they are our one window into Hektor's doings. And by the way, expect an unscheduled visit at the office tomorrow morning. Do not patronize Café Noir until that contact is made; you are under surveillance from Joonas's ubiquitous Dogs. So, just stay put. We bid you a fond good evening."

––––––––––––

Tömör was pleased with himself. Since his pivotal disagreement with the Great Ones and what he considered the Guild's whoring to them, he had been compelled to act in a symbolic fashion, as if to prove to himself he had the courage to stand up to what he perceived as being a higher authority. The specificity of his thinking process was indicative of a rare corruption amid Angels, for there was no such higher authority. Along that line, it had appeared that the Masters who walked out on their own volition, were tainted by the very affliction they condemned in humans; namely, a sense of bloated importance, and an acute disconnection from purpose. Tömör was one of the rare few among the disgruntled Masters, who neither had joined Hektor nor sought to erase the nature of their discontentment with the decision of the Ones. For that reason, he had favored assignments away from the limelight, at the confines of the farthest civilized worlds. In some fashion, he strived for invisibility, and paradoxically, that was exactly what made him visible to Le Lien.

The corrupt Angel had not anticipated he would end up becoming a pawn of Hektor in the process of associating with Joonas. He resented the subterfuge and took it as a direct affront. He wished for the Dove to pay for his irreparable error of judgment, but there was no exit for Tömör's rage; if the Hektor ruler fell, so would he.

The inner conflict made him vulnerable to distraction, and so, in one very short spurt of inattention to details, or perhaps, in a subliminal abdicative move, he sent his last message directly to the computer of Joonas' nom de guerre, down in Eureka, where it was consequently delayed by his assistant and decoded by Le Lien.

Tömör was proud of his use of the forgotten port and of his skills at scrambling his signature. Technically, in the event of interception, both the sender and addressee would show as one and the same, never revealing the provenance and destination of the mail. But that was only as good as the reliability of all the points along the route, and Paula Hunter's laptop was the undeniable weak link. Not that the Angel was required to have known of that vulnerability, but had he simply put the next level of care in the security of his mailing method, he could easily have avoided what the Guild considered a sloppy maneuver on his part.

Still, Le lien couldn't know who the sender was, even if it had been able to identify the point of origin via the use of sophisticated locating tools. But there were few ex-renegade Angels who consistently steered from the fray by strictly working solo. In fact, there were a total of seven, six having above-the-table records, which left Tömör as the obvious suspect. It was a matter of time before he would make the critical mistake of using the old port again, which by then was under stealthy surveillance. As bait, the records office in charge of cataloging new recruits, created a fake file of names and coordinates, in hopes it would be hacked by the perpetrator. Joonas had been insistent on making sure that the flow of new admissions should be steady and plentiful, due to the ever-expanding nature of the universe, and the high demand for Angel personnel; thus, he expected proportional delivery on Tömör's part. The corrupt Master, who was in the habit of keeping a tab on student records as they were updated, hastened to copy the bugged file and send it to Joonas, this time, to a different destination. The timing could not have been more perfect for Paula Hunter, who had decided to conceal the previous list indefinitely, as the new one easily replaced it schedule-wise. She was notified by Liv via Slaughter, that Cruz had received a new file; therefore to no longer worry about the undelivered one – she could now destroy it. In his zeal to prove his worth, Tömör had failed to heed the hiccup in the rhythm of the listing pattern – he was uncovered. At that point, it was just a matter for Le Lien to strategically position its pieces.

Slaughter and Flemmingson arrived at the office early. They linked their computers, powered them up, but neither Spencer nor Liv came forward to request an audience.

"I guess we'll just stay put as they told us," Geir offered, while looking out the window onto the street, where the usual bustle of homelessness went about its business. "Things are changing," he thought, for he witnessed most were wearing fresh clothes and rode new bicycles. Olaf's teaching had changed the world for the better. Society was incrementally reaching out to its needy and rejected in an act of renewed kindness, while actually benefiting all layers of lives and fortunes. "Love creates miracles," he mused, as Slaughter came to join him.

"Who would have thought?"

The friends stood there in appreciative silence, waiting for the much anticipated visitor. As it turned out, there were two of them...

When the men, alerted by a slight shuffle behind them, swung around, a young couple stood next to the closed entrance across the room, smiling at them.

"Greetings, Marshall and Geir; I'm Spencer and this is Liv," the man said.

"Hi, and surprise!" Liv said with élan.

The two seemed relaxed in their casual dress. They apparently had not used the door to get in.

"Sorry," Spencer forwarded, "but we can't be seen by Hektor, so we had to create a portal in your office to get to you. We hope it's an acceptable compromise."

"You are more handsome than I had imagined you would be," Slaughter said. "But yes, it's as good a grand entrance as it'll ever be – scare and all. I'm glad you decided to not resemble my dad after all."

"As to you, darling Liv," Geir uttered, "look at you; you are gorgeous, dear Lord!"

Liv wore jeans, a plaited shirt, and sneakers, while her flaming red hair was tied in a ponytail. She had no make-up and wore freckles like sunshine. Flemmingson enthusiastically called her "the perfect Icelandic tomboy."

"Now that we have been properly introduced, we've got work to do. Of course, as long as we're in character, no need for us to be inside the dreaded machines," Spencer laughed. "Again, the game's off with Cruz – getting Paula Hunter out is our priority. The traitor has been identified – it's a matter of choosing our time and place. The town will be crawling with Dogs monitoring every one of your moves. Joonas is desperate to get to the Fieldbrook portal, so he will jump at the slightest opportunity to hole you up and take your property away from you under the shaky, temporary guise of officiality. He doesn't care if he is breaking all the laws; he knows he has enough time to ruin you before the real authorities catch up with him, and by then, he will be out of reach, while his entire records at the Forest Service will be made inexistent. No files, no memories; he and his assistant will have in effect never been there. That being said, we will do the best we can to help you stay out of harm's way by distracting Hektor's Dogs, while Le Lien prepares for the execution of Paula Hunter's exit."

"So this is how it plays," Liv cut in. "Alexander Cruz will want to set yet another appointment. You'll agree to meet him and Paula Hunter at the Wild Cherry Market patio in Arcata, because you'll be doing business there that day – but you won't show up. Just as Joonas realizes you stood him up, his security will email the news that the Guild is after Tömör on suspicion of being a tool of Hektor, and that he is believed to be trying to defect to the group. It will be in Joonas's best interest to help the traitor escape, so we hope he'll ask his assistant to stay put until his return. That's when we intervene and take Hunter to The Triad's portal at the estate. Needless to say, your federal agent will not find Tömör, who by then will have been transferred to an undisclosed location. By the time he returns, you'll be calling him to let him know you're late, but would still like to meet. He'll want to kill you, but he will just offer to reschedule. Are you both still with me?"

"You're making it sound like certified history, Liv," Geir jumped in. "I sure hope it plays out as smoothly as you're trying to convince us it will. How do you propose to snatch the son of a bitch; isn't he going to snap like a cornered, wild animal?"

"You don't know his kind well, Geir. No, he will remain extremely calm and probably return to Hektor headquarters to regroup before he strikes again. He'll still want to access the portal at all cost, but by then his Forest Service cover will be blown, so he will need a new guise. Prepare for the unusual," she returned.

"I thought one of you said the Guild was going to surround him with a force field; did you change your mind, or did I get the timing wrong?" Slaughter asked.

"We didn't change our minds, though you are right to enquire; we will surround him, but our timing works on a whole different scale from your Earth-oriented perspective. Joonas, just like Angels and the Great Ones, experiences all presents simultaneously. His arrest can metaphorically happen both in your past and future – even perhaps intersect your present. He's not quite done here, but he will be busy on many fronts – and so shall we," Spencer clarified.

"Needless to say," Liv added, "the access to the Warrior's realms comes with an expiration date, and it's all happening in your time. So, not only will Joonas have to act fast, he will also have to be stopped from reaching the emergent Oneness from within that framework. But it's not the same as his arrest and the dismantling of Hektor, which play on multiple probable stages, and with different scripts."

"Furthermore, Joonas's Dogs will be stopping by your house and sniff around. We were there after you left his morning; so we made sure to conceal the portal with an overlay and verify that your safe was left unlatched with nothing but irrelevant paperwork inside. He'll be highly displeased with the scant results," Spencer added.

"Rest assured that we aren't abandoning the laptops, but we see no point in not meeting one on one while we can. It will allow us to be in touch more frequently, as well as mix with the crowd to spot who's spying on you. Does this meeting cover the essentials?" Liv asked.

Slaughter and Flemmingson looked at each other as if to cross-examine their thoughts.

"A lot of it is coming out of left field, but I think we can adapt. After all, we have seen some murky waters under that bridge over the last few months. We'll do as you advise. OK with you, Geir?" the detective queried.

Flemmingson agreed.

"Alright then, we'll be around!" Spencer declared, as the pair walked out through thin air.

After he put the list through the port, Tömör returned to the gate that was to take him back to Gliese 832c, where he was to complete his assignment. It was the last of its kind, for he had decided to forego guidance and sever his ties with Joonas by opting for "controlled erasure"; a seldom used process for Angels who desired to be temporary forgotten, while tethered to a "memory reference," essentially set as a glorified alarm clock.

Le Lien, which had just reallocated the portal to the network, had reconfigured the itinerary coordinates; consequently, the rogue Master found himself in a very different place. When he realized what had just happened, it was too late for him to engage an emergency escape.

A voice rattled the depths of his being:

"It is not in the name of a proper welcome that you should find yourself among us, Angel. You have broken the fundamental contract that until this spacious present, bound you to your unique signature and purpose. You have by the nature of your deeds betrayed your own core identity and done great harm to countless promising students of the Guild of Masters. Under the latter's authority and in conjunction with our own set of tenets, you are now stripped of your position of power and your skills have been taken away from you. You are detained in perpetuum or until a fitting assignment is deemed to match the character of your crime. You are presently in a state of suspension in a one-way quarantine zone out of the reach of your expansive field of mobility. You created your predicament; there is no punishment involved. This is the end of our message."

The universe abruptly collapsed around Tömör. With his sense of self-awareness and purpose, his immeasurable skills and unique signature, with all that filled him with pride and the taste of power, and every grand and minute thing about him strewn across impossible times and distances, fated to never regroup; he then understood how he was solely responsible for the tragedy of his demise. He resigned himself to exist within a vacuum, away from all grounding forces, quietly being returned to the womb in a blind and mute *unbirth*, until, at last, denied of all things that *are*, he became nothingness.

The mock list intercepted by Tömör and received by Joonas in the form of decryptable data embedded in ambient noise was composed of real names and places. It was hoped the Hektor founder would act on it immediately. He did exactly that, by using various identities, shapes, and codes under around-the-clock surveillance from Le Lien, thus revealing to the fullest his leadership in the case of the corrupted Guild students. The conditioned subjects were duly treated and kept out of danger – but Joonas had not broken Hektor protocol; he had simply exploited a vulnerability overlooked by the Guild. The Great Ones didn't find him in direct violation of his own core purpose, in spite of having trespassed into an area of great darkness, while forcing his group to walk in his steps. To a point, Hektor had been a healthy counterpoint to the Guild, providing balance in the field of distributed powers. But the way the Masters saw it, Joonas had sought to upset that equilibrium by conning Guild members into joining his organization, all the while vying for an emerging Oneness with the intention of corrupting it. It was perceived as an act of bringing dilemmic dichotomy to the steps of the original One – a war declaration against existence – and for it, his cohorts of inter-cosmic saboteurs had to be taken down.

But with great powers came the matching breadth of potentiality. In spite of the urgency of the threat posed to the Warriors' realms by Joonas, notwithstanding the collateral consequences looming over innumerable exposed realities, there were great unknowns in regard to the emergent properties that had yet to rise from the new Oneness. The Great Ones had no jurisdiction there; those worlds belonged to the Goddess Ma-l and her kin. It was a complex multiverse, alien in nature to the Oneness they identified with. Should Hektor subjugate the realms, the Ones could only intervene if conflict arose at the highest levels. In other words, they would only take Joonas down if his most foreseeable destiny was to create havoc within their own sphere of reality; outside of it, the rogue group was the concern of other consciousnesses, a matter best resolved between the Guild and Hektor itself.

The Great Ones were in the least enviable of positions when it came to dealing with Joonas and Hektor. As overseers, they had no place being the protectors of the Guild or the Oneness that birthed them; and in spite of having forced the rebelling Angels to step down, they had in fact given Hektor an opportunity to thrive – to which the latter was cognizant and privately thankful. They saw the detrimental and beneficial sides of intervention as equal forces not to be challenged. The fate of Hektor would be addressed only if it posed a direct or indirect threat to their domains; until then, Joonas was a villain who hadn't yet crossed that line.

Le Lien understood that the Great Ones would be watching and evaluating at a level that knew not to judge or invalidate. As their Oneness once evolved on a combination of myriad purposes; it was their choice to not intervene in the complex balance of that synergy. But the Guild operated under a different set of tenets fully integral to the equilibrium of the many universes it supervised and assisted; therefore it was empowered to take the appropriate measures to enforce these rules, even if it meant bringing Hektor down. It was also at a point at which it straddled both original and new Onenesses, a position it had no intention of losing by letting the rogue organization wreak havoc in a universe that was largely born of their labor. To Le Lien, it was unequivocal that Hektor was not to set foot in the Warriors' realms.

As presaged by Liv and Spencer, Alexander Cruz did indeed seek to set up an appointment with Slaughter and Flemmingson; and so, it was agreed they would meet the next day at the Wild Cherry Market patio over lunch. Paula Hunter had been counseled by Spencer via the one-way autodestruct system of emails that had kept her informed of the rescue plans since the original contact was made. She had been unable to respond, save for the occasional nod away from Cruz's scrutiny. She was ready but scared. Her previous Guild training had helped her stay composed under pressure, as a result of which the Hektor elder never came close to heed the smokescreen between his plans and what was geared to defeat them. If anything, he saw his assistant's recent submissiveness as a sign she was at last resigned to her fate of perpetual servitude to the group. But his vanity was in the way of his better judgment, for he had failed to become cognizant of the fact his victim had nurtured a visceral awareness of the rape and the corruption her mind suffered at the hands of Adam Basset, his short-lived alter ego, as more of his true personality steadily transpired through the oppressive grotesqueness of his guise.

Paula Hunter was ready to take the leap – her fears of a failed escape no longer paralyzed her thoughts; she had to get away from the tightening dead-end she had found herself at. There were definite unknowns before her, as well as the apprehension that she could be put to shame for her defection; but as new allies came forward, those who had only pretended to be on her side had steadily become the empty, broken shells of unkept promises and artificially induced hopes. She loathed what the fringe organization so hypocritically stood for. The Hektor elites were nothing but a self-serving cabal that saw neither shame in lies nor wrongs in the manipulation and the ruin of dreams.

If she ever were to be granted re-entry into the Guild, she had full trust in her capacity to expose Hektor's heinous neurological manipulations inflicted onto its recruits. She was taking with her the entirety of her accumulated knowledge from within the league of Dark Angels; that was how she privately savored her last day with Alexander Cruz.

———

Joonas had not gotten much out of Hunter's skills, or the scanning program in her laptop; he relied on hard-earned experience to define the ground zero of his work. He belonged to the school of logicism that saw the field of mathematics reducible to plain logic. Computers were only logical in the sense they displayed the already existing and applied reasoning of their creators; hence, he deemed them unnecessary. He liked having Hunter around as a symbolic presence; she was the token fallen student, the exemplification of his dominance over a race he despised, and of his powers over the will of the Great Ones. Unlike the majority of the young recruits that had fallen to his cohort of trained Dogs, he had consumed Hunter in the flesh, raped her while she was under the influence of the drugs he had added to her drinks. He controlled her wholly then, as he did again when he arranged to have her work for him at the Forest Service, and now, as his subservient assistant. She was with him to remind him of his status, to appease his restlessness towards the ludicrousness of the world that surrounded him. He didn't feel amused by the way Slaughter and Flemmingson had attempted to play him; he would make the two pay for the insolence they had dared throw at his person; for that, they would rot in the hellhole of their labyrinthine judicial system, as collateral damage issued by the dysfunctionality of a world they had created for themselves – it was a fitting retribution to the energy they had forced him to waste in endless posturing and gamesmanship. They were cornered, and nothing could prevent their downfall. All bets were off after their next meeting; he would arrange to have them both charged with the murders of Olaf Swyndle and Linda Sue Klein. He would then have all the time in the world to fine-comb the Fieldbrook property and overtake the portal into the Warriors' realms. With his ancient skills, combined with those of the Hektor elite, he would crack the Guild codes that gave the Angels proprietary access, and move the entire organization across, to seize the reigns of the new worlds. Blinded by his ambitions, Joonas only saw the one probability that had him succeed – it was, regrettably for him, only a close second to the one that laid a wide-open path of serious complications to his master plan.

Cruz and his assistant arrived at the Wild Cherry Market ten minutes ahead of schedule. They ordered some food at the deli and carried their trays to the patio that gave view onto the bay, all the way to the Samoa Bridge, with Eureka in the background. Paula Hunter plugged in the laptop and fired it up as she normally did before meeting. She feared some last second instructions would flash on the screen to let her know that plans were cancelled, but the secret page remained blank.

"We probably won't need the scanner today, Hunter, this is our last meeting with these guys; we're taking over," Cruz said, weary and distinctly detached from the implication of his words.

The ex-student was overtaken with anxiety, but refrained from making it obvious to her boss. Did it mean he had been ahead of the game from the get-go, having strategically placed his chess pieces all along, while readying himself for the play-ending move? Or, was he so imbued with power as to being completely oblivious to the counter-forces that were at work? She couldn't tell, but she recognized that focusing on doubt weakened her assurance that things were going to pan out. She needed to keep her computer on as per the instructions in Slaughter's last email.

"If you don't mind, we may still want to record the interrogation," she offered.

"Do as you wish!" he returned impatiently, looking up at the wall clock as it moved a tick past the meeting time.

Hunter's laptop beeped – the Hektor blazon filled the screen.

"Something from headquarters," she informed her boss.

She turned the laptop around for the cam to scan his signature before he opened the message. Alexander Cruz barely flinched, but rose up at once. He told Hunter to stay put and to let Slaughter and Flemmingson know he might be late for the meeting. She saw him, from behind the glass wall of the patio, hastily get into the USDA vehicle and take off. The two strangers who had sat at an adjacent table stood up and approached her.

"Quick, it's time to get out of here;" Liv said, as she grabbed the stunned ex-Guild student's arm. "We only have a very small window!"

Hunter picked up the computer and left her food untouched. The three walked hurriedly out of the market, jumped in Marshall's SUV, and drove off to the freeway ramp a few blocks to the north, before connecting with Highway 299 onwards to the Fieldbrook Road exit and the estate. They ran out of the vehicle, straight to the courtyard portal and vanished through thin air. The Triad, who had originally created the gate and wisely left it available in the case such a situation would arise, was now ready to erase its mark and prevent Cruz from reading its blueprint.

When the Forest Service captain returned to the market and saw the untouched food, he realized he had been duped. His phone rang; it was Slaughter informing him he had been delayed on his way to the meeting.

"There won't be another meeting for a while," Cruz simply said, looking emptily towards Humboldt Bay.

The cop returned to his SUV and hurried in the direction of the Fieldbrook estate. When he arrived, he already knew he was too late. He drove back to the Eureka motel, where he accessed Hektor headquarters via the portal in his room.

A few days later, the paper headlines cried foul play – a Forest Service vehicle had been found abandoned in a parking lot with one of its occupants dead in his room and the other missing. The USDA office confirmed that the SUV had been gone from their lot for a while, presumably stolen, since all of their employees were accounted for. Alexander Cruz and Paula Hunter were never part of them.

It was most certainly not the way Marshall Slaughter remembered the facts, since he had spoken with Groveland headquarters weeks before, to verify the legitimacy of the two agents. Either the USDA had lied, or two realities had momentarily overlapped – the one he and his friend Geir had been recently living in; and the other, where the rest of the world resided.

3 – THE LAST PORTAL

Ma-l, Saka, Vac, and Olaf stood at the top of the valley as the flames rose in the distance, pushed by the forces that had destroyed the mother reality. The snake, as the Goddess had named the raging fire, could only be soothed by the voice of compassion. It was not to be seen as the enemy; rather, it was to be recognized as a vital and necessary part of the creative thrust behind the new world that had emerged out of the defining paradox triggered by Olaf and Vac's intrusion into the impossible probability that cocooned the Warriors' realms. It was the destructive majesty that would open the seeds buried deep in the ground, to awaken the latent life. It was the cleansing energy that birthed the new from the old – it was not to be feared.

As they looked down towards the mouth of the valley, they witnessed a gigantic plume of smoke rise from the heart of the burning forest. Streaks of lightning pierced and tore the bulging contours of its emerging mass – and there it was, a giant copperhead, whizzing and hissing, twisting amid the raging winds. It stretched the distance to hover above the group.

The imposing gestalt asked threateningly, "You, who do not fear, tell me; why should I spare you from my wrath?"

Ma-l's voice rose as if amplified by a giant sound system.

"We do not fear the might, and we do not walk away from the power that defines you. We cannot thrive in the shadow of each other, or by hiding from what makes us. This is our world; we are all welcome here. There is much to build that will require everyone's skills guided by their unique purpose; and so, we must be thankful for our sacred diversity. We stand below you in peace, with the assurance that there is only authenticity in the forces that radiate from your core. Your place is among us, for we embrace your courage and relentless drive towards the purification of consciousness. It is through the Oneness which unifies us that I know we cannot be defined by the sparing or the annihilation of each other. You are well aware I could have called on the rain long ago, but we chose to wait instead. All of us here are humbled as well as honored by your presence. Peace is what we offer, love is what we serve."

"You have spoken from a true heart, Goddess; therefore I will assist you, and protect you and your guests. The honor is mine. May we live to revel in each other's appreciation of the creative powers that come from all the directions of wisdom. You may address me as you wish," the guttural voice rang.

"Then, if you do not mind, your identity shall remain Snake, in honor of the hidden beauty you represent. I could not possibly think of a more suited title," Ma-l said.

"It is music to my ears, Goddess, may your land prosper!"

The smoke retreated, recalled by the forest. The winds subsided, as the blaze rescinded its forward progress. The amber glow of the sun brightened and the blue of the sky deepened from behind the receding haze. The ground steadied itself, as the dance of tumbling boulders from the high cliffs and the deep rumble from the belly of the realm, at last came to an end.

The friends hugged and laughed. Vac howled in appreciation. The friends then hurried towards the orchards and the house. Ma-l's playful pack came racing towards them, leaving a dust cloud in their wake.

———————

By the time the group reached the house, Olaf felt his laptop vibrate in its pouch. The Triad requested an audience – all gathered around the computer.

"We have news from the team that one of the Guild's students forcibly enrolled by Hektor is in need of safety and must be transferred to your realm. Is it an agreeable arrangement?"

All turned to Ma-l who was deemed the authority in the matter, but she deflected the responsibility. A consensus was reached – it was an acceptable option, providing the realm was her most immediate safe harbor.

"She will be accompanied by two members of Le Lien, named Liv and Spencer, close associates of ours, who have been working on this convoluted case with Olaf and Saka's old Earth friends, Marshall and Geir. You may be pleased to know connections still exist in spite of limited access mostly enjoyed by migrating Angels. It's a long story that we will share later-on today with those of you unfamiliar with Guild history and Hektor. The student in question is Paula Hunter, a victim of conditioning that led to her defection from the Masters' program to the league abovementioned. And though technically, she no longer is an Angel, her training has left a strong enough imprint to afford her access to the portal through which we came before the mother reality collapsed. Again, there is much to tell, but we shall only concern ourselves, at this point, with the urgency of rescuing the student. The cliff access to the cave must be cleared from the rubble that is now blocking it, but there is time. As you all know, Earth physics are of no concern between the two Onenesses. By tweaking the timelines, hours in Saka and Olaf's old world can be turned to weeks in this one, and vice versa. But of course, when Paula Hunter and her guides finally arrive, they will have landed in a distant future – it's all a big present! We must admit to enjoying teasing our friend Olaf here," The Triad expressed, failing to convince the group there was indeed appreciable humor in that last comment.

"We'll make sure to prepare for their arrival in a *timely* manner. I'm delighted at the prospect of making new friends," Ma-1 said, satisfied.

Saka, Vac, and Olaf concurred. The Triad thanked everyone for accommodating on short notice.

"When it rains, it pours," Swyndle offered.

"Is that humor, or just an old adage that doesn't want to come un-stuck, Angel Olaf?" Saka teased.

"Dare I ask why the Goddess of Light still puns like her old self?" he countered with a wink.

Vac described how Hektor came to rise from the failure to come to a consensus by the team in charge of realigning the tribal energy that had waged war on the "Evil Ones." The Angel, who knew Joonas personally, wasn't surprised by his violent opposition to the Ones' request. The flawed human ego, as the Dove saw it, was in its last throes – saving it was pure madness. Vac explained that the formation of Hektor was perceived by some as an inevitable and potentially positive emergence. But in view of the latest developments, it was clear the group had overextended its welcome, particularly if Joonas was after much bigger game. Vac refrained from speculating on what kind of game that might have been...

———————————

For the next few days, the group worked relentlessly on clearing the trail up to the top of the cliff. Most of the platform to the cave was missing, and what remained was covered with rubble. The entrance was irreversibly condemned, making it painfully obvious that access had been forever denied. Vac took off along a precarious trail cut into the side of the cliff, and disappeared around a protrusion of the rock face. The three decided to have lunch while waiting for his return.

"What is stopping you and Vac from getting around these obstacles with the use of your skills?" Olaf perplexedly asked Ma-l.

"For one thing, you and Saka have quite a lot to do with it. Here, in the physicality of what we may call our collective realm, these skills are expressed through the strength of our bodies and the swiftness of our thoughts. It's true I'm able to manifest many things on my own, but I have chosen to accept you in my world, with the knowledge that it would limit my abilities to import expertise from other areas of my personal reality. With time, as each of us further defines their unique talents and purpose, it will be possible to extend these native skills into much greater tools. For now, I'm grateful to be able to create a few useful objects behind your backs, and occasionally rise to the task, as in our meeting with Snake. But Saka has already been nosing into my bag of tricks; perhaps she doesn't mind telling what she's been up to lately?" Ma-l teased.

"Since Great One Amaterasu gifted me with the stone and named me Goddess of Light, I have been working on defining my place, with the aim of unveiling my unique creative abilities. Out of the light, spectral forms rise, ideas that materialize when teamed with purpose. Shaping purpose is the task of love. I'm not there yet, but I will tell you when I come up with something we can all use. For now, if you see more butterflies in the garden, blame it on me!" she laughed, looking in the distance of the valley.

"That's lovely, Saka," Olaf said. "If any of them find themselves in need of an Angel, I could use the training," he added with heartfelt humor.

Vac returned, covered in dust.

"There's another way to the cave from the side of the mountain, but the trail is treacherous and missing in some areas. A rock slab sled off the face during the earthquake to reveal a passage. It also provides somewhat of a platform below it. Access appears easier from the opposite side," the Angel explained.

The group consented on exploring the means to clear a path to the new entrance from the other end. They were done for the day. They walked down the trail back to the house, where The Triad awaited their return for updates on the Paula Hunter case.

———————

"Here's the way it plays at the other end: the transfer will happen in two days. We've synched the timelines, making sure the lane will hold steady to that point," the trio described. "Make sure you're ready; if not, you must keep us informed with enough notice, so that we can recalibrate the coordinates. We've forwarded your written messages to your friends via Liv and Spencer, but for reasons bound to the chasm between the two realities, we're incapable of clearing the translation issue. It has been difficult to explain the principles of the information hurdle to their human logic; to them, a simple 'hi' at one end should translate into 'hi' at the other. Spencer is working on something that may open an alley, but he cannot promise he'll succeed, for it has a lot to do with how their psyches fail at making the necessary adjustments, due to being unable to conceptualize the nature of data transfer across two alien environments. For now, they have to trust our word that you all are well and readying yourselves for the student's arrival."

"We're hoping we can let you know by tomorrow. As it turns out, we're no longer able to access the cave from its original entry point, but Vac has located another possible way in," Saka explained.

"All is well, we're available whenever you need us," The Triad returned.

They gathered around dinner to discuss the plan for the coming morning. Olaf had baked stuffed squash and fruit pies – the team was in high spirits. Vac ate in his usual corner by the pantry, content of just being a dog around meals. He called it his private canine time. He once was asked to consider donning the human attire, but he felt no particular advantage to it – as long as all chose to dwell in the physical universe, he was satisfied with his end of the bargain. He had been thinking about his good friends, Axel and Ilia, who he assumed had found their places in the Warriors' realms, and how he and the rest of the group would connect with the remaining pocket realities. Unlike the Guild portals that linked all points of Vac's native multiverse, these domains posed a logistical challenge to the creation of a network that would join them all – there wasn't a point of reference. Even as he, Axel, and Ilia belonged to the group that pushed for extreme mobility across realities; they were faced with a dilemma with the new Oneness and its lack of history. But there was still plenty of time to figure it out.

The four took off early the next morning to clear an access path to the new cave entrance. Vac had been reflecting on the cavity's peculiar resemblance to the end room of Ma-l's tunnel. The possibility of other such caves implied a multiplicity of tunnels connecting in complex ways. He asked Ma-l if she knew of other rooms, besides the one they had been using in and out of her realm – she was positive none existed. He thought of it as an oddity worth earmarking.

It was midday when the four reached the base of the slab that had fractured from the cliff and sled down its face, revealing the gaping hole. Its surface offered many ragged edges that made for a relatively easy climb. The group opted to first take their lunch, an opportunity to address the logistics of taking the Guild student into their home. There were vivid concerns around her association with Hektor, and the reasons behind having to be moved to safety. Joonas's intentions were left to much speculation, including the possibility of imminent danger to the realms. They just would have to wait for the student and her protectors to arrive before getting filled on what The Triad had been leaving out.

It didn't take long for the friends to get to the top of the slab, where they found a wide platform only a few feet below the opening, allowing them to enter the half-domed-space that exposed a tunnel at its end. Saka provided the light – Vac went ahead. All kept their eyes open for side corridors or other rooms, but none came into view. The alternatively narrow and wide rock passage snaked aimlessly, as if unable to make up its mind about any specific destination; but it eventually settled on a faint glow, followed by a rolling growl that came from around a blind turn.

Vac stood facing a gaping inferno – it was clear they hadn't reached the anticipated target. A thousand feet below, magma rose and fell. From fissures high up in the blackened skies, lightning bolted, striking the heart of the molten rock, hurling it upwards with ferocious power, like the whip of an angry demon, cracking in dysrhythmic madness.

Ma-l brought the group in a circle, away from the raging abyss and celestial fury.

"I know what this is – we're at the entrance of one of the Warriors' worlds. It so saddens me to be witness of a spectacle that can only exist in reflection of the pain and anger felt by one of my ancient brothers and sisters in arms, a view that sheds light on a state of spiritual desolation that is beyond my words. My heart aches at such torment, and I fear the room by which we entered was the cocoon of that restless soul. This world is about to collapse, so I beg the three of you to follow me back whence we came; I doubt there's anything we can do to save this brave fighter; too much damage has been done by too long a trail of despair. This deity burnt at infancy and we must turn our back on its fate."

Saka, stricken by the grief that arose from within, couldn't hold the tears. She was born of the crippling solitude of the stone, having foreseen, as she came into awareness, the ravages of this tortured world in many of the probabilities that had lain before her.

Ma-1 led the group back to the other end of the long tunnel – it was night when they arrived. The realms had shifted like two plates out of alignment. The few hours had turned to many more. Olaf pulled out his laptop to connect with The Triad to seek counsel.

"Greetings – You are only a few hours off course. We're sorry you are discovering the intricacies of what interconnects the Warriors' worlds at such inopportune time. We advise you to stay put and retry the tunnel; its shifting properties indicate that it is linked to more than one place. Rather than side corridors as you first thought, there might be a system of portals that operates on the specificity of the destination. There's the possibility each realm uses a unique access to a shared réseau of connections. Angel Vac knows what we mean; we believe he can take it from here."

"I think I just figured out a way to connect with Axel and Ilia!" Vac uttered cheerfully.

"We'll sleep here tonight," Ma-1 said. "I too, believe I've understood the fundamentals of this network of tunnels and portals. After all, something had to have been put in place for us to enter in contact with each other upon reaching a certain level of creational mobility."

"I worked on many portal routes, but conceptually speaking, the realms represent a mystery. The technology couldn't be too far removed from that of my training though. It would no doubt be easier with Axel and Ilia around," Vac confessed.

"We will let you know what Le Lien comes up with in the morning; they have maps for just about

97

everything. Keep in mind we are dealing with a big place!" the voice in charge emphasized, failing once again at humor.

"With all due respect, I believe Le Lien is out of their league in this universe; but feel free to surprise us," Saka countered.

"As long as we have a foot in your world, we will assist you with everything at our disposal, even if the logic of our methods escapes you, Goddess of Light. Maps take many forms and straddle worlds that exist far beyond the reach of your consciousness; do not underestimate the work of the Guild. The Warriors' realms exist because we put them there, and though they certainly evolved beyond our capacity of observation, there are certain fundamental elements in their collective makeup that are still within the scope of our cognitive abilities. In all seriousness though, we promise that we will eventually manage to amuse you; it may just come from left field, as your friend Marshall Slaughter often said it did," The Triad concluded triumphantly.

"If you keep on putting it that way, you may succeed," Saka tagged on, laughing.

———————

Over a short breakfast of dried figs, nuts, and lukewarm herbal tea, the group reviewed The Triad's assertion that portals existed somewhere along the course of the extended winding tunnel to the volcano. On a variance of it, Vac hypothesized that such ways most likely converged to a manifold roughly positioned at the median point of the total length of the passage, a ratio that would be maintained regardless of the fundamental measure of each new tunnel explored. Ma-l proposed that, due to the elusive nature of its gaugeable length, the corridor they had traveled the day before could be concealing portals in the process of constantly shifting. Upon consultation, The Triad simply stated that Saka was probably right about the maps. In fact, Le Lien was in no position to help. It advised the group to stay vigilant and to please, not get lost in the maze.

It was all the more convoluted due to the fact they entered a tunnel through the backroom of another Warrior's realm – were they not? It suddenly and simultaneously occurred to Ma-l and Vac that they could still be looking at the Goddess's own rear cave, but owning to the fact the original exit into her valley was blocked, a portal into a different realm could have been activated. In that case, they were contemplating a useful coincidence, where the student and her guides would be introduced to the valley directly, without ever using the tunnel. Irrespective of these notions which amounted to little more than speculation, the group still had to locate the rear of the blocked exit into their realm.

Ma-l spoke.

"Vac and I will go first. We can work in tandem with my personal signature guiding us to the chosen place, and not just theoretically, I hope. At any rate, let's heed anything resembling a marker, or we may yet find ourselves in another realm. If I recall, yesterday Vac went first, but I led on the way back; why I believe we made it to where we started. So, it's possible that some 'revolving portal' automatically responds to my inner wishes when I pass, because of my intrinsic connection to the realms – same with Saka. After all, when Olaf and Vac first came into my birth cave, I was, flickering light et al, the one who led them out of the tunnel."

"I can't fathom what would have happened if you hadn't," Olaf thought aloud.

"I originally believed the system was strictly designed to allow for passage into the mother reality and beyond. Of course, you three's arrival changed all that. I had assumed I needed to get out of my realm to access the others, when it appears it can be done without leaving it. Believe me, this comes with great hopes – I was resigned to accept my kin had gone their separate ways. So, if our theories are meant to yield the results my heart yearns for, we have some serious work ahead of us," Ma-1 said intently.

"By the way, Angel Vac, your sense of orientation is nothing but trouble – the mouth of an about-to-erupt volcano?! Really?!" Saka teased the Master.

"There's a reason for everything, and purpose in every mistake. It just happens I have a fondness for the dramatic – ask Olaf," Vac countered.

All laughed and got up to ready themselves for a new jaunt into the tunnel.

"I suppose we need to stick together to prevent an accidental separation; so please, let's keep it tight," Ma-1 advised.

The Goddess went ahead, followed by Vac, Olaf, and Saka, hoping the two with the identical signatures would protect the ones in the middle. Saka's light, courtesy Amaterasu's stone, provided ample visibility; the group progressed rapidly along the rocky corridor, right up to the rubble blocking the way.

"Bingo!" Olaf exclaimed, "A bit shorter than the tunnel to the gates of Hell!"

"An understatement, Angel," Saka cut in, "but where was the portal?"

"This could be more complicated than what we anticipated, although Ma-l's signature holds true. I will have to reflect on this – there's the possibility of a distinct consciousness involved with the process of opening and closing these portals." Vac offered.

"Now that we know the gaping hole above the valley is actually the cave at the end of your tunnel – or is it the beginning, Ma-l; I never know? – we can presume the student and her guides will be fine," Olaf said.

"The beginning where it all started! So, assuming things are as they look, we can speculate so, Olaf. The student is due to arrive tonight; let's inform The Triad of our state of preparedness. Are we ready to commit to the transfer as scheduled, or should we further investigate for instabilities in the system? I suggest that we first retrace our steps, this time with Saka leading; then we'll have confirmation of the signature's reliability," Ma-l said.

Saka went ahead. Within minutes, the group came to the collapsed wall that overlooked the valley. Not even the Goddess doubted that she stood in her place of birth, a straight shot from the blocked end around the cliff. They informed The Triad of their readiness to welcome the visitors. With plenty of time before the scheduled night meeting, Saka and Olaf volunteered to fetch food and supplies. Ma-l and Vac hiked the horseshoe-shaped uplift of the valley, down to the head of the creek, where the first patches of water-loving shrubs grew. The hole of the cave above, a gaping mouth whose moan carried with it the millennia of gruesome solitude, the rise and fall of hopes, the near descent into insanity, and at last, softly, the flight that gave birth to dreams, a mouth whose breath bore the song of creation, filled the valley with love and life. The Goddess laid her naked body in one of the shallow pools, closing her eyes to free her senses from resistance and allow the elfin spirits to converge towards her core. She took in the reflection of a world that had rooted in her dreams and grown into a consciousness and purpose of its own – purpose beyond the reach of her wildest hopes. She was being rewarded by the miracle of her creation – her work – invited to walk among the fields of its own sowing. The cold water ran past her shoulders, around her breasts, above her belly, and between her legs, until she became the river that quenched the forests along her flood lines; and onward, to the sea where she cycled back up with the clouds that broke on the jagged edges of mile-high summits – and then into the stream again. It was a rare and precious orgasm that shook her core consciousness in similar ways the quakes had rattled her land and brought Snake to life. It was a dance of flesh, water, earth, and sun merging as one into the arousal of her senses – she was one with all.

Vac roamed along the creek, occasionally diving in its white waters. He was trying to put order to the elements of the portal configuration, bemused by the peculiarity of its mechanics. The standard Guild gates were connected in separate groups to a single matrix, but could run independently from it; each cluster taking over for any dysfunction within the whole, until repairs were made, generally by the diagnostic and remedial tools of other groups. In the case of the Warriors' portals, the Angel sensed an organic synergy between the realms, which dictated the priority of access. He saw the volcano as a sinister choice made by a gestalt of consciousness that deemed it the best option for the unknown traveler;

102

yet, these worlds were relatively new, with unlikely traffic between them. Again, Vac's thinking delved in hypothesis, since he couldn't fathom what stage of evolution these realms had arrived at; if they had evolved at all. The quasi-biological nature of the system lent itself to the speculation there was a unique and odd technological process at work, providing technology had anything to do with it. He would have to ask Ma-l, or perhaps Saka, if deep in the memories of their sedentary lives within the stone, some of the dream connections between the Warriors didn't bring forth the coalescence of an embryonic system that later matured into a complex réseau of inter-branching lanes and portals, as well as a unique awareness of itself. Had the collective reality of these worlds expanded into a consciousness of unthinkable breadth and potentiality? He returned to join the Goddess, who, a distance away, stood looking towards him and the widening valley beyond, as if, somehow, she had been aware of his thoughts.

The Ma-lian sun was setting when Saka and Olaf returned laden with baskets and blankets. The Triad had informed Le Lien that the elements of the transfer were in place and ready as per scheduled. Liv warned about the student possibly being in a state of shock, and thus to expect some form of emotional shutdown.

The group was prepared. They sat around dinner under the flicker of early stars that had joined the purple glow of the set sun beyond the valley. Vac revealed his thoughts about the ways of the realms, probing the

Goddesses for hints of their shared knowledge of ancient paths into the Warriors' dreams. Ma-1 answered by speaking of the days when she could hear the echoless and ghostly whispers of her kin from across the darkness of the stone. It happened during the first stages of isolation from physical life. Much later, these same voices would be silenced by the long hand of time, when the only noise that was heard came from her very thoughts. Those early whispers were the waves that carried the Warriors into the fields of dreams – waves, which later became known as the lanes. With spears and arrows left to the fires of battle, they sat peacefully in the grass, under the enrobing moonlight, sharing stories and songs. Then, almost mysteriously, they, one by one, left the gatherings, until the day the words stopped being spoken and the lanes ceased to run. Soon, Ma-1 forgot about the dreams – the era of Saka was born.

Could the paths that were thought dormant, or even dead, have grown into a complex réseau of caves, portals, and tunnels that opened onto unique realities, as the dreams of each Warrior evolved into universes similar to hers? Ma-1 couldn't tell, but it was plausible. Perhaps the wave lanes never stopped, and it was just the riders that ceased to come. If one were to seek them again, maybe, just maybe, the dream meadows would come to life again... Ma-1 took a deep breath.

The Triad informed the group that all was in place for the transfer and to expect their visitors to arrive within the next few minutes. Saka lit the backside of the cave as the countdown began. It didn't take long before they realized something had gone amiss. The Triad confirmed the two Angels and the student had entered the portal following precise coordinates – they should have reached their destination. Le Lien was positive, the timelines were synched. Even if the dates and hours had shifted off the charts, that data was irrelevant – they should have made it across!

"We must get back in there!" Vac urged. "This isn't what we assumed it was. Same as last time: Ma-1, you go first – Saka, you're last! We need to act before we lose them!"

By the time they made it to half the distance, they heard voices. Vac, who had never lost his cool, instantly discovered the meaning of relief – he took due notice. Their visitors had come to a stop at the far end of the tunnel, where thousands of tons of rubble had closed the original access to Ma-1's universe. Liv and Spencer laughed at the mishap, but Paula Hunter looked bedazzled. After a quick introduction, a line was formed with, again, Ma-1 and Saka at each end. Within minutes, the group was back on track, overlooking the mouth of the moonlit valley.

Saka turned to the student.

"You look like you went through the spin cycle, dear; we brewed something that will make you feel like your life is supposed to support you. Here, drink as much as you need and pass it around when you're done!"

Vac came to lie by Paula Hunter. He figured she probably could use the company of a friendly canid. She did – his presence grounded her instantaneously. She stretched out, put her arm around him, and then softly fell into deep sleep.

Liv and Spencer took turns entering code into Olaf's computer, while The Triad relayed the data to Le Lien HQ. The mission had been accomplished; it was now time to move to the second phase of the operation.

They informed the group that they would be leaving as soon as all were up to date with the rescued student's situation. For the next hour, they recalled the events that tied Marshall Slaughter and Geir Flemmingson to Paula Hunter: the interminable interrogations, the treachery of Tömör preceding his arrest, and of course, Joonas's vileness and his sinister plan to infiltrate the realms. The Great Ones, all the while, watching with their hands metaphorically tied to the pillars of protocol. The last bit of news was received with mixed feelings, especially since Vac had shed light on the rise of Hektor from the standpoint of his personal relationship with the rogue Master. They all, at various intuitive levels, understood the implications of Joonas' name being tossed around, and what it meant if the Ones were to not partake.

"We can't tell how the Dove, at the helm of such a vast organization, would be able to cross, but as long as the ghost image of the mother reality holds, allowing Masters to travel here and back as they wish, we have to consider the extreme risk this last portal poses. The Guild is firm, Hektor is forbidden in your realm," Spencer concluded, before he asked to be shown the way back.

"It's the one thing only the creator of this place can help you with at this point; so follow me," Ma-l said.

Liv and Spencer hugged and thanked everyone. The Great Goddess took them into the darkness of the tunnel, until the dullness of their steps could no longer be heard.

When Ma-l returned, all had the same question.

"How did you find the way to the end of your cave if this one is not it?"

"I figured it was just a matter of putting across the intention of getting there. As it turns out, and because of

106

the obstruction, it appears there is a shift that has happened in the way the portals are configured. This cave is not mine; it probably belongs to the Warrior whose reality opens onto the volcano. There's a definite connection between the blockage at the end of my tunnel and this gaping wound, a form of synchronicity. But focused thinking only takes me to the ends of our two worlds – not exactly an achievement, dare I say? With the dream wave system, we shared a space for our meetings; now that our worlds have evolved into their unique manifestations, the lanes, or in this case, the tunnels, should also take us to a common place. I don't know how Axel and Ilia accessed any of the other realms; either they had a partial knowledge of the system, or their immutable desire to assist triggered the tunnel consciousness into assigning a path to their journey. There's also the possibility that they never managed to reach their destination, but since they knew their way to this realm, I rest assured they're fine wherever they ended. Assuming there is such a gestalt in charge of the tunnels, I wonder how it's able to define its purpose with all the Angel traffic. After all, doesn't it look like, at this very moment, I'm the only Warrior who's shown up against great numbers of outsiders? I imagine it could be quite mind-boggling for such a consciousness to see its evolution tested under these circumstances."

"I am perfectly with you, Ma-l," Vac said. "But what happened to Axel and Ilia also concerns all the Masters who have transited to the realms. It may sound extraordinary to you, but we don't know what became of them. They don't possess the means to communicate with the Guild and none have returned via the portal tied to the ghost image of the mother reality. We can only assume they have found their place amid the Warriors, while others are waiting for their turns to join them. So, where are they, and why haven't Axel and Ilia gotten in touch? All the reasons to believe something's up."

"Then it leaves us to define what this entity exactly is, and how it impacts the reality of the realms?" Saka said.

"It's my personal understanding that this gestalt is what ties the realms together," Olaf cut in. "From having heard the stories of the battles on so many occasions, I'm arriving at the hypothesis that the Great Ones added their personal touch to the gift of creation the Angels handed the Warriors. I am seeing it as a way for the realms to stay connected, in the form a whole larger than the sum of its parts. So, in essence, the aforementioned gestalt could be seen as the Oneness of this new multiverse."

"I witness that Vac's training is befitting your intuitive knowledge, Olaf; it's a delight, as much as privilege, to be in such fine company," Ma-l said, smiling, with her hand on his shoulder.

She paused; collecting her thoughts.

"After we bring our sleeping guest into the fold, I suggest we explore these mysterious realities. I'm of course invested in finding out how each Warrior has fared; although, I must confess that my relationship with them was never defined, at least not until we met in the dream meadows. Before that, as per our training, we barely acknowledged each other emotionally. The tribal leaders deemed closeness between us detrimental to our purpose. For the sake of clarification, my reaction to the fate of my kin can only be in relation to my potential victories and failures while in the stone. As I said, and apart from a few exceptions, there were no real bonds between us. The battle and dream spirits existed integral to collective realities independent from each other, where individual passions never influenced our endeavors. But there's something that lingers as I speak. We assume the Warriors took in many Angels into their worlds, yet they failed at opening their doors to me – one of them – while ignoring the welcoming arms of my open realm."

Paula Hunter slept in the background of many unanswerable questions – she would soon be adding to them. Slowly, the friends drifted, until their minds were called by the songs of early morning birds, when the last of dawn stars glided past the far end of the valley.

———

It seemed natural that Paula Hunter would benefit from Saka and Olaf's supervision, based on the two's deep knowledge of the student's native world. The Triad had warned that her Hektor conditioning could backfire and instill a visceral compulsion to reject her new environment. But instead, she woke up like a youth with a bad hangover, trying to chase away the veil that had rendered her reality incomprehensible.

"Things happened so fast," she said. "Forgive me if I'm not exactly rising to the occasion."

Ma-1 handed her a cup of steaming spiced tea.

"It's our understanding that you were forcibly enrolled into Hektor by the individual that passed as your boss. His name is Joonas. As you should know, his reputation precedes him. We're sorry that you, as well as the multitude of Guild students in your position, had to suffer at the hands of a reckless and bitter fallen Master.

Because of their human origins, Goddess Saka and Angel Olaf will help you get oriented – both have roots in the area of your birthplace. It goes without saying that before we deem you fit to regain full student status, you will be subjected to steady evaluation. The Triad, the three Le Lien Angels in Olaf's computer, will communicate the results to the larger team. Your Hektor system laptop was confiscated by Liv and Spencer, and thus went back the way it came. You are now fully disconnected from the rogue organization; consider yourself technically safe, as long as the Guild stays one step ahead of the game. Additionally, because of the extreme urgency of your situation, you were given no time to tell your story and shed light on your level of involvement within that group. You are encouraged to divulge that information, while we'll help you with letting go of the emotional trauma that occurred during your exposure to Hektor and Joonas' influence in particular. We hope you understand this has little to do with trust, as much as it has with vigilance and common sense. We're well aware of the alien nature of finding yourself here, but bear with it; you'll be fine!"

"Each of us will tell our story. The one about Linda Sue should be of particular interest," Saka laughed. "For now, we'll return to the house where you will be assigned your own quarters. All commodities as well as tasks are shared – you'll be required to pull your weight. Rest assured most of it is more play than work, even if it's at times exhausting. For the next few days though, all that will be asked of you is that you rest. When you feel sufficiently strong, we'll know. And please, if you could strip out of that awful outfit, I believe Ma-1 has something for you. Of course I'm not talking about her bare skin and tattoos," she added with pointed humor.

Paul Hunter obediently let go her Forest Service garb. She stood, fully naked, disencumbered from the excessive ballast of her recent past. She waited for the Goddess to pick an outfit out of one of the baskets, aroused by the cool breeze that gently detoxified the immediate proximity of her form.

"Cleansing the self is a good start," the Goddess smiled. "My realm, unlike your world, doesn't have a dress code. Here's something that I believe will enhance your complexion!"

Ma-l turned to the rest of the group.

"Before we get going, I suggest we all hit the creek – I forecast a warm day!"

With her body drying under the early morning sun, Paula Hunter turned to Ma-l.

"You're not saying that the four of you are the only inhabitants of this planet, are you?"

"In a nutshell, yes, plus a pack of semi-tamed puppies at the house; and of course, a variety of wild mammals and birds," Ma-l answered.

"Two Goddesses and two Angels, am I right?"

"And the puppies," Saka, who was seating nearby, interjected playfully.

"Hierarchically-speaking, that takes me to the bottom of the ladder, I guess," the student remarked.

"Well, in a world of so few, it's hard to imagine such a short ladder. But no need to worry, there's no hierarchy in this place, just individuals doing their parts. The idea of a caste system is stigmatic of Hektor, only reflective of a desire by its founders to rule over souls they have robbed of their dignity. We value all levels of evolutionary knowledge equally. We understand that all parts of the whole rely on each other to exist and thrive.

111

It's obvious you haven't experienced love in a long time, dear one, but it will soon again fill your heart as your aches fall to the past," Ma-l replied.

"Thank you, I haven't heard such kind words since my days of training with my guardian, prior to being taken into the Guild," Paula Hunter returned.

"What's the Angel's name, and what did he/she call you?" Saka asked.

"His name's Leòn, like the city; he called me Pau, 'like the other city across the border,' he used to say," she answered with a smile.

"If you don't mind, this is going to be your name among us, it befits you," Ma-l said.

"I would love it," she returned, barely concealing the tears.

"Leòn and I worked side by side, but our subjects never crossed paths," Vac, who had joined in, added with pointed interest.

"Maybe I can breathe again," Pau said in relief.

Ma-l put her arms around her and gently pulled her head to her shoulder. She whispered something no-one heard. Pau hugged the Goddess in return, with the affection of an errant soul reunited with her long lost family of consciousness.

Marshall Slaughter and Geir Flemmingson awaited the news from Liv and Spencer. Their computers had remained silent. If it hadn't been for the reports of Cruz's death, they would never have guessed the rescue plan had worked. Geir had finally re-succumbed to his taste for sleazy bars – the friends were downing shots at the Shipwreck Saloon.

"What I don't understand is why bodies can squeeze through portals, but a plain English text can't make it in one piece to Olaf's computer at the other end," Geir lamented.

"You worry too much about this kind of stuff, mate; plus, Liv has already tutored us on the fact that we're at odds with a reality that, at first, didn't technically exist. Now it's in an entirely different system of existence, so what d'you expect? Case in point, in the past, when we sent them Van Goghs, they received Picassos, and vice versa; if you don't mind the crude analogy," Slaughter countered.

"Fair enough, but wouldn't it be nice to get news directly from them while there's still a path?"

"Spencer's working on it," the detective returned, intimating he had no interest in furthering a discussion on the subject.

"I gather I'm returning to Iceland, now that our friends have gotten things under control. I'll miss you and this place, as always."

"You can never stay away from here for too long, Geir, but let's wait for Liv and Spencer before it's safe to say the coast is clear. Cruz may be gone, but Joonas is alive and well, and if that son of a bitch is as desperate as Le Lien seems to indicate, we should hear from him sooner than later," Slaughter warned.

"Well then, I've got another two weeks before I'm due to lecture in front of the students that run the *Icelandic Society for Intelligence Research*; I'll stick around a bit longer to enjoy the beautiful Humboldt spring, I guess," Flemmingson practically slurred.

113

"Let's shack at the office tonight, I think we can count on Hektor to leave the estate alone for the night," the detective humored.

Marshall and Geir were about to go down to Café Noir when Liv and Spencer appeared by the office door.

"Sorry about the unannounced visit, but it's somewhat tricky to maneuver around time shifts and worlds stitched together with ghost realities. We hope you didn't have to wait too long. We're just coming back from Ma-l's realm; Paula Hunter did well under the circumstances. Again, your friends are fine and they were told you are too. They know what is happening with Joonas and they've been warned of Hektor's desperate attempt to bridge the chasm to their world," Spencer said.

"We've noticed this town is crawling with Dogs, which means Joonas is actively searching for the portal through which the object of his abuse was ushered. He more than suspects the student is with the Warriors, so his resolve to get across has intensified drastically. The elder accepts no failure; he no longer just yearns to control a universe, he is now waging a personal vendetta against the Guild, twinned to a visceral desire to punish Paula Hunter in ways that, we're afraid to say, are beyond description," Liv sinisterly added.

"We stayed here last night – does it mean Joonas' Dogs have been all over the estate?" Slaughter asked.

"They're all over you in ways you may not even comprehend. Under extreme situations, they are capable of infiltrating your system to the point of ubiquity. But we see it as a shot in the dark; you have no control over the placement and operation of portals – Joonas knows that. Call it compulsion, but to him, it's more a matter of bringing down those who have bruised his pride, than it is one of actual logistics. He believes he no longer needs you, but his intractability to see through what he considers unfinished business presents a peculiarity, in that you're still quite instrumental to him in finding the portal; hence, and in an ambiguous way, that's how he will get to it. Do you follow?" Spencer asked.

"It's evident we're not completely safe," Geir replied pragmatically. "In a paradoxical twist, his pride is both his blindfold and vision."

"Well said! Joonas's pride is what makes for the convolutions; he cannot accept the fact he was duped by lowly humans; thus, he's not willing to look into what extra value you may add to his pursuit. In more ways than one, he stands at the center of a paradox that casts its long shadow over the Guild," Liv said.

"We're keeping an eye on the inter-dimensional web for unusual fluctuations; make sure you do the same with your environment – and trust your intuitions; they are better equipped at detecting pattern shifts than your intellects on their best behaviors," Spencer added.

"We must return to Le Lien. We'll alternatively appear in person and via the machines, so stay close to these laptops at all times. You must keep us updated, should you have something to report," Liv finished.

Slaughter and Flemmingson bought coffee and croissants to go before heading north to the Fieldbrook house. The detective had a hunch something was amiss with the picture, to the point he regretted having spent the evening drinking and sleeping at the office apartment.

When the friends arrived, they were greeted by the landscaping crew.

"Weren't you guys scheduled for next week?!" Slaughter shouted, his window down, over the noise of lawnmowers and hedge trimmers.

"Sorry, the boss had to move the dates around – something came up," one of the men cried out.

It wasn't unusual for landscapers to shuffle their appointments around weather conditions, but this clearly wasn't the case, especially when the jump in schedule was totally off the charts.

"Say, since when d'you show up a week early; the lawn didn't even need mowing?"

"I know, but we're just doing our job," the man returned defensively.

"Well, in that case, mine is to make choices that fit my agenda. So, right now, I want you to pack your gear and leave the property. Come back next week as agreed, and call before you decide to change the schedule!" the detective slapped.

"I need to call the boss," the lawnmower man said, as if the phrase added leverage to his argument.

"You do that, and please tell him I want to speak with him," Slaughter challenged.

The man feigned professional standoff stoicism as he dialed the number. When apparently no-one answered, he told the detective to try the office later, and then ordered his reluctant crew to load the equipment on the trailers. Slaughter finally relaxed when he saw them leave in a small convoy.

"Are they usually that many?" Geir enquired.

"No, they're not even my fucking landscapers; my guys have marked vehicles. I memorized the license plate

116

of one of the trucks; I'm gonna check with some friends at the EPD to see if those numbers have a name," Slaughter replied.

While they waited for the data on the vehicle's ownership, Marshall and Geir went around the property to look for indicators of foul play. The stone courtyard and the fire pit still vibrated from the buzz of activity. The detective could tell, just by soaking in the energy, that there had been a concentration of movements around where the portal used to be. It didn't take much to raise flags when his senses had been tuned to heed the minute details that eluded the untrained eye, such as the disturbed charred sticks in the pit, the broken twigs along the paths, and the torn leaves and mud smears in suspicious areas. There were no landscaping details in the cobblestone yard; the fruit trellises that surrounded it and the kiwi arbors that branched out in three directions had been pruned in the winter, yet curious and unwanted souls had been nosing around the place, sniffing for clues.

The Eureka cop called back; the license plate didn't match the VIN for that truck model; in fact, it belonged to a totaled vehicle involved in a highway crash half a year before. Slaughter didn't even want to know whether they were going to find the suspect pick-up or not; he already concluded it would just lead to a dead end.

"No need to bother assuming the house wasn't combed," he told Flemmingson. "They're looking for traces of Saka and Swyndle's past, but there's nothing for them to find, unless they're after something that goes beyond the obvious, like old energy clusters in the spatial memory of the place... Did I get the science right?"

"Close enough," Geir returned. "I don't know what these guys are capable of, beyond mowing the lawn and pulling blackberry roots, but I suspect they have training that defies our understanding. I wouldn't be surprised if they had the means to read complex data out of thin air. But how is it going to help Joonas find what he already knows is no longer here? Are he and his Dogs adept at peeling layers to the point of reconstructing the past? With the mother reality gone, his only access is in the reenactment of the time frame, from the precise moment at which the portal was created by The Triad, to its relocation after Paula Hunter went through with Liv and Spencer. But that's a mind twister of the first order. That would mean he and his cohort could have made it to the realms as early as the time at which Saka and Olaf got there; sheer impossibility in the light of the fact he's still searching for the way across. No, he needs to find the coordinates of that portal, so that he can back-engineer his way into the realms. He's looking for ghost images."

"Then, based on the activity in the courtyard, I guess he's getting really close to obtaining what he's after. Time to bring this to Le Lien's attention, don't you think?" Slaughter urged on.

The friends hurried to link their computers – the Angels came on at once. There was a long pause after the release of the news. Liv spoke first.

"Thank you for your keen observations – it means Joonas has most likely already found what he's been looking for. The one thing we are certain of is that he can only operate from the standpoint of this reality, which is as you know, the only platform for us to access Ma-l's domain – through that one portal left by The Triad. It doesn't mean some of us weren't able to cross into the realms from our own system – but later on that. We have now relocated your courtyard portal and adjusted its coordinates, as well as assigned a scrambler to it. We doubt there's much of a ghost image left at your place to work from since the degenerative curve is steep and exponential, but if his crew got there in time to take a clear enough print, Joonas could well be on his way to the next phase of his plan. Based on what you gave us, we doubt your home is any longer of consequence, but it doesn't mean he will forget about you."

"Why can't you just move the portal to an entirely different reality, where Joonas' chances of finding it would be negligible, and thus eliminate the potential for his infiltration of the realms?" Flemmingson asked.

"For one thing, the portal's key identity is inseparable from its point of creation. There is a radius of tolerance that doesn't exceed a circular area roughly the size of Humboldt Bay. Even if we could move it to a remote world within a non-physical environment, the nature of existence is such that every known element simultaneously nests in all of its associated locations. For someone like Joonas, it would hardly be a feat to connect the dots. Placement is inconsequential – the art of concealment, on the other hand, isn't. We're sorry to say that in the event Joonas were capable of engineering a copy of the portal with his own coordinates, it would have to be accomplished within your area, and the closer to the original location the better his chances of success. So now, his next step is to find where we hid it. I hope we are clear on the nuances," Spencer concluded.

"Am I to assume the two of you against all of Joonas' Dogs, makes for a balanced fight?" Geir asked sardonically.

"The two of us are only the eyes of Le Lien; we operate at many levels. To ease your doubts, we're not the only Angels working the area. We are confident the balance of power tips in our favor. That being said, we're also aware that 'chance' is an elusive player easily attracted to the forces of desperation and the will of those with nothing to lose. It's imperative for Hektor to find terra firma away from Guild control if it's meant to exist beyond its present short, projected lifespan. Joonas knows too well his organization cannot thrive much longer with the Guild closing in on his shenanigans. The student fiasco and Tömör's treason have sealed the course of Hektor's destiny. And though the Great Ones may opt to not interfere in the Warriors' realms, on this side of the gap, they are intently watching. Another violation will pretty much be cause for the irreversible dismantling of the group," Liv clarified.

"Would it be too brazen to ask where you're hiding the portal?" Geir asked.

"There's no redeeming outcome in you knowing; only danger to you and the Warriors. So yes, it's too much to ask. You already are in this predicament for information you hitherto were barely able to process – the lesser you know all the better; though we understand your exposure was inevitable from the outset. What we can avoid now, will save exponentially in resources later; that should be clear to you both," Spencer replied firmly.

"Of course," Flemmingson returned.

"At this conjuncture nothing's cast in stone; we don't even know for sure if a print was ever taken of your backyard. What we're certain of is that your property cannot divulge anything beyond what has already been harvested; the Hektor founder either got what he wanted or has realized he was too late. Anyway, he'll be at it in whatever guise, with unthinkable resources; he's engaged in the peremptory process of seeing the organization's unspoken bylaws actualized in the form of out-and-out control of the core mechanics of this group of universes, the realms – or of another – as it proves those are currently the only remaining options," Liv finished.

The art of concealing articles lay in the concise placement of the item to protect. It didn't matter what had to escape scrutiny, whether it was a portal into an impossible dimension of reality outside the recognized realm of existence or a particular object of importance to a lonely soul; the methodology was identical. "Too far out of the way" exposed a singularity easily identifiable by some, while "too obvious" only worked for the things that lent themselves to be lost in the background clutter. In the case of portals, the busier the environment the better; and since the heart of town was rife with Guild and Hektor traffic, it was only fitting to place it where its already scrambled signature could further be masked by the kaleidoscopic weave of inter-dimensional light fields, the compression and expansion of space quanta, and myriad electromagnetic pulses. As long as it wasn't in use, it could be anywhere; so the middle of the busiest town square was deemed the safest of all locations, right under the gazebo at the top of the Snug Alley circular fountain.

Joonas was unsure of the scope of the area to survey, but he figured the boundaries of the county had to delineate its outer limits. While research was working on the various prints taken by the Dogs, he had time to close in on the relocated portal. The deep wilderness would easily unveil an anomaly, but rather than excluding it in his hunt, he chose to have the vast swaths of forested mountains inspected, courtesy weather service helicopters and equipment tied to the Hektor network. That step out of the way, he ordered the denser zones of activity to be circumvallated in overlapping groups, by positioning Dogs and instruments at strategic points of surveillance. It was then a matter of waiting for the inevitable glitch. While his net was busy cross-referencing field fluctuations and ghost signatures, Joonas kept busy devising ways to reenter Slaughter and Flemmingson's plane of reality. The guise had to be subtle yet creative. It was clear the Guild was behind the feat of rescuing Hunter, thus the two humans were likely under its protection – the mask had to fit the occasion. The physical world offered very few alternatives; full focus, requiring complete adaptation to the elements, or stealth, foregoing the bulk in favor of shadows; neither of which would fool any Master on a mission to locate him.

Joonas' dislike of computers made a u-turn when he came to realize that Hunter's laptop was in the hands of the Guild, precisely where he needed it to be. A quick check with Strata headquarters' technical department confirmed the machine was active and connected to the network, meaning the Angels were using it to monitor the group's activities. It made no difference to the fallen Master – he was well aware the Guild had been following their actions from day one, computer or not; and since none of his plan to access the Warriors' realm had involved heavy computing until the prints were made, he had no concern about his own steps being followed. The last place Angels would look for him was inside that very machine; pending, of course, the ability of Hektor cyber technology to allow for invisible forays into the deep strata of the Guild.

To Joonas's dismay, Hektor was nowhere near Guild advancements in quantum computing – the program that had to be designed to allow for some of his consciousness to be installed into the laptop, was to remain strictly experimental; meaning that it could work or not. The other downside was that the tech department was incapable of confirming to what level the machine had been compromised. The filing system's guard dogs didn't detect tampering, but then again, the roaming program was late on updates, due to the lack of reliable architects. It didn't surprise the elder, who was starting to reconsider his recent enthusiasm. Nonetheless, he ordered the department to immediately look into it, promising an outpour of considerable resources within the hour.

It also turned out the prints from Slaughter's house lacked definition. Joonas had once again acted too late.

When Liv and Spencer returned from Ma-l's realm with Paula Hunter's laptop, they were advised by Le Lien central to link it to Marshall and Geir's machines. First-tier Qwave technicians needed to bring it to its cloud lab for deep scanning and the installation of a series of one-way kennels to attract and receive the roaming Hektor surveillance dogs. Indifferentiable clones, save for their ability to reverse-survey the group's actions, would then resume with normal activity. In essence, the computer would be rigged in anticipation of Joonas seeing an opportunity to infiltrate the Guild network. In the tech-rich environment of the notoriously untraceable Qwave Industries conglomerate, it was standard procedure; but from Joonas's standpoint, such process didn't belong to the equation – he was simply incapable of conceiving how far he was being out-maneuvered by Le Lien's agents and Qwave technicians.

A few days later, Liv and Spencer paid another surprise visit to the office, where, once again, Slaughter and Flemmingson were readying themselves for their customary breakfast at Café Noir. The two Angels had brought Hunter's computer with them and told the friends to go on with their morning ritual, while they would work on the three laptops in their absence. Marshall and Geir obliged, relieved from not having to baby-sit the machines. They promised to be back within the hour.

The Le Lien agents connected the two Qwave computers to the Hektor laptop via custom interfaces and firewall hardware designed to sanitize embedded spyware and monitor the presence of new sniffer dogs. Guild tech had advanced its quantum technology to the point of having dispensed with the hurdle of running its gear at sub-absolute-zero temperatures. Its processing power was in the range of a thousand times faster than that of Hektor's, which allowed it to perform anticipatory action and nip malware while still at its embryonic stage.

The Angels immediately saw that a program was being installed in Hunter's computer. The Qwave sensors automatically attached themselves to it in the form of an invisible shell separated by a thin zone of space-time foam that relayed data by shape-shifting through gravitational gates one Planck area in aperture, a tool of the hybrid technology of codes and quantum mechanics, fully undetectable by Hektor.

The program in question was a host environment similar to the one Liv and Spencer used as a temporary consciousness-specific habitat – a vehicle essentially in line with the physical brain. What they noticed was an ambitious attempt at allowing the chosen guest to perform autonomously within the system, in a way consistent with the spirit-in-the-flesh experience of inter-galactic species. It meant the consciousness was locked within a set purpose akin to a fractal of its larger existence. Liv and Spencer deemed the experimental program highly dangerous to the guest awareness, especially in the light of the fragile architecture of the host environment. What they were observing was the creation of a virtual ship with dawning structural vulnerabilities, a vessel so haphazardly put together that it betrayed the pressure under which its builders were operating. The two Le Lien tech agents reluctantly concluded that they had no choice but to come to the programmers' rescue, if they were to keep an eye on Joonas's movements.

Upon returning from Café Noir, Marshall and Geir received the news that one of the two computers had to remain in the care of the Le Lien until further notice. Since Geir only used his for mostly emails and browsing, it was agreed Slaughter's would be the one to stay with the friends. Spencer would stand as the sole cyber-liaison when the agents couldn't appear in person.

The Hektor engineers at Strata Research were relieved by how well the pieces were falling into place – luck was auspiciously at play. Like most residents of the complex, these women and men were also Guild fallouts under the constant, omnipresent abuse of the founders. To them, the quality of life improved as time was bought. Some knew that the string of positive results didn't add up, but they saw no need in challenging a process that provided temporary relief from scrutiny. They assured Joonas the project was moving along successfully and that they would deliver on schedule.

"The league will not forget to show its appreciation in the appropriate manner," the founder promised, in the style of double entendre common to his rank.

The program was completed within a week's time. Joonas came into the lab with a group of founders to cross-check the technicians for possible foul play. The head programmer was unceremoniously selected for the test run and led by Dogs to the *suspension chamber*, where his consciousness would "safely" be connected to the software, for the creation of a contracting symmetry designed to fit the confines of the host vehicle.

At its end, Le Lien was monitoring the procedure. It knew from the signature that the guest wasn't Joonas, rightfully suspecting it was a dry run to verify the functionality of the program. It was clear that without the Guild's intervention in strengthening the frame and correcting artifacts of corruption, both the entering consciousness and the host space would have been destroyed instantaneously. Liv and Spencer followed the progress of the subject's mating to the program's matrix and the Qwave shell, taking note of how well the two technologies complemented each other.

Though Strata lacked the staff and resources to match Qwave's potency, it had moved in a direction that dictated economy over complexity, thus making some areas of computing extremely efficient, even if they lacked in raw processing power. Team Le Lien concluded that the fact Hektor was willing to take on the risk of endangering its subjects, in tandem with its desperation to create results, was grounds for its respectable achievements in computer science. Nevertheless, without Guild assistance, the host program was destined to failure; Hektor was still a way from gaining momentum on the Angels' quantum advances in applied technology.

The installation of the consciousness went without incident, save for the fact that the identity that found itself in the host program felt troubled. Guild neuroscientists considered full immersion barbaric. The alienation experienced by the unwilling participant had all the disorientating characteristics of an unwelcome acid trip. The subject held psychologically and started to maneuver around the computer environment. He found the port to the Qwave machine, followed the path that had been specifically laid for him by Le Lien, passed through the firewall, and entered the Guild laptop. From the standpoint of his consciousness, he found his surroundings similar to a complex array of tunnels and rooms, all of them labeled. Each was put in place by Qwave, markers fully adaptable to the particulars of the visitor's signature, so that Le lien could monitor exactly what was being experienced through all of his senses. He was scared, but his curiosity was slowly taking charge of his situation. He wasn't sure where he was, on top of lacking focused memory of his origin, but he was fully aware of what appeared to be a machine cocooning him. From that moment on, he gradually began to cognitively recall some of the specifics of his core consciousness. He retroactively recognized the patchwork environment of the Hektor computer by the arrangement of its architecture, but found himself in alien territory the instant he crossed the threshold of the firewall. At that point Liv and Spencer set up a directional banner that read, *Guild students this way.* He paused then followed the sign.

"Another one of ours most likely in need of rescue," Liv noted.

She took a print of his signature and cataloged it into a new ledger labeled, *Conditioned Defectors*, where a name would eventually join the encryption.

With suggestive input from the Qwave program, the subject began to understand that he merely was traveling below the surface of an untold universe of vivid landmarks connected to a wealth of history; and how, in the hands of Hektor, access to that world would prove so detrimental to the Guild. Liv and Spencer made a point of acknowledging the nuance. For safety's sake, they erased the memory of the banner, inconspicuously redirecting the traveler back to the firewall, the port, and then the Hektor machine. The technician felt suddenly yanked back into the suspension room, where Joonas and the group of elders were awaiting the news in inquisitorial stances.

"Compose yourself, my friend, you're in one piece," the founder said. "Now, would you be so kind as to let us know whether the experiment was successful or not?"

The Hektor engineer cleared the fog in his mind before assuring Joonas of its success.

"It's so much more than I had anticipated, there's a complete universe in there," the tech said. "The entire Guild makeup, its total knowledge and achievements are open like cities straddling several dimensions of reality. Anyone who can travel freely within it, will have access to great powers."

"Did you have a sense of being followed?" one of the elders inquired.

"I came across some of our roaming dogs, but I am certain I was detected by neither them nor the Guild," the engineer answered, knowing that showing hesitation at that point, would have been counterproductive.

"Very well," Joonas said, "go over the fine details again, until you are absolutely convinced that all glitches have been eliminated. I will let your team know when I shall return for the real mission. For now, take a day off in the manner of your choice."

It was clear to Le Lien that the next run would be more than a test. The team needed to prepare the field that would lead the Dove and his organization on a wild goose chase – one they preferably would never return from.

Hektor's ultimate goal under Joonas's leadership was to fight wars on two fronts: one to deny the human race its granted right to evolve into a peaceful and prosperous species, the other to invade and control the reality of the Warriors. In simple terms, the plan was to plant the seed of ruin in the furrows of humanity, before moving the entire organization across the fragile chasm that separated the two Onenesses. The one-two punch would sum up to a resounding victory against the Guild, as well as a calculated affront in the direction of the Great Ones. Hektor would then run the Warriors' realms unchallenged, with each elder at the head of a pack of Dogs and a throng of Guild defectors, in charge of a domain under serfdom rule.

Joonas thought of it as poetic justice, one that saw ravage and decay as purification and redemption. Like most fanatics, he would never think of himself as such. As much as all Angels understood the power of beliefs, and thus, trained to become the observers of change, the Hektor elders had adopted the maxim that change was to be imposed by the will of a strong and focused system of immutable tenets, thereby deeming flexibility a moral weakness. Joonas believed the Guild of Masters had failed at taking the reigns of command by serving worlds instead of using its massive skills to dictate their courses. He never thought the human race, or any species with inherent defects, were worth saving. He saw it as a waste of resources and a display of affected righteousness to gain the favors of the Great Ones. In that light, he considered the Guild vulnerable to the will of those who chose to not serve but lead; its failure to recognize his unflappable morality was what justified the creation of Hektor and brought forth the inevitability of conflict.

And thus, blinded by the unwavering glare of self-aggrandizement, Joonas could not see how precariously positioned his powers were, and how steadily the aperture of opportunity was closing.

4 – THE GREAT HALL

Ma-1 rallied the group for the next phase of tunnel exploration. Pau was exempt from all realm-related meetings until the expiration of her probation status. Since the ex-student was under Saka and Olaf's supervision, each had to alternatively be excluded from the mission. Vac, who needed to connect with Ilia and Axel, couldn't fill the role of guardian; he belonged with the Goddess, tied to the double duty of technical assistant and Guild communicator. But there was discomfort in leaving the Hektor rescue with either Olaf, who only had the limited skills of a Master in training, or Saka, who barely navigated hers as the newly appointed Goddess of Light. Both were vulnerable to foreseeable foul play by Pau, although no-one truly doubted her reliability. Mostly, the news about Joonas's intentions had everyone on edge, hence the extra vigilance. It was eventually agreed that both would stay behind with the guest. The Triad suggested that Leòn be located and asked to assist in the rehabilitation of his ex-protégé. It was deemed a brilliant idea, though Vac pointed that the responsibility for Pau's defection wasn't the Angel's to bear. Schedule permitting, it would ultimately be his choice.

Little had been mentioned to that point about the health of the portal tying the realms to the old world. Olaf was concerned that a series of crossings would jeopardize its stability. The Triad assured him that the integrity of the link, unlike that of the gateways in place before the collapse and subsequent separation, was not defined by traffic flow, but rather, by the inherent and slow degradation of the ghost image used to stimulate first-stage reconstructive rendering.

"Were it the case, we wouldn't heed the Hektor threat!" the computer voice squelched.

Because of the ill-defined specifics, Ma-1 and Vac chose to explore the tunnels in increments, with the principal aim of documenting each of their steps. The Triad would stay behind with Pau and her mentors, since there was no logical reason to take the laptop into the darkness of the underworld. Olaf remarked that without light and Vac being a dog, the idea of map-making was ludicrous.

Ma-1 looked at him wildly.

"It then rests on my foolish, blind self to scribble a few arrows and crosses on a piece of parchment in the grand tradition of treasure hunting," she laughed. "I'm confident the Master and I can adjust to the absence of light and memorize a few directions!"

Pau felt a mixture of excitement and shame at the prospect of facing the one who had seen such promise in her development. She had failed Leòn on so many levels! How would she withstand the emotional impact of the reunion? She admitted to feeling quite scared and fragile.

"It needs to be addressed sooner than later," Ma-1 had said. "Embrace the opportunity to free yourself!"

Leòn was contacted. The Angel was in between assignments – free to honor the request. He would connect with Liv and Spencer, who were in charge of guarding the concealed portal in Eureka. His crossing was dependent on logistics that involved acting before Joonas could sit in the cockpit of his host program and on keeping Hektor's Dogs at bay. But first, there were the Dove's cross-sweeping sensors that needed attention. Le Lien had mapped their locations, counting three of them scanning the critical area. But disabling just the three would inevitably alert Hektor and position the portal within the crosshairs of detection. It was plain that the entire scanning system had to be deactivated; something that couldn't be done by hacking the league's réseau, since Joonas would be alerted that the Guild was ahead of his intentions. It had to look like an accident – or better – a standard operating error.

Le Lien located the techs in charge of monitoring each active area for unusual energy spikes and inter-dimensional winds. They operated from a rented house overlooking the Elk River watershed, south of town, having commandeered the Humboldt Hills cell towers to use as relay points. Liv and Spencer quickly understood they only had to break into the standard communication system in order to render the sensors ineffective for the second needed to elude Hektor scrutiny.

Leòn sat in the shade of the Snug Alley Gazebo. He had the looks of a dignified elder who enjoyed his privacy in the company of a good book. After the Paula Hunter assignment, he remained in Humboldt to take charge of a charter program shepherding homeless offspring towards a better life. He was kind and gentle; his voice, steady and assuring. All the children under his wing succeeded at breaking free from the social and generational traumas of ruined families. Two of his most promising subjects made it to the Guild of Masters' training program; one was Paula Hunter, the other, coincidentally, Gerald Brinsk, defector and lab engineer at Hektor's Strata Research Ltd., in South Africa. Leòn was particularly adept at recognizing Dogs by the soft red glow of their auras. They walked inconspicuously among groups of pedestrians, minding their own business like standard denizens. They seldom were at rest; perhaps they were in between assignments, but never for too long. He doubted, considering the seriousness of locating the last Guild portal into the Warriors' realms, that any of them were presently inactive. He counted five within the vicinity of the fountain, but they went their separate ways until others emerged from side streets and alleys. They were directionless, oblivious to his presence, or what the fountain Gazebo concealed. Liv and Spencer were to join as soon as all the elements for a safe crossing were in place. When they arrived, they sat facing him in such a way that his back was to the wall of the adjacent building, and their bodies masked him from the square. At that moment no Dogs were in sight

"It is time," Liv simply said.

Leòn was gone and the portal quickly sealed. The two remaining Angels sat around for another fifteen minutes before getting up and walking down the spiraling path outside the Gazebo.

The Hektor team in charge of the downtown scanners registered the hiccup, but quickly assigned it to a common tower outage. They went back to their routine, not bothering to record the event in the incident log.

Ma-1 and Vac found their way to the back of the cave, where Leòn was scheduled to arrive imminently. The two Angels had met briefly during their time working the Eureka area; mostly when Vac, "the dog," strayed from his subject. Both had acknowledged the depth of their work with the Guild, as well as how far back they went in Angel history. It remained unclear whether Leòn would be willing to stay in the realms or resume with his work of helping the disadvantaged children of the rejected social groups of Earth, but the Warriors could always use an extra, seasoned Master.

Leòn made it to the room like clockwork. After a brief introduction, he, Vac, and Ma-1 proceeded towards the opening above the valley, whence they walked the long series of switchbacks down the trail; the guest all the while, unveiling the details of his relationship with the troubled student.

Paula Hunter was raised by medical parents. She was five when her mother, a child psychologist, suffered a series of seizures that led to the diagnosis of a large brain tumor. The surgery and subsequent radiation treatment left her with profound memory issues, accompanied by recurring, unpredictable blackouts. Her father, a pediatric endocrinologist at UCSF, forewent his position to stay close to his wife, only to gradually be swept by deep depression, until one stormy night, he walked to the end of the south spit jetty, straight into the mercilessly forces of the towering swells that came crashing against the concrete dolosse. His body was never found.

Pau remained in her mother's care. The meager monthly disability income added to the good graces of a generous landlady, who only accepted what they could afford in rent, barely kept them from ending on the street. The child's struggle developed from the existential nature of her relationship with the mentally and emotionally unfit parent. While most human subjects existed within a collectively-accepted set of psychological markers, Pau was put to the test by her constant exposure to unbridled, lateral thinking and a logic that had no roots in social commonalities. Her disorientation was brutal. What she intuitively uncovered about the brain, memory, and the nature of consciousness, positioned her in a place of questioning what her contemporaries accepted as truths. Her world ran counter to the powers that shaped her standard education, forcing a mounting of rebellion against social reality, and the building of a self-loathing platform sourced from perceived inadequacies. Then one night, Pau desperately called for help. Leòn heard her plea. He first appeared to her in her dreams, an Angel whose voice could be heard from across the background noise of her tumultuous thinking. Before long, she started to trust his omnipresence as part of her regular existence – it was time for him to step in. He soon applied for the job of assisting her ailing mother – one of many consecutive assignments – in the form of a white-haired, gentlemanly figure he so deemed perfectly fit to carry both wisdom and compassion. His goal was to simultaneously operate in the unofficial capacities of father and grandfather for the remaining of Pau's mother's life. He was present much beyond the terms of his contract, and by the time of his retirement, he offered to continue working as a volunteer. By then, it was no longer a job – he was family. Pau turned twelve the day her mother died.

Shortly after the funeral, as they collected their belongings, she rose and looked her guardian in the eyes.

"You've been an angel to me, grandpa Leòn; without you, I would either be lost or my mother would now be joining me," she said through the tears.

"Then you may call me Angel Leòn, my dearest Pau, I believe you've earned the right to be told the other half of the story," the Master returned.

By her eighteenth birthday, Pau was admitted into the Guild's students program. After parting with the Angel on the promise they would be reunited as colleagues, a portal took her to Qwave headquarters, where the bulk of her training would take place.

"A poignant story, Mater Leòn" Ma-l said. "What Joonas has done to her and all the other fallen students, is beyond description. Nonetheless, it's wise to assume the damage may be persistent in spite of her choice to leave Hektor. I'm in a position to unveil potential subterfuge, but my actions wouldn't be without harm to the trust between us, so I'm delighted you chose to help."

"She was one of my most talented subjects, one I came to regard as my own grandchild. I couldn't just turn my back on her," Leòn said.

As they approached the house, Pau stood, facing them, her dark hair blowing in the breeze. She appeared stately, yet fragile. She wiped a tear before running towards Leòn, stopping abruptly as if to reconsider, but then moved forward and wrapped her arms around him, resting her head on his shoulder.

"I am so sorry, Angel Leòn," she sobbed.

They held each other for the eternity of a moment lost in time. In that union, Ma-1 perceived depths that were only matched by her love for Saka. She was touched at the core of her being. At that very instant, the Goddess knew Pau would never return to Hektor.

When not busy with Pau, Leòn spent his time with Vac, studying the possible outcomes of Guild influence on the realms. Though, it was understood the Masters had no holding powers in the emerging Oneness, the fundamental nature of Angelhood was deemed agreeable with the new environment. When Vac questioned Leòn on his plans, the answer was categorical – he would remain by Pau's side for as long as it would take to get her back on track. When reminded that the last portal was dependent on the decaying image of the old mother planet – the Angel simply smiled.

"Be it then, my good friend; it appears you and I are destined to team up for the long run in the realm of this most delightful and accommodating Goddess!"

As soon as Leòn settled into the critical role of deconditioning his subject, Ma-1 and Vac prepared for their first expedition into the Warriors' realities. Since it was understood the tunnel to the volcano presented a liability that had to be corrected, the first course of action was to leave a marker at its threshold so that it could be avoided. The second part of the plan involved locating Axel and Ilia, in hopes they had found a realm tailored to their skills, and were not – as it was feared – lost in a mazelike reality of caves and corridors, reenacting the clickety-clang of turnstiles in perpetuum. If all went well, the Warriors, and the Masters who had previously crossed, already saw to the most suitable of arrangements.

Over time, Ma-1 and Vac had explored the many variations on which the realms could have evolved. It was clear the backdoors only existed in the defunct mother reality, where no access, regardless of probability, was provided that didn't automatically divert the unfortunate intruder into the old one-way encampments. Technically, all growth had to have come from within, bearing the characteristics of the entity confined to the solitude of the stone. One of the questions was whether these Warriors had reunited with their own earthly creations as in the case of Saka – something that evidently didn't happened with the world of the raging volcano – or evolved in ways bereft of the physical. The most perplexing of them was how many had actually found their footing and not succumbed to the crippling isolation.

Vac counseled Ma-1 on disassociating from her emotions towards the unknown side of the realms. He saw how close the collective of the Warriors still was to her heart in spite of the millennia. The in-the-flesh Goddess was the closest to being the arrow wielder of her past; she didn't even change the patterns of the tattoos that covered her nudity – she kept her native name and held onto her memories.

"I was a foolish fighter, but my heart was as big as the clouds that made our creeks flow through the corn. I love the woman and what she represents; she's like a dear child to me," the Goddess confessed to the Angel.

They found the threshold to the volcano on their first try. Ma-1 marked the location in chalk on the black stone – she named it "Despair." The revolving door that was theorized to access any tunnel in the system was thought to be positioned at the halfway point between each birth cave and its corresponding exit, as it proved to be the case with the arrangements of those of Ma-1 and Despair. What would follow was a matter of defining the threshold for each reality. As they progressed through their work, they could then rely on these identifying markers to guarantee trouble-free returns. In theory, the nature of these thresholds was such that each realm could be accessed from any other via the same revolving gate, always found at the half point of each tunnel. Until they deciphered the system, the two deemed it safest to return to their original entry point before crossing into a new realm. The thought of a gestalt of consciousness behind the complex array of inter-connective paths, brought into question the ability for such an entity to anticipate the traveler's intention and automatically assign a code to that journey. As the group had already speculated before, such a being could find themselves tested by the incapability of said traveler to name their destination – why it was thought Axel and Ilia could potentially have met a tragic end. But all was still speculation on a precarious edge...

Ma-1 already knew that her wish to access the back of her cave from the opening in the cliff face was all that was needed for her to get there. The specificity to her request and the fact she was also the creator of her own realm guaranteed her passage into it. That was simple compared to the multiplicity of unknowns she and Vac were about to meet; each with a unique cryptic access, only to be opened with the cognitive knowledge of its existence, as well as a precise image of the desired point of arrival. So where did the errant traveler end? Vac proposed that they either do without a clear destination or

– as he favored – proceed with the aim of connecting with Axel and Ilia. Ma-l agreed.

They returned to the top of the slab where they took their lunch. Vac reflected on the fate of Angels in a universe that had never known a need for them; where their skills could be diminished by a lack of purpose. Like all pioneers, they were faced with incertitude. It was a pivotal moment in the evolution of the realms; and as long as Hektor was threatening the precarious balance of their newness, Angels would have to assist. Later, who knew? For now, they would have to go with the flow.

"Ready, Vac?"

"Let's go for it, Goddess!"

———————————

After reaching the back of Ma-l's cave, they paused to ascertain they were transcendentally locked in as one. Vac took the lead, homing on his desire to reach Axel and Ilia as his inner compass. The tunnel dipped and twisted, rose and zigzagged endlessly, at times a narrow passage, at others a space as wide as an underground station. Just as the Goddess gathered the path was incapable of making up its mind, they came to a hallway lined with rooms, leading to a balcony that overlooked a majestic, circular hall buzzing with activity. The space resembled a giant, glassless cathedral carved into the heart of the mountain, its enormous columns supporting an impossibly high ceiling. Light was provided by a multitude of suspended energy sources that spread their luminescence in a diffused, enrobing ambience free of shadows. These elegant fixtures moved around

141

autonomously, continuously adjusting the balance of their collective glow, as the gathering below ebbed and flowed, parted and regrouped, as if belonging to a hive consciousness.

"We're definitely no longer in my realm," Ma-l pointed, utterly dazzled by the sight.

"I believe this is where we'll find our friends," Vac returned. "I trust those are the Angels that crossed before the collapse of the mother reality."

The vast congregation was composed of a majority of humanoids interspersed with canines, the two common guises of Angels in the material sphere.

"Out of my realm and in the flesh, my powers are very limited; right now, I'm essentially feeling extremely vulnerable," Ma-l confessed.

"Remember, your core consciousness isn't, and it still protects you," Vac assured. "You're among Angels, which is possibly the safest environment you could find yourself in – I would know. I believe this place is the center provided by the entity controlling the system of tunnels – a shelter city of sort, until the time comes for each Master to choose the realm that best befits the scope of their skills and purpose. I think this clarifies our mission here – should we proceed?"

Ma-l agreed. They started the long descent down a steep stone stairwell, each pair of half-turn runs alternatively providing access to the floors' main terraces from one side, and exit from the other. Additionally, these groups of stairs were joined at their midsections by a full-space landing lined with an intricately sculptured railing on its exposed side, offering yet another platform between each floor to enjoy the spectacle of the imposing hall. They counted thirty-three stories, each with an opening similar to the one they had emerged from at the very top. Another three identical stairwells equidistantly rose from the main floor.

"We're looking at a complex organism; I can't wait to get to the bottom of its conception." Vac marveled.

As they reached the intricately patterned marble floor, they were immediately greeted by Angels who couldn't contain their pleasure to meet them.

"The news of a realm Goddess among us tells of the awakening of a long awaited change," one female Master by the name of Ingrid rejoiced.

"We seek Ilia and Axel from *Portal Engineers*, have they been seen in this assembly?" Vac enquired.

"Their desk is directly across the hall. You can't miss it, it's always the one with the longest line!" one excited Angel replied.

"What is this place?!" Ma-l asked, open-armed.

"You may call it Guild Headquarters away from the Guild, except we really don't know what its purpose is, since we have been unable to find a way out. The hundred and thirty-two tunnels connected to the stairwells lead back to this hall in ways we are unfamiliar with. *Portal Engineers* has been working on it relentlessly, but to no avail," the Master answered.

"Thank you, Angel, we will help further look into it," Vac simply said, refraining from making a promise he sensed he and Ma-l might not be able to fulfill.

They walked the half mile to the other end of the hall, where a long marble desk lined with Masters accepted requests and suggestions. The queue moved quickly. It took little time before they faced a punked-out young female with a yellow Mohawk and pierced eyebrows. She smiled at Ma-l with a mischievous look.

"A tattooed Goddess – this is my luck!" she laughed. "I assume this is going to be good."

Vac stood on his hind legs.

"How did your last subject fare, big sister?" he inquired.

The clerk stood up.

"Oh my God, Vac, it's you! You look great as a dog!" she exclaimed.

"Angel Naja, this is Ma-l, realm Goddess; Ma-l, Naja," Vac introduced. "Naja and I worked in San Francisco's Lower Haight and Castro neighborhoods when the first publicized outbreak of AIDS spread around the city in the early nineteen eighties, a future of your old timeline," he explained.

"The company of Angels was requested," Naja added. "Vac and I worked on many cases to assist in the transition of innumerable victims into the spiritual realm. It goes without saying, Ma-l, that your presence here represents an opportune point in time, am I wrong?"

"It is my greatest hope that we'll be able to help unlock the inner workings of this complex system of connections between the active Warriors' realms, and what I'm beginning to sense as being something way beyond them," Ma-l replied instigatingly.

"For now, Naja, we need to get in touch with two of our old friends, Axel and Ilia, who are believed to be among you," Vac cut.

"They are indeed," she returned with a laugh. "Take the stairwell behind me to seven, twelfth door on the left; that's their dwellings/office area. Nice to see you, Vac, and a pleasure to meet you, beautiful tattooed Goddess," she added with a wink.

Axel and Ilia greeted Ma-l and Vac with the

intensity worthy of a fortuitous reunion between long lost friends. After visiting with the Goddess, while Saka, Vac, and Olaf's were back on Earth, the two Angels had gone on their journey to seek other realms with the intention of offering their services. When they came back to the mother reality, set on accessing these worlds through backdoors akin to the one into Ma-l's domain, they found to their dismay that they only led to the buffets of the infamous encampments, in maddening loops.

The existence of these gateways was rumored to have been the work of a special team of Angels, Masters who yearned to not forget the Warriors, and who wished to eventually reconnect with them at an auspicious point of their evolution. Yet, those dozens of portals, thought to belong to these fighters, failed to reach their realms, as if requiring entry codes. Perhaps these pioneers accidentally stumbled across a small window that opened into an impossibly distant probability. If so, what in that vision fed the necessity to see these realms rise? Was it the implausibility of Saka's emergence from Ma-l's yearning for freedom away from the isolation of the stone? Were these Masters aware of the one gate into the Goddess's realm, or did they mathematically arrive at the infinitesimal point of a chance encounter of unrelated events? Perhaps they simply sowed to the winds to see what would take... The thing was, there was only one detectable entryway into the realms – the one that led to Ma-l's reality.

Axel and Ilia went back to Guild Headquarters to consult with archives for maps of ancient portal routes in the far corners of the known universe, but were unable to find any data on the Warriors' worlds. They returned the back way into Ma-l's domain, just as the mother reality was caving in. By the time they reached the end of the tunnel, the entry into the Goddess's realm had been shut off by the quakes that shook her land. They walked back in hopes of finding side passages, but instead ended up traveling endlessly, far beyond the length of the original corridor. It went on for days, until their physical selves felt robbed of their vitality. Finally, and on the verge of leaving their dying bodies behind, they arrived at the Great Hall, where they were received by Angels who nursed them back to health. As it turned out, Axel and Ilia were originally able to reach Ma-l's reality because of their previous connection with her. All the Angels who had crossed before the collapse, had easily found the hall and settled there. Their travels had been unimpeded; their purpose clearly defined by a desire to help the realms; hence, they were naturally directed to the right place. It was determined that the consciousness that operated the system of tunnels was confused by Axel and Ilia's early intentions of reaching Ma-l, Vac, and Olaf.

The Masters concluded that the Great Hall was a space that had been reserved for them, for it catered to all of their needs and carried the mark of the great craftsmembers of the Guild. The first Angels to make it there attempted to return in order to prepare volunteers, only to be invariably brought back to their point of entry in the rear of Ma-l's reality – the only portal known to the Masters to have led into the Warriors' realms – all other backdoors hence having been deemed the work of carefully placed and mysterious rumors.

"It's not for want of trying, but since we haven't been able to collect much information about this place, who do you think the early Masters behind it were?" Ilia asked Vac and the Great Goddess.

"As Axel well knows, I was in the team of engineers at the time of the great battles, though, I only was peripherally involved with what you may call, 'work at ground zero,' I knew a few of the Angels who went on to protect the Warriors; they were the antithesis of Hektor, Masters fully dedicated to the cause of humanity and the request of the Great Ones. They were fringe Angels in the sense that they went beyond the call of duty, but they never dishonored their contracts, or violated the fundamental tenets of the Guild. They volunteered to bring an unprecedented level of compassion for the Warriors into their work, as well as irreproachable standards towards completing what they had started. Though, I was aware of the extent of these Masters' dedication to the cause, and of their relentless determination to reach their goal; it goes without saying that what they achieved at the creative level, goes far beyond what anyone could have conceived – the bottom of it has yet to be probed. What most had thought to be an accident of the highest order may, in fact, be no accident at all," Vac explained.

"My life in the stone," Ma-1 interjected, "never afforded me an outside view into the reality of the rock element, the deep strata of rising mountains carved by time and the hands of Masters. My worldly perspective was toward my soul, into the unreachable depths of my being. Those were my caves, my Great Halls. We, Warriors, traveled the wave lanes to the fields of dreams; perhaps they were like the tunnels, and perhaps not. Maybe, what we see here is the growth of the seeds that were planted a long time ago. I have a hard time extrapolating on a parallel consciousness that evolved along the lines of my own, unless it is born of the reality of our collective dreams, before we went our ways. But the Angels were the ones who locked our souls in the rocks of the exploded mountain. They didn't have to do it – we would simply have flown to where other souls had gone before. The purpose of their actions is thus engraved in our destiny."

"We all have our theories – some more colorful than others. We have harnessed our resources and probed the depths of Guild knowledge to get to the bottom of this, and honestly, I don't think we have arrived anywhere closer to understanding where we are than the first day we came here. There just isn't any way out," Axel expressed somewhat frustratingly.

"Well, there might have been a reason for it until now. I'm quite positive I can find my way back to my realm from here. If you two are willing, I can take you there with us to teach you how to commute between my valley and this hall. Believe me, it's a much shorter distance than the length of your unfortunate journey," Ma-l countered.

"I agree with the Goddess," Vac said. "We need to start somewhere. If you could inform your team of the plan, I believe this might help mesh the gears into motion."

Axel seemed relieved.

"I'll let the engineers know of our actions."

"All will have a chance to visit my realm, but in small groups; I insist," Ma-l laughed.

Axel, who had let go of his Warrior guise after the meeting with the Great Ones, stood before the Goddess.

"Do I need to abide to your dress code?" he teased, not necessarily in the best of tastes.

"Do as you wish, Angel! As it turns out, we have a young Guild student who was recently rescued from

Hektor, who just might enjoy the sight – for now, we are concerned with staying focused," Ma-1 returned, somewhat coldly.

"Hektor, hey? I guess we're due for some updating. I'll just go out as I am; kakis are the latest in realm fashion," Axel humored, failing to impress.

Ilia, who for reasons similar to Vac's had retained his grey wolf guise, offered to take the visitors on a tour of the Great Hall, but Ma-1 made it plain she wanted to return to her realm as to not keep her extended family at home waiting.

"I will teach the two of you how to go back and forth between our worlds; then Vac and I will return to our valley. But first, I need clarification. We came through the top opening across the hall. I presume that based on your experience, all hundred and thirty two gateways, including the one that tunnels off past your dwellings and stores, systematically bring you back into this place, am I correct?"

"You are," Ilia returned.

"Just assume," Ma-1 added, "that each of them leads to a realm, but since you don't know who the Gods and Goddesses behind them are, you find yourself in no position to establish an intellectual, spiritual, or plain emotional connection with them – you automatically get returned to the hall. Do you see my point?"

"It makes sense since we came in through the top of the diagonally opposite stairwell, just as you did, after our catastrophic failure to connect with your world," Axel forwarded.

"So, here we have it; it's thirty-third up, stairwell three for destination Ma-1!" she exclaimed. "You Angels can reach the realms from these headquarters; while we,

Warriors, can access them via some form of revolving door – elemental! OK, it's not proven science, but it's a start!" she closed exuberantly.

Following Axel and Ilia's update to the team at *Portal Engineers*, the group crossed the Great Hall and climbed the stairs to the thirty-third terrace. The three Masters followed the Goddess into the darkness of the tunnel, walking the dips and the turns through the narrow and the wide, until they finally made it to the opening above Ma-l's valley.

"Astounding!" Axel rejoiced.

"You understand, it's not my original entryway, but one that was borrowed from a lost realm. Now that you have a mental picture of both this and your hall, you may retrace your steps, and then come back once more so that we know you have succeeded," Ma-l suggested.

They went and returned. At last, the two Masters understood the fundamentals, as well as the organic nature of the system. It was a matter of time before the Goddess would connect with the other realms and update the assembly, hoping Warriors and Masters would be able to meet and operate from the Great Hall.

The friends parted.

Vac and Ma-l walked down the series of switchbacks towards the orchards and the house. A great weight had lifted. The sun on the horizon was swollen with the promise of rebirth.

The next day, Ma-l, Saka, Vac, and Olaf took off early for the tunnels. The Goddess's plan was to try to access the Great Hall from the lost realm of Despair. Vac wanted to introduce his ex-subject to the congregation of Angels, where it was likely his further education would take him on a regular commute. Since Leòn was in charge of Pau's training and rehabilitation, Saka wished to stay close to Olaf, as the bond between them had strengthen since the days of portal-hopping, prior to their return to their old world. She carried Amaterasu's white stone in a pouch tied to a leather strap around her neck that she likened to the heart of the light that cast its glow on the cave walls, to reveal the intricacies of the veins in the stone, as it refracted through the crystalline translucence of the prismatic gems that intermittently protruded from the strata, sending colorful rays in all directions. After they crossed the marked threshold, they proceeded towards the Great Hall on Ma-l's instructions. It was confirmed upon re-crossing, that they had entered a new corridor, as no markings were found. They continued along the new tunnel as it descended into the heart of the mountain. The smooth floor was soon replaced by stairs that down-spiraled into greater depths. When they finally arrived at the expected landing, it did not open onto the Great Hall, but rather, onto a vast chamber four floors high, supported by hundreds of marble columns. Numerous Angels worked at stations along its perimeter; behind them, a variety of classrooms, shops, storage rooms, offices, and laboratories spread in a circle around the space. They realized they had arrived at an underground facility below the main hall.

"Next time, remind me to get a layout of the place first, before we go on assuming we have counted all possibilities of entry into the Warriors' realms," Saka said with distinct amusement.

"I am sure one of Vac and Olaf's colleagues, here, will oblige," Ma-1 said, winking at her playful spiritual offspring.

They walked towards a young female clerk, whose striking looks veered sharply from Earth's norm. She greeted the group with gentleness and singing vocal tones.

"We all have been briefed about your last visit; it is an honor to meet. How may I help you?"

"Do all these openings loop back into here, or do they access the Great Hall as well?" Ma-1 asked.

"They only return to this area; entry to the main floor is via the stairwell by which you came; it's above the fourth landing," she returned.

"Are there any other levels?" Olaf inquired.

"There's a substation below, ran by a branch of Le Lien and a team of Qwave engineers," she answered.

"Thank you for your kindness, Angel, what is your name?" Vac asked

"Where I'm from, names are like the weather, they only last the length of a mood. You may call me Shade."

"An honor to meet a student in her native garb," Vac returned. "And if my intuitions are correct, one nearing completion of the Masters' program – congratulations."

The young Angel thanked Vac on a private telepathic channel, surprising the Master. He sensed something unique and powerful about her.

The group had planned on spending ample time visiting the main floor, intent on making introductions with the various teams, while getting a feel for the complex metrics behind a space engineered in anticipation of linking a congregation from the Guild with the Warriors of the realms. Ma-l felt compelled to ask herself the question of how the Hall came into existence, if not for the collective desire of the Warriors to seek the protection and council of the Guild. Was the shared consciousness a unique gestalt that had emerged with the single purpose of serving the realms? It was highly plausible, based on the nature of the near-forgotten dream meetings. She thought that perhaps the time had come to close the second chapter on Warrior evolution.

The first Angels to arrive had found the hall empty and dark, save for the floating luminescence that had guided their ways. With each Master, a new light came to life above the giant space, bit by bit illuminating the stairwells, the vaulted ceilings, and the main floor in between the columns, until no shade was left. All had crossed, unbeknownst to Ma-l at the time, through the backdoor to her reality. It became a matter of speculation as to why none of them were directed to her world instead of the Great Hall. Additionally, no portal was ever found with access into other realms, and most likely, none existed. Ma-l thought of it as an ingenious way of limiting the visit of unwanted entities like Hektor, but she wasn't fully convinced hers was the only portal into the Warriors' realities. Some of the elder Angels in the hall had to have the inside story, but who, beside the engineers, could have masterminded the entire design of the realms and put the Warriors in charge of stewarding them? Yet, Axel and Ilia had no idea. The possibility of involvement by a Great One came to mind, but no-one could confirm it. This was a very different Oneness with unique laws, where the most needed of skills was to adapt and allow other talents to take on the tones of their environment. Roughly, nine hundred Masters and students had made the crossing. They were divided into various teams, which beyond Le Lien, *Portals*, and Qwave, also included Healers, Guardians, and the *Department of Maintenance of Creations* among others. All shared duties equally. Supplies were inconspicuously provided by the arcane mechanics operating in the background. For all intents and purposes, the Great Hall was a small city, albeit one without a governing body, or the need for policing. *Realm Headquarters* pulsed like a well-oiled machine, preparing for the next phase of the journey.

There were two major questions on the collective mindset of the group. One, how to access the Warriors' worlds, and two, where among the Angels of the Great Hall, were those who set-up the realm system in motion? Though Le Lien was in charge of collecting general data on Angel activity, assignment, and location, it was unlikely its new branch, disconnected from the whole, was able to do much. The Triad, on the other hand, had a direct line to the main team.

Vac and Olaf joined with the surveillance team at Le Lien headquarters on the basement floor shared with the Qwave group, while Ma-1 and Saka visited with other segments of the assembly. The agents were incapable of providing data on the whereabouts of the founding Angels; on the other hand, they were extremely interested in meeting with their old The Triad colleagues. Since the collapse of the mother reality, the Great Hall had been fully cut off from the Guild, effectively ending the influx of volunteers and fresh news. Olaf promised to bring the laptop on his next visit.

Ma-1, Saka, Vac, and Olaf regrouped by Shade's station. They took their lunch, courtesy one of the service buffets of the main hall. It was without much surprise that the Goddesses observed the food dispensers were in all respect identical to those of the old encampments. She guessed that there had been fundamental, as well as mutually beneficial connections between the realms and the defunct reality, in more ways than imagined. The four moved on to assess the prospects of accessing the pocket worlds; Ma-1 suggested entering any tunnel with the intention of reaching the Warrior at the other end. She had known most of them before and after the battles; thus, she was confident the strength of her conviction coupled to her millennia of evolution within the stone, would activate the portals. She also sensed there was a relation between Despair and their arrival in the lower hall, deeming it plausible that the other fifteen openings of the combined four stairwells also led to lost realms.

They informed Shade of their plan to follow the corridor next to the one they had come out of earlier. Should they not return by day's end, her job was to contact Axel and Ilia.

The tunnel went upwards for quite some time, before it leveled to terminate in a low cave lit by a single shimmering, floating source. A strained voice abruptly resonated from all the angles of the space.

"I recognize the one among you, but the others are the beetles that feast on my bones. Begone evil doers!"

"What is your name Warrior?" Ma-1 asked gently.

"Your arrows broke like the wings of fallen eagles, yet you dare ask for my name?! Damned be the wickedness that brought your wretched soul to this place, to drink from the wells of my past, and leave my tortured heart to bleed into the gully that feeds the bane in the bowels of the mountain!" the screeching went.

155

"I am Ma-l, you once knew me, brother in arms," the Goddess forwarded.

"I know who you are; you died in the blaze caused by the Evil Ones. I saw your body burn like the summer straw struck by the sky fires. Why do you seek to trouble my dreams? Begone, wandering ghost, and never return!"

They swung around as one and left without another word. The Warrior couldn't acknowledge they weren't part of his nightmare – he had damned himself for eternity – there was nothing they could do about it.

The encounter had been sobering. They kept to themselves until they reentered the lower hall, where they gathered around one of the white marble tables spaced equidistantly along the precise geometry of the immense footprint of the Great Hall above.

Shade smiled at them from the distance.

"I still don't know who he was," Ma-l said. "He reminded me of a Warrior we called Badger, because of his combative spirit. He was never seen at the dream meetings, though his absence didn't surprise me. He was a fighter for the sake of fighting – much less so for the honor of protecting our people. But I can't be sure."

"One could say your intuitions have put a name to that developmentally arrested realm; *Badger* it is," Vac stated.

It was nearly confirmed that the low-level tunnels were paths to the failed or incomplete realms – the Warriors behind them, fading souls, dispirited by the alienation of centuries of confinement, laden by a lack of creative release. Their dreams did not reach far enough to harness the energy beyond the illusion of ensnarement; slowly, the candle of their hopes burned, before their eyes could open onto the resplendence of their first sunrise.

Pau and Leòn stood at the entrance of the upper orchard when the group finally made it back to the dwelling grounds. They looked relaxed; the student seemed at peace with herself. Ma-l was ready to give her a clean bill of health. Vac too agreed that she had returned to her Guild-bound former self. Leòn confirmed their views. To Pau's delight, a ceremony of reinstatement to Master training was proposed. They all walked joyfully the rest of the way to the house where dinner was awaiting them.

5 – LE LIEN'S DECEIT

Joonas readied himself for his first exploratory outing into the cyber reality of the Guild. He had already positioned an "aspect self" in the cockpit of the program, through which he was adjusting his focus. Le Lien received a confirmation of his identity – the entire team was on high alert. They needed him to feel assured he was traveling incognito – keeping him on a long enough leash, as to permit him to break a few barriers without sounding any alarms. The Hektor dogs would also have to stay out of the way; too much sniffing too close could potentially raise suspicion that the program was not stealthy enough. He had to be given access to what he was after; ultimately coaxed into believing he was getting nearer the Warriors' realms when in fact, he and the rest of Hektor were being redirected away from them.

Strata engineer, Gerald Brinsk, was monitoring Joonas' progress. The elder had to stay in the suspension room until the probe consciousness was fully embedded in the program. The ex-Guild student had had plenty of time to recollect his experience during his few days of rest, resulting in some confusion about the sign that had appeared in a flash. He remembered following it, and yet, he wasn't sure it was ever there. Had he wished for its presence as part of a deeper desire to defect from Hektor, the same way he had once yearned to leave the Guild? He made no mention of it to the other technicians; some of whom might have felt compelled to alert Joonas and jeopardize the momentary sense of peace that arose from being treated, ever so rarely, with a modicum of respect.

Was the Guild aware of the program? Brinsk felt uneasy about it. The design went better than anticipated – in fact, it went too well. While inside, he had recognized a level of sophistication that exceeded what he and his team had put in. At the time, he was scared and confused, but it all began to coalesce while on his break – the program wasn't working alone. Was the marker installed for the single purpose of identifying him from his response? If so, then the observers knew he was a defector. He suddenly felt caught between the two worlds of Hektor and the Guild, his inner compass unable to settle. He already had misled the Dove by buying time on the empty promise of delivery, but to what purpose? He was locked inside Strata, which in turn was sealed within Hektor; his chances of ever walking away from it were non-existent. But yes, the sign was there, if ever so briefly – his Guild training didn't lie. He felt drawn to it, as if an inner voice had shouted for him to run.

Joonas proceeded. He maneuvered through the firewall, unnoticed by his own dogs, and then entered the Guild network via Geir Flemmingson's laptop, presently under Le Lien control. Liv was inside her own program pod when the Hektor elder passed her by; she stealthily tacked herself on his tail, keeping Spencer and the rest of the team informed of his movements. The realism of traveling within the network was such that consciousness translated the experience with all the vibrancy of existing within a fully focused reality. Long boulevards with their rows of skyscrapers intersected with other major arteries at giant roundabouts and squares. These thoroughfares had names ranging from *Storage Avenue*, to the humorous *Memory Lane*, but Joonas had no capacity for humor, even when it arose from subjective interpretation.

He had emerged from the underground roadway that had opened beyond the firewall, and was now piloting his vehicle along the treed median of a major throughway. Beside a few other similar pod-like cars that traveled in both directions, the streets were empty – same for the sidewalks, which aside the occasional individual stepping out of their parked transport to enter one of the buildings, were devoid of pedestrians.

Gerald Brinsk had briefed Joonas on the capability of his vehicle to guide him, within the network, on input from his wishes; thus, he believed he was on his way to portal records. But the Hektor founder was far from aware he wasn't inside the Guild's infrastructure, instead, he traveled within a simulation created by the Qwave/Le Lien team assembled for the occasion. In all respects, the decor was faithful to the real thing, at the exception of the information it contained. His pod automatically parked along a massive building on *Access Boulevard*, its name mounted in imposing brass letters on a wedge-shaped, white marble wall at the center of its cobblestone plaza; it read, *Department of Portal Works*.

Joonas walked the distance to the glazed lower façade then entered through a revolving door. A casually dressed woman passed him on her way out, seemingly impervious to his presence. Liv followed, protected by a shield of invisibility that prevented detection of multi-layered energy-based effusions – a necessary concealment when dealing with a skilled Master. The Hektor elder reveled in his ease of mobility. He made the mental note to pass a compliment onto the lab technicians in charge of having created the program – a rare quality in the Dove.

Records, as in most Guild administrative buildings, were kept in the reinforced vaults of the basement floor. But rather than go directly to it, Joonas opted for the rooftop, for a view of the endless expanse of Guild accomplishment. He wanted to relish the pleasure of his intrusion with a vantage perspective of what he strived to weaken. He was rewarded with a sight that left him, and all that was Hektor, with a feeling of awed diminishment that he instantly turned to disdain for everything the Angels had edified; ironically unaware that he was experiencing an adjusted view of his own inadequacies in the form of self-aggrandizement.

The detail wasn't lost on Liv and the rest of Le Lien, since he was essentially traveling within the auratic shell of the program, whether in or out of the cockpit of his pod; thus, both his thoughts and emotions were being monitored with daunting accuracy.

Joonas took the express elevator, down the fifty-four floors to records, and entered a vast hall that could have been mistaken for the main library of any major city. He ignored the clerks sitting behind desks and computers along the way to where interminable rows of double-sided shelves spread their wealth of scripted and graphical information. A few individuals, likely workers, were dispersed amid the aisles, all seemingly busy sorting and arranging files. Since his intuitive skills were at no time alarmed by their presence, he allowed himself to dedicate the bulk of his energy to the task at hand: finding anything pertaining to the portals of the Warriors' realms.

Gerald Brinsk's monitors revealed that the embedding process had been successful. The elder was disconnected from the transfer equipment under the watch of a group of senior elite. The consciousness fractal that now lived in the matrix, performing as a metaphorical third eye, could be accessed at will. The program would allow the Dove's embedded self to function independently from its core consciousness as it sought to fulfill its purpose, which was to complete its assignment. In all respects, he was Joonas away from Joonas, separate, yet ever-connected – a spy-self within the very mind of the Guild.

"Give yourself a few days to adjust, Sir," Brinsk advised. "Before long, your 'probe self' will become second nature."

"Very good, I shall call him Joonas's Eye then. You served me and Hektor well, engineer, therefore I have added extra privileges to your list, effective immediately. Thank you," the elder said, as he left the premises.

Brinsk swiftly checked his status app and saw that his social ranking had been moved to the middle caste of members – a rare honor only bestowed upon those, who, in spite of their human origins, had shown exceptional contribution to Hektor. But as long as he would remain locked inside Strata, it was nothing more than an empty title. He strived to enjoy life outside the restricted area of his forced employment – the founder would have to show a lot more love before he was willing to return some of his own.

Meanwhile, Joonas's Eye was walking the aisles of the hall of records in search of the section dedicated to the realms. Le Lien had created one where none existed, a few levels down, inside a fake filing system of classified information. For that, the Eye had to first decipher the list of *Little Known Portals*, down to *No Longer Used Portals*, and finally, *Experimental Portals*, where the first mention of the Warriors' worlds could be found. With playful disregard to the Guild's single evidence of entry into the realms, the Qwave techs and the surveillance team had built a complex folder tallying obscure portals in innumerable probabilities. Although the defunct mother reality was referred to as one of the lost worlds, the access to Ma-l's sphere was of course omitted. The Le Lien files elaborated on secondary portals and lanes that led to those primary gates, such as the one in Slaughter's courtyard, or the various relay points found at Trinidad Head, Strawberry Rock, and Medicine Rock. Save for the mother reality, it specified that all main portals were scattered over the Siskiyou Mountains, under watch by the Great Ones. But Joonas was already aware of the fact, which was cause for Hektor to have arrived late in the game. The mother reality was gone, but the portals listed in all the other probabilities were classified as still active, even if the realms had now fully separated from the Oneness; in which case Slaughter's portal was only one of the innumerable ways to get to a primary connector, and thus inconsequential. The Eye decided he didn't need a stopover ride into the Warriors' worlds – he would instead concentrate on finding the real deal in the many realized versions of the Siskiyous, irrespective of earlier searches done by some of the elders.

Joonas' aim was to decipher the fundamental makeup of these portals. He couldn't use them, since they operated on specific signatures that Hektor members didn't possess, but new ones could be modeled after them. The group's entire gate network was born of the blueprint of the Guild's own, and aside from its cruder platform, it performed similarly. The elder was confident his organization had the technological savvy to duplicate the means to access the realms – if the Angels had a way into those worlds, so would he and his followers.

The main challenge was to not alert the Great Ones, who were overseeing the gateways. Le Lien found humor in the Eye's reaction to the discovery of the files, and in his thought process. In fact, those portals had only led to the terminal encampments scattered over the mother planet as a means to protect intruders from entering the Great Ones' domains, but with that world gone, they simply refused to open.

Physical laws prohibited the occurrence of a sudden state of non-existence, which wasn't quite the same as a void. Units of consciousness emerged as energy clusters into a combination of presents that formed a spacious environment. In essence, something that was couldn't possibly no longer be; it simply was or wasn't. Yet in a variety of scenarios, that "something" could easily have not manifested. In the case of the mother reality though, its collapse created a vortex that had all the appearances of a state of non-being. In reality, that world had only stopped belonging to a specific group of presents. As the result of trying to use these portals, the laws of electromagnetic repulsion would unequivocally deny access – a process which, unlike deletion, left the impression of acute activity by presenting a working façade Hektor couldn't question, while attributing dysfunctionality to signature error. It was Le Lien's intention to force the group into spending as much time and resources as possible on a project that was guaranteed to fail, while never surrendering why it did.

The Eye's next move was to obtain the schematics for the coveted portals. While records held the specifics of mapping the network, its science was in the vaults of *Portal Technologies*, in the engineering building located on an island accessed from the city by a series of slick bridges arching over a wide leg of the estuary that flanked its shores. Joonas' Eye left the *Department of Portal Works* and entered his ride – Liv stayed close behind. While the shell of the program kept a tight watch on his movements and reactions, the Angel kept on surveying the surroundings for artifacts, or other details of corruptions in the simulation program that could potentially alert the Hektor founder. There was also the possibility of an abrupt switch in pattern on the part of the Eye that needed synching without a single hiccup. Liv was best positioned to anticipate such a move.

The Joonas "aspect consciousness" informed his pod's console of his wish to reach his next destination. The vehicle took him leisurely across town, and then over a bridge to the aptly named *Isle of Gates*. The *Guild Crossways Engineering* building wrapped the semi-circle plaza meeting the end of the span, a space that graceful highlighted technology-based art and nature in an odd but harmonious marriage of two distinctly contrasting levels of creation. The Eye paid no heed to it as he walked the short distanced from his parked pod to the entrance of the three-storied, half-mile wide glass and titanium structure. *Portal Technologies* was located below the surface of the building's squat profile, on one of the median floors of the deep underground facility. Schematics and codes were locked behind security doors, but only at night. During daytime, the approval of the scanners was all that was required for entry. The Eye passed through them, undetected, as he had come to expect from the Strata head technician's skills and assurance.

A big part of Le Lien's plan was to uncover the Eye as soon as he had obtained what he was assigned to find, right after having relayed the information to his core consciousness. For that, they needed to make sure the greater Joonas was monitoring his probe and collecting data. The shell program had been designed to record and decode traffic between the two end points. Liv informed the team that the target was in the process of finalizing his mission – she was ready to sound the alarm across the system simulation as soon as instructed. The Eye scanned the mock blueprints of the realm portals, including the complex coding of the bio/auratic algorithms for signature detection, while the Guild's surveillance team screened the two-way flow of information, making sure it matched the contents of the files. It did.

As soon as Joonas received the complete data, Liv was given the OK to act. As the Eye walked out of *Portal Technologies*, the metal security gates slammed shut behind him, drawing the attention of the personnel that now looked fixedly in his direction. Liv ordered him to stop, but he instead ran to the elevators and managed to slip through the glass doors of the ground floor. Alarms were heard all over the building and on the Plaza. Once in his pod, he ordered it back to the Hektor sector, across the firewall. Liv stayed with him, keeping up with the steady flow of data between her and her team. It was meant to look like a standard procedure following an unlawful intrusion, so that, hopefully, Joonas would not discover he had been set-up. The chase was on with security pods on the Eye's back. He raced across the bridge, onto the main city artery, flying in a blur along the long rows of trees, circling gigantic roundabouts to sharply turn on skyscraper-lined avenues... The second he reentered the tunnel on his way to the firewall, Liv gave the go-ahead. An executive was immediately unleashed to destroy the Strata program and its Qwave shell. All went white around the Eye, as he, for the first time, experienced panic. In the fraction of a millisecond, he was deleted and the Hektor receiving hub was destroyed.

Gerald Brinsk's world collapsed as he witnessed his work, along with Joonas's offspring, shattered by the fire power of the Guild. The Hektor elder momentarily succumbed to faintness before quickly collecting his thoughts around his fragmented consciousness. He had gotten what he wanted, but his fury towards the Strata engineer was incommensurable; all recent privileges were immediately revoked; the tech's standing had now returned to bottom status. Gerald Brinsk had just walked through the gates of Hell.

Liv informed Le Lien that the network simulation overlay had been retired, and that no traces of the Eye's intrusion were detectable anywhere past the firewall. She then reassumed her post within the Qwave laptop.

———————

Slaughter and Flemmingson were preparing dinner at the Fieldbrook house when Liv and Spencer arrived unannounced.

"Greetings – and sorry for the impromptu visit," the female agent said, somewhat teasing.

After complimenting the cooks on the delightful aromas emanating from the kitchen, she continued.

"We're not expecting Joonas to actively search your area, since he appears to be busy with what we gave him; but until we eliminate the threat of Hektor to the Guild, your world, as well as the realms, it's best to assume he'll retaliate against you for the affront of losing the portal in your courtyard. From what we can forecast, he will be combing the Siskiyous in many alternative realities, for alleged active accesses into the Warriors' worlds. Of course, he was set-up for it, so he's doomed to fail, but we cannot underestimate what he is capable of, or what chance he may stumble upon. We have no native knowledge of these portals ourselves, since they were likely put in place by Angels that operated outside the Guild. Had there been records, they would have been found. The way we see it, his diminishing prospects for success will proportionally augment his thirst for retribution."

Spencer stepped in.

"Should you receive any formal mail, or calls requiring you to comply with obscure, official demands, or otherwise legitimate enquiries, you must notify us immediately so that we can counteract. At any rate, you mustn't take the bait. As you have previously been briefed, all subterfuge is fair game to Hektor – your system is rife with pawns teaming with their Dogs. We've set personal portals here as well as in your office – it's preferable that we're not seen together in public. So far, beyond inculpating the Guild, Hektor has been incapable of putting faces on those who orchestrated the Paula Hunter rescue; it's obvious we'd like to keep it that way."

"We understand," Slaughter said. "Are you guys staying for dinner, there's plenty for the four of us?"

"As a matter of fact, we'd like to keep you updated on a few other items; so, if you don't mind, dinner would be fabulous," Liv accepted.

The two operatives reported on Paula Hunter's rehabilitation progress under the supervision of her old Master, Leòn. The Triad had also forwarded the news of the group's expeditions into the tunnels, and the discovery of the Great Hall, alongside Ma-l's plans to locate the Warriors, under the vigilant eye of a gestalt of consciousness controlling portals and lanes.

The additional mention was made of rescuing another student buried in Hektor's Strata Research complex; although no plan had been laid yet.

"You may wish to help," Liv teased the hosts.

"In all seriousness, even though I would prefer not to bring Joonas back into the conversation," Spencer cut in, "his search for portals in the Siskiyous will soon prove to be fruitless, since all of them, at the exception of those in the mother reality, were mere byways to protect the gates of the Ones. Now, there is a little-explored yet perplexing possibility, which somewhat presents an oddity at our end: the plausibility of more realms beyond those of the Modoc Warriors. You may already know that the insurrection against the 'Evil Spirits' was global, so what stops us from stipulating that others were granted the same privileges as Ma-l's kin? In other words, other pocket realities may very well exist that may or may not be part of the new Oneness. From what's already established, there's a distinct group of realms acting as a complete gestalt, to which your friends Olaf and Saka's new world belongs – reachable via the one access presently under our control. But if the Warriors' realities were to form a larger cluster, counting these hypothetical groups, the possibility of a portal left open may be more than just theoretical. As long as the ghost image of the mother reality holds, nothing prevents Hektor from modeling its own gate after any left-behind throughway, thus allowing their hordes to infiltrate a group of realms – or them all. Joonas doesn't know that, so we hope he will stay busy with what is presently keeping him at bay. It's a dilemma – as much as we want him away

169

from here, we have to keep him from wandering too far off. Do you follow?"

Slaughter and Flemmingson nodded.

"Under normal circumstances," Liv added, "we wouldn't be sharing this information with you, but since, analogically speaking, you're caught in the crossfire, your safety depends on your awareness of the ebb and flow of danger. Again, Hektor isn't interested in systematically harming you physically, but incremental psychological ruin is far more damaging than torture followed by death. Should Joonas be so lucky as to not knock at the Great Ones doors, when he realizes he has been duped, he'll likely return to his search for our concealed portal. It may be beyond your understanding, but while he tried to infiltrate the Guild network, we were able to isolate a minute portion of his consciousness, which we duplicated. It allows us to monitor changes in his thought as well as his mood patterns; it's not much, but at least it gives us the means to anticipate his moves."

"Not to change subjects, but since Geir must return to Reykjavík, I've been thinking of joining him for a short stay to clear my thoughts. Of course, someone will stay here in my absence." Slaughter announced.

Spencer looked at him pensively.

"The timing seems auspicious for a visit, but if Joonas wants you, nothing will stop him from finding you there, you understand?" the Angel said.

"Of course, this will defeat the purpose of keeping him here, should he be seeking you; but we're dealing with multifold unknowns in regard to Hektor, with too many foreseeable scenarios for us to home on a specific one. So, in the end, your trip won't necessarily be a game changer. When do you plan on leaving?" Liv asked.

170

"A week from today – my flight's booked – but I can cancel if I must absolutely stay."

"No, please enjoy some time off; you very much deserve it. Remember to hug your laptop at all times," Spencer said with pointed humor.

"Incidentally, yours will be returned to you before you leave, Geir – I will remain a connection for as long as necessary," Liv added

"I hope you stick around for a lot longer than that, beautiful one," Flemmingson teased.

"By the way, Marshall; no need to look for a house-sitter!" Liv offered.

It took Joonas a few days to recover from the jolt of losing the Eye. The experience was akin to having had his consciousness scattered over every corner of the universe, with all connections stretched to their limits.

But he had work to do in innumerable probabilities – time was of the essence. He would work in tandem with a close group of elders, each covering a list of assignments across the vast spectrum of possibilities. Reports were to be collected by Strata Research to be inputted to the programs in charge of building Hektor's own array of portals into the realms of the Warriors, where the entire organization with its technology and social structure would relocate. Hektor science, like its Guild counterpart, was adaptable to the evolutionary environment of its host reality, in that it could tap from native scientific resources, as much as it was capable of creating its own platform where none existed.

Technically, the realms had a very limited number of foreseeable developments, since few choices had ever stood before them. In one variation, Olaf and Vac had not entered Ma-l's world, leading to Saka never reuniting with the Goddess. But what was the fate of a forgotten world that forever teetered on the outer edge of perceivable reality? Would the realms have collapsed with their crumbling mother universe, or would they have separated into their own Oneness, perhaps stifled in their evolution, to remain suspended in the quantum foam of their unrealized potential ad infinitum? The probabilities showing their backs to the Warriors' domains were dependent on present as well as future choices made along recognized timelines, but the concept of time was only loosely borrowed from the physical, insofar as the realms seemed reluctant to unveil the genealogical map of their makers and descendents. One might have seen these worlds as still gestating – in spite of the impossibly vivid realism of Ma-l's lush landscapes, or the dizzying intricacies of the Great Hall and its system of tunnels – to the extent that to the neutral observer, the whole makeup could have merely been the elaborate dreamwork of the She-Warrior, as she strived to distance herself from the alienation of her stone enclave. The vacuous nature of that possibility ruled itself out, on the premise that little of history had ever been seen to recede towards its source and completely vanish; although no-one would ever have known if it did. For all intents and purposes, the reality of the realms stood before a vastness of untapped potentiality.

Joonas surveyed the area originally explored by Olaf Swyndle. He came across more portals than the scientist had ever dreamt existed – all of them still emitting the signals of their specific signatures, yet none able to reveal the codes of what made them. He reached the end of Spectre Flat, where Swyndle and his dog had crossed into the inter-dimensional web. He sensed unusual vitality around the portal, which he mistook for a sign of a fully active gate into the Warriors' realms – he stepped through it. All turned impossibly white around Joonas, as his mind was sent reeling.

"How dare you, Dark Angel!" he heard, realizing way too late that he had inadvertently crossed into the Great Ones' domains.

He flashed on how much losing the Eye had slowed him down, painfully aware he hadn't allowed enough time for a sound recovery. He panicked at the sense of impending doom he had brought onto himself, as the voice rang again at the core of his consciousness.

"Joonas, the Dove, must have forgotten some essential rule – or perhaps he no longer cares for guidelines, while he covets the sacred Oneness of the new worlds. We may not have jurisdiction in the place you seek to make your own, but we do here, and you are in direct violation of fundamental tenets. But we sense you have erred out of blindness – a surprising development, if we may indulge – although, one not truly unforeseeable in the light of your psychological profile. Consider this your only warning – begone!"

The Hektor elder landed on his back, against the rubble at the base of the decaying cliff.

"I could have told you not to cross, but your kind never listens. If it is the lost world you seek, your lateness is epic, for the buffets have long been closed!"

The green Pacific frog leaped away.
Joonas picked himself up, visibly shaken and

utterly disorientated. He retraced his steps to the system of Hektor portals, dialed the itinerary to his dwellings at Strata headquarters, and seriously considered subjecting himself to an evaluation of his performance in executing the basic requirements of his game plan. His recent, successive failures had risen to an inadmissible level bound to greatly jeopardize its success. He couldn't afford to fail before the elders, the powerful ex-Masters who had entrusted him with Hektor's future, and empowered him to use all of the league's resources in the pursuit of finding solace in the Warriors' realms. The recent pressures from the Guild, following Tömör's treason, and the wrath of the Great Ones regarding his latest mishap, made it clear that Hektor could no longer operate in its existing locale; at least, not under his despotic approach to ruling. The more the snare tightened around his plan, the more imperative it became to reach its completion. The Siskiyous, in all of their foreseeable presents, didn't yield a single open portal, but it didn't mean probabilities along other timelines would also come up empty – the meeting with the elders would attest to it!

Joonas returned to active duty after he deemed his convalescence was a waste of his time. He combed another dozen variations on the evolution of the area of the Siskiyou Mountains, making sure to avoid the Great Ones' portals, before he came to the conclusion that all accesses to the realms were unresponsive to his signature. To add pain to injury, none of them could provide a model for the organization to build upon.

The information stolen from the Guild network was accurate, but the schematics were useless without the ability to activate the codes. The portals were the equivalent of computers with working bios, but lacking proper operating systems. The architecture and the host programs in charge of communicating with the destination points remained frozen. The best Joonas could make of it was that someone had deleted all entries into the realms. Based on his skills at reading the spatial memory left by portal activity, it was clear the deed was done well ahead of the Guild's possible knowledge of Hektor's intentions. He couldn't figure out the reasons behind the decision, since nobody appeared to have been cognizant they existed in the first place. According to his inside sources, the Great Ones even forgot about them entirely, or rather, had no interest in being reminded of their existence.

Even though Joonas had been part of the original team that saw to the concept of the realms and designed the seed technology that would make their evolution possible – much before it was revealed to him that the Warriors would become the beneficiaries – the portal system to protect and access them was built after his time by Angels whose identities, as well as whereabouts, were known by neither the Guild nor Hektor. The blueprints found in the *Experimental Portals* section of *Portal Technologies*, had most likely been deposited there by the Angels in charge of that program, without much ado as to their obscure activities. In other words, if the other scouting elders also came up empty-handed, he, Joonas, would find himself at the root of a very complicated situation.

———————

The Hektor conference didn't turn out well. Each member reported with the same predictable drum beat, under the somber cadence of mission failure: no known probability held the key to the entry into the Warriors' realms. Some of the most vocal speakers didn't hesitate to infer that precious time and resources had been wasted on a foolish pursuit. Joonas stood adamant that his plan was the guaranty by which Hektor, out of all foreseeable futures, would thrive, finally freed from an enclave circumvallated by Guild supremacy and the watching eye of the Great Ones.

An elder by the name of Dahbar, stood up and spoke in emphatic tones, "We have invested our trust in you, empowered you to act as you wished, with unlimited access to resources, on the premise you would deliver on your grand plan to hand Hektor full control of a brand new Oneness; yet you haven't to this day, come up with any justifiable reason for us to continue believing in your vision. I am in favor of limiting your powers, and if necessary, amending this self-fulfilling assignment, if palpable results are not presented to us within the next few days. Those in agreement, please raise your hand!"

Voices rose. Before long, a great uproar filled up the hall. Joonas shouted from across the conference table that Dahbar was in no position to seek a vote, and that he should leave the meeting at once. Dahbar refused on the technicality that Joonas had never been empowered to rule over Hektor, insisting that his stance was one of self-aggrandizement and delusion. Joonas called the Dogs to have Dahbar removed by force and stripped of his status.

The assembly quieted down, but remained divided on how much longer Joonas should be given to finish what he had started. The founder stood up, exasperated. He explained, in no uncertain terms, that Hektor had no choice but to go ahead with the plan or face extinction. He then called for an end to the meeting, swiftly retiring to his quarters, leaving behind him approval and discontentment to argue over the artifacts of orchestrated division. As usual, Joonas had fully anticipated the commotion.

———————

When Professor Jarred Gulliver rang the bell at the Fieldbrook Road estate, he was received by a lovely red head with a ponytail.

"Good afternoon – I am sorry for the intrusion; I thought I had the right house. I'm looking for Mr. Slaughter's residence."

"This is the Slaughter residence – and you are?" Liv asked.

"Very sorry – Professor Gulliver from UC Berkeley! I stopped by the office, but to my dismay, it was closed. I left a message on Mr. Slaughter's answering machine, letting him know I should be passing through town to consult with him on some personal matters. The young lady who teaches the yoga class, below the office, told me he lived here in Fieldbrook. A quick internet search and here we are! Is he home by any chance?"

Liv expressed calculated concern.

"I'm sorry, my husband and I are only house-sitting. Marshall is presently traveling and is not expected to return for another week."

"Most unfortunate. Would you be so kind as to telling me where he went?" the professor enquired.

"I'm not at liberty to answer that, but I could relay your message for him to call you back," she returned.

"It won't be necessary; I'm only in town for a day. I had hopes we would meet though; as you know, Mr.

Slaughter's investigative skills precede him. Sorry for the improvised visit!" the professor apologized, before wishing Liv a fine day.

Jarred Gulliver walked back to the classic plum-toned Jaguar MK X parked in the graveled lot, by the entrance to the circular courtyard.

Spencer joined Liv to watch the visitor drive away.

"I guess Joonas is back in town," he said.

"I wonder what the distinguished gentleman needed from Marshall," Liv added sarcastically. "Better inform him and Geir, as well as tell the team the chase is on. There's no doubt he's close to figuring out where our friends are."

"I'm on my way to Le Lien," Spencer said. "Please secure the place and keep me posted on what goes on with the boys in Iceland."

Spencer left through the portal, as Liv prepared herself to contact Iceland via the Qwave laptop.

6 – TRÖLLASKAGI

Joonas drove the Jaguar along Fieldbrook Road, towards highway 299. By the time he had reached the intersection, he had come to the conclusion Slaughter had followed his friend back to Reykjavík. He checked with Hektor portals to establish coordinates with the Icelandic capital and found that the most direct route would take him to the small community of Borgarnes, forty miles to the north of the city, where one of Hektor's Dogs managed a bed & breakfast.

Geir lived in a large L-shaped house at the end of *Stóriteigur*, north-east of downtown Reykjavík, a short distance from Route 1 to Borgarnes, the road that circled the island. He and Marshall were enjoying their after-dinner cognac when Liv called for an audience.

"Greetings – I hope I'm not intruding on a sacred ritual. Spencer and I just had the pleasure of a visit from a Professor Jarred Gulliver, who snooped by your office before he came to the house. We have all reasons to believe he is Joonas's new guise; we trust it won't take long before he catches up with you. Spencer is at team headquarters, trying to figure out why the trace didn't alert us of his return. We had an off-the-charts spike a few days back; since then, we've only received a very weak signal – we may have lost the probe. At any rate, ready yourself for an out-of-the-box encounter."

"Thank you, dear – but what makes you believe he hasn't found out who you are?" Geir asked.

"Good question, but Joonas is too preoccupied with trying to maintain his old Master's skills, to be aware of the fact he has long been outpaced by advances made in identity protection. Furthermore, he is incapable of admitting he is at a disadvantage from no longer receiving training updates from the Guild. In a nutshell, he is unable to even detect a young graduate," Liv answered.

"So, if I understand you clearly, he will appear in Iceland on faith that we're not anticipating his visit, am I correct?" Geir asked.

"There is no doubt he counts on me to inform you of Prof Gulliver's wish to meet, but he can't be aware that we know who he actually is. When he eventually connects with you in Reykjavík, he'll feign amazement at the synchronicity of the encounter. If I'm right, you have a lecture scheduled at the university branch of the *Icelandic Society for Intelligence Research* – there is a great chance a Berkeley professor will attend as well," Liv returned.

"In that case, I can't wait to feign having heard of him and his work," the philosopher humored.

"Very well," Liv added, "consider yourself warned. I'm at your service fulltime. Spencer and I will relay information back and forth between you and Le Lien, as soon as we home on Joonas's movements and intentions. Once again, you're finding yourselves at ground zero. The best I can say for now is, enjoy the ride!"

"Thanks, dear, send in the clowns!" Geir voiced with pointed sarcasm.

Liv cut out as Slaughter raised his snifter.

"May the fun begin!"

"I don't suppose our friend will be flying *Icelandair*. I wonder where the closest Hektor portal is located – *Grímsey Island* perhaps? Wouldn't that be poetic justice?!" Geir uttered, somewhat sardonically.

The lecture at Reykjavík University was only two nights away, which did not leave much time for Slaughter and Flemmingson to get psychologically prepared for the pseudo-unscheduled visit. It was followed the next day by a trip to the University of Akureyri, where the philosopher was due to attend a colleague's course on *Polar Law*. Geir would pilot the rented Cessna P210 to the northern city, with the intention of showing his friend some of the most spectacular views of the island's glaciers, its numerous volcanoes, and the dramatic coastline.

Joonas arrived in Borgarnes the morning of the lecture. Shortly after securing a car, he sat at an outside table of a local café to contemplate how to con Slaughter and his friend into accepting the Jarred Gulliver persona. He ignored the eerie spectacle of the black mountains in the background, though he found a certain subliminal comfort in their presence. Reykjavík was only thirty miles south as the crow flew, but *Þjóðvegur 1*, or Route 1, was a winding affair. He also had to get familiarized with the capital before meeting with the detective and the philosopher – time was of the essence. He finished his light breakfast then drove the Subaru towards the island's ring road, across the mile-long bridge that spanned the frigid waters of *Borgafjorður*.

The presentation room, where Flemmingson was to give his lecture, was bright and modern. Most of the students who ran the program were already there with their guests. Invitees, as well as ticket holders, were still filling up the lobby – a friendly brouhaha that was heard down the halls of the university. Although the program

181

was centered on industrial engineering and artificial intelligence, the professor's views on technology as seen through polarized human perception and the influence of beliefs, were anticipated. Eventually, all were seated. To the delight of his audience, Flemmingson introduced himself with an infusion of ample, field-tested humor, before he began addressing the main topic.

The lecture was extremely well received, even if some of the customary questions clearly unveiled the chasm between some factions of the scientific community and progressive thinking; but civility reigned above all, as all gathered shortly around drinks and crudités.

The philosopher stood in the lobby, conversing with a group of students, as Slaughter, across the ins and outs of traffic, entertained a couple showing a keen interest in visiting the Pacific North West, when Jarred Gulliver walked straight at them.

"Do I hear California!?" the man exclaimed. "It just so happens I arrived here from Berkeley this morning. Professor Jarred Gulliver – you must be the American!" he added, extending his hand to Slaughter.

The detective apologized to the couple then turned to the older gentleman dressed in the herringbone weave Harris Tweed suit. The professor spoke in a distinctly accented Oxford English, with just the right touch of eccentric flair thrown in the mix.

Slaughter shook the man's gloved hand.

"I'm somewhat to the north of you, but I was born and raised in San Francisco," he said.

Flemmingson pretended not to have noticed the arrival, using the students as a shield.

"How far north are you from the bay area, may I ask – Santa Rosa, Ukiah?" Gulliver enquired.

"Sorry, the name's Marshall Slaughter; actually it's Eureka, roughly a hundred miles south of the Oregon border," the detective replied.

"Eureka – detective Marshall Slaughter!?" the gentleman exclaimed. "What an incredible coincidence! I was at your house a few days ago, speaking with your charming house sitter."

It was time to bring Flemmingson into the fold of the conversation.

"Hey Geir, check this out; we have a man here, who was at the Fieldbrook property looking for me a few days ago!"

"Say what? How can it be?!" Flemmingson feigned.

The philosopher looked at the visitor with a perfectly rehearsed air of stupefaction.

"I don't have to introduce myself, I assume; but whose company are we blessed with tonight?" he asked with acted exuberance.

Gulliver slathered on his credentials with near-genuine panache. The friends agreed mentally that he played the part to perfection. All he needed was an old Bentley and a chauffeur he paid a pittance.

"What was the reason of your visit back in Fieldbrook, and what in God's name brings you here as well tonight, if I may ask?" Slaughter probed.

"For my first reason, well, I needed professional advice on personal matters that are best discussed in the privacy of your office; thus, I would propose to get back to it at the appropriate place and time. For my second, I teach a class on Artificial Intelligence at UC Berkeley. Since I had attended an impressive lecture at San Francisco State by my here colleague, Dr. Flemmingson, a couple of years ago, I believed I couldn't miss on the opportunity to be present tonight. But the coincidence of finding ourselves in this room is truly extraordinary; I would never have dreamt of running into you in Reykjavík after missing you in Eureka, Marshall. By the way, Geir, congratulations on your convincing argument on the nature of beliefs and perception; the mind behind the technology is still the human mind. I would love to extrapolate on the subject in private some day – a truly fascinating topic!"

"Thank you, Jarred, it would be my pleasure. But don't you think coming all the way to Iceland for a lowly lecture requires more than just a professional interest in the program; yours must border on unbound passion for the field. But yes, please, feel free to introduce me to your research; I assume you're going to be around for a few more days," Flemmingson enquired.

"Most definitely; will tomorrow do?"

"Regrettably, we're off to Akureyri to attend a friend's course on *Polar Law* – the next day perhaps," Geir countered.

"If there is any way I can join you, let me know; I would be delighted. I have heard many good things about the city – it would be a pleasure to visit it first-hand," Gulliver said, ever so casually.

"There's extra seating on the plane, if you're not afraid of heights; Marshall and I are on for some serious sightseeing before the late afternoon class. I'll be your pilot if it's agreeable with you," Flemmingson offered.

"Count me in!" Gulliver replied enthusiastically.

"Seven sharp at the *Reykjavíkurflugvöllur* cafeteria, that's short for the Reykjavík airport for domestic flights, in south town; don't drive all the way to Keflavík where you flew in; no chance of finding us there," Geir laughed, enjoying a fair amount of private sarcasm.

"Let's exchange numbers and synch our watches!" Slaughter advised.

The lecture audience had slowly dissipated, while the students in charge were putting final touches to the clean-up. Marshall and Geir informed Gulliver it was time to part. They made a point of not asking him where he was staying – it would have to pass for an oversight, considering it was, after all, Flemmingson's night. The friends drove back to north town in Geir's Volvo. Professor Gulliver, aka Joonas, aimed for the Reykjavík airport to book a room at *Hotel Gardur*, where he was to arrange a meeting with a group of Hektor Dogs and lay a plan of action for the Akureyri visit. Somehow, there was something about the island that resonated with the elder – he was determined to get to the bottom of it.

Back at Geir's house, Marshall poured cognac into a couple of snifters and turned to his friend.

"I hope you know what you're doing; I wouldn't trust that motherfucker in that plane, if I were you."

"Take it easy, Marshall, Joonas is here and we won't get rid of him until he puts his hands on what he wants. He sure isn't going to find it on the plane. Let's put Liv online to see what she has for us."

The agent came alive. She already knew Joonas had made contact. In fact, the meeting sequence had unraveled very much as she said it would.

"You pulled that one straight out of the book of the future, dear," Flemmingson remarked.

"We're Angels – probable outcomes are part of our environment. We don't always know the course of action on which a specific plot develops, but since we're pretty clear on what needs to be done – to stop Joonas that is – it becomes easier to predict the logical path and back-engineer events from a future point. Of course it's neither a precise nor a safe science, but the laws of average tend to work in our favor; it comes with experience. You made a good choice of playing into Joonas's game and not force him to resort to manipulation. As long as he thinks he's in charge, we know he isn't. Yes, we're aware of the flight to Akureyri; as it turns out, one of the university students is a Le Lien liaison who got wind of your arrangement with Professor Gulliver – he will also be attending the lecture on *Polar Law*. You may recognize him, but I prefer not to reveal his identity for now."

"So what's the plan, Liv?" Geir asked.

"We got the probe working again. In crude terms, one may say that it got jammed. We're of the belief Joonas was exposed to a force field of great magnitude, one that shook his psyche to its core, which in turn reverberated all the way to the aspect consciousness in our possession. We are investigating and have made contact with the Ones about the issue. The Great Goddess of Light, Amaterasu, has expressed a desire to see into our matters regarding Joonas. It appears she has a particularly intimate connection with your good friend, Saka. I shall give you more details when The Triad finds the time to elaborate – but I digress. We have picked up a heightened level of energy coming from the Hektor member that seems to be directly connected to the island. We believe he senses something of major importance to him, but we're fairly sure he doesn't know exactly what it is. Needless to say, it is of great concern to us as well, so it's imperative you keep this laptop in sleep mode in his presence, but definitely not within his reach or visual field. Keep it under your seat in its soft case; it's OK, it won't overheat – Qwave tech, remember! At any rate, we want to monitor Joonas from as many angles as possible. Vac has expressed to The Triad that he wasn't convinced portals similar to Ma-l's didn't exist. We have it from reliable sources that Vac knows substantially more than he has been inclined to tell – we're paying particular attention to whatever information comes from him. Unfortunately for us, he is an Angel serving another Oneness; his allegiance being to the Goddess of the realm. On the other hand, it's good news for the Warriors."

———————

Geir, Marshall, and Jarred met as planned at the airport cafeteria. The Berkeley professor wore the same suit he donned the night before, but forewent bow and gloves. Flemmingson explained that they were going to fly over a series of volcanoes, starting from the West Volcanic Zone, below the Mid-Iceland Belt, with *Vatnajökull*, the largest glacier of the island, then towards *Öskjuvatn*, a deep blue lake two and a half miles across, inside the crater of *Askja*; and finally, along the north coast to Akureyri.

"Give or take a detour here and there," Geir said with amusement.

"How many volcanoes are there on the island?" Slaughter enquired.

"It all depends on what you consider a volcano. Most, of course, are extinct. Some are below the ocean's surface off the coast; others are buried under two thousand feet of ice. Odd ones are long, deep fissures spewing lava like blood out of a flesh wound, while many are just exhaust shafts linked to larger volcanoes; but in all, I believe there are around one hundred and thirty, of which thirty are active, with eighteen having erupted since the first settlements. We're mostly concerned about the seven main ones along the east and north volcanic zones. There are four major zones, with the Mid-Iceland Belt tying west, east, and north ones. Volcanology is a big deal in this country and it can easily become extremely overwhelming. We'll get more specific as we fly over them," the philosopher explained.

"Well, gentlemen, I shall simply forgo the questions in favor of enjoying the scenery," Gulliver said chirpily.

"Then let's get to the plane, shall we?" Geir ordered.

It was a beautiful sunny morning, with just a few scattered puffy clouds spotting the sky. The Cessna lifted smoothly and quickly reached an altitude of eight thousand feet. The four main glaciers were visible front and sides of the plane. The first volcano on the list was *Hekla*, a majestic white-capped dome, nearly five thousand feet high, which had erupted in 2000. The land around it was grey from ash and lava rock. The deeply shaded western flank of the mountain was as black as coal, instilling a sense of eerie desolation that contrasted vividly against the blinding whiteness of the glaciers in the distance.

Geir aimed the nose of the plane due south-east to *Mýrdalsjökull*, the ice area that concealed *Katla*. On the way, they passed *Eyjafjallajökull*, a small cap that last flared up in 2010.

"*Katla* is a biggie," Flemmingson said. "It hasn't erupted in nearly one hundred years and it's overdue; also why it's being closely monitored for seismic activity.

Recently, melted ice from the glacier flooded the southern side, which forced the closure of the ring road; a strong sulfur smell has been emanating from holes in the ice. My take is that it's the next major one," Geir went on, educating his guests, while visibly enjoying his role as tour guide.

Gulliver spoke sparsely, expectedly refraining from asking questions about the land below them – it was clear he didn't care. He appeared relaxed and friendly, occasionally joking about nothing in particular. One of the Qwave laptops was under Slaughter's seat, to the right of the professor who sat directly behind Geir. Le Lien was keeping tabs on the interaction, but unfortunately for the friends, nothing would come out of it until they landed and retired to the rooms they rented for the night.

After *Katla* came *Vatnajökulsþjóðgarður*, the park that contained the vast ice cap beneath which hid the sub-glacial volcanoes of *Grímsvötn*, *Bárðarbunga*, *Esjufjöll*, and *Kverkfjöll*. Then, it was down to the *Hvannalindir* oasis and onto *Askja* and its crater lake.

Slaughter was speechless, awed by the breathtaking beauty of the land. It was life and death in an embrace of light and darkness, interspersedly interrupted by smudge-like swaths of red-brown and green tundra. The plane circled *Öskjuvatn* then flew over a milky blue *Lake Viti*, before it aimed north-east along the ashen regions of the fault line that split Iceland in half.

Gulliver was more interested in the history of the people of the island, than he was about the scenery. He kept on enquiring about native inhabitants and settlers, lore and sagas, tales that involved volcanoes and spirits. Flemmingson kept on reiterating that there hadn't been any native tribes before Celtic settlers from Ireland and

189

Scotland, most likely monks, first appeared. They were closely followed, in the ninth century, by Nordic colonists. It did not seem to persuade the professor, who kept on insisting that there had to have been others before them. Geir explained that there once was speculation of Asian and Native American blood in the Icelandic gene pool, but that never added to anything. Perhaps one day, the ice would recede enough to uncover vestiges of older settlements, but so far nothing had emerged.

"Your artiste, Björk, isn't exactly your typical Viking, or even your dark-featured Irish," Gulliver insisted.

"My dear Jarred, it's like saying that the Sámi people never visited Scandinavia; North Asian DNA is not uncommon in the Nordic gene pool; and who knows how much circumpolar tribes have interacted over the millennia? Our celebrity's heritage could have been introduced to Iceland as late as the seventeen hundreds. But from a scholarly standpoint, pre-eighth century settlers are a categorical no," Geir returned.

"Pardon me for savoring the odd jab at recorded history – too bad though," Gulliver said, resigned.

While the discussion went on, the Qwave laptop connected to the Le Lien's probe was monitoring and processing the professor's thoughts and emotions.

The Cessna followed the northern coastline westward from the small fishing village of *Bakkafjörður*, past the dark hills of *Fagranes*, on its way to the beautiful coastal community of *Húsavík*. Since the start of the flight, Slaughter had been relentlessly and meticulously photo-documenting the scenery from his cockpit window, while simultaneously loading the images to a Qwave cloud server linked to Le Lien.

At last, they flew the length of the mountainous *Flateyjarskagi* peninsula, along a deserted tundra-floored valley, towards Akureyri Airport.

Spencer was back in Fieldbrook; in conference mode with Liv and Le Lien. The detective had been sending pictures of the landscape as the team monitored Joonas's intellectual and emotional input. The conversation he had with Geir highlighted the fact he was after the conditions that prevailed during the great battles against the Ones – he sought to establish an ancestry that matched the time period of the conflicts. The probe and the various programs involved, perceived his intuitions as leaning towards the part of the island situated north-west of Akureyri. The team was left flummoxed as to what was magnetizing his senses. The peninsula to the left of the city was a jagged leaf-shaped landscape by the name of *Tröllaskagi*, one only explored by the few rugged individuals that dared to stray from the communities of its fjords.

There was no logical reason for an active portal to be found in such a desolate place. There were no tribes there at the time of the battles, and the closest gate into the domain of the Great Ones was near *Katla* on the other side of the island.

The student liaison to Le Lien was named Stefan. He followed developments in Artificial Intelligence on behalf of the Guild, with the aim of tracing significant leaps in human technology and making adjustments to the grading of the race's evolution. He was notified by the team to pay particular attention to Joonas's movements upon his arrival, especially in regard to Hektor portals and Dogs in the area. The situation was perplexing due to the fact that it was highly coincidental for the Dove to have stumbled across something that resonated at a deep intuitive level. Nothing was truly an accident though; his determination was bound to eventually yield results. But Le Lien still had the upper hand, as long as the team remained in the shadow, and Slaughter and Flemmingson kept on playing their parts to the high standard for which they had been known to adhere.

Liv and Spencer warned The Triad about it. The message was relayed to Ma-l's group, as well as the assembly of Angels at the Great Hall. If the Hektor founder were to indeed find an active portal into the realms, it was likely he would cross alone for a dry run, before letting the rest of his organization know. The probe had revealed some of the tensions that had emerged of late within the group of fallen Masters – Joonas was in no hurry to share his findings with the beleaguered malcontents inside Hektor. In the meantime, Le Lien had no intention of waiting for Gulliver to find what drew him to *Tröllaskagi* – the team had to get there first.

Jarred Gulliver left Slaughter and Flemmingson at the airport, for he wished to tour the city before they would regroup at the university. The friends took advantage of the break to go to their bed and breakfast to connect with Liv. When they did, she asked them to get in touch with the liaison at a downtown café, still not divulging his identity.

"No need for names at this point; you will know soon enough. The Angel has been scanning the area for Dogs and portals. It's no surprise that the city should host a number of Hektor moles, but their numbers are unusual. Joonas must have called them into service over the last twenty-four hours. There are two Strata-designed interdimensional gates in Akureyri, through which we believe most of the Dogs arrived. Another was found in *Húsavík* to the east, and oddly, there is one on the south end of *Miklavatn*, the coastal lake at the bottom of *Skagafjörður*, a fjord north-east of the town of *Sauðárkrókur*. We believe the latter gate was installed recently on orders from Joonas – that's where we need to put all of our attention. We have our own Guild accesses in the area, our most remote is at the head of *Stífluvatn*, an inland lake of the glacier-carved *Tröllaskagi*."

"Yes, the Troll Peninsula, the stuff of legend. No wonder Joonas is drawn to it!" Geir exclaimed.

"Your Icelandic sagas are one thing – portals where they don't belong, are quite another," Liv said. "But yes, I can actually see the humor, Geir. After you meet with the Angel at the café, he, Spencer, and I will visit the area of assumed activity. There are great chances Joonas will do the same. Le Lien will keep on using the probe to get a sense of where he intends on going beyond that portal at *Miklavatn*. That spot is directly in line with our own at *Stífluvatn*; we're almost certain it's where he's heading. I suggest you acquire a map of the region to get familiarized with its topology. The more you know about it, the better your chances of understanding how things play out," the agent added. "Furthermore, don't hesitate to probe him on his whereabouts during the few hours before the class; after all, it's part of social protocol. He

193

will mostly lie, but remember, he's being monitored. Lies, truth; it's all the same when it gets processed by Qwave technology – it all arrives at the same conclusion. Please, make sure to report on what he says to you – the probe doesn't relay speech. And by the way, I'm glad to inform you that you're momentarily off the hook – Joonas has bigger fish to fry for now."

"Yes, we sense the Gulliver character isn't really in Hektor mode like Cruz was. No questioning, no innuendos, as if the Wild Cherry Market incident never happened," Slaughter said.

"He has much on his mind; he also has suffered a couple more setbacks since then. It's not unrealistic to think that he may be getting weary of the whole situation. The team has informed us that he accidentally stepped into the domain of the Great Ones and was ejected with titanic force. The loss of the Eye was also brutal on his psyche. He is essentially doing his best to stay with the logical process of completing his plan; retributions can wait – that's our perception," Liv added. "But I must go now – let's connect after the class."

The laptop went silent and resumed sleep mode.

Marshall and Geir visited the office of the *Iceland Conservation Volunteers* with the intention of locating topographic maps of the Troll Peninsula. They were able to obtain a large photocopy of the blown up area that included the site of the Hektor portal, between the two lakes mentioned by Liv. They then walked back to the bed and breakfast to get prepared for the meeting with the Le Lien liaison.

Flemmingson remembered the student from the conversation he had with the group before Gulliver's interruption. He was one of the lively ones, he thought at the time; with boundless enthusiasm and pronounced leadership skills. If nameless introductions were peculiar, Slaughter didn't seem to care; he shook the Angel's hand with expressed appreciation for the meeting, and offered to buy the coffee.

"Because of our common connection with the University of Reykjavík," the agent said, "it's unlikely Joonas will find anything odd about our relationship. Iceland is a small place after all, as people cross paths with taken-for-granted regularity. That being said, I will be your physical contact here, so that neither Liv nor Spencer get compromised. You two and I are staying in adjacent B&Bs for convenience, while Joonas has booked a hotel room closer to the airport, where he can meet with his Dogs, out of sight from you both. I know Liv asked you to get a map of *Tröllaskagi*; you can additionally Google-Earth the area and use their satellite imagery to great effect. You won't always find the names you're looking for, but it can complement a topographic map quite nicely. The area in question is showing a high probability of hiding either a forgotten or misplaced portal near *Stífluvatn*. Use your intuitions when you explore it, they're as good as anything we have at this point," the nameless liaison concluded with a smile.

The two friends thanked him. He apologized for having to leave so quickly, pressed to get to his surveying job with Liv and Spencer.

Geir and Marshall went over the map, in addition of the satellite blow-up of the area. While the Angels were at an advantage with their own access portals, nothing stopped them from renting a four-wheel-drive and enjoying the back country. Route 82 would take them to the town of *Dalvík*, through *Ólafsfjarðargöng*, the tunnel that accessed the community of *Ólafsfjörður*, where they could catch Route 802 to *Stífluvatn*. It was a 53 mile drive that would roughly take an hour and a half – traffic being a non-factor.

Joonas came through the newly installed Hektor portal at the bottom of *Miklavatn*. The farm was run by a couple of Dogs, whose old barn provided an ideal concealment for his ins and outs. The energy signal he had received since his arrival on the island, had intensified. It was now beaming from an area ahead of him, towards *Stífluvatn*. The lake was roughly four and a half miles from the portal; an easy ride for the borrowed Mercedes SUV. It was the last stretch of Route 802, where it reconnected with coastal Route 76. Essentially, the two roads formed a loop around the Troll Peninsula; Marshall and Geir would approach *Stífluvatn* from the east, while Joonas reached it from the west.

The Hektor elder drove the length of the lake towards the increasing signal. Its strength stabilized to hold its level for the next two miles; then declined sharply as the road curved north-eastbound. He turned around; the wave picked-up anew for the same exact distance before it faded again.

Meanwhile, Le Lien was following Joonas's reactions through the probe, and concluded the area of interest was somewhere south of *Stífluvatn*. Liv, Spencer, and Stefan came out of the Guild portal at the dammed end of the lake then bounced via the directional pitch system, to another at the other end, near a trail across the waters from the road. They saw the SUV drive by, return, and then go around again, coming to a stop a mile south of the reservoir. Joonas's movements matched the coordinates from Le Lien and the probe. After a short while, the Mercedes returned to where it came then disappeared – the Hektor founder was done for the day. The team walked to the spot where Joonas last parked. Spencer searched the Qwave system; there were no registered Guild portals beyond that point for the next twenty miles.

"I wonder why he's sensing something we aren't," Spencer wondered.

"He's tuned to what he wants; apparently we're not on that frequency. If it's indeed a Guild installation he's after, something went awfully wrong with it," Liv said pensively.

Stefan's laptop informed them that Geir and Marshall were online.

"A quick word before we take off for the class: check that small reservoir to the south of *Stifluvatn*, Marsh calls it Keyhole Lake. You told us to follow our intuitions – that's where we're going, first thing tomorrow. We'll hike to it from the road and hang out there for a while – just a hunch," Geir said.

Spencer and Liv bent over the map on the computer, realizing with genuine amazement that the location of the keyhole-shaped lake was exactly the point of the wedge that corresponded to the section of road Joonas had been scanning. The probe had picked a heightened emission from the elder, the length of the two mile segment past the lake – a perfect arc to the circle of which Keyhole was the center.

"This is brilliant," Spencer remarked.

"Listen, go to the class then connect with the liaison when you're done; we may want to help you plan your trip to *Stífluvatn*," Liv added.

———————

Jarred Gulliver joined Slaughter and Flemmingson just in time for the lecture.

"Beautiful town," he said jollily, "I believe I shall stay around for a few more days to explore the countryside."

"We'll spend an extra day as well," Geir returned. "But we must fly back to Reykjavík to get Marshall prepared for his trip back to California. You're on your own, I'm afraid."

"Not to worry, old man, I'll manage. I'm only due back in Berkeley in a fortnight, so I might as well enjoy."

The Le Lien liaison arrived just as they entered the room.

"Professor Flemmingson, I was wondering if I would see you here; hope you enjoy the class!"

"By the way, meet my friends Marshall and Jarred," Geir said.

"A pleasure, Stefan Morganson; I too was at the lecture last night – small world. Forgive me, I must get to my seat," the student said, shaking hands as he hurried into the room.

They found their guest seating and waited for the lecturer to finish writing on the blackboard.

The class was an update on new regulations and amendments to *Polar Law*, as abrupt climatic changes that led to receding glaciers and rising oceans, wildlife endangerment, over-fishing, and rapidly increasing tourism were impacting the reality of the once isolated Polar life. Countries both in the north and south had joined to define issues and firm up guidelines. The university brochure best explained the heart of the course.

"Polar Law describes the legal regimes applicable to the Arctic and the Antarctic. It is interdisciplinary, placing emphasis on relevant areas of public international law and social sciences. Subject areas include: environmental law; the law of the sea; sovereignty issues and boundary disputes on land and sea; natural resources governance; the rights of indigenous peoples in the North; self-government and good governance; economic development; Arctic security and Arctic strategies; and land and resource claims in Polar regions."

After the class, Geir offered to treat Gulliver and Morganson to dinner, but the Berkeley professor declined on reasons of previous engagements.

"Making friends fast?" Geir probed, "Iceland will rob you of your heart if you're not careful. Well, do enjoy, my friend!"

"We may again cross paths before you leave, but now is a good time to part. Thank you dearly for the fabulous flight, it was most entertaining. And Marshall, I will be in touch with you when I return to California – I never forget my friends, plus I still have a need for your investigative skills," Gulliver said with a wink, as he shook hands before walking away.

"Dinner would be great – meeting at my place afterward? We need to plan our next move," Stefan said.

All agreed. Geir then invited them to follow him on a brisk walk, to one of his favorite restaurant in town.

"I believe you're going to like it – cozy, artsy; plus best seafood in the city!"

Liv, Spencer, Geir, and Slaughter met in Stefan's room, where the Angels had installed a temporary portal.

"Your intuitions were correct, Marshall, we have finally located an active doorway at Keyhole Lake. It's not part of the Guild network and, obviously, not one of Hektor's either; so we're left with the theory that it belongs to the system that was put in place by the protectors of the Warriors. What it's doing there is beyond Le Lien's guess, but regardless, we must now investigate where it leads, before Joonas gets to it," Spencer emphasized.

"We can only install temporary portals where we or our machines are. The closest official Guild access is at the end of *Stifluvatn*, two and a half miles in a straight line to Keyhole – we must walk that distance to it. We will then place our short-term gate nearby, but one of us Angels, will have to cross the forgotten portal to see where it leads. Spencer and I have already entered the realms to deliver Pau to Ma-l and her group, so it rightfully falls on us to probe its mystery," Liv added.

"Marshall and Geir, we count on you to get to the lake early enough tomorrow, so that when Joonas arrives, you can slow him down by distracting him," Spencer continued. "He doesn't know the portal is at Keyhole, but it's not going to take him long to figure it out. We don't have the means to deactivate it, since it is not part of our system, but we could try to shield it; so we need to buy time. Be there early then wait by the road a mile south-east of *Stifluvatn*; Joonas will be driving a grey Mercedes SUV – hopefully you will be ahead of him."

"Stefan, Spencer, and I will hike to the hidden lake after we're done with this meeting. We don't expect Joonas will feel inclined to do the same since his old Guild powers are not what they were; his night vision is by now barely better than yours. His skills of intuition are, on the other hand, quite formidable; it explains how he was drawn to that place after he detected its presence all the way from the capital. One last thing: do not offer to follow him when he readies himself for Keyhole – it would just be messy. When all is done, get back to your vehicle and enjoy the rest of the day around the Troll Peninsula; we will catch up again later," Liv finished.

"How can we not want to hike to the lake, or at least, stick around the area when it was our original plan?" Geir lamented.

"You're better positioned than we are at shaping your own destiny. We judge our advice to be sound, but if you want to be part of the action, we can't prevent you from doing so, regardless of the risks. You're wise enough to understand why you mustn't follow him, the rest is up to you," Spencer replied.

"We will play it by ear," Geir countered. "By the way, Stefan, thank you for trusting us with your name."

"I guess I had no choice – thanks to you for the clever trap. Joonas is a walking lie detector; there was no way I was going to jeopardize the moment – the time must have been right," he said laughing.

"Well, Liv made such a big deal of it – maybe one day she'll care to explain why she wouldn't tell."

"She had valid reasons," Stefan concluded.

"We don't have much time left; we must act now – good luck!" Liv closed, as the three Angels disappeared through their temporary portal.

———

It was past midnight when the three Le Lien agents made it to Keyhole Lake. With their temporary access in place, they could now reach the site instantly from any point within the Guild system. They scanned the gate with the use of a handheld Qwave devise. The portal was confirmed to be born of a variance of Guild tech, leading the three to agree its design was meant to serve the Warriors' realms, as it hid similar feedback properties to the one concealed by The Triad, under the Snug Alley gazebo, in Eureka. But since all original portals into the realms were now gone, it was obvious the Keyhole gate was not one of them; it had to have been part of an independent network, whose obscure purpose might not even have concerned the realms – the only way to know where it led was to walk through it.

Spencer stood in a tall hallway lined on both sides with grey doors. He looked back – the portal he had just crossed opened onto the vastness of red dunes as far as the eye could see. A unique symbol of mysterious origins was engraved on each of the doors. The hall opened at its far end through an arched gateway, offering yet another space with more of the same layout – and on it went. The seventh entrance to his right was left ajar, though no-one had stepped out. Spencer walked to it, entering what he, at first, thought was a room. To his surprise, he was met by a stately, elder woman sitting on a bench across a grassy area. She had been waiting for him.

"Welcome Angel; I am Amaterasu, Great Goddess of Light and philosopher. I've been expecting your kind. We don't have much time, as the dark Master, Joonas, isn't far behind you. You are not presently in the world of the Warriors; rather, you're finding yourself in an intermediate reality of my making. Each of the doors you see in the halls, accesses a version of my creative interpretation of the Warrior's realms, except for this garden, which in real life belongs to a very accommodating host. I've been made aware of Hektor's intentions long ago; as a matter of fact, I have been anticipating them. The Dove was about to discover your concealed portal through a near-imperceptible twitch in the ghost image, when, in the dream state, I merely suggested to your present subject, Marshall, that he was to consider a short vacation with his friend, Geir – a bit beyond protocol, I must say, but it had to be done. You already understand that we, the Ones, as a collective consciousness, are not to interfere with the process of evolution in a Oneness to which we don't belong; whatever Joonas and his organization do, beyond the boundaries of their present universe, doesn't concern us. That being said, it doesn't mean that we should never step in, or that laws are in place to prevent us from doing so. It's simply a matter of ancient principles getting passed along, as the universe, as we know it, expands. You are well aware that we weren't always Great Ones; some of us started as common deities, Angels, and sometimes both. I was what I am by the time of the battles, but I started an Angel eons before them. I was one of the firsts to go by the name – the Masters and the Guild were still a long way from coming of age then. My gift of light allowed me to see into the heart of All That Is. In that heart, I witnessed loneliness, and beyond it, I saw a path to insanity driven by the forces of cyclic redundancy."

Amaterasu paused as if to consider the time left.

"It was at the far end of the curve of light, into impossible distances, that I perceived an extremely remote probability onto which converged many of the same random events that had coalesced into the original Oneness. I assembled the very first team of Angels, whom I shared my vision with. We sowed the seeds of the realms, and when the time came, gifted the Warriors with dreams and blank life canvases; these dreams illuminated the darkness of their stony confinements. One such light walked out into the worlds of many eras and probabilities – she has now returned to the realm of the host I mentioned a short while back, the one who goes by the name of Ma-l. The main reason you have no precise knowledge of the original portal system connecting those realms, stems from the fact that many of us are no longer among the Masters; though we are still very much invested in what we have created. There is no secrecy about who we are; thus, I welcome you to share my words with your team. At this conjuncture, it's evident we are working towards the same aim. I extend my knowledge and skills to you, in the name of assistance and collaboration. My goal here is to send Joonas and Hektor into a world of illusion, one I hope they will never walk out of. But if they do, it will be at the risk of giving them what they want most – a way to the real thing."

"It's an honor, Great Goddess. I am in turn entrusted by my team to offer aid on all matters concerning the Warriors. But are you suggesting that you are buying time – possibly not enough to save the realms from Hektor?" Spencer asked.

"Exactly, and that's where you come in. If Joonas reaches those worlds, he will have to be pushed back. The system already established there will help you. There is rumor, among those in place, of a large gestalt, with enormous resources and a specialized awareness, which may have friends in unsuspected places – rumor, because of developmental inconsistencies, which I have no time to extrapolate on at this point. There is a considerable number of Angels that have yet to join; it is why the ghost image is to be exploited for as long as it is willing to hold – although, since the collapse of the mother reality, migration has stopped. Upon resuming, the Great Hall will keep on welcoming volunteers until, as foreseen, Goddess Ma-l, Saka, and the rest of their group unlock the lanes that connect the realms to each other; alongside all Angels moving into their assignments. So yes, analogically speaking, I am buying time, hoping Hektor will never be given the opportunity to infiltrate these worlds. It is the best I can do for now; please do hurry back; our timelines aren't synchronized and you don't want to be seen – good luck!"

When Liv, Spencer, and Stefan returned to the end of *Stifluvatn*, near where the grey Mercedes was parked along Route 802. Marshall and Geir's Jeep had long left on its tour of *Tröllaskagi*. It was six o'clock, and Joonas had just reached Keyhole Lake.

7 – HALLS OF DOORS

Spencer sent the latest news to The Triad, which in turn informed the group of Joonas's actions. Saka rejoiced at the revelation of Amaterasu's pivotal presence at Keyhole Lake, along with her mind-bending plan to divert Hektor away from the realms. She touched the stone through its pouch – she was available and ready!

Pau had officially rejoined the Guild; her student status reinstated by the chapter that would permanently remain in the realms – she had made the choice of becoming a member of the new world. Leòn had promised to introduce her to the Great Hall, where she would be put in the care of the students program, joining Shade, who offered to orient the newcomer. But Leòn had unfinished business to address; his ex-subject, Gerald Brinsk, needed rescuing from Strata. If he was to bring him back to the safety of Ma-l's universe, stealth was of the essence. It couldn't have been a better time for the operation, with Joonas about to get busy with Amaterasu's masterwork of realm simulations.

Liv and Spencer had returned to Fieldbrook, having practically converted Slaughter's house into an annex of Le Lien, from which they assisted in monitoring Joonas's actions. They also orchestrated the complex metrics to a safe passage for Leòn, who, in an unusual move for an Angel, breached into the Strata facility and yanked Brinsk from his cell via an experimental flash portal; a gate that existed in a state of excitation known as "static time," transparent to Hektor's detection apparatus. With precise input from Le Lien and Qwave, the entire mission took exactly one hour, seventeen minutes, and eleven seconds. Before Strata learned of the subterfuge, the ex-Guild student had already been evaluated for reentry into the Guild, far out of the reach of his tormentors. One of the reasons that made it possible for Leòn to break into the compound, was the general discord among the Hektor rulers that had spread confusion across the organization and distracted its surveillance Dogs. Hektor was experiencing swelling pains, which translated into signs of instability within the group. To add pain to injury, a coalition of Angels was in the process of organizing a rescue effort to free all corrupted students from the clutches of every department of the rogue league. The Guild was firming up its grounds in regard to what it considered a breach in protocol by Hektor, for having capitalized on Tömör's weaknesses and subsequent treacherous digressions. Furthermore, with Amaterasu officially involved in protecting the realms, which, according to her indisputable recount of their history, still existed under the clause of Guild projects sanctioned by the Great Ones, Hektor was deemed a criminal outfit that had to be righted without the possibility of an escape into the emerging Oneness.

Ma-1 had gathered the group – the subject centered on defining the consciousness that controlled the tunnels and portals between the realms. Further exploration had only yielded the discovery of stifled realities, where confused souls similar to Badger, crouched in the dark corners of their caves. The Goddess had been given clear access to these forgotten recesses from the four floors of the lower level of the Great Hall, sixteen in all; while all hundred and thirty-two openings above the main floor looped back into it in maddening randomness. She thought of the Warriors, put faces on their names, but was not given permission to visit their realms. There was an extra element of protection to the system that even her creator status could not breach. She was resolute on speaking with the energy gestalt that was protecting her brothers and sisters' domains, but she didn't have a clue on how to go about it – its alien origin provided very little on which to affix a conceptual anchor.

"Certainly, you must understand that the gestalt in question is the glue that ties the realms together; it's not just a system – it is the sum of all parts," Saka said.

"Yet, it's not integral to this world," Ma-1 replied. "Its energy spectrum doesn't embrace the realms as much as it touches them with the tip of its tentacles. When you travel along one of them, it flexes to connect you to where it deems your destination to be, or, as in the latter explorations, to prevent you from getting to it."

"It's evident its purpose is centered on allowing or forbidding access for reasons that are strictly bound to it. The original designers, if they can be found, must still hold the codes that set the course of its evolution in motion – perhaps, Vac can provide us with what he knows about it?" Olaf forwarded.

The Master asked to be given a moment of silence while he collected his thoughts.

"This is a question for Amaterasu, but I will answer it to the best I am permitted to reveal. I have never spoken of my involvement with the battles beyond brief mentions of being aware of why and how the Warriors were dispatched. In reality, I was an instrumental cog in the vision and subsequent design of the realms. The Great One was nearly done with her higher training, on her way to reach her next level of fulfillment, when she gathered her most avid followers and students to explain she had found a mate for All That Is, in the farthest confines of possibilities. It was crystal clear to her that without the realization of that potential, the expansion of the universe would be compromised from the rise of an inexplicable melancholia that would impregnate all layers of existence. We rode with her on the light that traveled indescribable distances, to what could be best defined as the end of time. We saw the birth of new universes that coalesced into a singularity. When we returned, we each assumed a role within a blueprint of our own design. The end part of it was for me to orchestrate Olaf's entry into Ma-l's realm, as well as Saka's return to it."

The group sat silent, while Vac continued.

"All will be explained to you in due time, but for now, we must come to comprehend the entity behind the lanes of the Warriors' dreams. First, it would never have existed if it hadn't been for the collective spirit of these soldiers; the single purpose of protecting the tribe was the perfect furrow in which the seeds of things to come could be planted. It was highly foreseeable that, eventually, these Warriors would seek to meet in the dream state. Amaterasu had cast her light, sowing the innumerable flickering stars that shone across the heavens above the gathering grounds. Without the collective nature of the dreams, the lanes could not have been conceived – they were the strands that connected these souls to each other, and only those who chose to be part of the meetings, are now the ones whose creations are integral to the larger réseau of the realms. Their dreams flourished to become mature realities, such as Ma-l's. The ones that opted to remain insular, never evolved beyond the confinements of their stony prisons, and, thus, stayed at the level of their original predicaments; they are best described as aspect personalities of their old physical selves, no longer connected to them, nor the reality of the realms. They may appear real to the observer, but they're only fragments of spatial memory devoid of self-awareness and purpose. Before we get to the gestalt in question, there were many tribes around the planet that battled the Great Spirits; those also were given equal opportunities to thrive. Perhaps, for them, conditions as well as timing were inauspicious, or cultural stigmas interfered; but none of these realms succeeded. Some of them evolved to the point of owning active portals into their embryonic realities; unstable and unprotected openings that eventually became traps to unfortunate, errant travelers, but which irreversibly collapsed to be reclaimed by their host realities. To our knowledge, only these present realms have thrived; or rather, it is assumed that beyond Ma-l's creation, others have thrived as well – we shall soon know how, and to what extent. The entity in charge of the tunnels and their various portals as we know them, showed a complex projected evolution at the time the collective dreams were set in motion. Amaterasu took us into probable futures, where we witnessed the growth of the energy gestalt that was born of these group dreams. It became aware of itself at the same time Saka emerged into her own. One may say that the two and Snake are cut from the same block of consciousness, or rather; one could easily assume they are the Great Goddess' children, cocooned by the collective awareness of the Warriors.

The tunnels that connect the realms are the physical manifestation of what links their creators spiritually. It knows when the time will come to open the portals and allow the Angels to find their places. It is also aware that there is another side to the Guild that looms over a number of foreseeable outcomes – Hektor was the inevitable antithesis to its birth, and its presence here would presage doom over the realms. For now it seeks to protect each of the worlds that lie below its watchful eye, and will only allow for the utmost necessary traffic to operate through its system. It knows it would not exist without the Warriors' domains, and most likely, neither would they without it. It is what makes the whole out of the parts – it is the function, the purpose, and the bond that holds these worlds into a coherent singularity. It is also the consciousness that beams its presence to the original Oneness with its wish to unite, and its messages have been received with unparalleled joy."

Vac paused.

"Now, understand this is one version of the gestalt's projected evolutions – I am inclined to opt for the most likely scenario. I hope that answered some of your questions."

The group collected for another minute, before Saka came forward.

"My understanding is that without dreams, nothing comes to be; and in the absence of creations, we are left to speculate the dreamers simply don't exist."

"As ethereal as it may be, we are the collective dreamer," Vac returned. "The nuance here is that we chose to separate from a unique Oneness, to form another amid energy clusters that only recently organized – including the Great Gestalt, as it deserves to be defined."

"Thank you, Angel," Ma-1 said. "I believe I have figured out how I may be able to communicate with it. Now, it's time to return to the Great Hall to check on our freshly rescued student and his heroic Master, Leòn."

———————

Gerald Brinsk was highly disoriented but overwhelmed with joy at realizing he had been freed from Hektor. Leòn would tutor him throughout his rehabilitation, until he was deemed fit to join Pau at the recently created Qwave inter-realm department, located in the Great Hall's substation.

The migration of volunteers had resumed. Portals and Qwave had finally succeeded in annexing the Eureka Snug Alley threshold to the Guild system, allowing crossings to be made directly from any terminal, and effectively putting an end to the freeze. There was nonetheless a fluctuation that, with each transfer, needed to be sequenced with the Hektor scanners. But the techs at Portals and Qwave had fine-tuned the program so that it ran automatically. Although the ghost image of the mother reality was steadily weakening, the throughway was thought to remain operational for the time necessary to complete the Angels' passage.

———————

Ma-1 needed all the privacy she could muster to establish communication with the Great Gestalt. She entered the corridor of Despair – the realm of the volcano

– and walked the long distance to the mouth of the crater to summon Snake from the boiling bowels. The elemental entity slowly rose from the magma, a smoking giant shedding slabs of semi-molten rock – he came within safe distance of the Goddess.

"How do I deserve the honor of your visit, Warrior?" the *he* element asked.

"The honor is mine, Snake. I am here on the intuition that you may be able to assist in matters that concern the integrity of the realms. You see, the Great Gestalt that governs the ways to the Warriors' worlds, has shut the portals in anticipation of an invasion by the Dark Angels of Hektor. As a result, I have been unable to connect with my brothers and sisters. I additionally find myself in the unfortunate position of not knowing how to communicate with it, but I'm of the opinion that you can. I also believe that you may impress upon its good graces to help me reach out to those whose worlds it links."

"Goddess: you, the Great Gestalt, and I know that we owe our existence to Amaterasu and the Angels that shared her vision. We also know that it – the gestalt – is the product of the manifold symbiosis that stemmed from the collective reality of the Warriors. I am the fire of the craters that swallowed you in battle, but I am here today, because you recalled me in your dreams. The Great Gestalt is the sum of the energy lanes of that group consciousness; its present role is to protect you in a way to protect itself. What I can tell you now, hoping it brings perspective into your inquiry, is that the portals will open as soon as there is more than one Warrior with the desire to meet another. So far, you are the only one who has exercised that wish. Keep in mind you possess knowledge the others may not have, that is, a direct awareness of the existence of the emerging Oneness. You've had the privilege of visitors who brought a backdrop to your reality – an honor that, most likely, has been denied to the rest of them. Remember the days before the Angel and his human friend arrived at the doors of your land; it may help you understand where the other realms may presently be at. Nonetheless, I don't see why the Great Gestalt would not grant you an audience if you asked. Perhaps, instead of fixating on the Warriors, you could focus your energy on what keeps the realms from coming apart and show your gratitude. If your were to extend to it the same love that you showed me when I engulfed your land in flames, you may be pleasantly surprised by the effect it may have – I am sure you don't need help in that department. When the time comes to deal with the Dark Angels of Hektor, don't hesitate to seek my services. You don't have to come all the way to here; a small campfire in your backyard will suffice to summon me – I enjoy quiet, intimate settings on occasion."

Snake recoiled to the bottom of the crater. The ground shook in warning of an imminent eruption. Ma-l returned to the Great Hall, where Vac, Saka, and Olaf were conducting business. She understood too clearly that she had failed at seeing the Great Gestalt for more than a conglomerate of caves and tunnels managed by a common program. At that key moment, and lost for understanding, she realized how much more dependent on each other all the elements of the realms were. Her original overview centered on her domain's relationship with the tunnels. Her world was not the hub – the reality of the lanes was. The entity in charge was in fact what kept her world from losing its tether to the collective makeup, and without it, she would be nothing more than one of the dispirited and frightened souls tucked against the back walls of their lifeless caves.

When the dream meetings ended, Ma-1 was left to reflect on her condition, with nothing more than the wish to end it. The collective spirit was lost; instead, she was forced to direct her energy inward on the pursuit of creating a better environment. What came of it was a reality vividly delineated by individual purpose and need. All that surrounded her was the metaphorical checksum of millennia of input, against which, she, at last, detected the obvious error in defining her place.

Her realm was only an individual endeavor, in the sense that its design relied on her unique creative skills; but without the collective experience, that world would have lacked the drive to exist. The thought was made all the more vibrant by the presence of her guests, who, through their personal contributions, had further colored their shared reality. Alone, she was able to imagine her realm, with them, she witnessed its realization.

Ma-1's entourage had become a common feature of the Great Hall, with each having interacted, in some form or another, with the teams that coalesced into the greater body of the "new Guild." At the exception of Gerald Brinsk, all had spoken before the assembly about the circumstances that brought them to the realms. Vac's speech was an eye opener on Guild history, with its emphasis on the battles and the emergence of Hektor. Other Angels, who partook in the preservation of humanity, came forward with their version of Joonas and his followers' dissenting views of the wish of the Great Ones; among them, an elder, female Master by the name of Qo'ai-Marael, who had worked alongside Amaterasu and Vac on "sowing" the realms. Pau's poignant life story and her work alongside Joonas were particularly strongly-felt. It became the standard by which Hektor was, from that point on, defined: a threat to evolution at large.

Ma-1 badly yenned to make up for her oversight of the Great Gestalt's primordial role in keeping the realms from coming unglued. A ceremony in its honor was overdue, though she sensed that rituals were inappropriate methods to getting the attention of higher consciousnesses – she knew it for herself, as she would never accept any token of adulation from her creations. She opted instead to confer with *It* in the privacy of her own thoughts, with the kind of intimacy deserving of the trust of deep-rooted affiliations. The Gestalt was as much part of her as she was integral to the interconnective reality of the realms. She left the group at the Great Hall to return to the tunnels and the back room that saw the birth of her domain. She sat in the silent darkness, surrounded by only stone and the weight of ages, traveling back to the place of first-recalled memories – to the lanes that carried her inner light to the leas of the dream meetings – all the way to that moment of awakening. It was long after she had died in battle. She became the infinitesimal fractal that carried the codes of existence into the vacuum of its inconceivable annihilation, to rise again to see the birth of a brand new universe. She became one with the absolute point of emergence, the spaceless and timeless condition of all coalescing presents and dimensions, the folding of the greater infinites into the smaller ones, until, at last, consciousness was freed from the echoes and ripples of both explored and unrealized potentials. At the immeasurable point of that metaphorical milestone, Ma-1 expanded again to find herself in a hall lined with grey doors. She intuitively knew the seventh entrance to her right led to her own realm. A voice rose from the core of her vision.

"You are inside a simplified model of the system that connects your realm to the others, Goddess Ma-l, one borrowed by Amaterasu for the purpose of sending the Dark Angel on an impossible quest. I deem it more hospitable than the cold darkness of the caves. You call me the Great Gestalt, but I prefer something shorter and less honorific – perhaps, a name like 'George,' short for, "Great Energy Overseeing Realms, Grots, and Entries." It comes with two g's as well. I see you chose the form of your ancestry, and that, beyond the stone reality of your rebirth, you built a world that approximates the one you came from. Not all is dark about me; it is why I have taken you here, to these brightly lit halls; but as you see, only the door to your domain is open, as it is in Amaterasu's version. It indicates that you only, Goddess, have allowed your world to be accessed by visitors. When Angel Vac and professor Swyndle entered through the backdoor of your reality, it was because you desired the company of others; a wish driven by a deep longing for Saka's return, and an instrumental detail to the emergence of this cluster of pocket realities into its own Oneness. Let me illuminate a point: unlike the original universe, which expanded from the perspective of the One, yours brought forth a singularity from the standpoint of the collective. That unique characteristic makes for the ultimate condition of unity. In my correspondence with the *All That Is* we all have come to be associated with until recently, the conclusion is overwhelming – it's a match! Now, you are expressing a desire to connect with your kin and their realities, and I am of the belief that, at this conjuncture, you might be wondering why your brothers and sisters have not forwarded similar wishes, for if they had, I have no doubt more of these doors would be open. If you chose to cross one of their thresholds, you would find yourself back in these halls from any of the others; just like the trickery of the Great Hall. This is not my doing; I have no powers beyond the management of the lanes, as you once called the system. If you desire access to these closed worlds, you will need to rediscover what it was that once connected the Warriors to each other, and then reach out to them. When you get to one, I am convinced it will become easier to find the rest."

"I was under the impression that the portals were locked to protect the realms from Hektor," Ma-l said.

"There is some truth to it insomuch that, unlike you, these Warriors do not have the help of Angels, a Goddess of Light, Snake, and the perspective of your advanced creational skills at their disposal. In reality, I do not know what exists behind these doors and what opening them would do to these realms. Yes, because of my position, I could breach the sanctity of these noble souls; although it would amount to an unprecedented violation I am incapable of committing."

"How, without the participation of all the realms, can this new Oneness qualify as the work of a collective?" the Goddess asked.

"Your open realm gave much vitality to the creation of the Oneness. It was foreseen that only through the coalescing of the elements that brought your world and the reality of the Great Hall into being, could the gears mesh to set the Warriors' spheres in motion. Active or not, these domains still display the characteristics of multiplexity that are inherent to the original collective spirit, and if only yours was to remain, it would yet be considered the end-product of a shared creational undertaking," the Gestalt replied.

"Am I to assume that those realms may not have evolved?"

"Not necessarily; they may simply have developed in ways that did not permit the expansion of the collective spirit – a natural reaction to the solitude of the stone. Eventually, these doors will open."

"With all due respect, I perceive a contradiction. I was able to open mine because of Saka and the exterior help from Vac and Olaf; yet, judging by what I just heard, it appears these realms are not to receive what was granted to me," Ma-l questioned.

"A paradox rather, since these Warriors cannot know what they need to know; yet, they must eventually know," George replied.

"One perpetuated by the notion that their realms are to remained sealed?" she countered.

"I have told you what I cannot do; you are free to make your own choices when you find the powers to open the portals. Unlike the Angel that visited Amaterasu's model of this hall, you can actually recognize the symbols on the doors. I am not at liberty to say more on the subject. One last item: you are of course aware this place is another way of looking from inside the Great Hall of the Angels – a more private space to allow you to work without distraction. Also, bring Saka and her stone with you next time you visit; there are yet a few more layers to the system you may wish to be aware of. I trust that you know your way in and out of this place. I am glad we finally met – until next time."

The echo of George's voice faded. The Goddess walked to the door that led to her world then realized that from it, she could be anywhere she wished – she was going to enjoy this place immensely.

———————

Ma-1 returned to her rear cave, making sure to secure the portal into George's hall. Eventually she would be able to access it from anywhere in her realm. It was essentially another dimension of reality parallel to the Great Hall of the Angels, with doors in lieu of corridors to reach the Warriors' worlds. There, she could meet privately with the Gestalt, or explore without the presence of the assembly of Masters. She recognized it was a gift from George – the expression of his boundless love. Ma-1 felt touched by deep-reaching emotions.

Suddenly, her world had grown a lot bigger.

She walked out of her cave to the halfway point of the tunnel, where the portal that led to Shade's floor was located. She then connected with Leòn, Pau, and Gerald Brinsk for a brief meeting, momentarily leaving the group to wander around the space and get a sense of what she had been missing. It finally occurred to her that the openings that did, in fact, reach into the back caves of the aborted realms and their tortured ghosts, didn't actually exist in George's hall – their doors would otherwise have been open. Ma-1 didn't believe she hadn't seen them because she hadn't been looking for them; no, they simply weren't there. She left Leòn and the students for the upper hall to join Saka, Vac, Olaf, as well as The Triad in Axel and Ilia's dwellings. She shared the news of her encounters with Snake and George, to the bemusement of the group. Although the mystery of the locked realms was partially solved, it did little to reduce the enigmatic quality of their silence. As Angels kept on arriving, they were faced with the incongruity of being unable to leave the Hall. The Guild and the Great Ones had given them their blessings, yet it remained unexplained as to why these Masters were to instead congregate in an underground city. Even the landscape of possibilities was devoid of probable outcomes, as if the new Oneness offered no scenario into its imminent future – the Angels had reached an impasse, while the door that had let them in, was about to close behind them.

Ma-1's entourage was spending consistently more time in the Hall. Vac was heavily involved with Qwave and Portals, while simultaneously tutoring Olaf onwards to his further education as a Master. A group specialized in Warrior and realm history had been newly formed on a recommendation from the Goddess, who had convincingly explained that it would eventually become the core organism in dealing with the emerging Oneness. Another branch was built around the rise of Hektor, in the light of its goal of overtaking the new world. The Triad transferred copies of the entire Guild archives on the rogue organization into the database of the Le Lien subdivision servers, down in the basement. Master Qo'ai-Marael, previously of Guild History, was in charge of putting order into it. Current technology had smoothly been integrated into the now complex daily requirements of the assembly, but *basement* could only produce equipment based on the scant supplies trickling between the two worlds. Access to physical versions of the realms was vital to the gathering of raw materials, but Ma-1 had made it clear she wasn't willing to go at it alone, for fear of losing the sanctity of a life she chose to keep away from the capricious nature of drama. She was reminded by Vac that her world was expanding into myriad emerging galaxies, meaning that her preoccupation with privacy was at best proprietary in character. She simply answered that she would look into it when necessity knocked at the door.

While Vac, Olaf, and The Triad busied themselves with Angel affairs, Ma-1 took Saka to the side to ask her to follow her into George's hall.

"It's the one item I kept out of the story," she said, "The Gestalt recommended that you accompany me with the white stone that Amaterasu gifted you with. It also obliquely alluded to dimensional layers still in need of exploration."

"I understand George's version of the Great Hall is meant to represent a more accessible means of linking the realms, yet you seem to leave open the possibility that it may not exactly be the case. Are you having second thoughts about the truth of it?" Saka enquired.

"The halls of doors make a lot more sense from the standpoint of our reality, but the fundamental makeup is the same. It's just a different view of the same thing, one that subtracts the Angel element and its influence. Whatever else it may contain or omit, it's best to see for ourselves," Ma-1 replied.

The two Goddesses left the Great Hall, walking the distance up to Ma-1's sanctum, which, as it turned out, was also Saka's official place of birth.

———————

George's space was a series of four halls in a straight line, each counting thirty-three doors. They were separated by high columned archways, and lit by numerous oblong skylights positioned along the ridges of the vaulted ceilings. Their walls were sober; painted in soothing, two-toned pastel colors: sage blue and moon glow. As expected, the entrance into Ma-l's realm was open onto the first hall, whose end wall exposed a purely decorative gateway motif that possibly was left as a symbolic portal into a never-to-be-breached unknown. From there on, the two rows of grey doors lined up to the far end wall, which also displayed a faux entryway. Ma-l pointed to the symbols on each of the entrances.

"We didn't have a written language, but we drew our names in the dirt, mostly with arrangements of lines and curves – sometimes waves. You can see mine wasn't very complicated," she laughed.

Saka smiled at the bare simplicity of the sign, knowing it contained a story as old as the ex-Warrior's world. As she allowed herself to drift, she realized it was also the one world, which, much later, cocooned Linda Sue Klein's reality. The thought of her previous life in Northern California, as secretary for the office of Marshall Slaughter, summoned a sense of comforting warmth. She recalled those times with acute fondness, endless moments of deep-rooted affection for her ex-boss and their common friend, Geir Flemmingson; and how those relationships had led to her becoming a permanent resident of the realms. "What are the two rascals up to?" she wondered, for she missed them dearly...

———————————

The two rascals in questions, some six hundred and forty-seven years earlier, give or take a few decades due to some unpredictable fluctuations between the timelines – and in an entirely different universe – had partially driven along Route 802 after having delayed Jarred Gulliver for as long as they could. They had now stopped for breakfast on the side of *Stifluvatn*. The Angels had left Keyhole Lake through their portal, oblivious to the parked Jeep between their two relay points. In their wish to avert an unfortunate encounter with Joonas, they trusted the two friends had gone around *Tröllaskagi*. Yet, Geir and Marshall had stubbornly stuck to their plan of hiking to the remote lake; they would give Jarred enough time to do his business before they would in turn go around the hills that concealed Keyhole. After they ate, they re-parked their vehicle out of view from the main road, and then waited. It took a few hours before Gulliver drove by, on his way back to the Hektor portal. They had no idea whether he had found what he was looking for or not. They then rode to the end of *Stifluvatn*, tucked the Jeep out of sight, and walked in the direction of the hidden lake.

It was past noon when they finally reached the place. There was nothing remotely inspiring about it. The discharge waters from the glacial pool ran in a small creek, into the larger reservoir below. Its shore were green with moss and low vegetation that clung to life in proof that no conditions were ever harsh enough to keep what insisted on growing from reaching the light. Keyhole was roughly six hundred feet across and less than half a mile long, yet it looked massive in the context of finding anything that could be as small as a standard door, while lacking the methodology to locate it. But in what appeared to have been an auspicious moment in space, the two walked directly across the threshold of the invisible gate, seamlessly finding themselves in Amaterasu's hall.

The Great One stood before them, ever-so-stately in her grey kimono.

"It wasn't exactly easy to get you to come to this place, but I'm delighted you were able to find your way to it. My name is Amaterasu. I am the reason why you, Marshall, are presently on this island. It's a long story, but please bear with me. Let me first say that I am well versed into all that is Joonas and Hektor. One may say, in your terms, that I have been following that organization for a very long time. Much credit has been given to those who've been instrumental in helping the realms come into their own, though it hasn't escaped me that both of you have selflessly served, while having been denied full disclosure, along missing the closeness of your friends. I am a Great Goddess, technically above the icons of your once relevant religions; but unlike my kin, I'm very adept at controlling light and preventing physical beings, such as yourselves, from ending up critically hurt by the radiant forces of our energy fields. I am thus able to scale down my powers; a useful skill that stems from my time as a Master of the Guild. By comparison, your friend Olaf needed the protection of the Goddess Ma-1 when he was exposed to the Ones across the portal of the Warner Mountains, in the mother reality of the realms. But forgive me for extrapolating on the convolutions of these overlapping realities; don't try to comprehend it all, it will soak in quite naturally. I am of course aware that the combination of your work with Olaf and Saka, your latest involvement with members of Le Lien, and your exposure to Joonas's various incarnations, has kept you updated on the case of the realms. But I am unsure as to how much of it has made perfect sense to you; such data is customarily beyond the reach of most of your peers; although you seem to have weathered the worst of it."

Amaterasu took a short break and then resumed.

"Saka and I go back a long way, although she only became aware of my existence while working as Linda Sue Klein on the disappearance case of Olaf Swyndle. I witnessed her rise, from a small scintillating light, to a force that shook the foundations of her host's beliefs when she left the heart of the stone to take on multiple physical manifestations at various chosen points along your timeline. Linda Sue was the apex of the cumulative energies that encompassed her human experience; one that brought forth a longing for a return to the source of her birth, where most of her powers were awaiting her. A short time before the collapse of the mother reality, I briefly stopped by Ma-1's domain to conduct the ceremony of the group's graduation. It was then that the host became Great Goddess of her realm; Olaf, a young Master of the Guild; Vac, well, Vac didn't need graduation, for there isn't much above him; and Saka was ordained Goddess of Light. She is now the keeper of the white chalcedony stone of fluid knowledge – the twin to the black onyx one that never leaves me. Normally, these stones are made of layers – a streak of white for the black one, and vice versa – but these are rare single-toned gems. They were gifted to me by the all-encompassing Oneness, on the implicit condition that they should only be separated for the purpose of unifying distant energies. That's the reason why Saka and I will always be one, even when great chasms part our worlds. Their combined might is such, that they are capable of bringing forth the collision of entire universes; their power of attraction exponentially increases against the forces that aim at separating them; and above all, the flux of information between them can never be interrupted. Before we move onto the next part of this meeting, do you have any questions?"

"How did you persuade me to come to Iceland?" Slaughter asked, as if compelled to break the spell with anything that crossed his mind.

"You didn't need to be convinced as much as reminded that you were due for a break away from the hardship that was starting to loom over your adopted town. Plus, Joonas was about to discover the portal that originally belonged to your courtyard, so he needed to be sent away. I am afraid you are in no position to come loose from the grip of the Hektor founder, but it's not necessarily a bad thing. To answer your question, I visited your dreams, but you predictably forgot, as it appears to be customary with your species," Amaterasu replied with an understanding smile.

"Did Jarred Gulliver ever find what he was looking for?" Geir inquired.

"Joonas did come in. I retreated behind the veil of these halls, undetectable to him. His thoughts and emotions were collected as he unceremoniously entered and came out through many of the entryways that, in this very version, open on worlds of my design. He was apparently satisfied with what he saw, which was substantially more than what he had expected. This isn't just a Guild portal that had to be painfully configured and duplicated, but a direct access into the realms – my version of them. Joonas will be back with a faction of Hektor; if all works according to plan, the entire organization will migrate through these grey doors into what they will assume are the worlds of the Warriors. That's all you need to know in that regard for now, for there are other matters that concern the both of you, which are, I believe, of great importance to your hearts. Please follow me for a moment of quietude in this beautiful garden, while I prepare for a small ceremony," Amaterasu said, as she led her guests through Ma-l's door, into the copy of her realm.

The Great Goddess pulled out the black gemstone from the pouch she wore around her neck. She held it in her cupped hands where it stood on its long point, defying gravity. It began to spin, changing from black to grey, and then faster, as it turned fully white, expanding into the radiance of an aura circling Amaterasu's extended arms. The garden filled up with light. Geir and Marshall felt their bodies lift from the ground, as their minds quieted from the soothing effect of the luminescence. Then, all senses ceased to return information.

Ma-l and Saka had entered the marked door to their realm from inside George's hall. It led to the circular grassy area surrounded by the low stone partition, between the upper gardens and the chestnut grove that served as a rest stop on the many hikes back from the top of the valley. The two sat on one of the benches built into the wall.

"It feels peculiar to access the gardens from across that door," Saka said, gesturing towards where the entrance had just been.

"We now have created a new portal into George's hall, no need for the back cave anymore," Ma-l returned with manifest amusement. "This could be fun!"

At that very moment, Saka's stone emitted a soft drone. She took it out of its pouch, holding it in her cupped hands. It stood on its point and started to spin. The gem shifted from white to grey, then turned black as the radiance of the day swiftly twirled its ghostly shape towards the strengthening vortex. All went suddenly dark. When the light returned, they found themselves in the middle of the circle, facing Amaterasu, Marshall, and Geir. Before anyone could speak, Saka noticed she now held the black stone, while the white one rested in the Great One's hands. She focused on the two humans caught in the grips of utter astonishment – there, they stood impossibly present, yet her mind was unsure. Her hesitation was brief; she ran to them, caught between laughter and tears, to end up squeezed in the middle of a giant hug.

"How is this possible? I never imagined we had a chance at meeting again!"

Ma-l and Amaterasu looked at each other with the appreciative stance of mothers in deep approval of their offspring meeting for the first time – they opted to observe silently.

"Welcome to our realm!" the young Goddess expressed with excitement.

She pointed towards the vista that stretched beyond the gardens, past the main house, far to the end of the valley where its forest met with the ocean father than the eye could see. She wanted them to stay, so that she could show them the land, and in time, take them to the Great Hall of the Angels.

All wished Olaf and Vac had been joining them to share that extraordinary moment.

"We hope there'll be other such opportunities," Amaterasu eventually interfered. "But for now, we're only allowed a small glimpse into what was until recently considered undoable; that is, the crossing of the great distance that separates the two Onenesses, and the exploration of the forces that will, one day, bring them into a union. The power of the stones makes it feasible, but I regret our combined skills are at this time incapable of harnessing their energy into sustained visits – we're still quite a ways from being able to generate permanent portals between our two universes. You may hug and kiss once more before we part. I impress on my human friends that their experience is real, and that their memories will not play tricks on them – it's a promise. Ma-l and Saka, it's a pleasure to meet again."

In a reversed process, the two parties returned to their points of origin, while the stones reassumed their native tones.

Amaterasu led Marshall and Geir back into the halls, thanking them once again for their contribution.

"Consider it a token of appreciation for a work whose ripples have touched the far shores of worlds hardly imagined by your species. You know how to get back here; the portal will be open when it is safe for you to cross. By then, Saka and I will have honed some of our skills in summoning the power of the stones – be well!"

Keyhole Lake stretched before them – it was time to get back to Akureyri and for Marshall to prepare for his return flight to California. They contacted Liv and Spencer via the laptop to explain what had happened.

"Most stunning!" Spencer said, "We count on a solid update upon your arrival. We're back in Fieldbrook, waiting for you. Enjoy your last day of vacation!"

The next morning, Geir and Marshall flew the Cessna back to Reykjavík for one last night together in Iceland. Fine cognac was poured in large snifters – a toast was raised in honor of dear friends in faraway lands.

8 – GULLIVER'S END

Joonas briefly returned to Strata headquarters, only to be served with the news of the disappearance of Gerald Brinsk. The elder was beyond himself, swearing to retaliate against what he considered to be an inadmissible affront to his person. He had remained in character as Jarred Gulliver, but his rage distorted the usually mild-mannered and endearingly eccentric traits of the English scholar to caricaturesque proportions. At that precise moment, the guise and the mood clashed in particularly vivid fashion.

"Who do you suspect did it?" he asked one of the senior members by the name of Vexter.

"It's somewhat embarrassing, but we're not even in a position to suspect anyone, since we were unable to detect the smallest trace of intrusion. He might as well just have walked out of here as if he'd been one of us," the elder replied.

"So, this is how we keep this institution protected? Since when do Guild defectors go in and out whenever they please?! Who was in charge of the Dogs at the time?" Joonas questioned – fuming.

"I'm sorry to say it was Dahbar, but you locked him up before his replacement was picked – by then it was too late. The Dogs were utterly disoriented without their usual compass – they didn't even notice the disappearance until days later, according to the lab team," Vexter answered.

"How convenient an excuse! Demote the entire tech crew for failing to report the absence in a timely manner, and get me the Tömör files on Brinsk and Hunter, will you!?" Joonas ordered. "Before you leave, arrange for an emergency meeting with the senior team; we must prepare for the execution of the plan – and I mean, the entire team, including Dahbar!"

Tömör's files were on Joonas's desk within minutes of the request. The elder knew there was a connection – it didn't take long for it to jump off the pages.

"Ah so, the two rescues were trained by the same Angel…" he thought aloud.

Joonas knew of the Guild's superior technology, so at a time of weakness within Hektor, it did not take much investigative acumen to connect the dots. It was the work of the Angels, and they had just given their game away – he had been set-up with the Eye. He was now convinced the visit into the cyber city, as well as the whole mapping of the portals into the realms, were constructs aimed at stealing time away from him. The realization came as a broad stroke of irony; on one hand, he was victorious in defeating the plot, on the other, the Angels had indeed wasted his time. The discovery highlighted the fact they had enjoyed a head start on all of his moves from the get-go. And so, to what extent did they anticipate his desire to infiltrate the network for the purpose of stealing the maps and blueprints?

He knew he had been played by Slaughter, who most certainly had help from the Guild, but he was unclear as to how it carried over from the Cruz persona into his real identity. At any rate, it was evident the Angels had kept tabs on him; his days and those of Hektor in the original Oneness were counted – it was a matter of time before the combined snares of the Great Ones and the Guild would converge on the organization. If Leòn and his two students were hiding in the realms, all the better to get to them as soon as feasible –

he would take care of Slaughter and Flemmingson on his way out, lock them in with the vermin, and deal with them at his leisure.

Not all senior members attended the emergency meeting. Joonas took note to make sure they would be arrested and hauled by force into the new worlds. Those present agreed, some wholeheartedly, others reluctantly, to the immediate move. Numerous portals were to be installed at Keyhole Lake, where league members from all over the galaxies would transfer through what would come to be sardonically known as *the forgotten access to the realms of the Warriors*. Dogs and bottom-ranking pawns would be bulk-carted as soon as organizers were done setting up hubs linked to their receiving platforms in each of the pocket realities. Joonas saw the Warriors as deities-in-title that would easily be subjugated or bribed. They would remain rulers-in-principle, on the premise their symbolic roles in the stewardship of their respective domains would keep the realms together as a whole.

It didn't escape the founder that with the level of Guild involvement circling his intentions, there most likely was foul play ahead. But it was no time to dwell on the technicalities of a subterfuge; he would adjust as he went. The realms were no program inside a computer, where down-scaling consciousness was required in order to access a mock reality. With over a hundred universes opening onto their unique infinities, each offering equally unique opportunities, there was no way an illusion of that magnitude was in the spectrum of feasibility. As far as Joonas saw it, these worlds all were in need of a ruler.

The strategy of overtaking the realms came down to simple math: Hektor numbered in the millions, while the Angels amounted to a few thousand volunteers; all in a reality where the equivalent of the Great Ones were ex-human Warriors with the wits of newts – it was the real deal and he wanted it. The Angels would be overwhelmed and sent back to the Guild, or used as bargaining chips – he then would rule over the entire Oneness until he became indistinguishable from it.

Naturally, Joonas wasn't aware that Le Lien had the equivalent of a wire tag on him – one with the sophistication to broadcast his thoughts and emotions with uncanny clarity to a fractal of his consciousness lodged within a Qwave program. The Great Ones were informed of the timing of the planned exodus. Amaterasu completely immersed herself in refining the imaging of the realm duplicates, hoping to be done before the imminent migration. The project was so titanic in breadth, that it demanded of the Great Goddess of Light full harnessing of her resources as a creator, and that the sum of her creations add up to a level of realism capable of enthralling the most vehement of disbelievers. She knew that the failure to convince Joonas would lead to dire consequences for the real realms, as the halls she had erected were identical to those gifted to Ma-1 by Great Gestalt George. On the other hand, there was no other option to prevent a critical invasion of the Goddess' domain; the only one with the vulnerability of an unprotected access. The closure of her world would prevent new Angels from reaching the Great Hall. Regrettably no distinct futures were foreseen without a complete congregation of Masters – Hektor was no substitute.

Amaterasu ascertained that all the doors into the mock realities, including Ma-l's, would be closed at the onset of the Dark Angels' exodus – just as they were when Joonas first visited the halls. The stone connection would no longer be made into the courtyard above the Goddess' gardens, as the copy would soon be overtaken by one of Hektor's rulers. But Amaterasu's creation was far from being a single-ended reality; the simulated Warrior's worlds were only one of many inlays patterned into the complex weave of its makeup.

The first Hektor contingent arrived within a week of the meeting. It was mostly composed of senior members primarily interested in checking their future habitat. They opened doors and poked around the fringes of a few realms, like prospective buyers checking real estate. There was nothing remotely invasive about them, but they were pivotal in validating Joonas's discovery and abiding by the final clauses of his master plan. With them in the fold, it guaranteed the founder's control of Hektor, subsequently firming his rule over the entire realm system. In return, they were each to be granted governorship of the world of their choice, with sovereignty over the lower castes appointed to them.

The primary reward was power – there had never been enough of it with the Guild and the Great Ones limiting Hektor's movement. In the realms, it was inexhaustible – infinite.

While the group's elite waded in platitudes among themselves, Joonas randomly picked a domain for an exploratory excursion with a team of Dogs. The place resembled Earth in many respects, but felt more like something remembered than the result of a chronological development, inasmuch that the elements of its evolution seemed fitted, as opposed to flowed into each other. It didn't bother the elder, for he assumed these physical worlds were the end product of the simple dreamwork of unsophisticated individuals. They were also virgin, which added to the element of desirability in his mind. The main goal of the inspection was to assess the authenticity of the domains. It was inconsequential how great Guild technology was, there was no way the Angels could fool him with a simulation. The sheer scope of the realm network was far beyond the reach of the Masters; it would have to be the brainchild of a major creator to lose him on the fine details, but at that level, it would no longer matter, since a creation of that magnitude would qualify as the real thing.

He was after specific signs of weakness: a thin haze in the tones, an aspect of pixelation in the focus of the image, a particular softness below his footing... He picked up two rocks, asking one of the Dogs to slam them against each other so that he could observe the way they shattered. In spite of his low regard for the Warriors, he recognized they had been granted deity status, with the ability to coalesce light and electromagnetism into matter; their worlds would thus carry the signature of their skills. The splash of water against boulders, the rustle of leaves kissed by the breeze, the sharp clacking of stones hitting each other – all had a unique pitch that could not be faked by even the best of Guild technology. He demanded of his Dogs that they eat the wild berries, catch rodents to spill and taste their blood... He listened to the songs of birds, counted the echoes that bounced across the valley – all had to meet the distinct parameters of the creation within which he was positioned, in the ambient present that embodied the precise time point of his experience. A simulation couldn't fool the senses born of the real thing. The physical self knew of its source; therefore any deviation on the theme would sound the alarm.

Joonas reentered the halls in one of the best moods he had been in a long time. The road of hardship had reached its end – Hektor was ready to make its move. The senior members unanimously approved. The rest of the league was to follow over the course of the next two months. Tömör, besides having handed over the list of students, had also leaked the lifespan of the mother reality's ghost image – the takeover could not have been better timed. The portal was secured, meaning it could no longer be deactivated by the Guild, as it was now annexed to the Hektor system, and thus fully under its control.

Amaterasu was pleased with herself. Her role was now to observe and make the necessary minute adjustments that would preserve the illusion of natural evolution within these realms. Most of it was set in motion to operate on its own, but it was a dance better executed with the choreographer in the room.

———————

Liv and Spencer, at the helm of team Le Lien, had systematically recorded every one of Joonas's moves, as well as the progress made by Hektor in the execution of his plan. They had fine-tuned the probe to the point of actually hearing him talk, while being able to analyze patterns between his thinking process and various levels of emotional activity. They also uncovered he was going to ambush Slaughter and Flemmingson before his exit, and then later, hunt for Leòn, Pau, and Gerald Brinsk while in the realms. Some of the spikes showed the threshold of sanity had been crossed; he was officially deemed critically dangerous to his preys. His aim was to bring ruin upon them – no holds barred.

The Eureka Hektor scanners had ceased to operate. Fewer Dogs were seen walking the streets of the city. Le Lien judged the portal fit to remain under the Snug Alley gazebo, as they didn't see a reason to relocate it. Angels steadily flowed through it, bringing the Great Hall to half capacity.

Marshall Slaughter resumed with his practice. And though he lacked the stamina to fully immerse himself in the routine, he just couldn't afford to abandon his paying clientele. He spent increasingly longer stretches of time working with Liv and Spencer out of his house, monitoring Joonas's inner workings in anticipation of foul play. The fact the elder had stayed in character indicated Jarred Gulliver was due to visit imminently. Like clockwork, he called from Berkeley announcing he was on his way to Humboldt State, wishing to connect about the matters he had previously alluded to.

The next day, the classic Jaguar pulled into the graveled driveway and parked outside the kiwi arbor surrounding the cobblestone courtyard. Slaughter waited on the deck for the visitor. Jarred Gulliver, dressed in his customary tweeds and signature gloves, approached the stairs in his usual easy stride.

"So, old chap, here we meet again!" he voiced with acute enthusiasm.

"I didn't think I would see you so soon; it seems we were at *Tröllaskagi* only yesterday. How did your hike go, uncover any mysteries?" the detective inquired in a playful tone, as the men loosely shook hands.

239

"It went well enough, though I'm not so sure why I wanted to explore that area; it just seemed so enigmatic at the time. It turned out it was a boring place, with absolutely nothing of interest," Gulliver returned.

"I understand, unless you're into lichens or ghost stories, the region holds little appeal; although its coast is quite spectacular," Slaughter added.

"I take it you mean, to the fullest extent," the professor agreed. "I came around early from the opposite end to the spectacle of a glorious midnight sun."

Slaughter refrained from allowing his thoughts to dwell on Gulliver's blatant lie, for fear of raising flags at the man's intuitive end. Over the months, he and Geir had trained with Liv and Spencer on how to dissociate from both emotional and intellectual processes in order to maintain full neutrality and effectively shield the self from intrusive probing – yet it had to appear as if the mind was still vulnerable to it.

"Please come in, unless you fancy having a drink on the porch," the detective offered.

"Actually, I wouldn't mind some fresh air; it's too beautiful a day to be inside. Has your lovely house sitter moved out yet?" Gulliver enquired, as Slaughter aimed for the kitchen.

The host returned with glasses and two bottles of local organic IPA. He picked up where they had left.

"She's still around going over her things, but she should be gone in the next couple of days. She's staying on the upper floor for now," Slaughter returned.

"Well, Marshall, I don't want to take your time away from more important things, but I'm here with a proposition: what would you say to the idea of going into business together? I have a fascination for your line of

240

work regarding the occult, I'm practically retired from my job, and I have a small capital that begs to be put to good use. You don't have to say yes quite yet, but I would be disappointed if you passed on the offer."

Slaughter silently processed the implications of Gulliver's proposal. "So, this is what Amaterasu meant when she said it wasn't going to be easy to shake Joonas off?" he thought, before vigilantly returning to the conversation.

"I get it, you're not referring to my regular, boring investigational work, but to my other business of sifting through graveyard data, and deciphering the mumbo jumbo of séances, am I right?" Slaughter asked.

"Correct, mate, I'm after fringe realities, the stuff that most people refuse to admit is around, as they compartmentalize their lives into sanitized cubicles. I want to walk the lesser-traveled lanes, the alleys frequented by the forgotten side of society, flirt with conspiracies, open the mysterious Pandora's Box that is the human soul... Plus, I know there is an untapped demand for that sort of work – it's a simple matter of relaxing the minds of those who've been asking the questions no-one wants to hear," Gulliver replied.

"You make it sound more compelling than it actually is; this is no Sherlock Holmes parlor mannerism, Jarred; it can be absolutely gruesome at times – nut cases et al," Marshall returned.

"It's because you work alone. Think about it, but please, don't make me linger," the professor begged.

"The offer is appealing – I will let you know shortly," Slaughter finished.

They drank their ales as they reminisced about the couple of days they had shared in Iceland. Geir came into

241

the conversation briefly when Gulliver asked about his plans, but it appeared the Englishman was more interested in the mundane details of life in Humboldt, or places to visit. It was clear that the partnership offer was the main point of the man's visit – he had opted to not dilute it with unrelated topics heavy on intellectual resources. He got up, put his shades back on and turned to Slaughter,

"Well, it's time to get to work. Don't sit on it for too long – until then, my friend!"

They didn't shake hands. Gulliver walked back to the Jag, this time, in a hurried pace. He drove away, followed by dust and the crunch of gravel.

"What was that all about?" Slaughter asked Liv, as she came down the stairs.

They connected with Spencer, who was back at Le Lien headquarters.

"It's obvious his offer is meant to put you in a position of vulnerability when you least expect it. He counts on the element of surprise to bring his revenge to a crest. Although, we can't know for sure, the data from the probe points in the direction of a Machiavellian subplot to his exit from his present guise. We expect he will write a similar script for Geir, or find a way to include him in yours. We don't have long before he makes his move, so utmost vigilance at all times is essential – consider yourself under a state of alert," Spencer warned.

Liv cut in before Slaughter could respond.

"In spite of his nonchalance, the Gulliver persona is under stress, exhibiting stigmas of deep emotional instabilities. Unlike Angels, who inhabit their characters from birth until death, in line with the biological, spiritual, and cultural guidelines of their chosen environments; in other words, assuming real lives, Hektor members hijack their guises without as much as a thought towards the mess they will inevitably leave behind. The reason why Jarred Gulliver is so different from Alexander Cruz is because neither of them were Joonas to start with. It's also the reason why you find the man personable, for the professor is indeed quite the gentleman. From the standpoint of the Guild, it has come to a sad state of affair; thus, it is why we believe Hektor must be either eradicated or sent to a place whence they can't return."

"I'm sorry for Jarred; this whole thing is fucked-up – and now the deal with the partnership... What do I say to him when I don't want anything to do with it?" Slaughter asked, somewhat under duress.

"You must accept; there are no other options. We'll provide protection to the best of our abilities," Spencer answered. "When we know that he's ready to strike, he won't be allowed to act on his wishes. We will rescue the professor as well, which may prove to be extremely complicated, under reasons you could not possibly comprehend at this time. But enough said!"

"I will inform Geir at once," Liv offered.

"So, what do you think Joonas intends on doing with us? Push us under a bus?" Slaughter asked somewhat exasperated.

"That would hardly be his favorite method of punishment," Liv answered. "We believe he will go for something somewhat viler, such as ruining your minds as he has so successfully done with the Guild students, and have you dragged into the bottom-dwelling castes of

Hektor, where you can exist as token reminders of his might over what he despises most: the human race."

"And how does he plan on doing that?"

"He has already started by aiming at confusing you, but your shields are holding. As long as he can't penetrate them, though you are leading him to believe he has, you're ahead of his game, hence in no foreseeable danger. But when he realizes that you're not willing to follow him into Amaterasu's realms, it's likely he'll have you taken by force by his Dogs, probably under an official arrest backed by an obscure warrant. But remember, time is not on his side; Hektor knows that they have a total of two months before the image of the mother reality becomes too weak to support the bridge. It doesn't matter if that detail is of no concern to the group's exodus, as long as they believe it is. Joonas has a lot on his plate, so if you manage to evade his methods, he won't be able to touch you. If for any reason, you and Geir end up being taken in the fake realms, there are ways to get you out, but it may blow the cover on the simulation and endanger the Warriors; so, focus is paramount! But I rest assured you already hold it dear in your hearts that the conflict must not extend to your friends Olaf and Saka," Liv responded.

"Since Geir is in Iceland where the portal is located, he's more vulnerable than you are – we must bring him back here immediately. Together, you will erect a stronger front to Joonas's hunger for retaliation," Spencer added.

"There's another factor that will work in your favor, in that, at this very moment, the Angels are pushing on with their campaign to rescue all Guild students. It's certain to disrupt the flow of Hektor's migration and make the organization less prone to dwell on details. It doesn't guarantee Joonas will forget you, but there's a chance the distraction will make him sloppy," Liv stated.

"You said you'll know when he's ready to strike, but how would I?" Slaughter inquired.

"There is a threshold to the execution of any plan that is preceded by its ghost image. Memory doesn't just belong to the aftermath of an event, it's encompassing of the event itself, in the way that it also radiates in the form of augury, a foretoken of what is about to happen. That being said, the Jarred Gulliver persona will be prone to betray the elder's critical move with signs acutely contradicting his normal mannerism; call them distortions in personality, if you wish – something Joonas could easily conceal in a better suit – but there is a price to be paid for the forced possession of identities: they fight back by imposing latencies on the way the unwanted hijacker controls his host. In a nutshell, Gulliver will try to warn you," Spencer explained.

"OK, I don't mean to be obtuse about this, but as far as I know, a psychological ambush isn't in the same league as a physical threat; the body reacts to danger with far greater speed than the intellect does to tricky wordsmanship, am I wrong? How do you predict when a particular arrangement of syllables is about to hit you full on? How is Jarred Gulliver going to warn me of something he may never see himself?" Slaughter asked with visible tension.

"I'm not saying it's something you can see or touch, or anticipate in the shape of coherent information. The human intellect is indeed afflicted with slow processing abilities, but the observer in you is not, for he embraces the power of vision of the intuitive – that part of you exists outside of time. So, in regard to the core of your question, the difference between physical and psychological is negligible. Do you follow?" Spencer returned.

"Very well, it's starting to make sense. Forgive me if I'm being thrown a bit off kilter by this rollercoaster of a deal. Who'd have thought the Swyndle case would have taken such a turn? I'd have imagined we'd be in the clear by now," Slaughter sighed.

"We don't need to remind you that your physical existence is yours to create, and that it was by choice that you became instrumental to the emergence of the realms, as all of us involved did. The minute you took the Olaf Swyndle job, you also entered into an agreement with yourself to pursue the course that would lead to your present reality. Had you turned it down, you and Linda Sue Klein would still presently be immersed in the routine of filing papers with the county clerk, Olaf would not have been able – and I mean that with particular emphasis – to cross into the mother universe; and upon collapsing, the latter would have taken the realms with it, while no-one, besides Amaterasu and a few Angels, would have noticed. Notwithstanding that you would currently be heading towards the extinction of your race, alongside a plethora of catastrophic shifts in the evolution of your planet, followed by the resulting aforementioned collapse. Does this clarify the nature of your present reality?" Liv added with unusual firmness.

"Thanks for bringing perspective into these matters, I hope you understand what it takes to be human," the investigator heard himself say.

"As much as we fail at it, we try," the Angel returned in a somewhat softer tone.

As Spencer left the conversation to return to Le Lien business, Geir called to inform Marshall he had been able to book a flight, but to please pick him up at SFO if he could, since there were no connections with Humboldt at his time of arrival. Slaughter agreed, relieved to have an excuse to get away from town and to not have to deal with Gulliver's offer.

When the Englishman enquired about the proposal, the detective was well on his way to the Bay Area, with a legitimate excuse behind postponing negotiations. He made no mention of Flemmingson. The professor was audibly disappointed; he regretted that Slaughter had not emphasized the importance of his offer, but he was willing to wait, confident the investigator could not realistically pass on it.

Geir and Marshall purposely leisured along the three hundred mile return trip from San Francisco airport. They stayed at bed and breakfasts; visited wineries and distilleries in Napa, Sonoma, and Mendocino; partook in the obligatory tasting, loading in the process the back of the SUV with freshly acquired assortments of the divine libations. There was no logical reason to not enjoy the life before having to smell the brimstone of Hektor.

When they returned to the Fieldbrook estate three days later, Liv and Spencer received them with the news that a police investigator had been enquiring about Slaughter's whereabouts, and that he was needed for a brief testimony on an old case that supposedly required clarification.

"I guess Gulliver's patience is running out, or should I say, Joonas is no longer willing to wait. I'd better call about that deal before he sends in the army," Marshall disdainfully said.

"A pleasure to see my favorite Angels in person once again!" Flemmingson warmly exclaimed, wrapping the Le Lien agents in a bear hug.

When Joonas's Dogs got to Geir Flemmingson's house in Reykjavík, they were met with the reality of his recent departure. The elder was also thrown off balance by the latest onslaught of rescue missions, which Hektor was incapable of containing. Short of a better solution, Guild defectors were temporarily excluded from the migration as to avoid utter disruption. He had been slow getting to the Icelandic philosopher; now it was obvious he was back in California with Slaughter to form an alliance that doubled up against his plans. Somehow, he was never able to set things right with those two, on top of which his guise's resistance was becoming a hindrance to his movements and the precision of his thinking. Perhaps, it was time to get rid of the old English suit and resume with the more appropriate, if ephemeral, all-purpose physical imaging of his Dark Master persona – an imposing presence cloaked in grey and black, that instilled a mixture of fear and respect in panic-prone humans. But there was still one more task: he wanted Jarred Gulliver to persuade Slaughter of agreeing to the deal. Joonas saw incommensurable, symbolic value to that partnership, as if it settled an old score the classic way. He wanted to defeat his nemesis at the human level, by downgrading him to below his physical value. Then, he could drag him into Hektor hell. By constraining the most unwilling of hosts to wage battle against an ally, it was his way of killing two birds with one stone, while indisputably sealing his supremacy over the species. At the close of the psychological dogfight, he would drop the guise, leaving the wretches to writhe in agony in the wasted discharge of their souls.

Slaughter and Gulliver arranged to meet over the details of the partnership. The detective had only agreed in principal, but how did it matter one way or the other, if the deal was to only be short-lived? It had become one of those inevitable details with inconsequential results that plagued the human experience; he might as well be done with it! Gulliver suggested that they meet with a prospective client and take it from there. Slaughter couldn't see the harm in it. So, the two scheduled an appointment with an old gentleman who claimed the upstairs section of his late nineteenth century Victorian house was at the center of some unusual activities.

They convened that afternoon. The client explained that he had been awakened every night for over a month, at precisely two o'clock, by the sound of steps and rummage on the upper floors. He took the men up the old wainscoted redwood stairway to the third story, where he believed the noises had originated.

Slaughter had not expected it would come so soon, but he suddenly felt he had once been there. He recalled hearing Gulliver say something before his head was abruptly sent into a spin. He felt his entire psyche being violently poisoned, to the effect that he likened his brain's chemical mass to the contents of a conical flask on a Bunsen burner.

When he came to his senses, he and Jarred Gulliver were lying on the floor. Spencer was bent over the Englishman's body.

"Don't get up quite yet, Marshall, you'll be fine if you let things settle for a minute," he said. "Liv's in there trying to keep Gulliver's vitals going until he returns to his body," he added.

"I don't feel so fine," Slaughter returned.

"Joonas almost cracked you open like a nut, but I was nearby to absorb most of the impact; you'll feel shaken for a day or two, but you'll be OK. We knew he was going to strike from the heightened readings from the probe; he's very much in a hurry. When he left Gulliver's body, he did so with such drag force that it pulled the vital spiritual energy out of it. Liv jumped in to keep it alive, while we now wait for the spirit to return. We also knew the professor didn't want to go – it's why Liv is preventing him from dying. His psyche was also critically assaulted, but again, she saw that the shock would be sufficiently cushioned. We expect he will recover, though it might take him a lot longer than you," Spencer explained.

"What happened to the client?" Slaughter asked.

"Oh, just a Hektor Dog; he simply walked out. He had no idea we were here though. For your information, the rightful owners are away for the day – it was a standard set-up."

"Pretty crude for mighty Joonas," the detective remarked.

"Many of Hektor's methods are crude, Marshall, but that doesn't make them less effective. He wanted you to wake up in a state of utter confusion near Gulliver's dead body, whose spirit was to live in the perpetual illusion that he was still alive, while not comprehending why he felt that he wasn't. As to you, he hopes you are wasted enough to wish to seek him and join Hektor. He'll check on you in the next few days, but we don't think he'll bother with a cover-up – he'll just show up as his imposing and clichéd self," the Angel further clarified.

"So what about Geir?" the befuddled detective enquired.

"Not to worry; he is in the company of two female team members who wished to meet him – you two are rock stars at Le Lien," Spencer laughed.

Liv appeared next to Spencer.

"He's back in body," she said, "we must help him down the stairs; I don't expect he'll be out of his stupor for a while. Marshall, can you walk?"

Slaughter got up and felt relatively stable. He held to the railing on his way down the staircase, as the two Angels cautiously carried Gulliver one step at a time. The unfortunate victims were loosely propped in the back of the Jaguar. Liv took the wheel, while Spencer kept an eye on the professor.

Back at the estate, Geir and his two guardians, agents Lillian and Vera, were cooking up a storm. The smell of roasted garlic laid magic on Slaughter's confusion; the detective was suddenly overtaken by a massive craving for Italian food.

"That was a fast recovery," Liv humored.

Geir quickly checked on his friend then hastened back to the kitchen upon confirming his status.

"Ladies, let's hurry feeding these hungry people!" he declared.

Gulliver was taken to the spare bedroom adjacent to Slaughter's, where he slept uninterrupted for a solid twenty four hours. When he woke up, he felt dizzy but responded coherently; that was all that mattered to the Angels – he had made it.

Geir reluctantly let go of Lillian and Vera, who had to return to their posts at Le Lien. The bubbly pair was a refreshing departure from the otherwise serious demeanor displayed by Liv and Spencer – the philosopher teasingly complemented the team on its good tastes in recruits.

"I have hopes for you guys," he said with a wink.

———————

The cheerfulness of that moment was to quickly dissipate under the weight of foreseeable events. Joonas would return to get Slaughter, while Geir was in distinct, yet unnamed danger. There was no way for the Angels to hide them in the realms, while guaranteeing they would ever see their world again; plus, Joonas's trace on them was too strong for the security of the Snug Alley portal.

At Le Lien's end, there was the looming possibility of Amaterasu's masterwork revealing its true secret, handing the codes of its makeup over to Joonas, who in turn would utilize the simulation as a fully functional mega-portal into the Great Hall, on his way to unlock the gates to the Warriors' domains. In a matter of days, the Angels would be rounded up, and either returned to the Guild or worse, absorbed by the rogue organization.

But Amaterasu's creation held, as thousands upon thousands moved on to establish sprawling encampments in many of its more popular pocket realities. A few among the most adventurous went on to build colonies on the distant star systems of some of the more complex realms. In spite of the migration's resounding success, the relentless sorties by Angel commandos to rescue their students were a blow to Hektor. But that fact alone wasn't enough of a distraction for Joonas to not ask himself one twin set of fundamental questions: where were the Warriors, and where did the Guild volunteers, already in place in the realms, hole up? Of course, as he had already theorized, the worlds themselves could well be the *Warriors manifested*, while the Angels would be scattered across these realities in too small numbers to be unearthed. Nonetheless, the founder felt unsettled by the lack of opposition to the invasion. The one consoling theory to his suspicions was that the Guild was perhaps too glad to see Hektor gone from the face of the original universe, even if it meant losing what it had tried to preserve. But Joonas wasn't completely finished with the Guild's precious Oneness. With the realms successfully overtaken, Earth's dominant reality would revert to its previously foreseen evolutionary process, and humanity, as well as secondary species, would collapse under the weight of irreversible errors, at which point the Angels would find themselves out of work in innumerable probabilities. The Guild would be met with the humiliating truth of its redundancy, where promises of infinite possibilities once stood.

At least, that was the way Joonas saw a certain palette of futures from the scope of a self-serving forecast, which was not necessarily what the Guild, the Great Ones, and the two Onenesses had in mind.

In the meantime, Le Lien had intercepted the Hektor founder's doubts, which were relayed to Amaterasu via the Ones. An Angel presence was required, or Joonas would soon call it foul play. The Triad was contacted and volunteers from the Great Hall agreed to help. A group of one hundred Masters was formed. It was small, but largely sufficient to appease Joonas. With the help of Saka, at a time when Hektor traffic had stopped and the invaders were tucked in their chosen realities, Amaterasu summoned the stones and moved the group into one of the lesser used realms – one of little appeal due to its still embryonic evolutionary curve. A few days later, the coalition was discovered by Dogs and rounded up. Joonas confronted the group, questioned some of its members, but either out of ancient respect for Masters or growing lassitude, he opted to return them to the Guild. Within a day, and with the help of the Snug Alley portal, they were back in the Great Hall of the realms. From that point on, Angels were found in many of Amaterasu's domains then freed. Joonas was not interested in starting an outright conflict with the Guild, which would most certainly stifle his hopes of ever controlling the Warriors' realities. The arrest and release of Angels became mere formalities that were regarded as necessary aspects of protocol. Honor had to be preserved as part of the code of ethics for all wars deserving of the name, including cold ones, as it was the case between the Guild and Hektor. That thought soothed the founder's mind, as he felt a sense of nobility rise from within his core. After all, what he sought above all was respect, and he wasn't about to question the fine points of its provenance, real or unreal.

Before the probe had sensed that Joonas was ready to get back to business with Marshall and Geir, Liv and Spencer, who had marveled at the story of the friends meeting with Ma-1 and Saka in George and Amaterasu's halls, reminded the two that they had an open invitation to revisit their experience, providing the crossing was safe. What better place to hide than right under the nose of the enemy; surely, the Great Goddess could accommodate a couple of guests? Gulliver, who had been transferred to the office apartment in Eureka, was steadily recovering under Liv's good care; Joonas no longer had any reason to be looking for him. If Marshall and Geir disappeared, the elder would assume they were hiding in the realms where he would eventually find them. And so, with the help of The Triad, Amaterasu was informed of the plan. The friends flew back to Iceland and crossed the Keyhole Lake portal under the cover of a Hektor system glitch orchestrated by the Guild. As it turned out, the halls concealed many levels undetectable by those in transit; micro universes that existed on frequencies alien to the realms, and only accessible via encrypted "soft zones" in the space/time fabric of their walls. Slaughter and Flemmingson were made to feel at home, in an environment that conveniently mimicked the comfort of the Fieldbrook house. They were also able to stay in communication with Liv and Spencer via their Qwave laptops. To their delight, their favorite cognac and snifters were included in the elaborate reproduction of their habitual décor; plus, given time and circumstances, their chances of reconnecting with Saka, Olaf, and Vac were about to increase exponentially.

Joonas didn't have to ring the bronze bell hanging by the front entrance to be given confirmation Slaughter and Flemmingson had left Fieldbrook. He stood on the deck, tall and imposing, wearing black slacks and a grey shirt; his hair was tied in a ponytail, and he kept his salt and pepper beard meticulously trimmed. It was his go-to guise when on short assignments; a form free of the encumberment of host-related issues. Within it, his senses and skills were at their sharpest, but he could only sustain it for the limited period of a few hours. It was all too clear the philosopher and the detective had gotten help from the Guild and had fled to the realms. He flashed on the image of Liv, as she opened the door before the Iceland trip. "So, she was one of them," he heard himself think. Those were also the very words the probe reported to Le Lien. She had been uncovered, hence could no longer serve as an open operative. Joonas finally rang the bell. Spencer came to the door to greet the visitor.

"You're obviously not the postman," the Angel humored.

"Indeed, I'm an old friend of Marshall's from City Hall; I just happened to be in the neighborhood. By the look of it, I gather he's not around," Joonas said.

"Correct, my roommates and I are renting the house for the summer. The owner said he was traveling to various places, but he didn't elaborate – he just left us a number where he said he could be reached," Spencer returned.

"Yes, I have it too," Joonas said. "Would you by any chance know where his previous house sitter is presently staying?"

"We never had the pleasure to interact; she stopped by briefly to pick some of her things. I believe she is traveling as well," the Angel replied.

"And would that be with him?"

"I doubt it; they didn't appear to have much of a relationship besides the house-sitting arrangement; but I could be wrong," Spencer returned.

Joonas probed the man for traces of Guild training, but found none. Spencer was one of Le Lien's expert members, a highly skilled Master with unmatched abilities at concealing and overlapping identities. The Hektor founder would get absolutely nothing out of him, except for what he was being fed. For now, Liv was out of the picture, while Marshall and Geir were on the run.

"Last I saw Marshall, he wasn't feeling so well – why I swung by. How was he when he handed you the keys?" Joonas investigated.

"I would agree he appeared disoriented and somewhat incoherent, but his Scandinavian friend was here to help. I think he might have been somewhat drunk at the time," Spencer lied.

"Well, yes of course, there is that. Thank you for your time. Enjoy your stay in Fieldbrook, it's a special place," Joonas said, as he turned around and left.

It wasn't until he had settled into a half-deserted Strata compound that the Hektor founder came to fully understand the implications of the presence of the female Angel at Slaughter's house prior to the Iceland trip – the plausibility of the organization having reached the real realms could no longer be substantiated.

9 – XARN

Ma-1, Saka, Olaf, and Vac entered George's halls. Since they had established on their previous visit that entries into the unrealized realms had been omitted, a quick verification assessed that, indeed, the grey doors could only accessed vibrant realities. A few tries at reaching these active worlds had only yielded results consistent with what was happening with the tunnels out of the Great Hall of the Angels: loops in various random configurations. The realms were closed. The two sides that could open them, namely the Warriors and George, were in no disposition, or lacked the willingness to do so. Ma-1 wanted to send a message across at least one of the portals, to let the Deity on the other side know that a desire for communication had been expressed. But the idea proved just as futile as the crossing itself. Recalling the dream lanes of the past provided no additional information in regard to bringing these worlds out of their stubborn silence. There had to be something else besides the series of halls and their doors. What about the faux end-wall gateways; what was their purpose aside from reminding the visitor that the builders had a change of mind? If so, what kind of vision did the architects have that later had to be left out of the design? Those were the questions Ma-1 asked herself and alternately posed to the group. The Goddess sensed something missing in the fundamental layout of the place; it was basically a hub with the single purpose of joining the worlds from a common point. As such, it was devoid of consciousness; merely a neutral zone defined by the wish of hypothetical travelers to cross from one place to another. But in essence, it was also a meeting ground, like the leas of the dream gatherings, theoretically capable of containing trace elements of the Warriors' collective spirit. Ma-1 imagined revisiting the time of the meadows when less and less participants chose to come, until finally, the lanes ceased to operate. George was right; the Warriors opted to end the collective dreams to focus on their individual realities, disabling in the process the throughways to the common grounds – they no longer wished to share a vision.

So, why did Ma-1 seek to connect? Surely, she couldn't have been the only one interested in knowing what was going on with her kin. She kept on falling back on the notion first explored with George – that the realms simply weren't ready. The Goddess wasn't fully convinced it was the case – how unready were they? Then there was the threat of Hektor that required a coalition to resist it in the event of an invasion; yet these Warriors were locked in the safety of their worlds, leaving a couple of Goddesses and a handful of Angels to push back the hordes of assailants? It made little sense in respect to the Warrior spirit; she knew these Gods and Goddesses would rise as one to combat Joonas and his followers. No, there was something else that hid in between what lay on the other side of these gateways and the halls she stood in. She began to sense the restless hand of trickery around her. The wish for the Warriors to connect had to be present, or else they had long left their worlds, meaning there was only emptiness behind the grey doors.

As discomforting as the notion was to Ma-1 and the group, it ranked high on the spectrum of plausibility. But there was the item of the thwarted worlds, the caves with the holographic images of the departed residents; these Warriors didn't partake in the dream meetings and the doors to their worlds were missing in the halls. And still, there was something else...

Ma-1 finally turned to Saka.

"I'm all over the map with this – it's definitely not the way I had envisioned it would go. Not very Goddess-like to admit to one's own vulnerabilities," she laughed. "Perhaps you have an idea, dear?"

While Vac stood to the side, Saka and Olaf felt relief in seeing Ma-1 regain her sense of humor. They understood the burden of reaching the Warriors had fallen on her shoulders, but it was a group effort that couldn't ignore the input of each of its members; for that, the Goddess's surrender was greeted as the voice of reason.

"I want to agree with you that there's another level to this," Vac suddenly cut in. "I don't believe George gifted you with a meaningless hub, for the single-ended purpose of proving to you that the realms were unreachable. It was shown by the power of the stones that there is a multi-faceted reality to these halls. Yes, Amaterasu's model is said to be a copy, but yet, by the nature of its complexity, from what I can make of it, it stands to transcend that unflattering definition. The Great Goddess is a creator of the highest order, only surpassed by the Oneness itself. That model of hers is nothing short of a masterpiece on the level of competing with the real thing, especially when we don't even know what that real thing truly is; while more than half of Hektor has already migrated to worlds they don't suspect are simulations. There's something greater than us interweaved in the cloth of this reality. George is a complex gestalt that, in my opinion, aims at becoming the sum of the individual realms, with the intention of taking nothing away from their unique nature, but gaining from their collective strength. Is it caught in the dilemma of its own origin, unable to free the source, for fear of losing what it has evolved into? Is Amaterasu aware that the Warriors are trapped, and thus using Hektor as a means to create a parallel universe through which the captive realms could be liberated? Ma-l, it is worth reiterating that Olaf and I breached the sanctity of your world, through which Saka was able to return – external actions that permeated the reality of the realms – at a time when George basked in the secrecy of the mother universe, never expecting such an intrusion would ever happen. That precisely defines the remoteness of the probability which sees to the realms emerging as a unique Oneness."

The group stood silent, as it contemplated the implications of the Master's words.

"Are you actually saying George is underhandedly misleading us, while potentially tightening the snare on Ma-l's domain and the Great Hall?" Saka questioned.

"I would think it wants the Great Hall and its Angel population, but I am leaning towards it wishing to shut our realm from it," Vac replied.

"Well, Vac, this all seems to be coming from left field," Ma-l interrupted, "I hope there is another variation on the theme, because frankly, I am finding this version quite oppressive."

"Forgive me, Goddess, I too dislike the sound of my own words, for it makes of Hektor our ally, and of what connects the realms our greatest threat. The paradoxical nature of our present predicament is climaxing into an unimaginable scenario. So yes, I do hope there's another version to my rant," Vac returned.

"Since you wondered if I had an idea," Saka jumped in, intent on answering Ma-l's original question, "perhaps I can ask the stone for a pointer."

"I trust you know what you're doing, but allow me to remind you that your connection with the stone is integral to your unspoken contract with Amaterasu," Olaf cut in.

"Point well taken, I will use caution and trust the stone to guide us safely," she answered.

Saka had barely taken the white gem out of its pouch when it started to spin in her cupped hands. Ma-l observed a distinct fluctuation in the makeup of the end wall closest to them.

"Hold that speed if you can," she requested, "there's a portal across the faux opening in that wall!"

The four walked to the location pointed by Ma-l, but only the Goddess was capable of perceiving the shift she had just described; she simply asked of them to follow her – Saka closest to her with the spinning stone stabilized at the frequency of the portal. They found themselves on the other side facing unending red dunes – the gate behind them was gone.

"OK, if this isn't a realm, what is it then?" Olaf pondered.

"Maybe Angel Vac cares to tell us when he was last seen in this world," Ma-l asked defiantly.

"Glad you asked, Goddess. As a matter of fact, it was eons ago, much before your time as a Warrior and the Great Battles. Amaterasu took us here, on the way to the end of all possibilities, where the probability of the realms precariously teetered at the edge of nonexistence. It was a stopover place then, but one she claimed was of great importance to her. As a Master, she had traveled farther than any Angel – having reached worlds we couldn't even fathom at the level of our collective development. She rode the light to its break point, and beyond, across the zones of pure consciousness. She could stand at the intersections of multiple time and space markers simultaneously – it was then that she taught the many of us the art of inter-dimensional journeying. This place was where we recollected our thoughts and forms. I believe we're presently in a remote corner of the domain of the Great Ones – of course, it also means that we're no longer in the realms. I hope I was able to shed light into your inquiry."

Ma-1 almost apologized for being rude, but she instead composed herself, privately promising to stop acting like a spoiled child. Obviously, Vac had skills and experience far beyond her reach, and thus was deserving of the respect earned by teachers and protectors. She knew the extent of her strength, but she also had to learn to accept her limitations and embrace the collective spirit. She was no longer ruling her universe alone; the group was integral to it. She recognized at that precise moment that perhaps she wasn't totally ready to open her world to the cloistered Warriors.

"Are you suggesting we're presently standing in Amaterasu's domain?" Olaf asked, puzzled.

"At the time, it was a different place, a long way from becoming part of the Great Ones' collective sphere of existence. I believe it was a space Amaterasu was in the process of creating, similarly to how Ma-1 formed what would become her pocket reality; or the one she is presently building for Hektor – and I mean that more than just figuratively. All Great Ones create on a very large scale; that is what defines them," Vac answered.

The stone had stopped spinning. Saka had no idea how to locate and reactivate the portal in the opposite direction. She had made the choice of surrendering to the safety of the white gem; in so doing, she accepted they were meant to reside in the dunes for as long as the stone would remain unresponsive. That doubt was quickly erased when it began to vibrate anew. The Great Goddess of Light was seen walking towards them, with her two guests, Marshall and Geir.

"Welcome, Goddesses and Angels," Amaterasu voiced from the distance. "Vac, you remember the place, I'm sure?" she added, as if amused.

She encouraged the two parties to hug and catch up with old times, capitalizing on the occasion to take Vac to the side for a stroll in the dunes.

"Have they asked, and have you told?" she enquired.

"They know as much as they need to, and their questions are in line with the evolutionary table; though I wonder if it was wise on my part to share my doubts about George – Ma-1 was particularly disturbed by it," he replied.

"Well, it's important you tell your side of the story, even if it proves to be otherwise in the end. Perfection is not a class that was taught at the Guild, and certainly not a term by which the Ones live. A static universe isn't what we have in mind. What's critical is that they don't end up doubting you and that you keep on answering their questions to the best of your abilities.

None of them are familiar with permutable truths, or that the more layers are accessed, the more opposite scenarios play off each other. It takes a fine set of skills to fluidly dance to the waltz of possibilities. In the meantime, it pleases me to be able to connect these friends to each other; their participation has been flawless. I don't expect Marshall and Geir will join the realms, but their world will greatly benefit from their influence, whether they know it or not. Of course, I must commend you on your work, for I have great hopes the two of us will soon witness the rise of the new Oneness with an overwhelming sense of undiluted bliss – and perhaps from this very place," Amaterasu evocatively said.

"It appears the Hektor exodus is going well, but we got wind from Le Lien that Joonas has become distrustful of the authenticity of your creation," Vac said.

"It was expected of him; the character would distrust the real realms just the same. He knows there's nothing he can do without losing face at this point; I rest assured he will let the process follow its course. But he'll try to locate the portal into yours and perhaps succeed; though his organization will not be behind him. He can either rule in a world tailored to suit his kind, or battle the forces of George's labyrinth and Snake's fire with a few of his Dogs. We both already know he'll opt for the latter," the Great Goddess returned.

"Talking of George, what should we do about it?" Vac asked.

"Nothing for now; as long as Joonas doesn't pose a threat to the Warriors, we can assume it will get over its insecurities. But the time for the reunification is due and the true emancipation of the realms must begin – we shall see how far George has crossed the line. Meanwhile, I must return to my work. I have to admit it is taking all of my resources, but I want to ascertain all the glitches have been taken care of. I have a reputation to maintain, even if I am the only one to report to," she laughed.

"One last detail – there was the fear that if he ever discovered the subterfuge, Joonas would be able to extract the codes out of the simulation and back-engineer his own portals into the realms; was that ever a truth?" Vac asked.

"It was a possibility contemplated by Le Lien, but it no longer is. I am building a universe, not just a gate into an illusion. The only opening left between the two Onenesses, besides the lone portal dependent on the ghost image in Marshall's town, is between the stones. The gap belongs to a sacred space only accessed by All That Is, the Great Ones, and their guests; it's the one lane that connects the two universes to each other – Saka and I are in charge of each end. I'm confident we have touched all bases, dear one," Amaterasu ended.

The two walked briskly to the group, their shadows backlit by a setting copper sun. The image of these old friends, with their distant and mysterious past, struck Ma-1 on the intuition that there was so much more to discover about the history of the realms and their greater purpose than she had first imagined.

Amaterasu informed the group that the meeting was ending, instructing Saka on how to lead her friends back into George's halls.

"There will be other times; until then, I count on you to keep on seeking ways to reach the realms. Only through the gate of purpose will the end be found – remember the source of all creations," the Great One said before she took Marshall and Geir back to the dunes.

The white stone began to spin in Saka's cupped hands, indicating it was time for Ma-1 to guide the foursome across the portal into the Halls of Doors.

Joonas's visit to the Fieldbrook estate was quick to alert Le Lien about the Hektor elder's awareness of the true nature of Amaterasu's work. Although he lacked the specifics, he leaned towards a possibility of involvement by the Great Ones. That thought, as speculative as it was, had implications far beyond what he had anticipated, essentially, that his organization was being quarantined. It meant that Hektor's forces weren't even worth battling; that the group was insignificant in the eyes of the Guild and the Ones, but that out of the charity of their hearts, they were willing to let it thrive within the confines of a mock reality; in other words, a prison, for lack of a better qualifier.

Joonas understood he had been played by powers beyond his control. Too many of Hektor's senior members had already relocated into their designated fiefdoms; thus, a reversal was inconceivable. It was clear the organization would be banned if it chose to return, and punitive proceedings engaged for past ills inflicted on Guild students, as well as wrongdoings towards humanity. It implied perpetual solitary confinement for its founding members, followed by the deconditioning of the Dogs back to their original selves as functioning members of human societies. It would sum up as a lost war without a single battle, a humiliating defeat of expectations and greater purposes at the hands of what instigated them. It was an ultimate blow to the all encompassing Joonas, to his evolution as a force that rose from dissent. The course of history no longer had a need for Hektor – unless history was written in a fake universe.

Joonas's personal reality should have collapsed to the realization, but rather, his rage grew exponentially, while his thirst for retribution magnified beyond registrable intensity. His pride had evolved into its own gestalt driven by unrestrained fury against all that aimed at limiting its expansion and squelching its appetites for control. Then, he would have to forgo Hektor. He would reach the Warriors' reality on his own and strike at the heart of their collective existence. He would not settle for a token rule over a mob of narcissistic pseudo-Lords, inside a universe tailored to curtail his true powers. He was going to take his war to where he could fight it, at the core of what he despised most – the very reason for being where and who he was. At that very point, the probe which had allowed Le Lien to track every one of the elder's moves, thoughts, and emotions failed. Joonas's rage had taken him over the top in such a way, that the extreme spike severed the aspect consciousness from its source. Without the vital link, the probe simply died. Joonas was on the loose, dangerous and untraceable.

———————

Before the fall of the mother reality, the first contingent of Angels accessed the Great Hall via Ma-l's back door in the Siskiyou range. At the exception of Axel and Ilia who had wished to connect with the Goddess, all Masters were directly shown to their new headquarters, where they formed the nucleus of what would eventually be known as the Assembly, while the Great Hall would be referred to as Angel City. After the collapse, access became limited to the one portal left by The Triad in Marshall Slaughter's courtyard, for the specific function of serving as an emergency gateway, and only because of the newest in technology that provided linkage to Ma-1's realm via an extracted ghost image. The Guild, with the blessings of the other Great Ones, contacted Amaterasu with the purpose of seeking her help in creating a permanent throughway, using the connecting power of the stones. For that, someone was needed to harness their energy at the other end; thus, Saka was chosen for that role based on her credentials and natural talents. The Halls of Doors were built, not by George as it was first thought, but by the Great One herself. They were originally conceived as a two-way route for Angels to travel to and from the world of the realms, but when it became obvious the gates into these realities were to stay shut, and Keyhole Lake was selected as the entryway into what would instead become the domains of Hektor, it was decided that the traffic of volunteers to Angel City would have to resume via the Snug Alley portal as soon as its safety was ascertained. The problem lay in the gazebo also being the subject of Joonas's obsession, leading to the portal finding itself at the fulcrum point of a precarious balancing act. George's gift of the Halls to Ma-1 was on Amaterasu's expressed recommendation, with the principal purpose of creating a passage between the two Onenesses. The Great Goddess anticipated the Gestalt would see that gift as one it could supervise, and consequently control as far as the doors into the realms were concerned. After all, those entrances were in the image of the system of caves, gates, and tunnels that were directly linked to it. What George could not administer though, were the halls end walls, the hidden layers among which Geir and Marshall resided away from the Hektor founder, and the lane between the stones.

Joonas had lost the Eureka scanning system as well as his ability to hijack bodies due to the lack of technicians and Dog scouts available to him. His excursions into the physical world in his temporary guise limited his time of operation, though his senses remained unimpeded. He no longer cared about Hektor's migration, but he nonetheless ruled over its progress, justifying his frequent and lengthy periods of absence on pretexts of matters of the highest importance. On top of it, the organization's portals were failing one by one, for they lacked the automation and recognition capability of the far more sophisticated ones of the Guild system. So, as if to add pain to injury, Joonas had to stealthily borrow his rides from his nemesis – that was when he noticed concentrated activity around Old Town Eureka.

For reasons of visibility, he hadn't been able to use the Guild's high-traffic lanes for his search of the portal into Ma-l's realm, but slowly, over time, he homed on ten square blocks of the downtown area, his instincts eventually leading him to the plaza hosting the spiraling cascade atop which the Snug Alley gazebo rested.

Joonas immediately understood that the portal had been synched to his scanners to evade recognition, but he doubted that while it was installed in the courtyard of the Fieldbrook estate, it had carried such steady traffic. It became evident the Guild had systematically followed all of his moves, inside or outside his disguises, and though he missed on the knowledge behind the various metrics of identification and trace technology, he intuitively came to suspect the Eye for having provided the link to Guild surveillance. If his current position was known, he had no logical reason to hide; on the other hand, if it wasn't, risking a crossing would be pure madness. It was a psychological standoff, yet he stood at a loss on whether his opponents were strictly in his mind or in the real world. At any rate, he wasn't about to venture a sortie into the realms without preparation and a team, even if it had to be done commando-style. Once again, and with all the cards in play, arose the distinct possibility that he was being set up.

From the comforting safety of the dwellings provided by Amaterasu, Marshall Slaughter called Spencer to enquire about Jarred Gulliver.

"How is our boy doing?" he asked.

"He's back to his old self, getting restless. He asked if he could go over clients' files, because apparently, it wasn't just Joonas who wanted to conduct business with you – the request was genuine," the Angel replied.

"Who would have thought!" the detective remarked. "Nothing can truly surprise me at this point... Well, since I agreed in principal, I don't see why I shouldn't let him have a go at it; it couldn't be any worse than what happened last."

"I'm sure he will be delighted; though he's not going to be allowed to go out due to the high risk of Joonas sniffing the Old Town area. One of our portals picked up his signature as he was piggy-backing another user. It would not surprise us if he had found the gazebo by now," Spencer returned.

"Do I have to remind you that Cruz was a regular at the office, and that perhaps, keeping Gulliver holed up in there may not be the safest of options?" Slaughter remarked.

"Yes indeed, but neither is the house the ideal hideaway. One of us keeps him company at all times, besides, we have Lillian back on the job to run errands for him; she is very skilled at lifting the morale of traumatized subjects. On the topic of safety, we got wind from Liv that Geir has been able to visit his home in Reykjavík at regular intervals; it appears the Great One isn't concerned with the presence of Joonas on the island," the Angel pointed.

"Yes, she has observed the elder has been seen more and more infrequently through the portal, thus suggested that if Geir had business to attend, it was possibly the best time to take care of it. So yes, he commutes back and forth," Slaughter explained.

"Fair enough, although staying on the side of caution is still very much protocol; we have had plenty an opportunity to study Joonas's in-depth profile, so we can assure you that he will not rescind on feeding his bruised pride. Gulliver is relatively safe, since he technically is no longer alive. You two are to a point as well, but only because he believes you moved to the realms. It goes without saying that flaunting your presence around is hardly a good idea. One third of Hektor remains in your world. Many of the Dogs are still fully operational and reporting for duty. I assume Liv has already warned Geir, but it's not a given; she's being kept busy at headquarters since she's now compromised. As to me, I'm on a portal commute between the office and the house, just in case you wondered," the Angel said before logging out.

Upon hearing that Joonas was closing in on the Snug Alley portal, Ma-1 and her team prepared for the imminent incursion. The entrance to her realm was via the back end of Despair, which led to the volcano and part of Snake's underworld. It was unlikely the Hektor founder and his Dogs would find her domain from that direction. On the other hand, the Great Hall of Angel City was most vulnerable. Le Lien assessed that George wouldn't be able to distinguish the Dove's signature from that of a Guild Master. The Goddess intuited Joonas would first be looking for Pau, Gerald Brinsk, Marshall, and Geir; but unless he managed to operate in stealth mode, he would easily be overwhelmed by the power of the assembly. He, of course, was unaware Slaughter and Flemmingson were tucked away in a dimensional layer only a few figurative inches from Hektor. He was left with a limited amount of scenarios if he aimed at doing the most amount of damage without the push of his organization's muscle behind him. Besides operating in the background and doing his dirty business with his ex-captives, it was unclear how he would get to George and persuade the gestalt to open the gates into the Warriors' realms. The powers of Masters were untested across the line that separated madness from sanity.

The group agreed, Joonas would probably use ruse over self-sacrifice; an assumption that was confirmed by Le Lien's time and field-tested diagnostic tools.

Snake was ready, but George had only returned Ma-l's requests to connect with silence. The Gestalt had seemingly opted out of the discussion on how to protect the tunnels, instead adopting the uncommunicativeness of the shuttered realms. It made the Goddess all the more resolute to find a path to the Warriors. She knew too well that her kin wouldn't stay passive before a threat such as Joonas and his Dogs, even if their use of arrows was forever behind them. A fallen Angel would not be allowed to rise among them – that was the simple, indubitable, unwritten, and unspoken maxim behind the collective might of these ancient people.

So, what exactly was George doing? The realms could easily protect themselves against the threat of a single dark Master without an army. The Warriors were creators with formidable tools at their disposal; the simple act of crossing into their domains was warrant for an unleashing of power on par with that of the Great Ones – something did not add up.

Ma-l returned to the Halls of Doors. She had come to understand that the strength of the stones was in linking the two Onenesses to each other; hence, it was of no value in connecting her with the Warriors. Saka had her role well defined, and Vac's loyalty was to the Guild in regard to honoring the clause of minimal interference. She needed to reflect privately on defining the elements of her greater purpose – it was obvious she was the only one with the inner reach to open the portals.

In spite of its reluctance to activate the ways into the realms, George had made it clear that for Ma-l to re-access the old lanes to the dream meetings, she had to tap deeper. The Goddess had traveled the paths to the grassy meadows, just as others, back then, had from their unique places in the stone. But had she ever ridden back with any of them to the darkness of their secluded existences? Had she invited anyone to follow her into hers? No, each lane was private. The dream environment was akin to Amaterasu's halls, or Angel City, or George's gift where she presently stood facing the open door into her gardens. What hidden common denominator was to reveal itself in a moment of unimpeded clarity? What did these doors, lanes, tunnels, and portals, all with the single purpose of connecting the Warriors to each other, conceal from her, a Goddess of the realms?

The thought came to her, vivid and magnified: the lanes had stilled when the last of the Warriors stopped wishing to meet – they would start again with a single yearning to resume. She had to revisit the meadows, like she had revived her meetings with Saka by the stream. That connection could not be affected by George's resistance to open the portals, for it was at the source of its own existence where any tampering would jeopardize its integrity. The Great Gestalt would have no choice but to weather the effects, as Ma-1 rode the wave lanes back to the gathering grounds. She sat at the center of the first hall, her back to the end wall as she faced the rows of doors on both sides. She closed her eyes, mentally returning to the end of her cave, letting herself fall into a deep meditative trance.

Ma-1 stood by the entrance of the dark recess. She waited as she always did before the scheduled meetings. The wave was felt like a released vacuum from the depths of the tunnels. It was followed by silence, and then a slow, deep drone – the heart of the mountain had come alive. The sound steadily got closer, but not louder. It arrived as an active omnipresence outside the opening of her cave, an invisible conveyor belt one could hop on at will. She paused before stepping on to commit to the ride, musing on how funny dreams were, trying to mimic life in ways that strayed so far from it. Why couldn't they just be dreams – like dreams were before the world came into existence? But then she reminded herself that universes were born of them. She smiled at the silliness of the thought.

The ride would be short – like one between two stations – but she could, if she chose, make the blur of sceneries traveling the other way last. When she stepped off at the foot of the path, she knew she had reached the right place – nothing to do with memory. Certain actions were automatic, reflexive in a curiously focused way; riding the lanes was one of them. She didn't wish to understand – it just was what it was. She walked up the dirt trail to the meadows. There they lay, exactly the same as they ever did – lush, green, and radiant under the golden glow of late afternoons. The sun always set as the Warriors gathered ahead of sharing songs and stories. They did so, well into the night, until the time came to part from under starry skies.

It wasn't quite sunset yet when Ma-l found herself standing in the exact place that had once defined her dream center of power. A gentle breeze moved every blade of grass in an improvised wave dance, bouncing light in a million fluorescing particles. She was mesmerized, overtaken by the simple magic of a moment made of very few parts. Saka had said that pleasure came in very small packages – she was right. The dream rose as if from small boxes released from wrappers tumbling away, carried by the invisible play of air fairies, until they vanished beyond the edge of the meadows. The sun slowly found its way towards the crest of the trees lining the setting side of the image. The woods darkened, until their details became lost in blackness. Ma-l lay on the grass, looking at a sky patched with flocks of puffy, purple-bottomed clouds which she endeavored to name, only to drift within the dream within the trance. When she opened her eyes, a tall, male Warrior, equally naked and tattooed as she was, stood above her, his body bathed in moonlight.

"I thought you would never wake up," he said.

Ma-l sat up, dazzled by the deep voice. She realized where she was, while unable to understand why she had fallen asleep. How long had she been venturing down the paths of sub-dreams, into depths indefinable by the laws of the environment that contained them?

"I have no idea how long you have been waiting, Ma-l, but I chose to come to these old gathering grounds on the recognition that it had been too long since I last heard of anyone. Someone needed to do something about it. I see by your presence that I wasn't the only one stirred into action," the Warrior said.

"You now are a God of your realm, Xarn, are you not?" Ma-l asked with acute apprehension.

"Yes, I survey my world from the top of the high mountain; if that's what you mean. I began working on it, soon after our collective dreams ended. What about you, Goddess?" Xarn inquired carefully.

"I'm relieved, dear friend; I too have been building a world, but in a better image of our old one. I now have permanent guests to help me with it," Ma-l returned, as she emerged from the mental haze.

"My guests are my creations, they're my family, my tribe; though they are scattered in many villages down the canyon that leads to the sea. I too chose the physical sphere as my dominant theme, but I do admit it wasn't always my favorite option," Xarn added.

The two Warriors sat side by side for the following days and nights, enthralled by the finer and greater details of their individual journeys. Xarn had remained unaware of what Ma-l knew about the history of the realms, their makeup, the Evil Spirits versus the Great Ones, Snake and George, as well as the collapse of the mother world. It took great effort and concentration for him to arrive at an understanding of the presence of the Angels, the threat of Joonas, and the time shifts between various overlapping realities. But Xarn assimilated the news with dignified patience and openness. His grounded presence helped Ma-l settle into a cadenced delivery of the information she had collected since inviting Vac and Olaf into her realm. She felt deeply puzzled by what he had to share about his world, his unique approach to creating, his outreach to realities she was near-unable to comprehend. He had been aware something had shifted when his land also suffered from flood and fire, but he harnessed the forces, and soon his realm began to heal. Ma-l explained how Amaterasu and George's halls operated; pointing out that upon her return, the door to his realm would be open into them. She would visit first, and then take him to her world and the city of Angels. And so, after they deemed they had left no stone unturned, they held each other in a long embrace, before returning to the lanes. Ma-l came out of her trance to the sight of a newly opened door in the middle section of the first hall. Xarn's realm was unlocked – George remained silent. The Goddess reentered her world in search of Saka. Both had business to conduct.

———————

"Where were you!?" Saka inquired. "It's been nearly a week since we last saw you."

"I would normally ask you to mind your own business, but there's a matter of the highest importance for which I need your insight and unique talents; are you available?"

"You're going to explain before you assume I'm fully prepared, aren't you?" Saka returned.

"I'll share the details as we go, but it won't take you long to realize what has happened when we get to the halls," Ma-l said.

They crossed the nearest portal to the hub – Saka immediately understood what Ma-l had alluded to.

"Did you do it, or did it happen on its own?"

"I think I did it, but it was practically a tie; my friend Xarn and I met once again at the dream meadows, after over a millennium since the cessation of the gatherings. Are you willing to come with me?" Ma-l asked.

"Before I answer your question, is Xarn a Goddess or a God? And dare I ask if the deity in question comes with the usual garb – perhaps a few tattoos to boot?" Saka posed, waxing mild sarcastic.

"For the sake of mobility, the Warriors wore no clothes during battle, and tattoos were for camouflage. Time to let go of your previous world's incomprehensible views of the human form; so, are you with me or not?" Ma-l asked, matter-of-factly.

"Who's not, Warrior? Let's do it!" Saka jubilantly exclaimed.

The two Goddesses crossed into Xarn's world to be met with a breathtaking vista. They stood on a high mesa overlooking a canyon; behind them, tall peaks carved by winds into delicate sculptures of red and purple strata rose like specters. Among them, the rubble of some of the collapsed giants was a reminder that the land was once brutally shaken. Ma-l and Saka walked along the ridge to the trailhead that led to the gorge's lush bottom, and through which snaked a slow, transparent river interceded by stretches of white rapids and the drops of majestic falls. It was a long hike to the wide area of green meadows in the distance, where the new corn followed the creeks that emerged from the base of giant cliffs. No structures were seen, but openings in the walls of the canyon betrayed a life inside the stone. Ma-l was surprised Xarn had not detected their presence, as she had when Olaf and Vac crossed the gates to her land. But the thought was quickly dispelled by the diagonal approach of a large coywolf who passed them as if on springs, never losing sight as he began circling them. He suddenly stopped, then ambled towards them, until he finally came to a halt.

"I have been to the top of your world, but our ways did not cross. There is much about the path between our two realms that I cannot explain. Xarn has entrusted me with the surveillance of the high land in anticipation of unwanted visitors. He said a Warrior would come in peace, but you are two; though I sense you are related by more than blood," the coywolf telepathized.

"We are Saka and Ma-l; do you have a name?"

"I am Wolf, in the image of a once prolific canid in the world of the Warriors. I am the only one of my kind in Xarn's realm, perhaps there are others in yours," Wolf answered inquisitively.

"There's a close relative of your kind in our domain that goes by 'coyote.' Wolves may come, but a Goddess' workday is never long enough," Ma-l replied.

"I gather you are the Warrior of the two," Wolf pointed. "Xarn asked me to show you the way."

"Shouldn't we inform Vac and Olaf of our whereabouts before we go any further?" Saka pleaded.

"If you wish to be the messenger, then you must return to let them and Amaterasu know. Of course, I would love for you to stay by my side, but I rest assured you understand this is my calling. I'll do my best not to make you wait," Ma-l replied.

"I'm dying to meet Xarn and his family, but I trust there'll be other times. This is only the onset of a long series of rekindled relationships between Warriors. My calling is to serve the realms to the best of my abilities, starting with the sharing of news; and since I'm the light that travels the farthest distance... well, you know what I mean. Nice meeting you, Wolf – until then!"

Saka turned around and left for the halls.

Ma-l and her guide safely traveled the series of switchbacks that closely hugged the cliff wall, until they reached the bottom of the canyon a mile down-river. Everything about Xarn's world was bigger and bolder than the Goddess's valley, but she recognized elements carried over from their native reality in both. The snaking rows of multicolored corn along the creeks were one; and so were the subtle tones in the rock formation, as well as the clear open skies. At the widest part of the floor, fields and meadows stretched on both sides of the river. Wolf came to a stop at the foot of a long suspended walk bridge that spanned the rushing waters.

"This is it," the guide said, sniffing the air.

The Goddess stood, her grey-streaked black hair dancing in the breeze, waiting for signs of the Warrior, or members of his tribe.

"Where is the host?" she asked.

"This is an intense and symbolic moment that cannot be rushed – Xarn is likely burning sage in his stone dwellings, intent on lifting his spirit to the level of the occasion," the guide returned.

The God appeared through an opening in the cliff, beyond the meadows. He walked the distance to the bridge, paused, and then crossed steadily, easily offsetting the harmonic bounce the structure. When he got to Ma-l's side, his eyes were moist with tears. He and the Goddess held each other for an immeasurable length of time, until they finally let go and smiled like old lovers in need of no words to tell all they had to share. Ma-l was overwhelmed with emotions from meeting in the flesh for the first time in millennia. Although, their statuses as deities of the realms afforded them the luxury of not being dependent on physicality, the very nature of the encounter could not go without it. The two had been very close in the past, not as lovers, since their allegiance to protecting the tribe forewent all sexual activities, but the attraction had always been there and further matured with the dream meetings. The shadow of longing vanished from the background of their reality; they now existed in a present of intense merging that went far beyond the closeness of their bodies, yet without excluding it. He lifted her as she wrapped her legs around his waist, slowly lowering her body until he was fully inside her. They made love standing, surrendering to the climax of their mutual affections while bringing forth the first indelible contract of the joined realms.

———————

The news of Xarn's opened domain was met with mixed reactions. The talks about the reunification of the realms had been going on for so long that its qualitative emotional value had been depreciated to that of existing in the blurred background of dormant expectations. At least, that was how it appeared to Vac and Olaf. Amaterasu was delighted to hear the Goddess had had a breakthrough, and hailed her remarkable achievement as a decisive moment in realm evolution. The Angels of the assembly received the information with great relief. At last, a purpose-defining moment had arrived, and the thought of being able to leave the Hall rose with the promise of freedom through the expansion of individual and collective consciousness; a Master's way of saying they were glad to finally get out of the stone confinement of Angel City.

In spite of her support, Amaterasu joined in with Vac and Olaf in not getting overenthusiastic over Ma-l's headway; too much too fast had its disadvantages. She also knew the union of Xarn and Ma-l could have deep and far-reaching ramifications, with the power of transcending the course of established probabilities, to the point of sending the new Oneness into distances unbridgeable by the stones. It amounted to a paradox that rendered the gems useless,

283

for the nature of their purpose was to only prevent a separation by hostile forces – not a natural one. Additionally, there were powers at work that could not be foreseen. The new world of the realms was bereft of law and governance. Much unpredictability resided in its makeup, pressuring those who wished to keep the two universes connected to adapt rather than usher without compass. Amaterasu saw no choice, but to take time away from her work with the domains of Hektor, to meet with Ma-l and Xarn.

The other matter of perplexity rooted in George's silence. The Gestalt had ceased to communicate, forcing the Great One to face the plausibility of trouble ahead. Amaterasu had become aware that the emergence of the George consciousness was the end-result of an unforeseeable flaw, first thought to be a kink that would eventually iron itself out. The tunnel portals were a system intended to grow with the demand for traffic, as the realms emerged into the next phase of their evolutionary process; not one equipped with the potential for self-awareness, followed by a desire to control its destiny. That detail came to life in parallel with the expansion of the Warriors' worlds, as George curiously saw itself as one of them through their dormant connections. It was recognized as yet another of the many impossibilities that came to manifest through the rise of the realms. George didn't just see itself as a part of the system that birthed it, but as its all-encompassing Oneness; even though it eventually realized its true place. It lived amid a set of double standards that deeply concerned the Great One. The point was highlighted by its intentions to convince Ma-l of its utter dedication to the safety of the Warriors, while methodically cutting their means to communicate with each other. The paradox was exposed by the fact the Warriors' strength was at its mightiest amid the collective settings; thus, any attempt at justifying their cloistering for the sake of safety was nothing short of a logical fallacy. She sensed Ma-1 had intuitively seen through the game, or she wouldn't have sought contact with the entity. In perspective, Amaterasu wasn't concerned about the realms forming an alliance – it was overdue – rather she feared George wasn't ready to accept that step in evolution, being instead driven to act erratically, pushed into a corner by irrational angst. It was partially the reason why she handed the halls over to it, as a gift to the Goddess, thus soothing the Gestalt into believing the offering would keep Ma-1 away from the tunnels. It was of course a back-handed way of making the Warriors' worlds more accessible to her, while providing the illusion that she would stay out of the way. The possibility George might have caught up with the subterfuge, in the light of the Warrior's reconnection with Xarn, was fodder to disquietude.

Amaterasu contacted Saka about her desire to bring Ma-1, Xarn, and Vac together for a meeting of chief importance to be conducted in her domain, away from the Gestalt's sensors and the potential danger of Joonas's intrusion. She trusted Ma-1 had brought her Warrior compeer up to date. The realm deities had to be added to the fold of knowledge, to be made participants in what was essentially a complex blueprint conceptualized by the original Oneness; then carried to realization by her and members of the first Angel team – the whole of it based on a vision brought forth by the gift of light. Much had happened in time's terms, while much still needed to be integrated to the final phases of the execution of the design. But the concentration of simple elements had engendered a set of complicated issues that were on the verge of tipping the scales in favor of a tragic undoing – she couldn't let that happen! Amaterasu understood that the fragile set of probabilities that had birthed the realms had been circumvallated by much stronger ones, which considered that their place in line had been manipulated. But that concept could only have taken roots in the mind of a creator; hence, that creator had to stay focused. Hektor had been subdued, its fate now irreversible in spite of Joonas still in the throes of old acrimony and roaming the possibilities for avengement. George was to be dealt with on a much subtler platform. The halls were a temporary patch, for they couldn't function on their own. Without the Gestalt's collaboration, they were reduced to a mere gateway between her and Saka. All would consequently revert to the labyrinthine reality of the tunnels, endless, random series of loops connecting the central hub of Angel City ad nauseam, until, eventually, George would find a way to close Ma-1 and Xarn's worlds, forever trapping the Masters. It suddenly occurred to her that Joonas might very much enjoy that development.

Wolf was standing by the portal when Saka crossed to fetch Ma-1. The Great Goddess of the realm had been absent for yet another week, moving the status of the meeting with Amaterasu to critical – the Great One couldn't wait any longer. The coywolf was glad to see the visitor. He forwent the stalking ritual in favor of a direct question about the canids of her world.

"You're welcome to come back with us to check it out; providing Xarn's OK with it, that is," she offered.

"I think he understands," Wolf returned. "He and I have had related longings for finding others like us. We all are one of a kind in our realm, eternal, though lonely. But now that Ma-l has shared the corn and the water, we know others will come to complete us."

Saka didn't know how to process the guide's words, but she realized how much they had struck her depths when she felt the tears running down her cheeks.

"That level of loneliness is alien to me. I was born in Ma-l's cave, but unlike her, I chose to explore the horizons of other realities outside the realms. But now, I see that without the gift of light, it would have been impossible for me to leave – I'm not sure how I would have survived," she confessed.

"Many of us came into awareness in the blackness of the cave, just like you did in your world. Xarn, the villagers, and I dream-conceived the land before it slowly manifested from the inside out. When we made our first steps, we were like children overwhelmed by play. Xarn imagined worlds without physical shapes, ambiances that cocooned consciousness like dream pillows, but he always returned to the warmth of the flesh and the cold air that filled our lungs. We settled into this form, as Ma-l did in her domain," the coywolf explained.

"Ma-l was unsure until the first visitors came, then she made up for it. This realm must precede hers from what I gather," Saka remarked.

"She was the first one to open her gates, so who's to say?" Wolf corrected.

When they reached the bridge, Ma-l and Xarn were standing side by side. Others had joined them, but there were no distinct humanoids among them. Most seemed to be of mixed breeding, some of radical crossing – there were no two alike.

"Hey Saka," Ma-l greeted, "I guess the time has come for me to rejoin my world. Xarn and I needed the space, so I'm glad you didn't come earlier. I'm sure Amaterasu must be anxious for my return, right?"

"I'm glad to see you, Ma-l. I understand what has happened and why it had to – you two aren't just friends, are you?" Saka probed, as she hugged the Goddess.

She turned to Xarn, extending her hand to touch his arm.

"You're beautiful, Warrior – it's a great honor to meet you," she said with uncanny passion, as she looked into his eyes. "I'm Goddess Saka, deity of light, holder of the white stone. Consider me at your service when I'm not serving Ma-l and the realm."

"The pleasure is all mine, Goddess, you are my eternal guest," Xarn returned.

"Great One Amaterasu wishes for us three, as well as Angel Vac, to come to her domain to discuss in private the more pressing issues of the realms. She deems the meeting a matter of great significance; she counts on you, Xarn, to make yourself available. I trust Ma-l has explained how to reach the halls," Saka conveyed.

"She has – I shall be there before this world's nightfall," he returned.

Wolf stepped in to explain his absence, while on an important, personal visit to the "other realm."

Xarn smiled.

"Come back to us with wondrous stories, my friend; my time to travel to Ma-l's home will come soon," he kindly answered his eternal companion.

Xarn stood by the suspended bridge, watching Wolf and the two Goddesses steadily walk up the trail to the mesa. He waved one last time before swimming across the river. He felt complete – he and Ma-l had laid out the paths to the rest of the realms.

———————————

Soon after Ma-l and Xarn met, the timelines of their realities came into alignment. Night was falling on both realms when the four gathered for the meeting. Xarn materialized just in time across the threshold of the grey door marked with his tribal name. The Goddess had taught him the art of installing and linking portals to the Halls from anywhere in his universe, so as to not have to walk up the long trail to the mesa when time was in short supply.

The white stone spun in Saka's cupped hands; the gates into Amaterasu's land opened on rows of undulating dunes bathed in the light of the copper sun.

From the distance, the Great One resembled a flame dancing on the hot sand, the air around her waving outwards in a radiance that betrayed the great powers contained within her form. She stopped before the group, looking at each of its members with uncanny intensity. Her salt and pepper hair reflected the red of the sun in cadence with the breeze that warmed and dried the land. When she finally spoke, it was in a tongue only heard by ears that belonged to times long gone, or possibly, those of a very distant future, *word sounds* grouped in clusters that triggered multiple, concurrent, intertwining meanings. It was duly noted that the translation of her speech, essential

289

to the untrained mind, was unfortunately less accurate in conveying subtlety and nuance.

"Greetings, and thank you for being here – I am delighted by the presence of a God of the realms among you. Welcome, Warrior Xarn; it's been a long journey! Much about the birth of the new world has been explained and carried over, so I don't wish to delve into further details about that phase of its evolution. The principal subject of concern at this moment is the reluctance of the system of portals to serve the Warriors' greater purpose of emerging as a vibrant collective of creators. Deprived of their vital connections, the realms have essentially been robbed of their right to exist as an all-encompassing Oneness. The Masters assigned to assist in their development have been trapped inside the Great Hall. That unresponsive system of tunnels and portals is referred to as the Great Gestalt; though lately, it wishes to be called George. It is inherently good-intentioned, but a latent and potent fear of being denied the specific consciousness it came to possess through a kink in its evolution, made it reluctant to assume the functions of its original purpose. It is not a natural consciousness in the sense that what made it was taken from the collective pool; those parts, which coalesced into a whole, rightfully belong to the Warriors. But it isn't the way George sees it, as it has come to recognize itself as the sum of it all – a unique Oneness on a par with ours. In order to protect itself, it recourses to locking the Warriors in, while prophesying that the doors to their domains will open when they are ready. It is instead inflicting great harm, while gathering strength from the devolution that was triggered when the projected time point of the emergence was missed. George is an oddity of the highest order, and though we do not adhere to the maxim that sacrifice must be made for the benefit of the whole, too much is at stakes in its case – it must be neutralized then returned to the level of its intended purpose. Its consciousness must thus reassume its role within the Warrior collective, where it will again become an active participant in the makeup of the new Oneness and the expansion of the realms. Now, there's no doubt that the opening of Xarn's world has sent traumatic ripples towards its core, and it is most likely thinking of ways to lock both live domains. I don't have to remind you that the outcome would be of catastrophic proportions, but it can never be stressed enough. There are ways to disable George, but the results would be just as dire. In truth, it must consent to its own dismissal. But before we can figure out how that is done, there are two places it can't touch: the halls which are of my making, and the dream lanes at the source of its existence. Theoretically, the instant the Warriors gather in the dream meadows and agree to unlock their worlds, the doors should swing wide open into my halls, consequently activating the portals inside the tunnels to the Great Hall of Angel City. I hope we all understand that these doors and portals cannot function without the Gestalt abiding to its initial purpose of serving the wish of the Warriors, Angels, deities, and their guests to freely travel between the realms. Without George, my halls revert to only connecting and holding the two Onenesses together with the help of the stones. Any questions before we continue?"

Ma-1 came forward.

"There is this ongoing notion that the access to the realms via the tunnels is contingent on using the Great Hall as a connecting hub, when in fact I have been able to cross over to various tunnels using portals unrelated to

Angel City. There is a system of gates that I am sure, functions independently from any of the halls. Vac and Saka can attest to it, since it is how we found the Masters after having entered an aborted realm named Despair. I am seriously contemplating the possibility that the tunnels to the arrested worlds are not controlled by George; they are dead to it, so no longer on its radar. In fact, they don't even show up in your halls; so you would know. If we bypass the hubs, we theoretically also go around the core consciousness. Does it make any sense?"

Vac turned to Amaterasu.

"Ma-1 is correct; the defunct realms are now part of the Gestalt's deep subconscious. Because of its present concern, its energy is spent within the periphery of what it recognizes as its primary existence. If Ma-1 and Xarn manage to map a subsidiary system, connections between the realms could be made without its knowledge. Full integration could at that point be implemented to the subsystem into a fully functional replacement of the Gestalt. It would in substance be an extraction of the indispensable codes of the original system prior to its corruption – though it remains unclear how these codes would be retrieved. With the realms linked that way, and bypassed from the core consciousness, any attempt on George's part to close any of them would instead permanently defeat its vital functions – the gestalt would technically shut itself off, by disconnecting itself from a purpose no longer aligned with the Warriors' needs. Does this make any sense?" the Angel asked.

"Well, it does, and am I glad we got this group together; those are hardly questions!" Amaterasu laughed. "I'm proud of you all as you should know. It is true that the arrested realms were intentionally omitted from my

292

halls for obvious reasons. I commend you on your observational skills, Ma-1. Tell me, Xarn, have you and the Great Goddess already started on a map of the subsystem?" she asked.

"We have, Great One! Additionally, we figured out a way to divert George's concerns and fears away from the tunnels; that is, we, Warriors, gather in the dream meadows without opening our realms, in hopes the Gestalt sees the threat diminished. He'll just have to assume we want to keep our gates shut. The plan may appear overly simplistic, but we strongly believe George isn't the evolved consciousness we originally thought it to be – it is only powerful because of what it holds captive. That being said, the intension is to buy time, while we work on mapping the new system."

"I am once more very pleased with your collective way of thinking; this is what your entire universe is about. I commend you on your unique skills at the service of the whole; thank you! Now we haven't heard from Saka yet. Tell me dear, how can you top what has just been said?" Amaterasu asked with visible humor.

"I thought you would never ask," Saka laughed. "Well, if there were an easy way for me to reach the Gestalt, I would be delighted to entertain him with a simple explanation of why Xarn's realm is now open. George is a scared child, but I believe he understands love. I need to persuade him that the bond between Ma-1 and Xarn is so strong that the doors could no longer stay closed. If I didn't believe it myself, I would not offer."

"I believe it too," Amaterasu smiled, "although, I admit it comes as a bit of a surprise – a pleasant and possibly, an auspicious one. I will try my best to summon the Gestalt."

"I am delighted the arrangement is agreeable to all," Ma-1 said. "Xarn and I have long been waiting for a chance at closeness; that time has come and it feels right in the context of the unification of the realms. That being said, as far as the Warriors are concerned, we should be prepared for some very unique interpretations of reality, judging by the far-from-subtle differences between our two worlds. It's very likely some of them have entirely opted out of the physical experience."

"We all can be physical or not whenever we desire; we clothe our creations based on purpose," Amaterasu added. "The dream state may look physical when it is far from it. It's all a matter of perspective, but all of us know that already. When the time comes, let us all embrace the wonderment of the experience. For now, extreme circumstances, which aim at interfering with the progress we have come to expect, are to be dealt with. Besides George, which by the way, both Vac and I refuse to refer to as a *he* – and I suggest you start dehumanizing *it* as well – there is Joonas and his pending crossing to assess. It's more than probable that he'll find the Great Hall, since the Gestalt seems to show a keen interest in populating Angel City, on top of being unable to tell the difference between a member of the Guild and one of Hektor. Consequently, you must protect the students and their guardians at all cost – no margin for error is provided in their respect. Additionally, he will not be allowed in my halls under any circumstances; so in case I have to shut them, you'll have to learn to connect via the subsystem of tunnels – you get the drift. The Gestalt will tolerate some level of traffic between my doors, but it'll block all other accesses under its control. The earlier you get it figured out, the better. Furthermore, there is a foreseeable scenario that involves an alliance between Joonas and George when the latter realizes that the former is banned out of the Great Hall. Another close probability is one of conflict between them. In either case, without an advanced mapping of the subsidiary system, we cannot allow for the two to meet. I believe we have addressed the important points. One bit of advice: refrain from frequent visits – it is best that you spend extended periods at a time when you must work together. On a related matter, I suggest Wolf stays at Ma-l's for a while longer ahead of his return – any questions?"

The group agreed on regularly meetings for updates on inside progress and outside developments. Amaterasu left for the depths of her dunes under a sky heavy with stars. Saka deftly reopened the passage into the halls of doors. Since Xarn offered to resume with the mapping of the subsystem at Ma-l's place, the four found themselves standing in silence, overlooking the radiance of the Goddess's valley.

Joonas had just returned from a Hektor meeting; and while the organization seemed pleased with their new world, he was all the more convinced he had been played. The fact was no Warrior had yet come forward.

The Snug Alley portal was heavily watched. He had gathered enough Dogs for the mission, but the logistics for a successful crossing were still undefined. Without Tömör on the inside, he had no clue as to what to expect when he got there. He just contented himself with watching the flow of traffic, recording the patterns of its rhythm, as well as the breaks he could exploit. There was one: a series of recurring gaps, exactly one day and seventeen minutes apart, with a length of precisely eleven minutes and twenty-seven seconds. The point was to determine the nature of the sequence and how it affected the safety of the passage. He was able to assign the pattern to the automatic synching of the timelines between the two ends. During that period, travelers were put in suspension until the two sides of the portal came into alignment. Joonas observed that the Angels ceased entering two minutes before the calibration started, and then resumed, a time likely due to an operational latency occasioned by the unimaginable remoteness of the realms. The Dove saw it as a dead zone that could be exploited away from the scrutiny of Guild detectors. But if he and his Dogs could technically manage to cross unnoticed by the system, there were still considerable logistical and safety issues in play.

The gates were designed and managed by *Portal Works*. The entire réseau was monitored at all times by an array of highly sophisticated halometric sensors that were able to recognize the travelers based on their unique auratic signatures. Only Guild Masters and their students could technically activate a crossing, but Hektor seniors were allowed to borrow lanes to reach areas that were not covered by their own system, under an obscure clause that belonged to an ancient treaty between the two leagues. Oddly, since the portal to the realms fell within the exception, automatic access would be granted to Joonas, but not without him being recognized and barred. The only way he could cross incognito was within the few seconds ahead of the synching process, while the sensors were in off-mode. The stratagem only allowed for one extremely skilled single user to pass. It was also the only window non-Angels could slip through; one the Hektor Dogs could exploit at the rate of one passage per day. Unfortunately, there was no room for error – one misstep and the traveler would be lost in the sub-layers of the system, amid roaming hijackers and thieves, as it was the case for a brief moment with Olaf Swyndle and Vac on their way to the mother reality. The Guild had worked relentlessly on closing the breach into the underworld, but to no avail – the complex physics of time alignment did not factor in harnessing unruliness into submission; besides, the creators believed that allowing for some breathing room was a necessary part of the process. Time was created to be subjective, to both expand and contract simultaneously from the vantage points of two or more observers – somehow, something was bound to slip through the cracks.

The vulnerability was deemed reliable, but it would take too long for more than a dozen Dogs to make it to the other side; therefore Joonas opted to limit his army to a crack team of weathered infiltrators.

It was just a matter of not being seen at the gazebo, but after the first Dog made it through without sounding the alarm, the Dove felt confident the crossing would succeed. There were thirteen of them against a projected two thousand Angels at the side of an unknown number of Warriors and their tribes, but he wasn't seeking battle; he only longed for the one vulnerability that would throw the realms off balance and send their future reeling towards a portentous destiny.

If Joonas had known about the Great Gestalt, he would most likely have had a radically different plan. The twelve Dogs made it safely, but only to find themselves confined to a quarantine area reserved for visitors lacking direction or identity; for all intents and purposes, the place was an encampment in the grand style of those of the mother reality, with their classic buffets and bare-bone conveniences in a setting that approximated the feel of being outdoors, while offering no way out. The general consensus among the team was that it could have been a lot worse. And so, Joonas's Dogs opted to make the best of it until their Master eventually showed up – but then, the best became exponentially better when it was discovered that the buffet doubled as a fully stocked bar.

When Joonas arrived, his Dogs were nowhere to be seen, while he stood at the highest point of one of the four stairways overlooking Angel City. After surveying the site long enough to gauge the power of the Hall, he retreated to the tunnel behind him, where he found a room that suited his purpose. He recognized it as being modeled after one of the old Guild's resting places for Angels returning from difficult assignments, an asylum where privacy was paramount. Furthermore, it was unlikely Masters in the area would recognize him, since no-one was warned of his arrival. He could then take his time to explore and retrieve his team. From what he observed, there wasn't a doubt in his mind that the Great Hall was the hub that interconnected the realms – the real ones.

––––––––––––

Le Lien informed The Triad that the team had lost the probe – Joonas's whereabouts could no longer be confirmed. Although his presence had been detected around the Old Town's square a couple of weeks back, nothing came of it – he had simply moved on. Since few Dogs roamed the area; it was deduced that the elder had not sought to use the portal.

Liv wasn't fully convinced the Dove had resigned himself to the fate of his organization. It was clear he had seen through the subterfuge, but since he couldn't lose face by reversing the course of the exodus, he went through the motions and acted the role of the captain who would leave the ship last. She contacted *Portal Works* for a look into exploitable vulnerabilities. The returned call acknowledged that portals linking significantly divergent timelines were subject to inconsistencies that required continuous calibration. When Liv studied the time differential between Eureka and the probability known as the mother reality of the realms, she learned that it had, at some point, forged its way into the future, come to an apex, and then reversibly sought to stabilize. Consequently, it left a gap of six hundred and forty seven years between the two worlds, necessitating a system adjustment of seventeen minutes per day at the time of its collapse. *Portal Works* explained that while it was possible to transit during synching – although in suspension – the traveler remained under continuous surveillance by the same identification-reading apparatus used across the whole system. The explanation included the case of the hypothetical "careless rider" attempting to cross within the period immediately preceding the synching and finding themselves irreversibly drawn towards the unmentionable layers that loosely defined the underworld. But *Portals* omitted to extrapolate on a little-known flash vulnerability sitting at the calibration point. It took the Le Lien operative a closer look at the index of the complex and extensive field specification manual to notice it. When Liv called again for verification, she was told that the only instance ever recorded of a recovered crossing under the definition, was performed by Angel Vac under conditions that were unpredictable at the time, since the corridor operated randomly and independently from the main network – it had since then been incorporated and stabilized. Historically, the vulnerability was first encountered during a routine checkup, and then soon exploited by inter-dimensional marauders and other underworld denizens. *Portal Works* insisted such a secondary network could not access the realms, rather, it would send the traveler far off-course. In other words, and in spite of the relevant information, the department's computer chose to not answer her question.

Liv brought her findings to Spencer. It took the tech a few days to recognize the full meaning of the vulnerability: if a traveler crossed the portal at exactly one second before the synching began – the only time at which the sensors could not operate – the subject would enter the suspension zone, detected by neither system nor existing travelers. Even if the sensors could tally and identify riders who had entered within the two-minute cautionary period, they could not for those who had exploited the stop-frame property of that minute window – they simply would cross unnoticed. Spencer contacted *Portal Works* who returned his review with the affirmative that if such a traveler should be so lucky as to get the timing right and possess the extreme skills to team with the sheer recklessness required to execute such a stunt, it could be done – success rate: unknown.

Consequently, Le Lien notified The Triad that if Joonas ever made it to the realms, he would either be alone or at the helm of a small team. It confirmed what Amaterasu had speculated; the greater threat was in an alliance or conflict with the Gestalt, not in an overwhelming Hektor presence.

The Great Hall was put on high alert, with volunteers on watch at every tunnel entrance. The young Master in charge of the topmost access of *Stairway Three*, set camp in the room directly across from Joonas's retreat; a detail that didn't escape the Hektor elder, and which confirmed he had been suspected of having reached the realms. He heeded the warning, though he saw it as nothing more than a logical furtherance of circumstances, with the possibility of an added logistical asset in the form of the young Angel across the corridor.

The Master on duty, who went by the name of Shido, was a graduate from the Earth island of Japan, in a remote, second-generation outer probability of Marshall Slaughter's world. His reality had split ahead of the Great Battles, and once more further down its timeline, before yet another catastrophic conflict. It was known as the *Peace Universe*, due to a collective consciousness and mass belief system that found no use in war and discord. He was a mild-mannered male in his late twenties who belonged to a pedigree highly suited for the role of Guardian. In spite of his age, he had been on numerous, difficult assignments; hence his familiarity with the recovery periods following traumatic missions. It was his choice to watch the thirty-third floor of *Number Three* for mostly sentimental reasons. While he noticed the occupancy across the tunnel, he chose to abide to the internal laws of sanctity for healing spaces by deferring enquiry about the tenant. He would simply wait for the resting Master to introduce himself.

301

Joonas let a day pass before he deemed the time was right for a move. He walked across the corridor to Shido's dwelling, dressed in the same outfit he wore when he last visited Slaughter's house. His imposing figure contrasted sharply against the delicate features of the young Master. Before the Angel had a chance to recognize the Hektor signature, the elder had penetrated his mind with a verbal algorithm that instantly severed the connections to his body's motor functions. Joonas took over, while leaving his own image behind in a state of fragmented suspension undetectable by space scanning devices, to be retrieved at his convenience. Shido, the Master of inner peace, internally assumed the grounded stance of meditation; there was no energy to waste on resisting or fighting – the intruder would eventually be forced out by the high tides of his private storms. In the meantime, he would quietly observe.

Ma-l had shown Xarn how to access Despair from his own back cave, a way that would lead him directly into her realm without George's knowledge. The same arrangement was possible from any of the abandoned or arrested worlds, but Despair's back room already opened directly onto Ma-l's valley, while its volcano shaft was where Snake dwelled.

The call to the dream meadows had not yet been returned, but neither deity was concerned by the silence – at least, not as long as they were in the process of reassigning the lanes to a new hub. Snake was summoned. He was informed of the Gestalt's interference and of the possibility of Joonas's presence in the system. The formidable elemental entity's interest was awakened by the mention of a need to create a new network of tunnels that would bypass George. He, to their amazement, proposed using Despair as its hub.

"Know that fire reaches the deepest and hiddenmost places! Behind these walls exists a great natural hall that has been waiting to assume its purpose. I shall carve an entryway into it from every one of the realms. Each single flame that burns in these dimensions of reality is an eye that belongs to me. Upon your return, the new hall will be ready in the model of its counterpart. Did I ever mention to you that the city of Angels is where the Gestalt's core consciousness dwells? The greater the traffic, the mightier its strength!"

"You just did, Snake," Ma-1 returned. "It occurred to me as well, but your input serves as official confirmation. As to the carving, how do you propose this new hall will awaken to its purpose?"

"Trust me on that, Goddess, I inhabited these caves since the days the mother reality was formed; I carved the tunnels and the back rooms from the blueprint of your dreams – I know a thing or two about consciousness and purpose – this hall will serve all of you well. The Gestalt will slowly revert to its code base, until it no longer knows it had ever existed. Now, you two go on to map the way between Angel City and the new hub; I believe you will find the entrance to Despair below the Great Hall – it will be your link by which the slow and steady transfer of the Masters will commence. As per now, all new Angel arrival from the old world will be redirected from your back cave to the new place. You may inform the Assembly of the changes."

Snake retreated to the shaft. Ma-1 and Xarn returned to the Goddess' realm; none of the movement and subsequent activity was noticed by George, who was busy trying to understand what had just happened at *thirty-three* of *Stairwell Three*.

10 – AMATERASU

At their next meeting in Amaterasu's domain, the group consisting of Ma-l, Xarn, Vac, and Saka worked on refining the logistics of the migration from Angel City to the new center. Snake had matched the original blueprint to the finest details, including its two underground levels – the two Halls were identical. The tunnel between them had been enlarged to accommodate the transfer of equipment. The Qwave unit was the first to move in, since it was in charge of cloning the ingenious light system of the Great Hall, then the entire assembly would migrate in trickle mode as to not alarm the Gestalt, until it would, in theory, be too weakened to pose a threat. Joonas'S absence from all spheres remained a mystery that made Amaterasu all the more suspicious that the Hektor founder was operating in the background. She pressed for utter vigilance on the part of the assembly to make sure he hadn't infiltrated their ranks under guise, or worse, by having overwhelmed one of them.

Meanwhile, Axel and Ilia had received the memo from Le Lien via The Triad, about the little-known vulnerability in the portal system that could have been exploited by Joonas and his team, and thus were advised to look into where, in the Great Hall, such a deed could have landed the Hektor member based on his unique signature. A series of computations confirmed that, had it been the case, Joonas would have been naturally attracted to the recovery center on top of stairway three – a straight line from Ma-l's rear cave to which the Snug Alley portal was connected. As to his pack of Dogs, there were no places in the Hall for them to remain unnoticed. A Le Lien security team was immediately dispatched to Shido's post, where the young Master was found in his usual meditative state.

"I didn't think relief was due for another few days," he said, as he lifted his gaze towards the foursome.

"We are enforcement; the intruder is expected to have come this way. Do you have anything to report concerning an unexplained occupancy, or a scrambled signature?" the surveillance tech asked.

"As you know, we do not breach the sanctity of a recovering Master. Two arrived this morning, but they haven't left their quarters," Shido replied.

"You must be referring to Angels returning from assignments in the other Oneness – were you not briefed on monitoring arrivals and reporting them to us?" the tech further inquired.

"I was not briefed on a change in protocol; the laws of privacy infer these Masters are beyond suspicion," the young Angel returned.

"The laws rightfully apply to Masters, but not to fallen ones. You are correct though; you weren't advised to break protocol. Only recently have Angels been admitted to the realms directly from their completed work – we're still adjusting," the Le Lien official apologized.

The real Shido persona shifted in his inner pose. Joonas couldn't have known that the Master's consciousness was linked to the larger gestalt that connected all residents of the *Peace Universe*; many of whom had joined the Guild over the millennia, of which over a dozen presently lived in Angel City. While Joonas's guise was being distracted by enforcement, Shido informed his team of the hijack. But because of the vast distance between the remote probability, where the core consciousness resided, and the Oneness of the realms, notwithstanding the weakened ghost image of the mother reality to further add latency, the peace Angels of the Great Hall would not receive the message until the next day. By then, Shido had been relieved from his post, having been kindly directed to the basement, where Pau and Gerald Brinsk had resumed with their training.

The young Master walked straight to Shade's desk to seek directions to the trainees' room. The recent female graduate came from a world that operated on emotional nuances alien to most intra-universal species; she immediately perceived a discrepancy between the Angel's aura and the visceral qualitative behind it – the signatures didn't match. She instantly shielded herself against possible invasion then telepathically sent an alarm signal to the Le Lien quantum supercomputer. At that very moment, Pau came to the desk to retrieve information for the class taught by Leòn. Shido froze. Shade acted on the predator's reaction by urgently ordering the student to fetch the teacher. Pau left, but returned all too soon with the Master and a barely recovered Gerald Brinsk, the three unaware of the snare about to close around them. Shade was buying time; she understood too well what was going on – something she could not allow to happen. Joonas felt distracted by her; he loathed the effect she had on him. He turned his back on her to face the trio. "One strike, three birds," was his last thought before the compounded impact of the Le Lien team forced him out of Shido's body. His consciousness was sent reeling back towards his real image where he had left it, expelled out of the Great Hall with such power that when he finally recovered his compass, he found himself in the extreme darkness of three linked figure-of-eight tunnels designed to make the user falsely believe he was nearing destination, while caught in the wicked redundancy of a perpetual series of mutating loops. The Dove's loosely reconstituted image had force-traveled through the rocky mass of the mountain – he felt horribly bruised but in luck to still be in one piece.

Shido had pulled out of his meditation unscathed. He stood up, smiling at Shade.

"Thank you, sister, your skills are only matched by your beauty."

Shade smiled back.

"It requires equally beautiful talents to maintain control under the dire conditions of being hijacked by a ruthless Fallen Master. Thank you for keeping the two signatures away from each other – I would never have known otherwise, my dear Sir."

The Le Lien team called the recovery unit for Shido and advised for the class to be cancelled.

When she finally surrendered to the shock of Joonas having come that close to ruining her, Pau had to be escorted to the newly formed *Student Trauma Center*.

Before they parted, Shido turned to one of the Le Lien officials.

"So, was it my message, or Shade's reaction that prompted you to save the day?"

"Both arrived at exactly the same moment. My take on it, Angel Shido, is that great minds think alike – perhaps you two should spend more time getting to know each other," the security tech replied with a smile.

The Triad was immediately updated on the latest developments. The news quickly reached all concerned parties: Joonas was either permanently subdued or somewhere in the tunnels, forever banned from Angel City, theoretically deprived from entering any realm.

George had been following with keen interest.

Jarred Gulliver had sufficiently recovered to take daily walks along the streets of Old Town Eureka. His recent experience had come with much invaluable perspective into his life's mission as it reconnected with purpose. He had not minded the confinement of the office – Lillian and Spencer had been exemplary caretakers – but he was delighted to be able to breathe some fresh air by the boardwalk, while observing the ritual of seagulls, pelicans, and seals during the feeding hours brought forth by the tides.

He had made closing arrangements with Berkeley, where he would teach a series of final classes before the ceremony of his retirement. Spencer had returned the vintage Jaguar that had been garaged out of sight in Fieldbrook for the length of the convalescence. Jarred had taken the opportunity offered by his few remaining days in Humboldt, to explore the area to its fullest. Marshall had come home from Amaterasu's. He was back at the office, catching up with his clientele. He and Gulliver had limited time together, but they valued their interaction whenever they could. They agreed to engage in business details, but only after the professor's retirement date.

Before he returned to the US, Slaughter enjoyed a peaceful stay at Flemmingson's house in Reykjavík. The friends revisited the Keyhole Lake portal on one more occasion to meet with Saka and Olaf. The prospect of a stable inter-dimensional lane powered by the stones warmed the heart of these two men, who had privately feared that the connection would eventually be irrevocably severed. It was hoped that they would be able to spend sizable periods of time in the realms, while reversibly, the portal would offer the possibility for Saka, Olaf, and Vac to journey to their old grounds. All hinged on Amaterasu and the young Goddess of Light's skills at harnessing the power of the stones.

The threat of Joonas's return to Eureka was minimized by the fact *Portal Works* had reconfigured the Snug Alley gateway into a one-way corridor. Amaterasu would be handling return traffic via a redesigned version of George's halls attached to the New Guild Center. The existing two sets of halls, one at Keyhole Lake – also the realms of Hektor – and the other, gifted to Ma-1 by the Great Gestalt on behalf of Amaterasu, and operating in parallel with the tunnel system of Angel City, represented the two ends of the lane set by the stones. The third one, in the making, would eventually replace George's halls and bypass its irresolvable dysfunctions. Upon finalization of the Masters' relocation to the New Center, the Gestalt would find itself too weak to fight back, at which time all the doors in its halls would permanently be erased, and the old tunnels rendered inoperative. Angel City would by then be empty, the myriad lights strewn upon its great space forever dimmed back to darkness.

The realms of Hektor were to remain connected to the old world. Upon revealing their true nature, the choice would be left to the organization, of either thriving in their allocated space or returning to face the tribunals of the Guild. The doors between their realms were to forever remain open, while concealed layers would facilitate traffic between Keyhole and the realms, as well as serve as entry into Amaterasu's domain.

Although Liv and Spencer's roles were no longer defined by the threat of Joonas, they returned to Fieldbrook with the regularity of those who had fallen in love with the place. They also called on Geir and Stefan in Reykjavík; it turned out that the Le Lien student liaison at the *Icelandic Society for Intelligence Research* had become quite fond of the philosopher's company.

It was likely that with the threat of Hektor gone, Olaf Swyndle's old world was free to steer itself away from imminent catastrophe and thrive. It was truly a different place from the early days of the case, one where the Angels felt that the old secrecy of their existence was about to become obsolete. And there were Lillian and Vera who too revisited Fieldbrook and Reykjavík for cookouts with old friends. The gap between the spiritual and the physical was closing, while a prosperous probability was in the process of becoming a vivid reality for those who chose to follow that course. Marshall and Geir did so through their work, dedication, and openness in the face of many unknowns. Their reward came in the form of a best-ever life scenario – one for which they had come to steadily nurture the gift of appreciation.

But all was far from being blissful in the realms. Amaterasu had made it clear in a following meeting, that as long as Joonas was known to be inside the system, he posed an unquestionable threat, regardless of his status. She cautioned against precocious elation related to his

311

defeat, as long as George was still in its prime. The Angel City organizers were facilitating a seamless transfer to the New Guild Center, but it required finesse, assisted with patience, to not arouse the Gestalt, until the point at which it would no longer matter. The Great Goddess very much desired to witness the progress, but her presence would have demanded that she cross from her halls before accessing the subsystem of tunnels – a foolish risk that was unworthy of the thrill. The new Halls of Doors were being built by Qwave, since Amaterasu couldn't be present to create them herself – it would take time before she could again visit the realms. The perceived lesser traffic between Xarn and Ma-l's worlds had desensitized the Gestalt from its initial paranoia – it simply let go of the idea of shutting the Warriors in. Saka never had to intervene on behalf of the two deities, for which the Great One was thankful. Wolf, who had very much enjoyed his stay in the "other realm," was now commuting via the new lane between the two open realities; the coywolf was on a mission, but all refrained from asking. Amaterasu thanked everyone for their impeccable team work and promised that upon overcoming the remaining hurdles, she would invite the group into her domain for a unique perspective on universal reality – which translated, as the guests were concerned, into a special treat.

Joonas lay still. His thoughts echoed against their bony enclosure. He could no longer find the strength or the logic to seek revenge on Shade and Shido – so much of his anger had turned precious energy to waste. He had tried to progress along the dark corridor, but the experience had left him with the sense of traveling along a path of linked pretzels. He sat on the coldness of the stone, resolved to be absorbed by his incomprehensible fate. By then, the migration of Hektor had been finalized – there was no return. If the other elders saw through the trickery, they showed no intention to challenge it – it was real enough for them. His team of Dogs was lost or destroyed, while some of the vital skills he possessed in the previous Oneness were ineffective in the tunnels. He couldn't move through the thickness of the rock walls; his body had become a heavy, sluggish mass pulled downwards by the force of gravity. He had lost his drive to carry Hektor and resume with the game of power – all had turned to posturing, privileges, and backstabbing. The nobility of his original concerns around the dangers of saving humanity had taken on the cloth of lunacy and moral decadence. He was a renegade, forever cornered by his innumerable failures at making his point clear; failures born of unchecked anger and bloated pride. In his time, he had been recognized as one of the most successful Masters; a visionary on the level of Amaterasu and other Great Ones. His once might was severely diminished from the ravages of out-of-control passions, the last of which made him aware of his lost powers in the face of the skills of young Angels. He could have been the one to train Shido and Shade, to help them discover their unique gifts; instead he stood to despise them, wishing to ruin their noble minds. It wasn't the first time Joonas faced his own demons, but it was the one during which all others converged. What had he learned from Hektor besides assimilating and acting the traits of his imagined foes? He was the enemy. The Guild was right; humanity deserved to be given a chance. It was not preferential treatment, but a reverential acknowledgement of what was owed to all species. What he battled so feverishly was a projection of his own perceived inadequacies, which simply resulted from a lack of self-love. Taken into the whirlwind of what he had created in Hektor, he ignored the inversed growth of his repressed qualities; and just like the ego he despised so much in humans, the repression formed into a gestalt that overwhelmed common sense in favor of status, turning dignity to affected pride. At that very point, he understood he was in the right place and time; only the sustained confinement of the stone could heal him as it had the Warriors. He had fought against what he feared most; his own humanity and the ego seed of his birth. He was reared amongst the women and men he saw descend into the bowels of worlds created by corrupt minds. It was an ancient reality much before the Great Battles – a portent of what was to come. His young visionary heart was overtaken by the absurdity, the hypocrisy, and the injustice of what he had witnessed – he fell into despair. He was rescued by one of the earliest Angels, then immediately admitted into the newly formed Guild, where he was brought back to psychological and emotional health. He was a promising and extremely skilled student who eventually rose to become one of the most respected Masters. His protector and tutor was an Angel by the odd name of Vac.

───────────

The Great Gestalt watched Joonas for a while. It did not comprehend what the energy around the entity that had been forced out of the Great Hall was. Why was a Master expelled with such power from the Assembly? George tiptoed around the Hektor elder. "Where does he come from; where should he be sent to?" it thought. It couldn't read minds – only signatures – yet it wished it could understand this odd Angel's internal conversation; it seemed so fascinating and complex. But George felt tired, drained by an inexplicable sense of lassitude. What was going on?

Joonas had perceived the presence. He knew what it was without even guessing, just that it wasn't meant to exist. He had been a nemesis of the realms for too long to not recognize another; but this one was born with them, or rather, was a product of them. An opportunity to get out of his prison had introduced itself; this time around, he was going to do things right.

"Who is the one that crawls in the blackness of these tunnels and leaves traces of his thoughts for all to read?" Joonas asked.

A moment elapsed before George responded.

"I feared you would never ask, stranger, I am the Great Gestalt of the realms."

"And what does the Great Gestalt of the realms do, exactly, to deserve such a godly title?" Joonas asked.

The entity paused.

"Why should you express insolence, Angel – if it is indeed what you are – when I represent both extremes of your fate? But to answer your question: I am the consciousness that links the realms to each other and without which they could not thrive."

"Umm, I haven't been in this universe for very long, though long enough to observe a lack of traffic between the so-called realms. If the links you mention had

315

indeed been there, you would presently be doing your job and probably not be wondering about my person. So perhaps, you should start by telling the truth." Joonas taunted, relishing the fact he had nothing to lose.

"I have never had the privilege of being addressed in such a way; I honestly find it curious. What have you done to deserve the right to live without a single fear?"

"I have stopped hiding from them. It took me years beyond your age to realize how simple and painless it was," Joonas returned.

"How dare you call yourself older than me; your vulnerability betrays an immature evolution!"

"If it had been completely up to me, you simply wouldn't exist, and neither would the entirety of the realm system. You are the mere byproduct of the work of those I opposed. From what I see, you are failing at your own purpose, something I am familiar with; but if only for what we have in common, I'm glad we've met," the elder countered.

"I don't know what prevents me from killing you," the Gestalt spat.

"What prevents you is your inability to do so. You have no powers besides interfering with the destiny of those you stole from, through deceit and abject logical fallacies. I can read you like a book; you are incapable of even shielding your own thinking process from me. If you spoke and lived the truth, I would be unable to do so, but your existence is a lie and it's my specialty to make liars talk and writhe."

From that moment on, the Gestalt forgot about the realms and tunnels. It became blind to the Warriors, the dream lanes, Amaterasu, and Ma-l – it was in the throes of an all-consuming rage that knew no bounds, its powers rippling through the halls and the caves. The Angels and deities present in the new center accurately guessed that George had met Joonas at last.

Vac, in a rare instance of sharing without being asked, took Ma-1 to the side to disclose the details of his critical involvement with young Joonas's rescue and education. The Goddess was shocked by the news.

"Amaterasu knows of it," the Angel added.

"Why would such a pertinent historical detail be systematically hidden from us from the start; it's beyond my comprehension?!" she voiced with distinct disappointment.

"When you get over your earthly emotions, you will understand how much that knowledge would have changed the course of the destiny of the realms. I didn't have to tell you now either, but *now* is the right time," Vac returned stoically.

"An alliance between Joonas and the Gestalt means the end of the realms – we are not ready with the codes for a complete switch-over to the new center, don't you get it?" Ma-1 retorted.

"Joonas is an integral part of the making of the realms, then and now. Everything exists on the precarious balance of opposites – it never is one side or the other, but I trust you know that," Vac added.

"You speak of illogicality as if it were elemental logic; who trained you to show such impassivity in the face of imminent disaster?" Ma-1 heard herself say, before she internally stabilized.

"The potential for disaster is the great impetus behind all creative endeavors; but since you asked, no Masters existed to train me. It all hinges on Amaterasu's promise; this is as far as I am at liberty to tell. Now I must absent myself to take care of important matters – please inform the others."

Vac turned around then quickly disappeared into the darkness of the tunnels.

Ma-l was left to ponder on Vac's last remark, "It all hinges on Amaterasu's promise." What was that supposed to mean? She composed herself, for she knew better than to come unstitched at such a critical moment. She connected with the organizers and advised them to accelerate the transfer flow; finesse was no longer the norm when the storm brewed ashore. The new hall had long been completed, but the tunnels out of it lacked the codes embedded in George's unlocatable mainframe. Unfortunately, neither she or Xarn, or anyone at *Portal Works* for that matter, knew how to write new ones. It was actually the unsolvable part of the plan that had been left to chance, and the main reason why Ma-l felt hopeless in the light of a possible alliance between Joonas and the Gestalt. And why did Vac leave? The codes were locked in the past; they existed as a live honeycomb network that defined George's place in the realms. The Gestalt didn't know them, it just responded from a reflexive standpoint. Most likely those on Amaterasu's team wrote them. So, who were these early Masters, and where were they? Vac had told Ma-l that the early seed programs had evolved symbiotically with the specific environment within which they were sowed, so even if the builder was found, the codes could have mutated beyond decryption – the likely cause for what the Gestalt had

318

morphed into. The outcome was only foreseeable up to the first turning point, which was left to be defined.

Ma-1 called Olaf over to report on what had happened, intent on probing the budding Master for insight into what he knew of Vac's mysterious history – something somewhat out of character for the Goddess.

"Vac is a master of disguise; not because he seeks to hide, but because his knowledge is so broad that his presence dissolves behind it. The dog outfit is the ultimate camouflage, charming, friendly, loyal, and above all, one that forfeits the requirements to engage intellectually. He can be both a guide and a follower, free to neither ask nor answer questions when on assignment. To understand Vac is to unlock the origins of the Oneness – I don't mean that lightly. He has been known to rise from an era preceding the concept of time, and even travel where consciousness has no hold. Yet, I have seen him as a playful puppy, rolling in the grass, barking at butterflies. To define Vac is to name each marker between two extremes, only to realize their sum represents but one point within a larger set, until you come to understand that trying to grapple with the idea of extremes is a waste of resources; thus, you resign yourself to roll in the grass with him, and then you discover that you are experiencing the perfect moment. To know Vac is to not behold what he's made of, but to be with him as one. No two presents are alike, and no adjacent truths resonate equally. If he says Joonas is fundamental to the process of freeing the realms, one must deduce that Vac is instrumental in making Joonas that way. With all due respect, I advise you to not challenge his wisdom."

"Are you saying that Vac lured Joonas into founding Hektor?" Ma-1 asked, incredulous.

"If he did, there would be good reasons for it; that's what I'm saying," Olaf returned.

"Well, Angel, you make me feel like I have lost some grounds in my education; perhaps I should have spent more time around you and your ever-so-resourceful teacher," the Goddess said, resigned.

"I owe my education primarily to you and our teamwork around creating the physical representation of your realm. Your choice of taking on the human form has undoubtedly slowed you down, but it has not diminished your skills. You are feeling human emotions which I find endearing, but you are, above all, a force by which I orient my compass, and around which our shared universe orbits. Even if Vac turned out to be a super-Angel, or a Great One, or the One; remember, he works for you. His history will be clear to all of us at the convergence of the elements that define our collective purpose. For now, we need to return to this precious present."

Olaf put his arms around the Goddess, holding her close. It was a great hug, well-deserved and rightfully sensual.

When they finally came apart, Ma-l looked at him with teary eyes.

"What is taking Saka so long to unwrap your passions?" she teased, as if regretting not to have done it herself.

"Saka is not to blame for it; I'm sure you know that," he returned with a smile.

Perhaps it wasn't so coincidental that, at that very moment, in a separate part of the center, Saka and Xarn were also disengaging from a passionate embrace, for reasons not entirely dissimilar. It was only natural that under the burden of uncertainty, the Gods and Goddesses of the realms would be seeking comfort and reassurance in each other. It was obviously essential that love should flow between those who were most pivotal to the liberation of the emerging Oneness.

———————

The Gestalt's energy was breathing hard down Joonas's neck.

"It appears you wish to become part of the rock walls that surrounds you, Angel. When they close on your body, perhaps you will show me some respect."

"You live an illusion that has little or no impact on my reality. The vision you stole from the dreams of the Warriors has no power away from them. Go ahead and close these walls. Enjoy the sight of splintered bones, spilled blood, and liquefied organs, until this body becomes one with the stone. But I will still see through your lies, untouched by what you think is real to you," Joonas said with calculated derision.

"Then let's put your arrogance to the test, shall we, and see how intact it comes out!"

While the Gestalt concentrated on moving the tunnel walls around him, Joonas probed the abyss of its mind into its ancient past, all the way to its seeding stage, to rewind and analyze the course of its evolution. He then witnessed a degradation of its makeup as if blocks were being removed from it. Joonas understood what was happening; the Angels were deconstructing the Gestalt by reallocating the realms to a new hub. In other words, there was another hall and the Masters were moving into it. Joonas also knew they didn't have the codes, since he was the only one in position to retrieve them, in addition of having been the original builder of the seed programs. By the time he had collected the pertinent data, the walls had made contact with his body. He left it and let its scattered image be absorbed by the mass of the stone, unscathed, as it slowly traveled across its thickness to the other side, into the space of another tunnel. Before he chose to rejoin his form, Joonas spoke to the Gestalt.

"You see, or perhaps you don't, but I am alive and you're still a lie. I suggest you awaken to the reality of your predicament. As far as I can tell, you have lost the lanes."

"Your words are nothing but Angel trickery; I am the lanes and the Hall of the Angels – I am the Great Gestalt of the realms – and to prove it, I will forever lock the two open realities," George exclaimed arrogantly.

"I do not need proof of your ineptitude; rather, unlocking those which you have shut would show true valiance. But whatever you're about to do, I advise that you think of the consequences," Joonas warned.

"Your advice is unwelcome!"

Those were the last words spoken by the Gestalt.

Joonas's spirit left the stone to rejoin the scattered pieces of his image. Vac was there waiting for him.

"Thank you, Master," Joonas said. "You were just in time – I don't think I had the strength to get out of there alone. It's been a long road since we last worked together; now I think I need a rest away from everything. I have the codes you need – I figured I owed the Guild. Somewhere amid these now-defunct tunnels, there's a cave Snake carved specially for me when we first came up with the concept of the new Oneness – just in case I needed to heal. Such a time has come. I shall reconnect in due time, and who knows, then, what will have happened of the realms – I can't wait to witness their evolved stages. Farewell Vac – give my regards to Amaterasu!"

Joonas turned around and vanished in the darkness of the tunnel.

As soon as George shut itself off, the openings into Ma-1 and Xarn's realms in the Halls of Doors closed forever. Their corresponding accesses in the Great Hall also ceased to function. The last of the Angels walked into the tunnel of Despair, as the lights faded behind her.

In the newly completed Qwave-built model of Amaterasu's new Halls of Doors, Saka stood with her cupped hands, holding the spinning white stone. The Great One entered, as Angel Vac presented her with the key to the adjusted codes.

"A special gift from Joonas," he said

She smiled.

"He'll enjoy the sabbatical," she simply returned.

The key was a scintillating light that lifted from Amaterasu's hand. It rose to mid distance of the cathedral ceiling. The One joined the tips of her fingers, bowed her head down and whispered three words that tailed off in a soft and long reverberating drone.

Naslent Damashir Umbadenindram

The hovering glow burst into many shooting lights, each choosing a door on which to engrave a name. Ma-1 recognized the symbol she had drawn in the dirt of her native tribal village.

"This is my personal access to the realms, but you are all welcome to use it whenever you need a change from the darkness of the new tunnels," Amaterasu announced, before she continued.

"Now, we all know his name has not always been associated with the honorable side of morality, and some of you have come to fear him viscerally, but without his unique skills and dedication at the early stages of this project, as well as in the last critical minutes that preceded the dismissal of the rogue Gestalt, we wouldn't be here to inaugurate this place. So, in his honor, and as my return gift to him, I find it fitting that you should all be standing in Joonas's Halls. This is my final word on it, as you must accept that without its two main counterparts, no whole is ever complete. Finally, so that you further get familiarized with the symbolism of it, the white stone will operate in the Halls of the Dark Angel, while the black one will spin at the source of all light – it is a wish that I hope will remain unchallenged."

Amaterasu, followed by the group that had gathered for the opening ceremony, exited through the portal that accessed the main floor of the New Guild Center. When the Great One suggested to change the name to something more colorful, she was told a contest for a new title was in the works. Saka, Ma-l, Olaf, and Xarn then showed their guest around the facility. On her request, she was led into the tunnel of Despair, to the opening overlooking the shaft of the volcano – Snake was summoned.

"As official representative of the Great Ones, I am here to thank you for your pivotal part in making the realms happen. Not only did you work on the original tunnels, but you carved new ones to accommodate for unforeseen developments. You are a hero among us, Snake. There is no doubt these worlds will embrace your elemental powers as ours did since their birth. You have my eternal love," Amaterasu said.

"There are no words to describe the pleasure of your presence amongst these modest dwellings. I am forever at the service of the realms as I have been your loyal servant from the depths of time. I already know I will enjoy this new Oneness immensely, judging by the way I have been treated – love goes a long way. So, thank you, Great One, for having entrusted me with an important part of your vision – Snake never forgets."

The fire entity retreated to the molten depths of the volcano in a hissing rush of smoke and flying sparks.

The group returned to the Center. It was official: the realms were the new Oneness, ready to expand from the core of a collective consciousness pooled by the creators of each of the pocket realities.

Saka turned to the group.

"What do you make of the lack of response to the invitation to meet in the dream meadows?" she asked, looking around, unsure of the timing of her question.

"The Gestalt had successfully closed off the lanes, consequently stifling the dream sequence long ago. Ma-1 was able to reawaken them because of her unique skills and position, but also because the entity had become negligent about them. By the time Xarn appeared in the meadows, it was too late for George to respond and prevent the realm from opening," Vac answered.

"Are you saying that the Gestalt arrested the development of the realms in their infancy?" Olaf asked.

"Their collective development suffered, yes, but not their individual ones. There will be some catching up to do, but I believe, from what I have witnessed of Ma-1 and Xarn's universes, that the personal evolution of each realm has reached a level well above the planned benchmarking point; a growth that will undoubtedly counterbalance any deficiency at the other end," Vac returned.

"Xarn and I will go back to the meadows to summon the Warriors until they come. The new lanes were reconfigured to the specifications of the times of the early gatherings, so we hope our voice will be heard," Ma-1 said.

Amaterasu turned to the group.

"It is more than plausible that the cessation of the dreams was perceived as a reluctance to meet, when it was in fact the work of the Gestalt that prevented them from happening. There will be questions before actions, but with time and perseverance, I have no doubt all the doors will unlock. It needs to be pointed that those which were to never open, served us well by offering the biggest gift of all: a new center, new tunnels, and Joonas's Halls – just to show that nothing is ever wasted throughout the creational process."

"I was under the impression that the Masters were to populate the realms. But now I understand they will remain in the Great Hall until there is a demand for them when the Warriors open their gates. It would appear that Vac and I are residents of Ma-1's, but how are we needed at this point? Certainly not in guiding and tutoring two Goddesses; am I missing something?" Olaf questioned.

"Olaf, I must speak with you in private about this," Ma-1 returned. "As to Vac, he is welcome to make my realm his home whenever he needs one, for I sense he doesn't belong to the Center. But I must confess; I'm unsure of where he truly belongs."

"You are right about the belonging part, Ma-l," Vac responded. "Anywhere is where I am, but your offer pleases me – a home away from home, where a piece of my heart forever resides, is always best. I will need to travel and likely be absent for long periods in time's terms, but I'll be glad to join the warmth to your company – a dog always returns to where love is given."

After its tour of the Center, the group casually returned to Joonas's Halls and the portal that was to take Amaterasu back to her domain. She stressed that her invitation was still standing, although she needed some time to sort things out. She would let everyone know with due notice.

Ma-l expressed her wish for a grand gathering in celebration of the opening of the realms.

"I offer my home. It would only be fitting for all the actors to be present," she put forth.

The company approved with shared enthusiasm. Amaterasu promised to fetch Marshall and Geir, as well as Liv, Spencer, Lillian, and Vera from Le Lien for the occasion. The Triad, who were about to lose the laptop connection, let everyone know that there was the possibility they would appear in person. Applause ensued.

It was time to part. Saka accepted an invitation from Xarn into his realm – the two hugged everyone and left. Vac opted to go with Amaterasu – there were important matters to be sorted out over the next couple of days. Ma-l and Olaf stood before the portal with the realization that, for the first time, it just would be the two of them back at the house.

"Well, I don't know about you, but I miss my place. So, if it's OK with you, I would love for us to leave now," Ma-l said intently.

"Then if you don't mind, I'd very much like to take the old way through Despair and hike down the valley; I miss the trail. Are you up for it?" Olaf proposed.

"You beat me to it, professor," Ma-l laughed.

As they stopped by the creek on the first stretch of the descent, Ma-l wrapped her hands around Olaf's neck, searching his eyes.

"There is a right time and place for everything; I believe it has now come to us," she said, as she began to loosen his clothes.

He smiled.

"I would love to return the favor but you are already undressed," he teased.

"Humor can't mask desire – not now," she said softly.

They held for a very long embrace until the whirl of their combined passions spun them into its dance. They made love again and again, until their bodies surrendered to the sweet exhaustion of extreme release – they fell asleep in the grass. They had become one – a tattooed Goddess and a bedraggled new Angel – in a world that had set its roots in the uncanny meeting of once unforeseeable elements.

———————

Saka was so overwhelmed when she first met Xarn that her mind immediately strayed from the course of reason. Just when Ma-l had finally found her mate, was the young Goddess swept by her mounting passions – she felt utterly disoriented. Though she was borne of the light cast by Amaterasu, she tapped the fluids of life from the furrows of the realms. She had returned to her birth grounds after a long journey that had taken her to universes so unthinkably distant, that they had fallen off the bounds of memory; yet she prevailed. At the other end, Xarn arrived to the fields of dreams by lanes that were condemned to never come to life again, and he too persevered in seeking to rejoin the fold of the collective. Ma-1 stood between them as the catalyst to their meeting. Saka and Xarn had taken nothing from the Great Goddess; rather, Ma-1 had unconditionally handed the gift of love to both. In doing so, she freed the playing field from ancient, erroneous preconceptions, leaving her to give, from the depths of her heart, to the one most capable of returning the kindness.

And thus, for the days that followed, the two couples explored the one most primordial and fundamental impulse of known existence; the drive to bond and partake in the pushing of universal boundaries. It wasn't in the mating of similarities, but rather, of dissimilitudes, that the complete whole was formed. The laws of attraction made sure of it, as long as love had a space to thrive.

Vac returned to Mal's realm first, with the news that the guests had received the invitation to the grand gathering – Liv would be coordinating the shuttling to Keyhole Lake. He also got wind that Qwave was working on linking quantum computers between Guild headquarters and the realm Center, by latching onto the frequency spectrum of the two stones. As it turned out, the tubular energy between them consisted of an ultra-complex interweave of lockable languages that served as a corridor to the transfer of massive amounts of data at speeds that approached the impossible mark of zero lag over infinity – or instantaneity. It was good news for The Triad who had found its niche as a computer entity – the techs had felt somewhat unready to switch assignments.

Saka rejoined the family the next day – she was radiant. With the help of newly installed portals, the access into Xarn's realm was the equivalent of walking into the next room, at least for those whose signatures were registered in the system. The young Goddess had felt a tinge of remorse, but Ma-1 didn't give her the time to nurture the feeling.

"It's OK, darling; I knew it the instant you two met. I too, at that time, became aware of where my own heart belonged. All along, I thought you and Olaf were meant for each other, so I refrained from following the yearning in my soul. All of it is an exercise in synchronicity for which I am grateful. The moment is our most precious asset; we must cherish it for an eternity."

"I gather it took me by surprise. I have a history of failures around the affairs of the heart; I never thought I would ever let anyone in again. I think Olaf knew that, and he respected my space," Saka said, unable to hold the tears.

"Olaf had his own personal reasons not to seek the intimacy of a close companionship, but when a Goddess's love fills her land with the scent of a million blooms, a lot of healing can happen. Though, I do admit, I first needed Xarn to trigger the manifestation of that love deep within my core," Ma-1 explained, turning to Vac.

"I understand this may well be an inappropriate question, but tell me, Angel, have you ever had a mate?"

"You ask then I must tell, but only to a point," Vac replied. "Many of us are, what you may call, 'married to our work,' so a natural leaning towards self-love is indispensable. It is by far the most difficult form of intimacy; definitely the one most easily confused with narcissism. Because of a vast array of assignments that demand immersion in the affairs of many species, we do find ourselves, with random regularity, involved in relationships that require the expression of the affections you are referring to, albeit temporary and very much in line with incarnational contracts. But I assume you mean, a mate at the eternal level of an Angel's reality. So, in that light, and because I am uncertain of the timing, all I'm permitted to divulge is that yes, there is a special someone to whom my heart belongs. You must understand that my original form has left me long ago, and that the true nature of my being no longer depends on the physical universe – it's the same for all of us, but I am referring to focus-specific experience. So, sex as you know it, is only a very small part of the love expressed at my level. When you and Olaf transcend the flesh, you will have a better understanding of what I'm getting at. As to the name of my mate, you must wait for a specific alignment of conditions, before you are permitted to know. I beg you to refrain from enquiring any further about it," Vac added with pointed firmness.

"I won't Vac," Ma-l said. "But I must confess that with every one of your answers, I find myself looking at a greater unknown. How many steps are left before we can start calling you the ultimate Oneness?"

"Your question touches on the fundamental, philosophical notion that since all of us belong to the Oneness, we all are the One. How do you define the steps you speak of? Do they go up to the top of the pyramid, or down into the multitude? Are they part of a ranking system based on the merit of having abided to a predetermined set of tenets written by some hypothetical authority – like commandments? For now, you're a Great Goddess of the realms questioning a crossbred Labrador; so who's closer to the ultimate One?" Vac replied.

"I didn't intend on subjecting you to hyperbolic doubt, just that you always seem to be so much more than what you show – and I mean from the standpoint of both specific and universal knowledge. I do understand we all are more than our particular selves across any chosen assignment," Ma-l replied.

"Then yes, my present undertaking brings me closer to the Oneness than my last one did, which was to make sure Olaf wouldn't trip all over himself; it's all subjective," Vac added, letting the Goddess know he was done.

Ma-l and Xarn returned to the dream meadows. Just as Amaterasu foresaw, nothing came of it at first, but on the seventh call, the lanes came into motion. Soon a figure appeared at the bottom of the trail. She was young and slender; her muscles were taut like springs ready to uncoil. She was an archer like Ma-l, part of a special team of swift and precise shooters. She walked up steadily, with no hurry in her movements. Her body was also tattooed, but she wore a loose, light brown, one-piece top of mid-thigh length that hid very little of her beautiful form. She stood before Xarn and Ma-l, looking at them incredulously. She remained silent for the longest time, while she searched for something in their eyes.

"Do you not trust the truthfulness of your dream, Warrior Enola?" Ma-l asked.

There was a long pause.

"I counted the cycles from the moment I was denied these cherished gatherings, Ma-l; it's difficult for me to awaken to a hope that was lost long ago. But why only the two of you?" the young Warrior inquired.

"It's a very convoluted story that must be told in its rightful settings; for now, we need to reconnect in order to rekindle the family spirit. We imagine that just like us, light came to the darkness of your isolation and guided you to the great outdoors of your realm. Now the time has come for all the Warriors to unlock the gates of their lands and thrive as a great collective of creators. Goddess Enola, our homes welcome you; doesn't yours wish to open its doors as well?" Xarn asked prudently.

Enola paused to weigh in the implication of his words; then she suddenly relaxed and smiled.

"I thought I would never hear a voice outside my head ever again, though it probably is still in it, but I recognize the nature of the dream; therefore I know I'm real inside it. So, confirm this please: if I say yes, I'll awaken to be graced by your visit; then you will show me the way into your realms, am I right?"

"You are perfectly right," Ma-l returned.

At that precise moment, a door opened into the second section of Joonas's Halls.

The next day, Enola was introduced to the two realms and the new Great Hall. Ma-l sent Saka to inform Amaterasu of the fabulous news then immediately started working on preparing for her Grand Gathering. A group of elder Masters – though their looks had nothing to do with the distinction – expressed the desire to meet with the new creator to discuss her needs and what she wished to see further accomplished inside her universe – an action that would become standard with every new awakened realm. The aim was to dispatch Angels, either permanently or on an assignment basis, to advise on the creational process and follow through with maintenance. Enola smiled, admitting she could definitely use the help. In a thought-provoking twist, she also expressed a keen interest in joining the rank of Masters. The question, "Could an Angel double as a deity?" resonated through the New Guild Center for days on, until Vac put an end to it by affirming that if a Master could become a Great One, the reverse was a perfectly acceptable option as long as it was a step in evolution. Amaterasu saw much humor in it – only good things could come of it.

Enola's energy was magnetic and vibrant. The Warrior was soon taken in by the younger Angels, who looked up to her as they expressed their wish to be part of her team. Her realm was unique in that it contained no mobile life forms, but every structure was a meticulously conceived art piece integral to a city that spread its rich colors and reflections to the edge of a flora just as resplendent. An omnipresent, playful consciousness was felt everywhere, seemingly following the guests as they passed under glittering mosaicked bridges, traversed spiraling tunnels, and swam across limpid waterways. Enola was a visual artist in the grandest of tradition. She claimed the colors came to her at first, murky and faint, but she soon found ways to wash off their opacity with the fearless hope that swelled her heart, and the relentless drive to give them a proper sun with which to interact.

Unlike Ma-l and Xarn who favored some privacy, she embraced visits and reveled in the wonderment her creations aroused in her guests. Within the span of a few days, the entire assembly had come to her city, while many promised to make it a habit to return. Her greatest hopes were to populate her world with similarly joyful and colorful spirits, myriads of autonomous counterparts to their effervescent surroundings.

Now that it was clear the realms were coming into their own, Amaterasu advised not to rush the process. The three Warriors were to resume with the gatherings at the meadows, until one by one, each door came unlatched – but only at a pace that flowed along the natural beat of the new Oneness. It was obvious that the foreseeable diversity of creations would keep all captivated for the ages.

As part of the preparations for Ma-l's Grand Gathering, it was arranged for Marshall and Geir to arrive days ahead to partake in the grunt work – something the friends had persistently insisted on. Everyone who had been pivotal in making the realms a reality was expected to be present – the sole exception being Joonas. Slaughter had thought of calling Gulliver in Berkeley, but refrained on the basis that the trauma inflicted by the abduction was probably all he could take for a while.

Marshall was so delighted about his ex-assistant's new-found love, that in return, Saka put her index finger on his forehead and promised he would be next.

"The light never lies," she said, laughing. "But you know what Marsh, I had hopes Linda Sue would

335

eventually sweep you away, but it turned out the girl was wounded beyond repair – I hope you forgive her," she added with a wink.

"Make that two wounded souls," he replied candidly.

Liv, Spencer, Stefan, Lillian, and Vera had also made the trip, but were temporarily being kept busy at the recently formed Le Lien branch of the New Guild Center, where Olaf's laptop containing The Triad now resided. Lillian and Vera promptly reassured Geir and Marshall that they would soon be reporting for kitchen duties.

The new Qwave connections were at the testing stage, running under an experimental cluster of programs meant to shield out the many resonances emitted by the quantum foam environment and the locked languages the data traversed through. It was an exciting time for the Guild, one that aroused the vitalizing passions of olden days among many Masters.

Vac needed to absent himself to tend to important matters, claiming he would be back for the festivities. It went without saying that Snake was in charge of the bonfires that were to burn throughout the many nights. Ma-1 and Olaf harvested from the gardens and the orchards, only finding scant opportunities to escape from the mounting frenzy. Lillian eventually joined Geir in the kitchen, where the two could be heard laughing to no end. Pau made a surprise visit, with the intention of crossing paths with Marshall. She was naturally part of the guests, but the party was still five days away – she wanted to connect before it would become impossible to find enough privacy for what she needed to share. She and Marshall took off, after his kitchen shift, for a walk along the creek dividing the valley. She was shy and quiet at first, but the detective intuitively granted her the space to find the pulse of her courage.

Pau finally spoke.

"There's a great deal of apologizing owed to you, Marshall – Paula Hunter was a walking affront. Although, I could go on saying that I wasn't myself then; that would be nothing short of a cop-out. It was me alright – I was that bitch! But you know, I'm happy now. Without you and the way you handled the situation, I wouldn't be here to thank you – so thank you, and I hope you can forgive me. Now, as part of my further training, I'm required to perform quite a bit of repair to my past, so I thought it would be fitting to ask you if you would be willing to take me in as an assistant at your office. It's not being forced on me; it is my choice. I don't think it would hurt if I brought some Angel energy to the old town. I owe it to myself to prove that I am a very different person from that smug character; besides, I owe it to you as well to demonstrate that there is more to me than spite. I won't be offended if you turn me down, although I would be deeply honored if you accepted."

"I thought you abhorred the smell of fish that blew in from the docks," Slaughter teased.

"That was part of being a person hating her life, I guess; now there's something almost comforting about it," she modestly replied.

"You know, Pau, in some twisted way I've always liked you. I can't say I didn't feel sorry for you, but I admired your bravado, because it was the way you demonstrated your courage. I recognized from the get-go there was something out-of-whack in your relationship with Cruz – his energy was oppressive, and I saw you battle his influence. You were in a tough place, so I never took your verbal jabs personally. If you don't mind the humor, that personality fitted the suit it lived in; after all, you were a cop and I've been around them all my life – my dad was one, rough but kind," Marshall returned.

"I was blessed by that very kindness you showed my person then – I hope I can make it up to you. I'm also very happy to see you and Geir here; it's nothing short of a miracle that the realms were given a chance to prosper. You know, in the end, Joonas almost managed to destroy me – his presence took me off-guard – but when he finally saw the light, he redeemed himself like a true Master. There's always much goodness below a surface of evil; most of the time, it turns out to just be a role. Angels don't do roles; they do assignments, they do missions; they act out of purpose for the benefit of the species and the worlds they serve – it's the nature of my training. Someone like me could be fun in your line of work; I'm referring to your second business, of course. It goes without saying that I'm still a student – assignments will come later. You may call this request one from left field, or a longing for the overdue adjustment of a personal detail," Pau added.

"I can tell you're dead-set on this. I'm sure you're aware that you'd be filling in for Saka – a hard act to follow. I was never able to hire a replacement for her position because of it, but somehow, I trust you may fit the requirements. It's mostly straight office work, but occasionally, an odd case demands that you travel in time to impossibly distant realities to retrieve a lost client," Slaughter humored.

"Right up my alley," she laughed.

With barely contained elation, Pau thanked Marshall for trusting her. She then took his hand and did not let go until they made it back to the house. Saka saw them arrive from the distance. When the two reached the kitchen, she was first to welcome them back. The young Goddess smiled at Pau; then she turned to Marshall.

"The light never lies, remember?"

On the eve of the Grand Gathering, guests arrived early. Axel and Ilia were among the firsts, soon followed by the Le Lien crew led by Liv and Spencer, who brought The Triad with them. Shido and Shade sat on a bench in the circular yard, below the olive grove, to take in the sight of the valley before joining the festivities. They had been working together with Pau on reorienting Guild defectors under a new rehabilitation program aimed at reuniting victims with their original training. They also had signed up for kitchen duty alongside Lillian and Vera.

Amaterasu arrived with Vac, who was followed by another black Labrador.

"Sir Vac," the dog said, "I believe I was once here, but I recall I was lost then – am I lost again?"

"No, Sam, you're never lost among friends; besides, your human caretaker, Maggie, will never know you were gone for more than a few minutes, chasing that squirrel inside that bush," Vac replied with pointed humor.

Saka came running.

"Wow, Sam, of course you had to be here; without you, we would never have known Olaf was safe!"

Sam turned to Vac.

"I remember the human female from a hike we took together long ago. I like her, though I do not know what she is saying," Sam confessed.

"She likes you as well, my dear friend, but not to worry about what she says, even though it concerns you and your deeds a great deal. Let me simply put it this way: you mean much to our hosts; thus, I advise that you take in the experience to its fullest and stick around for a while; you never know what the future has in store for us," Vac said conspiringly.

"I like it here, Sir Vac, it's just that my business is elsewhere," Sam countered.

"Then, consider it a vacation; business can wait! Feel free to roam and enjoy the food – you know the place," Vac said joyfully, before joining in with the group.

Sam returned to the waterfall where he once found the portal that took him back to his world. This time around, the circumstances were very different – he resigned himself to their reality. He drank from the pool; then just as he was about to turn around, he came face to face with a green frog.

"I reckon we once met, Sir," the amphibian said. "'Twas by a much smaller pond; formed by a rivulet perhaps. But I do have a secret to share. Just between you and I, it matters not how far our destination is, or how lost we are: home is always a lot closer than we think. Trust me on that – doors are everywhere!"

The frog leaped and vanished behind a rock.

Sam walked back to where the food was – he felt considerably relieved.

It might have just been coincidental, but at that precise moment, Saka turned to Marshall to ask, "Marsh, you remember the story of the green frog, the one in the eye of the papier maché fish sculpture, and later at Spectre Flat? Shouldn't it be here tonight? After all, it was part of the actors that helped us solve the case."

"You claimed it was a hallucination," he replied.

"That was what I thought then, but I don't have to doubt myself anymore; I saw what I saw and heard its words loud and clear," she returned.

"I'll have Pau look into it," he humored.

———————

Ma-l's Grand Gathering went deep into the night, and then into the following days. It actually lasted the whole of a week. Though Xarn's world was only reached by those with invitations, Enola's was open to all; the guests poured in and out through the conveniently placed portals. It was a true celebration of the realms, the capping of a multi-millennia long, first-stage fulfillment – a baptism symbolic of a promising release of endless possibilities. The event was thoroughly documented by a team of historians from the Guild, who didn't miss a beat on the intricacies of what connected the elements to each other. It was the culminating point of the work of one Great Goddess and her group of talented Masters, for the benefit of all the parts that formed both Onenesses; a monumental task that allowed for Marshall and Geir's world to prosper away from the fate of the lost mother reality. Amaterasu presided over a small ceremony to congratulate all the participants, starting with the original members who initiated the concept of the realms, and then those who followed with the rescue of the Warriors' souls from the fires of the battles. There were the portal makers; the tireless administrators of the unfortunate encampments; all the players behind the scene, who dedicated their resources to the project; all to be praised

341

for their relentless work. Of course, there were the final actors: Olaf, Geir, Marshall, Saka, and the countless Angels from Qwave and Le Lien who pooled their courage, skills, and experience together. Slaughter and Flemmingson were rewarded with limited access to Guild portals; limited only in the sense that those that would endanger them were kept off-limit. They were also granted honorary members status, which opened the doors to working relationships and other partnerships with Angels, with the clause that upon reaching the end of their useful physical lives, they could enroll in the Masters' program. Both were profoundly touched by the gesture and left the limelight with teary eyes. Lillian was seen taking Geir away from the gathering to an undisclosed location, while Pau and Marshall spent the rest of the festivities in each other's company. It was clear that the main theme was about unions and their collective sum, one that was at the very source of all existence.

Eventually, all guests returned to their worlds and assignments. Somehow, Sam found his way back on his own, a feat that did not escape Vac and Amaterasu.

"He must have met a certain someone," the Great One humored.

"Sam's heart and his boundless trust always take him where he needs to be; many lessons lie within that one simple truth – just brilliant!" Vac marveled.

―――――――――

As promised, Amaterasu invited the three Warriors and their close entourage to her domain. Enola was accompanied by a young Angel, who could easily have been mistaken for an art institute student also playing in a punk band. His name was Lev – he had just returned from an assignment in London's Camden Town and was still in persona.

"Lev has ideas I would love to implement to my realm. He chose to move in permanently, so now I have an official resident," Enola proudly revealed.

Amaterasu smiled as she welcomed the young Master. The group walked over the warm, red sand, until they came to a depression that concealed a verdant oasis. The host took her guests down a powdery trail onto level ground, where the first of the vegetation poked through the parched earth. A wide path lined with date trees and tobacco-like greens growing out of their bases – the space between them carpeted with succulents – led to a pyramid-shaped structure made of glass and osmium blue steel, reflecting the copper glow of the sun in shades subtly shifting to the rhythm of their steps. The Great One's planet rotated on its variable, tilted axis in such a way that the fire orb never rose past mid-point, before it descended again below the horizon; and so, the light always shone in rich, deep golds, ambers, and reds akin to some of the most glorious autumn sunsets avidly sought by photographers in Olaf and Saka's old world.

Amaterasu's home was imposing, yet conveyed a sense of lightness that defied its footprint. They entered through a trapezium cut in the triangular incline of its face, into a long hallway that led to a stairwell which terminated onto an open terrace set below the remaining twenty feet of the summit. From anywhere around the four corners, the celestial view was one of rare unimpeded majesty. The sun was setting, as stars lit up the skies in a divine tapestry of scintillating colors.

Amaterasu gathered the group in a semicircle.

"When I first saw this place on my first voyage, I promised myself to return. Every time I did, I got closer to the realization that one day it would become my home. It is now part of the domain of the Great Ones. Back then, it was a little-known corner of the universe. It may be of interest to Olaf and Saka, that it resides exactly at the halfway point between their version of Earth and the collapsed mother reality, at a crossing of probabilities. It was a convenient place to reorient the light on which we traveled. It is important for everyone to understand those journeys weren't simply dependent on time and distances, but also on a broad and mostly untethered awareness of potentiality, which necessitated breaking across the membrane separating explored and unexplored possibilities, to trigger options into emergent probabilities, until the explorer's perceptual field became reversed. All viable outcomes are, as you know, fully manifested realities in their own rights – the focus of experience dictating which one we make our primary. One must let go of the system of beliefs to free the mind of the boundaries between all foreseeable ends. The mother reality, for example, <u>was</u> a future probability of Saka and Olaf's Earth, one which until recently stood on a direct course with their world's fate. When Olaf's work was introduced to their time, the knowledge it contained ever so subtly – yet, so fundamentally – changed the structural makeup of mass beliefs, that it steered their reality away from its course towards horizons of better prospects. You all naturally understand the principals by which all of creation is thrust outwardly from the self, as it was demonstrated by our Warrior friends. We all build our unique spheres from the same standpoint of oneness by which our individual truths are conceived. Also, one may say that each realm emerged singularly from the collective consciousness that imagined it, as *it* and its likes also rose collectively from the singularity that wished for their existence: a unique gestalt that knew of no other like itself, one that yearned for release from the confines of its isolation. It dreamt of an Angel – a savior that would find a seed in an impossible place, before Angels, places, or seeds ever existed. But its dream became so strong and resolute, that purpose rose from within, onward to gaining specific awareness. The name was Amaterasu, Angel of Light. And so, very much in line with the original consciousness, the new awareness wished for another like itself – Amaterasu requested the creation of a second Angel. The One obliged, and along came Vac, Angel of Possibility. Thus, in a nutshell, was born the Guild of Masters, though our mastery was still to be put to the test. Time had not been conceived, while physical universes were a long way from being formed; yet, the Angel of Possibility imagined that nothingness had to have a counterpart; out of it came unlimited potential or 'everything.' The Angel of Light shone her metaphorical lantern on the infinite expanse of visualized possibilities and located, in a place where light could no longer cast a shadow, a very remote probability on the fringe of *absolute absence*. It existed at the end of an inconceivably long, linear course, even though it was also right before her; and out of that paradox, time emerged. It was thus seen that the probability in question was set in a future universe that only light could access; hence, the concept of space simultaneously surfaced. Those were the very first steps of the physical version of the Oneness. We had to look along the outskirts of the farthest possibilities to find the worlds that were teetering at the edge of the abyss of forgetfulness, before we could bring them back in the fold of time, to the very beginning of it, a point at which we came across the concept of the realms. The singularity we refer to as the One wished for more creators, as it saw a great need for them. So, it asked me to take over that role as the first Great Goddess of Creation. It also told me that there were two stones to be retrieved from one of the future worlds, the black onyx and white chalcedony gems, that it stated symbolized the great paradox of its existence. It advised me to come back to this place; I found them buried in the sands on which I built this very home. It said they were its gift to me, that they would eventually bridge the gap between *it* and another like itself. It then urged me to create others in my image. When I discussed the possibilities with Vac, it was agreed that more Angels were going to be needed. These future Masters were not created inasmuch as they arose from the pool of potentiality across the eons, thus the original team was born, among them, Joonas, who came from an early tribe of Earth which existed in a relatively close future from us. He was rescued by Vac and brought into the fold of our time. I was conceived as light; energy, when combined with the forces of attractions, also known as an immutable quality called love, and propelled by the winds of purpose, became the source of all existence. I was seen, in your terms, as the female symbol, the mother of all births. My stars were strewn across myriad possibilities, while Vac became the male counterpart of the emergence process. The black and white of the stones, seen as an intertwined singularity, was the great impetus behind the dilemma of life, as the latter appeared to straddle opposite yet complementary forces. Without their symbolic encryption, the necessary thrust to propel dream into existence would never have realized. The three Warriors among you are creators of your own, so none of this is alien to you, but your origins have far greater depths than the story of the Battles; hence, part of your further training is to hear it from the mouths of those who were there when nothing and everything existed as one, as what is best defined as the original paradox. There were no before or after, and neither was there any containing space, only a wish dreamt by a gestalt that had no origin and no end; yet, we prevailed, for we are here today – not days following the celebration in Ma-1 and Olaf's realm – but many millennia before it, and many more thereafter, in a place unbound from time, and when you close your eyes, in no place at all. Prepare to meet the One."

END

EPILOGUE

Inevitably, the news of Joonas's disappearance reached the realms of Hektor; it was capped with a fitting ceremony in his remembrance. His team of Dogs was forever locked in the cold stone in an arrested state, petrified in the pose of their last round of cheers.

Amaterasu's creation had been so precisely crafted that even upon revelation of its true nature, the organization deemed it on par with the best of realities worthy of the name; Hektor was honored to call it its own.

The Guild and the rogue league came forward with a treaty that allowed for some of the approved Dark Angels to become honorary Masters. Many came forward and were seen working in tandem with Angels on many teams. Those who remained ruled their worlds as they wished.

The old Strata headquarters were turned into a recruiting center, under the Guild's condition that only ethical practices were to be employed in both orientation and training. All Hektor actions outside of its domains were conducted under Angel surveillance and enforced by a common code.

Tömör was released from his artificial state of suspension and assigned to a post on a distant Hektor realm planet ruled by Dahbar, one of Joonas's main opponents inside the league. As the two found a liking for each other, the exiled Angel was appointed governor of a peaceful island amid semi-tropical settings that provided much healing to the once errant Master.

Eventually, the ghost image of the mother reality lost the force to carry the last original portal into the realms; Snug Alley was reoriented towards another extremely distant future probability that showed promise in linking with the origins of time – a popular destination for the adventurous Angel and the few among the first generation of humans to interact with the Masters.

Jarred Gulliver invested substantial capital in Marshall Slaughter's secondary business and became a partner. Pau was delighted to work with a surviving abductee of the Hektor elder and found much comfort in knowing that ample positivity could live behind the face of evil. She theorized that the good eventually prevailed over Joonas's corrupt character and that he was turned around when purpose redefined itself. Pau moved in with Marshall, livening up the feel and general sense of unkemptness of the old Fieldbrook estate to an unparalleled level of resplendence. After she graduated, she took an easy assignment in town as Jarred's counselor. The English gentleman was never told her story, since Angels didn't volunteer information; but oddly, Gulliver refrained from telling his as well. Although he professor suffered regular spells of panic from his trauma, every day, he grew stronger in every way. The business thrived and rapidly became a labor of love for the team. Its new name:

Private and Beyond Investigation Ltd.

Geir and Lillian visited Eureka on a regular basis. The two couples often took trips together to Keyhole Lake, to connect with Amaterasu, Ma-l, Olaf, Vac, and Saka; as well as pay visits to Xarn and Enola.

Liv, Spencer, Stefan, Vera, and her new partner, Angel Bluefeather, stopped by on occasion to spend a few days at the estate. The Triad reported with predictable reliability, as new Qwave laptops replaced the old ones.

Of course, much was about to happen in the realms. It was hoped the Guild would document every moment of it. The story of Ma-l's Grand Gathering was published in a small book which became a hit among the Angels. It was rumored copies had found their way into some of Earth's bookstore.

www.ingramcontent.com/pod-product-compliance
Lightning Source LLC
Chambersburg PA
CBHW030636260626
47157CB00007B/2346